THE GERSHOM SCROLL

By the same author:

Fatal Tears, Book Guild Publishing, 2013

Errant Angels, Book Guild Publishing, 2013

Feelings of Guilt, Book Guild Publishing, 2014

THE GERSHOM SCROLL

Further Journeys of Rupert Winfield

Stuart Fifield

Book Guild Publishing
Sussex, England

First published in Great Britain in 2015 by
The Book Guild Ltd
The Werks
45 Church Road
Hove BN3 2BE

Copyright © Stuart Fifield 2015

The right of Stuart Fifield to be identified as the author of this work has been asserted by him in accordance with the Copyright, Designs and Patents Act 1988.

All rights reserved. No part of this publication may be reproduced, transmitted, or stored in a retrieval system, in any form or by any means, without permission in writing from the publisher, nor be otherwise circulated in any form of binding or cover other than that in which it is published and without a similar condition being imposed on the subsequent purchaser.

All characters in this publication are fictitious and any resemblance to real people, alive or dead, is purely coincidental.

Typesetting in Baskerville by
Keyboard Services, Luton, Bedfordshire

Printed and bound in Great Britain by
CPI Group (UK) Ltd, Croydon, CR0 4YY

A catalogue record for this book is available from
The British Library.

ISBN 978 1 910508 00 8

For MC and KD, who never wavered...

PROLOGUE

Petra

The Royal Palace, AD 108

'And you found out nothing further ... other than this ... no information from those who were carrying it?'

'Nothing, apart from the literal meaning of the words,' replied the tall, muscular tribune, resplendent in full dress uniform. 'Despite our persuasive methods, they professed not to know anything.'

The glow of a fiery, setting sun flooded across the broad expanse of the wide balcony. It filled the opulent throne room with a russet light that set the heavily ornamented columns and wall friezes alight with the shimmer of gold leaf. In the streets of the city, beyond the palace walls, a palpable sense of urgency filled the air, almost as if the divinity of profit was aware that there was but a short time left for trading before the sun finally set.

Lucius Sentius Corbulo, proconsul of the lucrative province of Arabia Petraea, looked down thoughtfully at the small marble tablet he held in his be-ringed hand. These were dangerous times. He put his wine goblet to his lips and took a long draught of the deep ruby-coloured liquid.

'You say this is written in the Nabatean script? Perplexing...' he said softly, his brow furrowed.

Since the death of the Nabatean king, the Eagle of Imperial Rome had settled itself comfortably on to the highly profitable nest of the ancient city of Petra and its surrounding countryside. There had been hardly any objection from them about what had, in effect, been a Roman military conquest by stealth. The Nabatean kingdom had long ago been built on commerce, where profit was their only consideration. It made very little difference who occupied the palace, as long as trade kept flowing and the money kept pouring in.

'The question is this, Tribune,' continued Corbulo, studying what to him were the incomprehensible marks on the tablet, 'should we keep hunting until we find something? The last thing I want here is a repeat of the trouble they had in Judea,' he muttered.

He remembered the problems Pontius Pilate had been faced with several years before, when a religious fanatic had stirred up trouble with the vague promise of a redemption and forgiveness other than that which came from the emperor in Rome. Corbulo had no wish to deal with outbreaks of similar religious or civil unrest in his province. In any case, the Nabateans were nowhere near as troublesome as the Jews that Pilate had been forced to deal with.

He took another draught of wine. On the other hand, he thought, if the Nabateans are somehow involved in a plot against us, then this tablet could give us early warning, if its meaning can be made clear. If they are not involved, then why is this message inscribed in their script ... and why did those who were carrying it resist at the checkpoint?

'What is the state of the city?' he asked, gesturing impatiently out across the balcony.

'Calm,' was the stark reply. 'Everything is as it should be.'

'It would not do to upset the status quo,' continued Corbulo.

He had his legion, Legio III Cyrenaica, which was more than capable of suppressing any dissent by the populace, but, despite such a comforting thought, he remained warily mindful of the enormous amount of trouble a handful of fanatics could wreak.

'Remind me once again what the inscription says,' Corbulo said softly, waving the tablet towards the tribune.

'It is an exhortation to the Jews to rise up. At the command of their one god, who assures them of victory, Gershom will lead them to their own kingdom, which will stretch from Judea to Petra.'

'And who *is* this Gershom? Is he known to us?'

'It is a common enough name amongst the Jews and is associated with one of their prophets, the one they call Moses. Gershom was one of his sons. The inscription on the tablet could refer to him ... or not. We have no way of being certain.'

'What interest would the Nabateans have in this Gershom ... or in a land for the Jews?'

Another silence descended on the vast room. Corbulo still held the marble tablet in his hand and was patting the top end of it against his lips, deep in thought. As a military man, he preferred a known enemy; one that could be seen. The unknown, unseen foe was quite a different matter and was one for which he had very little taste.

'Keep looking and let me know if you find anything,' he added, pointing the tablet at the tribune as he walked past him towards one of the two arches that gave access to the room. 'We cannot afford the luxury of irresponsible complacency.'

As he left the room, he tossed the marble tablet towards a long, ornate table, behind which were seated two scribes. He completely misjudged the distance to the table as he threw the tablet and it fell short, landing upon the marble floor with a deafening clatter. It bounced once and the bottom right-hand corner fractured and broke off.

STUART FIFIELD

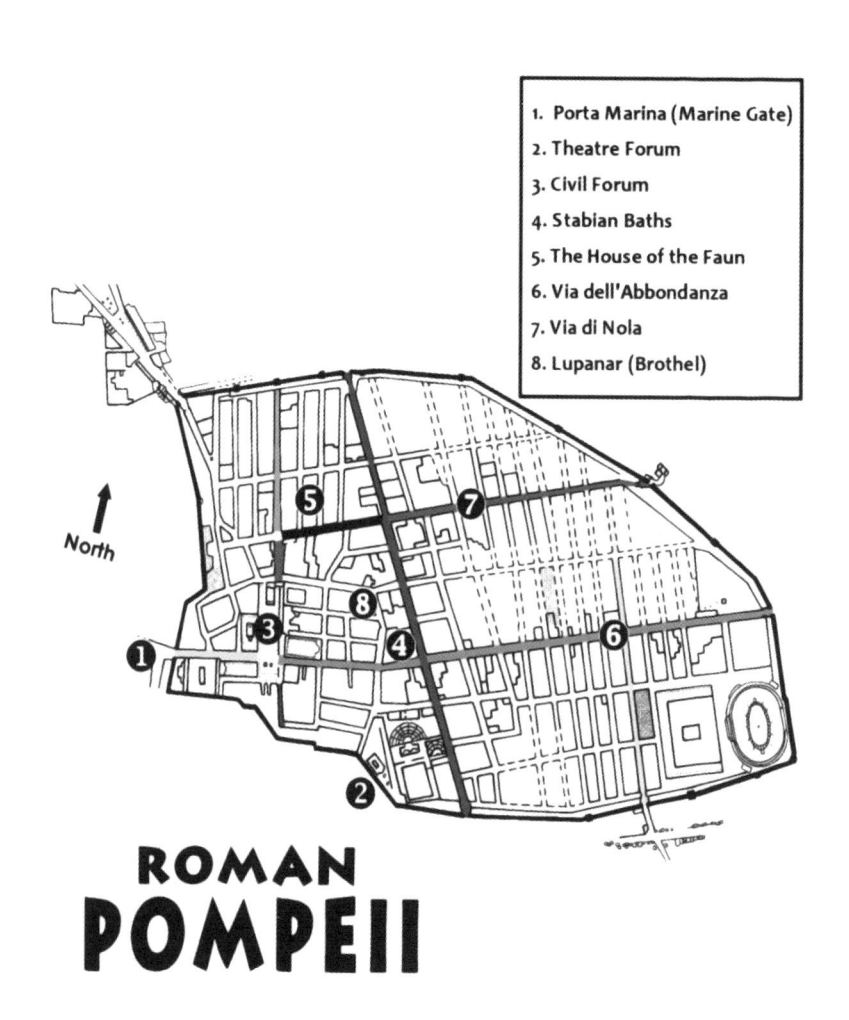

1. Porta Marina (Marine Gate)
2. Theatre Forum
3. Civil Forum
4. Stabian Baths
5. The House of the Faun
6. Via dell'Abbondanza
7. Via di Nola
8. Lupanar (Brothel)

ROMAN
POMPEII

1

Pompeii

Thursday, 9th October 1930

Close to the shores of the Bay of Naples the town of Pompeii was once again coming to life, ready to face another day in the shadow of the majestic, sleeping volcano that smouldered nearby. The modern town was, in reality, two distinct settlements joined together by geographical proximity, but separated by nearly two thousand years.

The new town, which had only been established towards the end of the previous century, grew up around the central Piazza Bartolo Longo, the spacious dimensions of which were faced by the Sanctuary, a provincial church with the substantial proportions of a basilica. A certain *Signor* Longo, a lawyer by profession, had come to the village in 1872 and it was the news of his saintly good deeds and, more importantly, the miraculous cures effected through the numerous interventions of the Blessed Virgin Mary that had largely encouraged the growth of the new town. A considerable annual income had also been generated for the Sanctuary. Even the Vatican soon began taking a very special interest in the town.

Pompeii had become a *civita* in its own right at the end of 1927. Now it looked forward to an era of prosperity and growth, as did the whole of Italy, under the charismatic leadership of Il Duce, the blacksmith's son who had swept to power five years before, much to the alarm of the more restrained powers at the western end of Europe. However, not everyone in Italy welcomed or approved of the forceful methods used by Il Duce's followers – the *Fasci Italiani di Combattimento*, the Italian League of Combatants or simply the Fascists. Foolishly, perhaps, those who disagreed with them soon learned that having a conscience had suddenly become a dangerous thing. To the passing tourist or even the average citizen, these authoritarian methods were not generally in evidence in the quiet, clean streets of the new town. Life followed its usual pattern: the faithful would continue to flock to the Sanctuary in their thousands every year, ensuring a steady flow of income; the average resident would continue the daily struggle to put food on the table. It was mainly the ever increasing army of tourists, who descended like a swarm of curious bees during the season, which would be entranced by the other, much older Pompeii: the one that nestled in the countryside, shoulder to shoulder with its much newer namesake. To the typical resident of the new town, the ruins were just that – ruins.

As for Vesuvius, if it decided to once again set its mind on the total destruction of Pompeii – both the new town and, for the second time, the old town – then there was very little that could be done about it. The populace had long ago learned to live with that thought.

It was just ten o'clock on the first day of their visit when Rupert Winfield and his friend Doctor Stephen Hopkins set out to discover the lost world of ancient Pompeii. After enjoying a leisurely breakfast at the Grand Hotel, they strolled up Via Roma, away from Piazza Bartolo Longo, towards the marvel that was the reclaimed ancient city of Pompeii. They entered through the Porta Marina, the Marine Gate, where, in ancient times, the sea had lapped close by; now it was several miles distant. Thanks to very careful excavation, more and more of the buried town was awakening from its two-thousand-year sleep and was, once again, revealing itself to the curious world. It was almost noon before they reached the shade of the trees on the south side of the ruins next to the theatres and the Triangular Forum.

Stephen had found the steep climb up the uneven stones of the road a little taxing and had been obliged to use his thick black cane to support himself on more than one occasion, as the unevenness of the terrain got the better of him.

'Thank God for that,' he said, as he sat down on the low wall that formed one side of the border of the Triangular Forum, 'those roads out there are hell on the old leg, I'm afraid.'

Large dressed blocks of stone had been carefully set down to form the city's extensive, paved road network. The ravages of time and of seismic activity from the volcano had made them uneven.

'Perhaps we should have taken a carriage or taxi from the hotel,' said Rupert, unscrewing the water canteen the hotel had given them for their outing, 'it was much further than I thought it would be. Sorry.'

'That's all right, my dear chap,' replied Stephen, rubbing his left leg above where the lower part had been amputated. 'We can't give in to these little inconveniences now, can we?'

The site had been surprisingly busy that morning. Groups of tourists had criss-crossed the ruins, some being herded on by the official guides, others on their own, following the instructions offered them by their Baedeker or other tourist guidebook.

'Well, it certainly makes a change from ancient Egypt,' said Rupert, as he removed their packed lunch from the haversack he had been carrying. 'I wonder what the hotel has prepared. It was thoughtful of them, don't you think?'

'Absolutely perfect, my dear chap; perfect food, perfect setting and perfect company. So this is where it all happened, is it?' asked Stephen, pointing across the Forum in the direction of the remains of the theatre, as Rupert started to investigate the contents of the prepared food parcels.

'Yes. This is where culture was provided to the general public in the form of plays and poetry readings. I read that an audience of nearly five thousand could be accommodated at any one performance,' replied Rupert, pointing through the retaining wall, on the other side of which lay the auditorium.

'Just so that I get it right in my own mind ... this forum is not *the* forum, is it?' asked Stephen, laying one of the food parcels on the wall between them.

'No. This one was to accommodate visitors to the theatre ... theatre*s* actually, because there are two of them. And there was also a temple dedicated to Hercules and Minerva ... over there. The real forum, where justice was administered and where all manner of economic affairs were conducted, is the one we walked past as we came up the hill from the Marine Gate,' replied Rupert, who had read about it in the *Baedeker Guide for Southern Italy and Sicily* he had purchased from Foyles bookshop before they left London. 'No doubt some affairs were legitimate and others not quite so.'

'So not much has changed over the centuries then,' quipped Stephen, 'and in any case, what is it about ruins that creates such interest?'

'It's undoubtedly a sense of mystery. Think of the lives lived in and around them...' replied Rupert, making a sweeping gesture, '... and of the secrets those people might have had...'

'Oh, come on...' said Stephen, looking at his friend incredulously, 'you don't mean to say that you actually *believe* that?'

'Of course I do ... and why not? Everyone needs a little

dash of romantic mystery in their lives. When we think of the inhabitants of any historic site, we need to accurately record the evidence of what we find, but we also need to consider the mystery of the lives those people might have led.'

'That'll be the archaeologist speaking, will it?' said Stephen, punching his friend gently on the shoulder.

'It will,' Rupert replied, smiling at his friend. 'We must never forget our trip to ancient Pompeii. It is from shared memories, such as these, that contentment in later life comes.'

'That is a very profound remark to make for so early in the day,' replied Hopkins, good-naturedly. 'So your professional recommendation is that I should focus my thoughts not only on the unevenness of the roads in this place, but also on the mystery of the lives these long-dead inhabitants might have lived. They must have had some wild parties...' he concluded, moving his leg slightly.

'How do you mean?'

'My dear chap, can you ever recall seeing an erect penis being used as a direction sign before?'

'Stephen! I explained to you that they indicated the way to the brothels ... That's what it says in the guide. So there's no mystery attached to that at all. It's perfectly obvious, actually,' Rupert responded, taking a bite of his *panino*.

Stephen laughed, holding his own *panino* in his hand.

'Then I will concentrate on the more mundane mysteries of their lost lives, such as how they managed to contend with *that*,' he continued, gesturing towards the nearby volcano with his chin before taking a bite.

After lunch they investigated the Temple of Apollo and strolled around the forum proper, before crossing to the eastern side and the ruins of the administrative buildings. From there, they wandered off down the Via d'Abbondanza, the Street of Abundance, towards the Casa del Menandro, where a hoard of over a hundred priceless silver objects had recently been discovered. Their progress had been slow but steady. Being mindful of his friend's leg, Rupert eventually suggested that they walk on the pavement, rather than on the road, as the surface was not quite as uneven.

'Thanks for that ... thoughtful as ever, but it takes more than a few Roman boulders to keep an old soldier down!' Stephen remarked, turning to smile at his friend.

'They are not actually Roman ... That's what it says here,' replied Rupert, pointing at the page he held open in the guide. 'Pompeii only became totally under Roman control around 89 BC. Then it became a sort of Roman colony and it was run by local people who were friendly to Rome.'

'Oh ... I see,' said Stephen, who had always found the unravelling of different layers of history more than just a little confusing. To him, a Roman was a Roman. He refrained from asking any further questions as to who might have built the streets.

As the afternoon wore on, the number of tourists in the ruins also diminished considerably. Eventually, as they strolled slowly along one of the pavements, they found themselves totally alone. The atmosphere was such that Stephen recalled Rupert's earlier remark about those who had lived and died in the town and the secrets they might have had. For a moment, even he thought it possible to feel the slipstream of a passing chariot or to hear the creaking of an ox cart delivering wine amphorae to one of the numerous shops that lined most of the principal streets in the town.

'Here we are...' announced Rupert, as they stopped outside the Casa del Menandro, '... He was a highly respected Greek playwright,' he read, before lowering the book. 'I wonder if any of his plays were performed at the theatres?'

The house itself proved interesting enough, although none of the silverware was on display.

'Right then ... off this way,' continued Rupert. 'It will eventually lead us back to the Triangular Forum.'

'Where do all these fancy names come from?' asked Stephen, as they strolled along the pavement. 'Did that Menander chap actually live in the house that now bears his name?'

'I really have no idea. He might well have done. Most of the names are modern and come from the archaeologists. A significant find can give that location its name ... so you have the House of the Large Fountain, the House of the Lyre-player and so on. They're not the names the Pompeiians would have given to things.'

'I say, my dear fellow, can we have a breather for a bit? This low wall is just too convenient...'

The two of them sat down, Stephen moving his leg until he found a comfortable position for it.

'Is it getting worse?' asked Rupert with concern.

'Not at all,' Stephen reassured his companion. 'It is simply *I* who needs to still get used to *it*. That's all.'

Sitting in the shade of the buildings out of the hot sun, they took the opportunity to have a much needed break for refreshment and to enjoy the peace and tranquillity of the site with the views of Vesuvius in the background. It looked so peaceful as to make any concept of the disastrous, cataclysmic eruption almost beyond the bounds of imagination.

'According to Baedeker,' Rupert announced, ' "Vesuvius last erupted in 1906 ... for over two weeks it pumped out molten lava, plumes of smoke and clouds of ash." Not quite on the scale of AD 79.' He looked up from the guide and stared at the volcano. 'I say! ... I'm not sure *I* would be too happy about living so close to such a potential time bomb.'

'Me neither, old chap. Mind you, there was a little activity up there last year, so who knows when it will go again. Here's another titbit of information. My Uncle Cecil told me ages ago that the Italian government asked that the Olympic Games they were due to host in 1908 be relocated, as they needed funds to rebuild the area damaged by that 1906 eruption. Allegedly, it was a convenient excuse as they couldn't afford to host the Games anyway and that is why London unexpectedly held them. I doubt, though, if that is in your guidebook.' Stephen chuckled.

The two friends sat in companionable silence, each with their private thoughts about a town and its people being buried by the output of such a powerful force of Nature.

'Shall we make a move? I'm ready for the next spot of sightseeing after that rest. Even the water tastes different here,' said Stephen, replacing the stopper on the water flask before handing it to Rupert, who returned it to the haversack. 'It must be the minerals.'

'Talking of which, they were really quite civilized in the water department,' said Rupert, as he buckled down the flap of the haversack and replaced it on his back. 'Have you noticed the lead water pipes in the pavement?'

'I have,' replied Stephen, 'and have you noticed the regularity of these large water troughs on each of the main roads? They had to be fed with pipes of some description. I reckon that, if the volcano hadn't got the townsfolk first, then the very real risk of lead poisoning would have. Their constitutions must have been quite robust!'

They walked on a little further, before Stephen spotted something written on a wall.

'There's no mystery attached to *that*,' he said, pointing to the almost faded graffiti. 'I can't make out the end of it, but the beginning is clear enough...'

Rupert turned his gaze back to the pages of the guide.

'All it says here is that you can still see the remains of

graffiti, mainly political, at various points throughout the city,' he said, 'but there are no translations or anything like that.'

'I am not in the least bit surprised, my dear chap. That message is one that would not sit too easily on an editor's conscience,' responded Stephen, lifting his cane to point in the direction of the writing. 'Through the benefit of a sound, classical education, I can tell you that the Latin reads as follows: "I will not vote for Marcus Adrianus Lorrius. Before I do, he can suck my...".' Stephen's voice trailed off as he lowered the cane. 'The last bit is too faded to read.'

'Oh, that's a pity...' said Rupert, looking at the writing. His Latin was not good at all. He had never had an ear for languages.

'Oh, come along now, my dear chap,' replied Stephen, a twinkle in his eye, 'surely you can put two and two together. You know how broadminded the Romans were ... as you are always telling me.'

'Oh ... that.' Rupert chuckled.

'What's your opinion on the chaps with the knitted caps and dangling tassels?' asked Stephen, abruptly changing the topic of their conversation.

'You mean the ones with the black shirts and breeches ... and the tassel that dangles on a long string from the centre of the cap?'

'More like jodhpurs than breeches I'd say, but yes ... them.'

'I've noticed a few standing around in small groups. I thought they might be guides of some sort, except that we saw some of them out in the *piazza* last night ... and there were a couple of them at dinner as well ... dressed in military jackets and without the tassels, but their facial expressions were just as severe and arrogant. Why do you ask? Do you have any idea who they are?'

'Oh yes,' replied Stephen, keeping his voice low despite the fact that they were the only ones in the street. 'The king is head of state, but the real political power in Italy rests with the Prime Minister ... this Mussolini fellow. He is also head of the Fascist Party and those fellows in the black outfits are not simply members of his local Guild of Undertakers, hanging around on the street corner in the hope of picking up business.' He stopped and cast a furtive glance about them, before continuing in a whisper, 'They are his strong-arm boys ... a law unto themselves. Oh, and one other thing, Mussolini is very friendly with Herr Hitler. They both think along similar lines, as I understand things.'

'How do you know all of that?' asked Rupert.

'Eyes and ears, my dear chap ... remember Egypt? Eyes and ears,' he repeated, tapping his nose in the gesture of one who possesses knowledge.

'Is this your Uncle Cecil in Whitehall talking again?' asked Rupert, but Stephen simply smiled.

'Lead on Macduff! Where to next...?'

2

Pompeii

Thursday, 9th October 1930 – One hour later

They had set a course up Via dei Teatri, past the Stabian Baths, on up into the maze of streets and then on towards the so-called House of the Faun. By the time they stood outside the considerable expanse of the house, it was early afternoon. In the near distance, barely six miles away, the volcano still brooded ominously.

'Well, well ... look at that,' said Stephen, as they neared the first of the two entrances to the house. 'That's really quite imposing, isn't it? The columns go back towards old Vesuvius in the distance ... and there's that pool thing in the entrance ... with a little statue in it. Look,' he said, pointing.

Rupert was busy turning to the relevant page in his Baedeker, but managed a hasty glance.

'Yes,' he replied, 'and that pool thing, as you call it, is called an *impluvium*. It catches rainwater and stores it. This is what the guide has to say about the rest of it,' he continued, quoting the printed text: ' "... The House of the Faun is a very large domestic dwelling ... It dates from around 180 BC ... It occupies the entire block on which it is built ... contained many lavish mosaics and exquisite statues ..." This is interesting ... the famous Alexander Mosaic, which is estimated to have over four million tesserae, the tiny bits of glass or coloured stone used to make a mosaic, was found here ... It says that most of the finds are now in the Archaeological Museum in Naples.'

Whilst Rupert was talking, Stephen decided that with a little careful positioning he could take a very worthwhile photograph. He visualized it framed by the entrance to the ruined house, with the atrium and the *impluvium* in the foreground and the volcano as an imposing backdrop.

'All done,' declared Stephen, a few moments later. 'I think that picture will be one of the better ones for my photograph album,' he continued, smiling at Rupert as he closed the leather camera case. 'It's a pity about that group of people in the background over there. I couldn't avoid getting some of them in the frame. I think that the scene is better without people in it. They might be able to enlarge the image when they process the prints ... That should cut them out of the picture, as long as it doesn't upset the proportion of everything else.'

They resumed their progress down Via di Nola, towards the eastern end of the ruins.

'That was really very silly of me,' said Rupert, stopping abruptly.

'What was?'

'Not taking a photograph back there ... You were quite right; it is a very picturesque scene. Perhaps those people have moved off now and I can capture it without them in the exposure. Can we go back for a minute?' he asked, already unslinging his camera and removing its leather case.

'Well ... I tell you what, my dear chap; at present the old leg is twitching away faster than a rabbit's whiskers. You nip back and take your photo and I'll have a sit down and wait for you in here. In this ... what *was* this, do you think?' he asked, pointing towards an open-fronted building that had a counter running parallel to the pavement.

The counter protruded from the left-hand wall towards

the centre of the room, and in the top were several large, round openings, some of which still held the remains of large clay jars.

'It was a shop,' replied Rupert, without having to consult the guide, 'a food shop. I read in the guide last night that most Pompeiians bought their food from the shops in the town ... Sort of early fish and chips, I suppose,' he said with a laugh. 'Look there, see those hollow tiles running around the outside of the counter,' he continued, pointing to the broken ends of the square tiles, 'they would have had hot air flowing through them, to keep the food warm.'

'Or to make it go off even quicker in the heat and dust,' quipped Stephen.

'Well, not really, because...'

'Your photograph,' said Stephen, pointing back up the road down which they had just come. 'Don't leave it too late otherwise the sun will have set!'

'Very amusing,' replied Rupert, as he closed the Baedeker and gave it to his friend. 'Whilst you are sitting comfortably on that low stone bench in the corner, perhaps you'd like to read up a bit on Pompeii? There are nearly thirty pages of very useful information to choose from,' he added, as he turned and strode off.

On reaching the right-hand entrance to the House of the Faun, Rupert adjusted the focal length and set the shutter speed of his camera to match the light conditions, but found that he was unhappy with the picture he saw through the viewfinder from that angle. He walked on a few more paces until he reached the left-hand door, from where he found he could compose a far more aesthetically pleasing image. He pressed the shutter release just as a group of men suddenly appeared in his viewfinder. They walked out of the house and into the street, nearly colliding with him.

From the shaded seclusion of his stone seat, Stephen looked up from the Baedeker. He had chosen a page on

Pompeii at random and had almost finished reading it with some difficulty in the low light, when he suddenly become aware of the sound of a disturbance – shouting and the sound of running boots echoing off the stones of the street. He put the book down on the bench next to him and crossed the darkened interior of the shop to investigate. He had a split second to take in the view that met his inquisitive gaze, make a decision as to what to do next and carry it out. Hopkins flattened himself against the shop wall, keeping very still, his mind racing. Had his eyes deceived him? Surely, they had been wrong? Gingerly, he edged closer and closer to the shop's open frontage, until he could just see around the corner of the wall without being visible himself. His eyes had not played tricks on him.

Rupert was standing in the street in front of the House of the Faun. He was surrounded by a group of uniformed men, some in the all-black uniforms of the Fascists and others in the smart uniforms of the Carabinieri – the paramilitary police. One of the Fascists had Rupert's camera in his hands and was pulling the film out of it, exposing it to the light and totally ruining the images it contained. Although he was surrounded, no one seemed to be physically holding Rupert. There was a great deal of shouting – none of which Stephen could understand – and much gesticulating. Further up the street, beyond the animated knot of uniforms surrounding a bemused Rupert, a tightly packed group of men, all dressed in smart suits, was walking away briskly in the opposite direction, towards the forum.

Stephen flattened himself against the shop wall once again, torn between wanting to protect Rupert and ensuring his own survival: but survival of what? He found he was unable to move, his mouth was bone dry, his breath had started to come in shallow gasps and his heart was racing. He recognized the signs because he had experienced all of these symptoms before – amidst the blood, trenches, barbed wire and carnage of the Western Front. As those memories came flooding back, his body reacted in the way it thought best to allow him to cope with this unexpected, acute anxiety: he was frozen to the spot. In this state, he was unable to think clearly or to spring into action, as his body and mind tried to blot out the horrors of a war that should have remained in the past.

Eventually, after only a few seconds, his adrenalin started to flow, his military training came to the fore and he was able to rationalize and start to form a strategy.

The film, he tried to reason in the garbled, over-animated way humans do when faced with unidentified danger. *Why the House of the Faun ... and Rupert's film ... why have they destroyed the film?*

Silently, he crept away from the front of the shop, back towards the rear of the structure where there were dark shadows and where only the very feeblest of light reached. With sweaty hands he quickly removed his camera from its case and rewound the film. Then he took it out of the camera, making sure that the lightproof backing paper was securely wrapped around the end of it. Despite the rear of the shop being in cooling deep shade, beads of sweat had formed on his brow. Picking up the heavy walking stick, he released the catch of the ornate silver handle and removed it, before sliding the roll of film into the hollow central compartment, which, in the past, had held a king's ransom in uncut diamonds. It fitted perfectly.

For a split second he looked at the short, bright stiletto blade that protruded from the ornate, bird-shaped handle. He hoped that he would not have to resort to using it. With a sigh he returned it to its chamber and clicked the handle securely home once again. He crept carefully towards the open front of the shop and deposited his empty camera inside the deepest open-necked jar he could see.

The whole process of removing the film and hiding the

camera had taken no more than a minute, although it felt much longer. Once again, Stephen flattened himself against the wall of the shop before carefully peering round the corner of the opening and up the street. It was empty. He walked as quickly as he could towards where, only minutes before, he had seen his friend standing, surrounded by the threatening group of uniformed men.

'Welcome to the New Italy,' he muttered, acknowledging that those same uniforms represented the heavy-handed authority of the state.

Now there was no sign of anyone. The street was strangely silent apart from the sensation of his heartbeat. He felt much more in control of the situation, but then Stephen suddenly felt a twinge of something. What was it? Fear – anxiety – conscience – apprehension? He was not sure, but he did not like it – not one little bit. *Where to now?* His mind was working furiously. Faced as he was with the warren of ancient streets that surrounded him, Stephen felt totally helpless. *Quo vadis?* he mused, rather aptly, as a smile flashed across his face before disappearing into furrows of worry, concern and helplessness.

A sudden movement caught his eye. A cooling afternoon breeze had started to pick up and it was playing with something yellow – a long, fluttering strip of paper that was flapping along in the gutter. With some difficulty Stephen stepped off the pavement and into the road. As the paper snaked towards him, he squatted down and caught it, then, with his trophy grasped securely in his hand, he retraced his steps to the safety of the shop. Once inside, he looked at the crumpled contents of his fist. It was the lightproof backing paper from a roll of film – Rupert's roll of film. One of the Blackshirts must have torn it off the roll when he has wrenching the film out of the camera.

So I definitely did not imagine it!

What at first seemed like a nightmare was in fact very

real. It had happened – and not more than a few minutes before.

Stephen made his way to the Marine Gate, but found no trace of either Rupert or the Blackshirts he had seen outside the House of the Faun.

Stay calm now, old chap, he reassured himself, fighting against the rising tide of apprehension he felt welling up from his stomach. You wouldn't be able to recognize them even if you did see them. Bully boys all look alike in their fancy toy-soldier uniforms. But his attempt at humour did nothing to improve his disquiet.

Enquiries at the Marine Gate proved fruitless, his questions being met with shrugs of the shoulders and a flood of Italian, nothing of which he could understand. By late afternoon he was faced with no alternative other than to take a taxi back to the hotel. Totally illogically, something in his mind told him that he would find his friend waiting for him there.

Back at the hotel he suffered more disappointment: Rupert had not returned. As Stephen tried to assert control over his rising panic, he decided on the only course of action he felt was left open to him.

'Good afternoon, *Signore*,' said the receptionist, from behind the ornate marble-and-mahogany reception desk. 'Did the *Signore's* expedition progress well?' he asked.

'I would like to make a telephone call, please ... Is that possible?' asked Stephen, ignoring the man's question.

'But of course. To where would you like to telephone?'

'London,' replied Stephen.

'I will enquire for you, *Signore*, but there is usually a delay before a connection of long distance can be made,' replied the concierge in his almost perfect English.

'It doesn't matter how long it takes, as long as I am put through at the earliest possible opportunity.' He hoped that the nervousness in his voice was not too obvious. It would not do to arouse suspicions of any kind in a country full of swaggering, authoritarian bullies.

As Stephen sat in the foyer waiting for his call to be put through, he began to question whether he had done the right thing by putting the safety of his film before that of his friend. Why had he suddenly done that? It had been a decision made, as it were, in the heat of battle. In the ruins of the once-thriving ghost city, he had been faced with a totally unexpected situation and had reacted, almost automatically, according to what his physical and mental instincts had told him; only after that had his military training kicked in. But had his instincts been correct? Should he have gone to Rupert's assistance immediately and just abandoned his camera with its film? He wrestled with the vagrancies of hindsight and concluded that he had acted appropriately after all. In any case, what had been so important about the film in Rupert's camera that the Blackshirts had reacted so violently by destroying it? Had it been witnessing that single action that had subconsciously made him protective of his own roll of film? More important still, where was Rupert now?

This is Italy, not some barbarian outpost of the Empire in the middle of nowhere. People didn't simply disappear! There must surely be a perfectly logical explanation for things, he reflected. There has to be! He found little solace in his ponderings. Instead, he found himself harbouring dark thoughts about having failed Rupert in a moment of need. Had he compromised his friend's safety through making the wrong decision?

As he sat and waited, he continued to torture himself with these doubts. He had also started to develop a severe headache. When he next looked at his watch it was nearly five; in London it would be nearly four o'clock, so his uncle should still be at his desk.

This time, it is I who need your help, Uncle.

3

The Middle of the Atlantic Ocean

RMS *Olympic* **– Wednesday, 15th October 1930**

The first-class passengers on board the ageing liner *Olympic* were engaged in their morning pursuits, all of which were extremely leisurely. Even the deck quoits and the shipboard variation of shove-ha'penny were relaxed, laughter-filled affairs. There were no outward signs of any aggression or driving desire to win amongst those passengers who happily played these games. The activities were simply there to while away the time until luncheon.

Like a society debutante, the ship had just turned twenty-one. She was really a huge, self-contained floating city, constructed years before by an army of ant-like workers using thousands of tons of steel and millions of rivets. During the five days it took to cross the sometimes bleak wastes of the North Atlantic, the degree of luxury offered to passengers by the White Star Line was in direct proportion to how much they had paid for their ticket. The luxury and service offered in first class was breath-taking. In third class, or 'steerage' as it was derisively referred to by those rich enough to be spared the experience of ever having to travel by it, the case was dramatically the opposite: comfortable at a pinch, but far from luxurious. From the top of her tall masts to the very bottom of her keel several hundred feet below, *Olympic* was a floating microcosm of the class structure that had held the Empire together for over two centuries. Following the catastrophe of the Great War, this structure had slowly begun to disintegrate and yet, on those of Britain's great passenger ships that had survived the conflict, there seemed little evidence of this. The oceans no longer hid the threat of sudden underwater attack and these great floating steel cities once again ploughed their way backwards and forwards across the Atlantic, very much as they had done before the catastrophic days of August 1914. They seemed to have largely escaped the post-war notions of levelling equality that had gripped most of the rest of battered Europe. Within the confines of the watertight hulls, each passenger was allocated their place and each soul knew, no matter how resentfully, exactly where that place was.

Alexandra Hawkhurst – or Alex, as she preferred to be called – and her brother, Lawrence, both knew perfectly well where their place lay within this clearly defined social structure. Owing to their wealth and connections it was very near the top.

'Steward,' called Alex, holding up her hand to attract the man's attention, 'may I have a dry Martini cocktail, please?'

It was a taste she had acquired in New York and she continued to find the heady aroma of this aperitif most appealing.

'Certainly, Madam,' replied the white-jacketed crewman, as he turned away to carry out Alexandra's bidding.

As she lay on her deck lounger, enjoying the pleasant sunshine, she became aware of loud voices in earnest conversation.

'...anyway, I just told him straight that it was not enough. I simply *had* to have more...'

There was a slender, well-tanned elderly woman lying on the lounger to Alexandra's left. She was heavily made up and was wearing far too much jewellery to be simply relaxing in the sun. She spoke in a very loud voice, heavy with an American accent.

'Hell no!' she continued, '... I ain't taking it lying down! I warned the loser about his wandering eye after that last time down in Michigan. I told him: "Honey, being married to you ain't always a bed of roses," I said, "and you think that you're a stud stallion or something? P-lea-se!! I've seen bigger ones in a gherkin jar!"'

The woman had a voice that was designed to carry, no matter what its volume, and she made certain that it did. Both she and her companion, who lay on the lounger to her left, dissolved into uncontrollable floods of raucous laughter.

Alexander Hawkhurst squirmed behind her sunglasses. It had been pleasantly quiet when she had settled herself on to her lounger, but her two neighbours had arrived shortly thereafter and their subsequent conversation had shattered her contentment. From behind the discreet anonymity of her glasses, Alexandra looked disapprovingly at this loud-mouthed woman, sparkling in the sunshine. She was obviously extremely wealthy, but what she possessed in monetary terms she woefully lacked in breeding and manners.

'Your drink, Madam,' said the waiter, as he held out a small tray in Alexandra's direction.

'Thank you.'

She would have her drink and then, if her brother had still not returned, she would find herself another place to sit, far away from her loud neighbour. Alexandra laid back, drink in hand, and concentrated hard on ignoring the irritation to her left. She thought instead of the outfit she had decided to wear for the afternoon – a light cotton blouse, white cotton Bermuda-style shorts and plimsolls. Then, sitting forward, she gazed first across the open expanse of deck, which lay between her and the stern, and then upwards. High above her, *Olympic*'s two tall masts pointed up at a clear blue sky. *That* was where she felt most at home; up there in the peace and tranquillity, safely encased in an aeroplane, moving through a foreign, yet welcoming environment. Today, that environment held the promise of yet more fine weather to come. Although winter lurked on the horizon, like some unwelcome actor waiting in the wings for his cue to enter, the weather was particularly mild for the time of year and there was hardly any wind off the ocean.

Other first-class passengers were also enjoying the fine weather on deck. Like Alexandra, they were dressed to fulfil their desire to absorb the sun's rays, though they were careful not to overstep the rigid boundaries of decorum and good taste as far as appearance was concerned.

Alexandra stole another glance at her loud neighbour, who brazenly continued telling the entire deck her most intimate details.

The sound of laughter and chatter, of people enjoying themselves, floated up from the games courts. As she lay fighting to blot out the sound of the voice to her left, Alexandra strained to see if she could catch the sound of her brother's voice wafting up amid the general merriment, but she could not. She adjusted her sunglasses and looked at her watch. Still no sign of him and she had only a couple of sips of her drink left. Then it would be time to move. The sun was already approaching the point where it would arch over the top of the ship's four funnels, before hanging there majestically and commencing its decline towards the western horizon behind them. The sunlight, which flooded the entire games deck, would then start to retreat into shadows towards the ship's bows.

To Alexandra's right was an empty lounger, on which lay Lawrence's navy jersey and cap. She turned her head and gazed at the items, wondering what her brother could be up to. She tried to concentrate on her copy of *Harper's*, which lay propped open on her knees in front of her, but her mind soon drifted elsewhere, fixed on other things far more significant than the temptations offered on the pages of the magazine.

They had enjoyed a good trip – no, she corrected herself, they had enjoyed a *very* good trip and she could not wait to get back to the factory and just get on with things. She closed the magazine, dropping it on to the deck. Reaching behind her, she retrieved her shoulder bag from where it hung from the back of the lounger and took out her cigarette case and lighter. Her father had never accepted his daughter's smoking, but then, as her mother had often joked, her father had never really accepted the fact that his pretty little daughter had the iron determination and will of a successful businesswoman either. That had been some years ago. Both parents were now gone and the family business was owned and run by Alexandra and her brother Lawrence. She smiled at the memories. It was only then that she realized the two deck loungers to her left were empty. She had been so lost in her own thoughts that she had not noticed the loud woman's departure.

'Thank God for that,' muttered Alexandra, before returning to her memories.

Hawkhurst Aeronautics had started in a shed, shortly after the Wright brothers had proved that machines that were heavier than air could not only fly, but could also be controlled in their flight. By the time the Indian summer of 1914 had arrived, Alex's father and his unmarried brother had become the British equivalent of America's Wright brothers, and they were soon demonstrating their British-designed and built aircraft at the newly established air shows across the country. Now, as a result of the constant demand for new aircraft and new ideas that had originated back in the dark, dismal days of the carnage of the war, the firm and their reputation had grown almost beyond all recognition. There was no doubt about that. If proof was required, it was in the pages of their sizeable American order book, particularly orders for their new Hawkhurst Avenger machine, which, because of its lightweight aluminium airframe, was capable of record-breaking speeds.

You would have been very proud of us, Father, she thought, as she hid her bag under the lounger. There was nothing of any value in it; her father had taught her to always put things in a safe place. Still clutching her cigarettes and lighter, she got up and made her way across the broad expanse of deck, which was as wide as the average village high street. She reached the railings and, nestling herself between two of the lifeboats, took out a cigarette and lit it, putting the gold case and lighter into the pocket of her shorts.

Alexander Hawkhurst was a woman ahead of her time and enjoyed a huge zest for life and for living. She had considerable business acumen, influence and power and, as such, was also something of an oddity, being a woman of note in what was largely still very much a man's world. She turned her head and, leaning out slightly over the railings, could just catch a glimpse of *Olympic*'s foaming wake streaming out behind the speeding ship, pointing the way back to New York.

'Hello, Sis,' said a voice to her right, which took her by surprise. 'Got a fag for me?'

She took out her cigarette case and lighter and handed them over. 'I was beginning to think that you'd got lost.' She took a draw on her cigarette, at the same time giving her brother a quizzical look. 'And then I thought you might be down there,' she said, sticking out her chin in the direction of the games area. 'I listened for your happy laughter, but, alas, there was none,' she said, with mock reproach.

'No, I was up that end,' Lawrence Hawkhurst said, pointing

towards the bows. 'I met some really interesting people ... We were sitting up in the lounge, chatting.'

'I see,' answered Alexandra, looking down at the water below them, 'and will you be chatting to them again?' She had had plenty of experience of those her brother dubbed his *interesting* friends. 'Female, are they?' she asked, already knowing what the answer would be.

Their father had asked Alexandra to always look after her younger brother – he was not as serious as she was; neither was he as clever. Their uncle, who was several years younger than their father – an afterthought was what he jokingly called himself – had shared the same opinion. But he had gone off in his Royal Flying Corps uniform one day in 1917 and that had been the last time they had seen him. Their father had never recovered from the loss. Years later, here she was still looking after her little brother.

They stood between the lifeboats, smoking their cigarettes and chatting, until, eventually, Lawrence turned the topic around to the subject of their trip.

'This wasn't a holiday, Law,' she sighed. 'You *know* it was important for us to expand into the American market. There's a lot of fierce competition over there and we have to break into that market if we're going to keep expanding. It was a business trip, not a holiday.'

'Yes, I know that, Alexandra.' He always addressed her by her full name when he was in earnest about something, 'but I was just thinking of that holiday you spoke about. Do you remember?'

'Yes, I remember,' she replied, wondering when her brother would grow up enough to take the future of their business – of their livelihood and their passport to the luxury they were presently enjoying – more seriously.

'You said that, if the trip was a success, we'd take a break to celebrate ... Well, we did very well to get the orders. I'd say the expedition was a *complete* success, wouldn't you?'

For a while she said nothing. She was used to him and could sense his growing excitement as he waited for her response, but she resisted the urge to either encourage or discourage him. Lawrence was her only brother, her only real family, but that did not mean that she was about to give in to his every whim.

'I did say that, didn't I?' she said, turning to him. 'I suppose we could manage a bracing week in Skegness when we get back. We'll have to sort the orders out first and make sure they are all in process of completion before we do, though.'

'Skegness?' he repeated, incredulously. Even after all these years, he was never quite sure when to take his sister seriously or when she was simply jesting and playing with him. 'I was thinking of something more exciting and for a bit longer than just a week,' he replied, somewhat crestfallen.

'Yes, I'm sure you were,' she replied, not unkindly, 'and where was it you were thinking of then?' she asked.

'Well, Caroline has recently been to Jerusalem...'

'This Caroline is one of your really *interesting* people, I presume?' she asked, lifting her sunglasses and smiling at him with a knowing look in her eyes.

'Well ... er ... yes,' he answered, knocked slightly off balance. 'She said it was really terrific and very interesting. I was thinking, it would be good fun for us to go there. She said there are loads of other places to go and see, as well ... but she didn't because her family didn't want to. They're quite religious and just stuck to the religious places.'

'And how long is this going to take?' Alex asked, lowering her sunglasses and staring down once again into the water. 'We mustn't forget that we have orders to fulfil and a business to run.'

'Well ... about a month, probably,' replied Lawrence. 'So, surely Richard could keep an eye on things for that time?'

Richard Stirling, their mother's distant cousin, had been

brought into the firm in the absence of any children on their uncle's side.

'Richard is an aeronautical engineer and a very good one ... but an engineer, nonetheless,' she replied, turning to look at him. 'He's definitely *not* a businessman!'

'Yes, I know that, Alex, but what harm can be done in just a month?'

Again, she said nothing, but remained gazing down at the vastness of the Atlantic.

'Look, Law, things are starting to look cloudy over Europe again.' Alexandra had become serious. 'Despite what the politicians told us and continue to tell us, the war did not do anything at all to end all wars. In fact, the last war left such a mess that there's even talk about us heading for another one ... and sooner than we think.'

'Another war?' repeated Lawrence loudly. He was startled at the prospect; he had still been a child during the last one.

'Quiet!' hissed Alexandra. 'Keep your voice down. We don't want anyone else to hear.'

Turning his back on the ocean, he surveyed the decks about them. Although they were full of passengers, no one seemed to have heard his outburst. He was about to remark on this, but his sister prevented him.

'Yes, war!' muttered Alexandra. 'If we do go on this trip of yours, we need to be absolutely certain that the time is right for us to do so. In the not-too-distant future everything could be ... well, a bit up in the air, at least as far as Europe is concerned.'

'Oh, I see,' said Lawrence. 'Was that a pun? Us and up in the air, I mean...'

She did not answer, but fixed him with a tolerant, though disapproving gaze.

'All right, Alex, I understand what you are saying,' Lawrence continued, subdued a little by her response to his attempted witticism, 'but if we can get going on these American orders and get them started, then do you think that we can...'

As he turned to face his sister, his attention was distracted by a huge, navy-blue rectangle of bunting, in the top left-hand corner of which was the Union Jack. As he watched, the flag quickly ascended the main mast to an ensign hoist, about three-quarters of the way up. Above that, at the very top of the main mast, the pointed flag of the White Star Line – a huge white star on a red background – had also suddenly burst forth.

'Look at that,' he said, pointing, his previous sentence forgotten in mid-delivery, 'Why are they putting the flags up?'

Suddenly, from the forward funnel, there came the long deep-throated blast of the ship's whistle, which caused Alexandra to jump.

'Steady on, Sis, it's only the ship's hooter,' said Lawrence, laughing.

Almost immediately, there was an answering boom of a much deeper, far more resonant whistle, ahead of them and off to their right. As they turned to look towards *Olympic*'s bows, they were aware of the railing becoming crowded with the other passengers, all eagerly pointing and waving at the approaching ship.

'That could well be the proof of the point I was trying to make,' said Alexandra, as she looked at the sleek, squat, black hull of the huge ship that had suddenly appeared as if by magic off their port beam. The smooth lines of her hull gave the feeling that she was like a thoroughbred racehorse, champing at the bit to let loose the considerable power of its muscles. The bow wave she created curled back in a noble, unbroken sweep of foam-capped water, as if to announce that the ship was the symbol of both the new decade of the 1930s, and of a new age of even faster and more luxurious trans-Atlantic travel.

'Take a very careful look and tell me what you notice

about that ship that makes her radically different from ours,' said Alex.

As the other ship sped effortlessly past *Olympic*, its flags flying and its whistle blasting a return greeting in the time-honoured tradition of the sea, Lawrence studied it intently.

'It's German,' he replied, seeing the billowing flag: the Iron Cross superimposed on equal horizontal bands of red, white and black. 'She's the *Bremen*...' he continued, pointing to the large white letters painted on the sharp bows and the large letters that seemed to grow out of the upper superstructure. 'Those sleek lines of hers are built for speed and would make a first-class aircraft design. She really is full of confidence. Look at her ... You can smell the arrogance.' He paused as he studied the vessel intently, but the seriousness that had given rise to his last remarks had already started to evaporate. 'And she's only got two funnels, and squat ones at that,' he added, chuckling, 'not like us, with our four tall ones.'

'You know, you really are an ass at times, Law,' replied his sister, despairing yet again at her brother's inability to remain serious about anything for more than a few seconds. 'For goodness' sake,' she hissed, 'what do you see in front of the second funnel?' she asked, pointing.

For a moment he said nothing and then, slowly, he answered her. 'My God, it's got a plane ... a seaplane.' His voice was a mixture of disbelief and wonderment.

'Exactly, and that is why I said that the clouds could well be gathering over Europe again. Our grand old lady here', she said, gesturing around her, 'is of an earlier age; she's a thing of the past. A bit of a dinosaur, actually, in comparison to *that*. And *that* has been built by the side that *lost* the war...'

She let the rest of her sentence drift out and over the side, to be sucked towards the now-disappearing stern of the German liner.

'So … do you think there's any chance of our holiday, then?' said Lawrence, venturing back to his previous topic of conversation.

Alexandra Hawkhurst slowly turned her head away from the disappearing liner and looked, not unkindly, at her brother. He was quite tall for his twenty-four years and not unattractive, especially when his face was covered with his broad smile, as it was now. Despite acknowledging that he was quite brilliant behind a drawing board, or at the controls of an aircraft, there were times when she could quite happily strangle him; it was impossible for him stay serious. .

'Well?' Lawrence queried, somewhat bemused by his sister's silence and her tolerant, yet questioning gaze. Knowing how his sister's mind worked, he added, 'Do you think we can? After all, if there is a war coming, we should at least have a bit of fun before we have to get really busy with the business. Just the two of us…'

'Perhaps, Law,' she said, 'perhaps … We'll just have to see.'

4

Paris

Gare du Nord – Friday, 17th October 1930

The train gave a jolt as it started its journey out of Paris, towards the north. For two of the passengers it represented the last leg of a journey that would return them to the safety and security of England. Beyond the comforting warmth of the railway carriage the weather had taken a turn for the worse; the clouds had darkened and, away to the west and distant Normandy, they hung menacingly low on the horizon. It looked as if they were in for a rough crossing once the train reached Calais in a few hours' time.

Stephen smiled at Rupert, as he looked at him across their first-class compartment.

'All right, my dear chap?' he asked.

Rupert, who had been staring out of the window contemplating the distant dark clouds, was lost in deep thought wondering if there was any hidden portent – a sign of some sort – behind those distant shapes and their ominously dark, brooding presence.

'Yes...' he replied, smiling back.

They had the compartment to themselves. Indeed, they had had every cabin and compartment to themselves since leaving Naples.

'... I'm fine thank you ... now...' There was a pause, '... Thanks to your Uncle Cecil,' he said, returning his gaze to the scene outside the window. 'Is that really his name?' he added, almost as if he were asking the question of his reflection.

Rupert had asked his friend the same question on several occasions in the past, but every enquiry about his uncle had been met with a wall of silence and secrecy. There would be a time in the future when Stephen would introduce Rupert to his uncle and the rest of his family, but that time had to be carefully chosen.

Stephen thought deeply before replying. He is my soulmate, after all, so why keep things from him? Am I ashamed of what we are? Or am I ashamed of him? Is an archaeologist perhaps not good enough for the rest of my family? 'I have never given you a satisfactory answer, have I?'

'"Only on a need-to-know basis and trust me, you do not need to know." I think that is how you usually phrase it,' muttered Rupert.

'Now look here, my dear fellow…' began Stephen, but then he let his voice trail off.

He continued staring at their reflections in the window of their railway carriage and drew on the analogy that, just as they were cocooned within the safety of the speeding train, they were actually living their lives in the protective embrace of a self-imposed barrier from an unforgiving outside world. The constraints of the law and of society required it to be so; to compromise those constraints would not only bring shame and dishonour upon them and their families, but it would ultimately bring unbearable unhappiness to himself and Rupert as they risked being subjected to ridicule and imprisonment. Certainly, for the time being, they were so wrapped up in the enjoyment of each other's love and friendship, that they had no need to project or justify their relationship to the outside world or, indeed, their own families. But they could not stay isolated for ever. Perhaps these opportunities to travel on these expeditions provided the necessary cover; the outside world would just see two men on a journey – two faces in a railway carriage – passing by – and not get close enough to question or to speculate.

He realized that their recent excursions together had created a unique bond of love and trust between them; he also realized that any subsequent adventures would deepen this bond. He smiled to the window: this bond was a much needed comfort to him and gave him the stability he needed after his hideous war experiences. In fact, he could not remember any time in his life when he had been as happy as he had been since meeting Rupert. His contentment at waking up beside him every morning was beyond the power of words to describe. Stephen was suddenly overcome with embarrassment. Of course, he trusted Rupert and he recognized that he needed to start being more honest and open with his friend. Perhaps now they could also establish a more permanent base from which they could slip in and out of that, potentially hostile, outside world.

'My dear fellow, perhaps the time is ripe for me to answer that simple question of yours,' he replied, completely changing what he had been about to say. 'No, that is not my uncle's real name, although, of course, I do know what it is. As far back as I can remember I've always just called him Uncle ... with a capital *U*. He's very high up in Whitehall. Remember that business in Egypt?' prompted Stephen.

Rupert did, but the memory was still a little raw and he did not deflect his gaze from the window. 'So where does this *Cecil* name come into the larger picture of things?' he asked.

'William Cecil, Lord Burghley. He was Queen Elizabeth's Secretary of State and chief supporter back in the 1500s and he controlled a small army of people, including Francis Walsingham, who was the Queen's spymaster. Remember your history?' asked Stephen, raising his eyebrows. 'I suppose that's why Uncle chose to use the name. He, too, controls a lot of people and he always *did* have a sense of the historical-theatrical.'

'I *thought* it might not be his real name,' answered Rupert, smiling through his reflection, 'but I'm still very grateful to him whatever his real name might be.' Then in a matter-of-fact way, he added quietly: 'They didn't harm me at all, you know. It was just all that shouting and the endless questions. I couldn't make them understand that I didn't have a clue what it was they were talking about. I don't mind admitting that I was getting a little worried by the time you showed up.' The smile had gone from the reflection, to be replaced with a deep-seated seriousness.

'Well, let us just say that Cecil owed it to us after that business in Egypt, shall we?' replied Stephen as he, too, turned and stared out of the window as the outskirts of Paris passed in a blur. 'And, yes, you are quite right, if it hadn't been for him...'

He left the sentence unfinished – both of them knew the extent to which they were indebted to the power of unseen authority. Cecil had pulled the strings and everyone had jumped – and quickly. In the comfort of the first-class carriage, thundering towards the protective barrier of the English Channel and the security of home, the events of a mere eight days before in the ancient, excavated city of Pompeii seemed to have occurred a lifetime ago.

Rupert's disappearance was unexpected and without obvious reason. Once back at the Grand Hotel, Stephen, who had attempted a desperate but fruitless search for his missing friend, had eventually been called to take the telephone call he had placed to London.

'My dear boy ... what a nice surprise,' boomed his uncle down the line, which was not a particularly clear one. 'You're lucky to have caught me. I'm off to the Club, y'know. What's that...?' he barked, as Stephen related that afternoon's events and told of his panic which, despite his resolve not to allow it to, had started a tiny fire of apprehension in his stomach that was starting to spread. 'Right, my boy, leave this with me. Give me the telephone number of your hotel ... and stay there. Just sit tight and wait for me to contact you ... Do you understand, Stephen?'

Uncle had used his name, which was something Stephen could remember him hardly ever doing. He took comfort from it, as it was something that only ever happened if his uncle was in deadly earnest.

'Make sure that there are no attempts at schoolboy heroics – that will probably only make things worse.' And with that the line went dead.

Stephen put down the receiver. Alone in one of the tiny telephone cubicles of the Grand Hotel, he felt as he had done at the end of the war – helpless, overwhelmed and scared. Under his jacket his cotton shirt was blotched with the tell-tale signs of apprehension.

'A satisfactory connection, *Signore*?' asked the receptionist politely, as Stephen emerged from the cubicle and crossed the foyer back to the reception desk.

'Thank you,' Stephen replied, his ears still ringing with the crackling, muffled voice that had spoken to him from the secure and impervious safety of the heart of the Empire in distant Whitehall. 'There will soon be another telephone call for me. Could you please make sure that someone informs me of it the moment it comes through? It could be at any time and it is of great importance.'

'Of course, *Signore*, we will summon you the instant that it is connected.'

Stephen mumbled a few further polite responses to the receptionist's conversation, although he had not been listening too closely. His mind was filled with other, more important things than polite chatter. Unwittingly, he had lapsed into the familiar pattern of action he had adopted in the heat and chaos of the forward dressing station, crammed in under the drab canvas of the large tent with the crazily swinging Tilley lamps and the incessant thumping of the distant artillery. Now, as then, he began to question himself. What was it that had made him think that whatever he had on his roll of film was so important that he had to spend time hiding it when his friend was being harangued further up the street? Had Rupert captured whatever it was on *his* roll of film, thereby provoking the heavy-handed reaction from the Blackshirts? There was something decidedly peculiar about this whole affair. Caught in a limbo of unexpected uncertainty, Stephen Hopkins, surrounded by the sumptuous luxury of the Grand Hotel, had not the faintest idea what it could be.

Stephen felt that his head would burst, as thoughts and voices raced around and around inside it in ever-decreasing circles, only to crash somewhere in the centre of his brain. Despite his attempts to stop it, the whole process would then start all over again, each time dragging him deeper and deeper into the pool of disquiet and unease that filled the pit of his stomach.

In his mind's eye, Stephen saw himself climb the ornate staircase – up to the second floor to reach the secluded sanctuary of his room. He knew that when he reached it he would be safe; but what of his friend? He also knew that when he entered Rupert's room, which lay through the connecting door just on the other side of the wall, he would find it empty – just as empty as the feeling he could not control in his stomach.

As he sat in the foyer chair waiting for the summons back to the telephone cubicle, he tried hard to stop thinking. Eventually, he got up and crossed to the desk.

'Could you please send cognac up to my room?' he asked.

'Certainly, do you require a small or a large measure?'

'Er ... the whole bottle ... and two glasses. Thank you,' he replied over his shoulder, as he turned and started to climb the stairs.

Upon reaching his room, he poured two glasses of cognac; one for himself and the other filled in readiness for Rupert on his return. Stephen downed his glass immediately and before refilling it, he threw himself into a comfortable armchair that was positioned next to the high French windows. Instead of looking at the splendid view out over Via Roma and beyond to the Piazza Bartolo Longo, Stephen stared straight ahead at the door, through which would come either the person he loved the most in the world or a summons to talk to his uncle. He shrunk into the secure womb-like embrace of the leather armchair as he embarked on this desperate vigil – something told him that it was going to be a long night. As the level of the spirits in the bottle sunk lower and lower, so did his state of mind.

Every noise, every footfall out in the passageway, caused his heart to beat faster. Hoping it would be the summons to the telephone and news, every passing sound had turned out to be a false alarm. He dived deeper and deeper into the bottle. As the bell of a distant clock struck the last note of eleven o'clock, the half-empty bottle stood on the round, glass-topped table next to his chair and glared at him admonishingly.

'Where the hell are you?' he mumbled to himself, but the alcohol made it difficult for him to determine if he was addressing Rupert, his uncle or the bottle.

The French windows were still open. The once balmy afternoon breeze now had a chill to it and Stephen's attention was drawn to the fine voile curtains, which hung down from under the pelmet several feet above him; they were billowing out gracefully in response to the breeze's gentle caresses.

In his intoxicated state, Stephen saw them as grotesque clouds of deadly gas – the gas that he and his fellow doctors had been faced with at the Front and for which there had been no real treatment. Those deadly, silent clouds had a yellowish tinge; these clouds, though, were white. The colour made no difference: there was still the feeling of helplessness he had felt when the blinded, hacking casualties had shuffled their way towards him, hoping for the help he knew he would not be able to give them. He reached once again for the bottle.

'Christ, old man,' he muttered to himself, 'you're losing your grip!'

He had not been reduced to such a state since the abyss of the Battle of the Somme, where everything had seemed to be in danger of being overwhelmed, and the fear of panic had first risen in him – the same panic he had once again felt earlier that afternoon. During the war, during the times when he did not have the luxury of a couple of days' leave away from the smell of blood, antiseptic and putrefaction, his fear and rising panic had only been driven back by the bottle. Slumped down in the armchair with the voile curtains billowing gently, Stephen Hopkins felt it all happening again, except that the nightmare of the field hospital was replaced by the opulent surroundings of a luxury hotel.

Friday dawned bright and clear. The sun had climbed high enough to capture the streets of both towns in its warming embrace and to dispel any lingering suggestion of the impending winter. In the crisp light of the new day the voile curtains hung down limply. The eager first fingers of sunlight crept through their fine mesh, across the short distance to Stephen's chair and up, to tickle his slumped face. They awoke him from his stupor.

'Ru-per-t...' he mumbled softly, without thinking. His speech was slurred and it was only with some considerable effort on his part that he finally managed to open his eyes.

He stretched, expecting to reach out and feel the warm body of his friend in the bed beside him, but the room was silent and still. There was no bed, no reclining body lying tantalizingly under the cotton sheets. Stephen looked around slowly and finally managed to focus on the bottle standing on the table; it was almost empty. Ominously, next to it stood the unused second glass. For a few minutes he sat and stared at it, his memory a scrambled kaleidoscope of billowing cloth, forlorn emptiness and mustard gas. Then, with some difficulty, he looked at his watch – it was just before seven-thirty. His mouth felt like it had been roughened with coarse glass paper.

'Must get a move on!' he mumbled through slurred words, as his battle to fully regain his senses continued.

Gripping the arms of the chair, he tried to get up, but his left leg gave way under him. It was a violent objection to having had the artificial limb strapped to it overnight. He had never thought of removing it, as he knew he would need the mobility when the receptionist sent for him. Now, because of it, he had fallen forward heavily on to the marble floor.

'You bloody fool!' he screamed, through a closed mouth heavy with the stench of the previous night's self-pity, '... you bloody, bloody fool.'

He turned and used the chair to claw his way up off the floor and to stand, shakily at first, in front of the French windows. *What sort of a friend do you call yourself? Right now, you are all Rupert has – and look at you...*

Turning his head, and with some difficulty, he focused on his unkempt reflection in the large overmantle mirror. 'You bloody fool!' he repeated, but this time, out loud.

By a quarter to nine Stephen had bathed, shaved and put on clean clothes. His head still felt as if a legion was on manoeuvres within it, but he had nevertheless resolved to take steps of his own to find Rupert, despite the clear instructions his uncle had given him. Although he was not really hungry, he went downstairs and forced himself to eat a sizeable breakfast. Considering the amount of alcohol in his system, he decided that it was the best thing to do. Then, with a need to be doing *something*, he informed the receptionist of his intended movements and set out once again for the excavated ruins of the Roman town, but this time by taxi. He was so fixated on finding his friend that he did not pay any attention to the dull ache in his stump. By ten o'clock, he had purchased an entry ticket and was well on his way back to the House of the Faun. There were already several parties of tourists wandering around the site. As Stephen progressed up the pavements and through the ruins, he noticed the occasional group of black-shirted men standing idly about, fired by the arrogance that their uniforms gave them; they made no effort to blend in with everyone else. Then, as he rounded a corner, he saw a little group of official site guides. Stephen took the opportunity to ask them about his friend.

'...yesterday ... er ... tall, like me ... blue trousers ... er ... and a hat, a white hat...' He tried to make himself understood through a combination of hand gestures and by pointing to himself, but his questions were met with a sea of blank, uncomprehending faces – except for one.

'I see a man ... how you say ... *egli sembrava cosi* ... he look like that ... at the gate—'

'When was this? Which gate?' Stephen interrupted, excitedly. 'The main one or the Marine Gate?' he asked, turning to point in the direction of the *Porta Marina.*

'There,' the guide said, pointing away to the top corner of the site in completely the opposite direction, '*alla porta della Via dei Mri* ... er ... how you say? ... The gate to the Villa o...'

'*Basta! Dica niente più!*' one of his colleagues muttered suddenly in a snarled whisper. '*Attenzione! I Fascisti!*'

The result was electrifying. Stephen's informant suddenly

turned noticeably pale under his swarthy complexion and turned to walk away, waving his hand in an absolving manner as he did so.

'*Fato sbaglio* ... I make mistake,' he said, as he turned the corner and disappeared from view. By the time he had done so the rest of the guides had also disappeared into the fabric of the ruins and almost immediately Stephen found himself alone on the pavement, save for a stray dog.

'Don't suppose you've seen him at all, have you?' Stephen asked and immediately felt foolish.

The dog barked back at him a couple of times, wagged its tail and then it, too, was gone, trotting off down the street towards the Forum.

Stephen reached the House of the Faun and, after a very careful examination of the scene from the pavement outside both of the entrance doors, was none the wiser as to what could have given rise to the previous day's incident. It looked exactly what it was – the partially restored ruin of a rich Pompeian's villa. He then returned to the ruin of the shop to retrieve his camera from the deep jar in which he had hidden it the previous day. With a heavy heart and a head that still maintained the faint drumbeat of the departing legion, he slowly retraced his journey to the entrance gate, empty-handed save for his camera.

It was nearly midday before Stephen found himself standing once again at the reception desk of the Grand Hotel on Via Roma.

'Has anyone telephoned for me yet? Or is there a message?' he asked hopefully, looking at the key to Rupert's room, still hanging on its hook behind the desk.

'The *Signore* has no messages and there have been no telephone calls,' replied the receptionist. The man was polite – everyone seemed to be polite – but there was a steely indifference in his eyes. It was not the same man that had been on duty the previous afternoon. That man had had the light of compassion in his eyes; this one had the glow of arrogant superiority.

'Thank you,' Stephen replied, not knowing what to think.

He had hoped to find Rupert back in the ruins, but that was ridiculous – he would hardly have been out there all night in the open. Then he had hoped against hope that his friend might have just strolled in off the street and asked for his room key, as if nothing had happened. That was even more of a forlorn expectation. And why had there been nothing from his uncle?

Surely, something must have been done by now?

Stephen had a pretty shrewd idea of how slowly, yet thoroughly, the wheels of government revolved, but that was hardly a mitigating excuse for the long wait: his uncle should have contacted him by now. Hopkins became aware of the receptionist, who had remained standing behind the desk looking at him with an air of polite expectation.

'Is there something else I can help you with, *Signore?*'

'No ... thank you,' Stephen muttered again, 'I will sit over here and wait.' He crossed to one of the comfortable chairs that were arranged throughout the foyer and sat down heavily. Despite the tiredness, he would sit and wait. He had no idea of what else he could do.

Two hours later Hopkins still sat in his chair, staring at the dark rings that had been left around the inside of the empty cup which stood in its saucer on the table before him. It was the second espresso he had drunk since returning to the hotel. He had developed a taste for strong black coffee during his time in Egypt, but then he had usually downed his cup when the liquid was hot, unlike now. He had taken only small sips at irregular intervals, as his mind dwelt on the seeming helplessness of his situation. As he sat vacantly looking at the dried rings of coffee residue around the inside of the cup, he realized that his bladder was telling him that it was time to empty the consequences of his over-indulgence. He rose from the chair, picked up the heavy black walking stick with its secret contents of stiletto blade and exposed film, and turned to cross to the gentlemen's lavatory, which was on the far side of the foyer, tucked away to the right of the reception desk.

'Mr Hopkins?' an English voice asked, easily pronouncing the *H* of his name, something that Italians found quite difficult.

Stephen had drawn almost level with the desk and was taken a little by surprise. The voice was deep, confident and soothing, and it belonged to a slim, tanned man of about thirty, clean shaven and smartly dressed in a dark suit. He carried a hat.

'Yes,' Stephen replied, turning to see who had asked him the question.

'How do you do, Sir? My name is Elkington. Would you mind accompanying me, please?' the visitor continued in perfect, unaccented English. He gestured towards the glass entrance doors, through which could be seen a large black vehicle waiting outside. It had drawn up alongside the broad pavement opposite the hotel entrance and it displayed diplomatic corps registration plates.

Stephen hesitated – bristling, as if preparing to face some unexpected, sudden danger.

Elkington noticed. 'It's quite all right, Sir,' he said, smiling reassuringly. As he did so he extended the hand which held his hat behind Stephen's back, as if to cut off any chance of escape. 'Cecil has sent me.'

Twenty minutes later, on the steps of Police Headquarters, they were met by the Superintendent of Police for the region, resplendent in full-dress uniform. With great ceremony and waving of hands they were escorted up the stairs to his office, where they found Rupert sitting in a chair, a half-empty glass of water in front of him. Looming ominously over all of them, in the centre of the whitewashed wall above the superintendent's desk, hung an enormous photograph of Il Duce, who leered down arrogantly from beneath his steel helmet at the minions beneath him.

'Hello, my dear chap,' said Stephen, almost without thinking, as he fought back the urge to rush across the office and embrace his friend, 'where on earth have you been? I was worried,' he added, by way of a very serious understatement.

'Hello, Stephen. I'm fine ... Phew! It *is* a relief to see you, too, I must say,' Rupert said, standing up and smiling warmly at Stephen. The connection in their eyes relayed all the fear, hope and joy that had been experienced by each of them. There was no need for further conversation between them.

The superintendent addressed them in an unbroken flood of Neapolitan Italian, which neither Rupert nor Stephen could understand. They stood next to each other with bemused expressions on their faces, but close enough to feel the thrill of their chemistry spark between them. Unperturbed by their incomprehension, the superintendent continued his performance, as if he were the main character in an opera by Donizetti. For his part, Elkington stood quietly to the side of the superintendent's desk, calmly listening. The policeman finished his oration, an event which he had signalled by a sudden silence and the cessation of his animated hand gestures, which he had performed almost constantly since the car had drawn up at the foot of the steps some minutes before.

Elkington took the opportunity to translate the gist of the speech for the other two.

'He says: Il Duce is truly sorry about this most unfortunate misunderstanding and would have been here himself to embrace you in the true spirit of brotherhood all Italians feel towards their fellow men, if only he did not have to attend to important matters in Rome.'

The translation was delivered in a flat monotone, which was in sharp contrast to the bluster of the superintendent. Neither Stephen nor Rupert failed to notice the slightly raised eyebrow on Elkington's face, nor the faint hint of a smile around his mouth, as he finished the translation.

No sooner had he done so, than the superintendent started up again, hands gesticulating wildly, sometimes pointing to them, sometimes pointing to the photograph above them, sometimes pointing nowhere in particular and yet everywhere at the same time.

Half an hour later and after a glass of wine, which the superintendent insisted they share in order to further cement Anglo-Italian relationships, the three Englishmen found themselves once again in the vehicle being driven back to the Grand Hotel. Relieved to be in the safety of Stephen's room, they sat comfortably discussing the situation.

'Of course, you do realize that the superintendent's performance was little more than a pantomime: pure theatricality,' Elkington said, as he looked at the other two. 'Don't be taken in by it and don't believe a word of it. They made rather serious fools of themselves over this entire affair. The superintendent's performance was their way of trying to recover some of their lost dignity. It is very important to the Italians to save face. One always has to be seen to be in charge, no matter how farcical the situation.' Turning to Rupert, he added, 'And you say that you were treated well?'

'Apart from the bully-boy stuff at the House of the Faun, yes. There was a lot of shouting and far too many questions, but I hadn't a clue what it was they were asking. They produced someone who claimed to speak English, but he didn't seem to have much of an idea of what I was saying and his translations of the Generalissimo's pronouncements were next to useless. As I've said, my Italian is non-existent, I'm afraid, so I was no help at all.'

Elkington chuckled, but it was a strange mixture of understanding and agreement, with very little genuine humour.

'I'm not sure what caused the greater irritation,' continued Rupert, 'my lack of understanding Italian or their chap's lack of understandable English!'

'Something must have tipped them over the edge to try the bully-boy tactics with a foreigner,' said Stephen. 'Any idea what it could have been?'

Elkington hesitated slightly, turned to look straight ahead out of the French windows, and then replied softly, 'I'm afraid that's the way things are going here at present. It's a kind of shoot first, ask questions later attitude. There *has* been a lot of good progress over the last few years, but it's come at a price and there are still far too many poor in the country. Vast amounts are spent on the military, which causes dissent amongst those who favour a more egalitarian national budget. Everyone is on edge and scared of being reported. That's where the chaps in the black outfits come in – *I Fascisti*, the Fascists. The way things are going at the moment, I would not be at all surprised if, sooner or later, the entire population will be obliged to become card-carrying Party members. There is very little in the way of personal liberty, but that is not the face of the new Roman Empire that Il Duce wants the world to see. So what do you think it might have been that *you* saw? What do you think might have driven them off the deep end like that?' he asked, suddenly turning back to Rupert and thereby changing the subject.

'I have no idea,' Rupert replied. 'I just took a picture through the doorway, with the volcano in the background, and then ... just as I made the exposure, these men suddenly appeared from the very back of the ruin, through one of the doorways, and nearly collided with me. At least, I think they came through the doorway, I didn't really see where they came from. It was all so quick. I suppose that they could just as easily have come up the street.'

'Not from my side, they couldn't,' Stephen said. 'I'd have seen them.'

'Did you recognize any of these men? Would you be able to recognize them again if you saw them?' Elkington asked, but without much confidence that there would be a positive response.

'Not a chance,' replied Rupert, looking at Stephen. 'As I said, it all happened so quickly that I didn't have the chance to take anything in. Through my viewfinder I could see the ruin with the volcano in the background, then these chaps appeared in my field of vision and then ... Well, you know the rest. Sorry.'

'It's a pity they destroyed your film. That would have told us quite a lot, I shouldn't wonder,' Elkington continued. 'If they hadn't thought it necessary to take your film, none of this would have happened in the first place.'

Stephen tightened his grip on the handle of the heavy black cane. Something told him that the next person to possess the film, which he had hidden in the cane's empty secret chamber, should be his uncle. He added nothing to Elkington's comments.

'I really don't think that there is anything further to be gained by you both staying on here in Pompeii,' continued Elkington. 'Cecil has asked me to get you out of here as soon as possible, so I hope you have managed to finish your sightseeing.' He chuckled again, but this time with humour. 'Before I left the Embassy in Rome, I took the liberty of checking a few things regarding your travel. The *Kenilworth Castle* is sailing from Naples tomorrow at noon ... She is one of our ships. That will get you to Marseilles by Tuesday. It's via Genoa, but the stop there is a very short one. Then I've booked you seats on the train through France, over the Channel and back home. It's first class all the way, to give you privacy and a chance to recover. If you can make sure you're packed and ready to leave by eight o'clock tomorrow morning, I'll come and collect you. No point in hanging around. I suggest that you stay put here in the hotel tonight,' he added, as he rose to leave. 'They won't try anything else, provided that you keep a low profile. I'll let Cecil know you're all right.'

A sudden, screeching shriek from the train's whistle pierced the air. Stephen and Rupert were both jolted back to the present and the soothing, hypnotic swaying of the railway carriage. As the train thundered through the rolling French countryside, chewing up the miles to Calais and the Channel, the landscape grew flatter. The two occupants of the first-class compartment had not spoken for some time, each choosing to lose themselves in their own memories and fill the compartment with a companionable silence. In the distance the low black clouds that were clinging to the far northern horizon as the train left Paris had made territorial gains on the sky and were covering about a third of it.

'What are you thinking about?' asked Rupert, who had noticed the deep furrows that seemed to have crept across his friend's forehead.

'The war,' replied Stephen softly, without turning his gaze away from the flat fields that filled the view through the wide carriage window. The endless flatness was broken only by the occasional row of trees, marching away across the fields as straight as the ranks of a guards' regiment trooping their colour. 'It was all around here, you know,' he said, more to himself than to his friend. 'The war...'

5

Norfolk, England

The Vicarage, Great Massingham – Wednesday, 22nd October 1930

'There you are, Vicar,' said Mrs Brightwater cheerfully, as she placed a large, white plate on the tablecloth in front of him, 'your egg and rasher, as usual.'

'And, as usual, it looks delicious,' replied the vicar, lapsing into the familiar routine. He brought his hands together and started silently reciting his usual prayer of gratitude for the sustenance he was about to consume. He had been doing it for so many years that, although sincerely meant, it had now become automatic.

'Thank you, Mrs B.,' he said, as the substantial form of his housekeeper waddled like a friendly duck out of view.

'I'll bring your slice of toast and the tea through directly,' she added, her voice fading down the corridor that led to the kitchen at the back of the old building.

The Reverend Theophilus Fairweather, DD, was a man of simple tastes. As the only child in a strict, God-fearing family he had been taught the value of frugalness and prudence in all things from a very early age. Thanks to this austere upbringing, the watchword during the many years of his long life had been moderation. That explained the single fried egg and rasher of bacon on his plate, so insignificant as to be almost lost in the encircling expanse of plain white china. He sighed gently.

Sitting at the table, savouring the fresh farm egg fried in freshly churned farm butter, he took the time to look out of the window at the fields that surrounded the back end of the vicarage. The parish church of St Denys and its vicarage were almost exactly in the centre of the village, hemmed in by the surrounding buildings. However, from the window of the dining room on the eastern side of the vicarage he had a view of rolling open country, which, from that single viewpoint, gave the impression that he was in the middle of nowhere. He watched the birds swooping across and down on to the fields and contemplated their freedom. He had spent his whole working life telling others to have faith in the intangible, the unprovable and the unquantifiable. For his part, despite encouraging others, he felt that he was sliding further and further into a dilemma which, he felt, was beginning to stifle him.

It had often been thus over recent months. This dilemma, which had been building for some time now, was always at its worst on Sundays. Then, he would mount the worn steps to his pulpit and spend some considerable time expounding on the messages of the Gospels or of Lambeth Palace to a congregation which, since the recent war, had grown steadily smaller; what was left of the younger generation had seemingly lost interest in organized religion and had drifted away. This realization had startled him somewhat. He had been brought up within the strict, un-giving religious fabric of unquestioning belief. The comfort he had always experienced through this inherited belief had suffered something of a bruising recently; he had been forced to try and reconcile himself to a newer generation which, for whatever reason, seemed to be questioning the old values and teachings to the point where they appeared to have largely abandoned them altogether.

After nearly forty years of loyal service to the Church, the Reverend Fairweather had maintained a predictable and unimaginative approach to his chosen path; that was the very reason he had never risen above the rank of a humble parish vicar. In all honesty, he had never questioned his lack of advancement. Of course, there had been opportunities for promotion, but, because of his retiring nature – his *boring* nature, as his bishop had once recorded in a diocesan report on him – he had never succeeded to anything more demanding than the parish in which he had now been the spiritual guide for the last sixteen years.

Even his relationship with his housekeeper had been unimaginatively exemplary – friendly, but always correct and formal, thus avoiding any possible breath of scandal. The rigid boundaries behind which he lived his life had even extended to never enquiring as to what her Christian name might be. He had no reason to know it – she was simply the reliable housekeeper, Mrs Brightwater or, after her many years of devoted service, simply Mrs B. He did not need to know anything else.

'Here you are, Vicar – a slice of toast and a nice hot cup of tea,' chirruped the affable Mrs B., as she emerged from the passageway carrying a small round teapot and a plate. The teapot was covered with a woollen tea cosy that she, herself, had crocheted last Christmas. 'Take it whilst it's hot. It always gets the day off to a good start.'

Sometimes he thought that Mrs Brightwater had the tendency to act rather too maternally. He fancied that if he closed his eyes and let his imagination wander, he would open them to find his mother standing in front of him, talking to him. She, too, had been dominatingly maternal. From her perspective, Mrs Brightwater harboured the opinion that the vicar lacked a feminine touch in his life. As she perceived the situation, a companionable female would put a spark into him.

Although Mrs Brightwater thought that the Reverend Fairweather might be bereft of this important component in his life, for his part he had never even entertained the idea. In his youth, as a newly ordained priest, he had had the teachings of the Bible to sustain him. That had been just as well, as he had always found making friends of either sex a difficult thing. Perhaps it was as a result of his upbringing; perhaps it had been because he felt uncomfortable outside the reassuring boundaries of his own company. Whatever the reason, he had never managed to attract a companion with whom to share the sometimes arduous voyage of Life. Now, as he stood looking over the threshold of old age with its implied threat of retirement and a reduced income, he was experiencing a quandary of faith. Not even a lifetime's interest in the origins of Christianity, supported by a considerable knowledge on the subject and by a substantial library of related books, was of any comfort to him any more.

For years he had wanted to visit the sites in the Holy Land and Middle East on which the pillars of his earlier faith had been built, but, despite careful saving and frugal living, he had never quite been able to amass the requisite funds necessary to enable him to embark on such an expensive undertaking. Now, as the shadows lengthened on the horizon of his life, he had given up all hope of fulfilling his dream, contenting himself instead with delivering his regular monthly evening lectures on his favourite subject in the church hall. Even if he would never be able to visit those far-off places, he could at least *tell* everyone about them.

As he pondered the meaning and possible future direction of what was left of his life, he carefully scrapped the smallest possible pat of butter across the slice of toast and was busy unscrewing the top of one of Mrs Brightwater's jars of strawberry jam when the vicarage suddenly filled with the jangling clatter of the front-door bell.

As he ate his toast he became aware of an exchange of pleasantries between his housekeeper and what sounded like the post boy. Was this yet another instance of him languishing in the tedium of his life whilst listening into the lives of others?

A minute later, as he completed his breakfast, his reveries were brought to a close by the sound of the front door being slammed shut, to be followed by the sounds of his housekeeper pounding along the corridor towards the dining room 'Here you are ...,' she said in her officious way, as she removed the dirty side plate and knife from in front of the vicar and replaced them with two envelopes, '... the morning post.'

Both letters carried Norwich postmarks and one of them bore the coat of arms of the Diocesan Office.

What on earth can they want now?

Letters from the Bishop's underlings, or even the man himself, usually carried unwelcome tidings of some sort. The other envelope was far more interesting. On the back was written the return address of Burton, Burton & Rogers, Solicitors.

The following day, in response to the polite summons received by post, the elderly Reverend Fairweather made the twenty-one-mile journey to the city of Norwich. He now sat very straight in a chair opposite the desk of Mr Samuel Burton, senior partner in the law practice of Burton, Burton & Rogers. Refreshments had been brought in on a tray and the niceties of polite conversation observed. Having refused the offer of a custard-cream biscuit which, in his opinion, was a rather extravagant luxury, the clergyman sat quietly stirring his tea. He had been in a similar position once before, when he had been in his mid-teens. Then he had accompanied his aged parents to a similar solicitor's office when they had been summoned to the reading of his late aunt's will. Stirring his tea in this office, whilst waiting for Mr Burton to finish shuffling through a pile of files and papers, he wondered if a similar reason had been the cause of his own summons.

He immediately admonished himself for such thoughts; speculative greed is not a worthy Christian attribute. *One should not allow oneself to even consider monetary gain!* In any case, who would leave him an inheritance? As far as he was aware, he was the sole remaining member of the Fairweather family.

The moral stance taken by his conscience echoed through his head as he watched the senior partner open a large, rectangular envelope. The papers that were withdrawn from the envelope were few in number. After they had been unfolded, and the creases smoothed out, Mr Samuel Burton cleared his throat and, smiling at his visitor, began to read.

' "I, Catherine Mary Patricia Louise Bullerton, née Woods, being of sound mind and body, do hereby bequeath and bequest…" '

In reverential tones that would have done the Reverend Fairweather proud during one of his Sunday sermons, Mr Burton carried on reading the legal terminology that was the preamble to the contents of a last will and testament. There were several large legacies to ex-servicemen's institutions and other charities, as well as some small bequests to family servants and retainers. The Reverend Fairweather sipped his tea, thinking to himself that this man, who must have read hundreds of wills in his time, was not that much unlike himself. Both of them were actors: one in the pulpit; the other tied to the red ribbons of the law.

As he listened to Mr Burton, the cleric allowed his mind to wander back to the simple question of what on earth such a document could have to do with him. He knew of one or two distant relations – scattered thinly to the four corners of the Empire – but, to the best of his knowledge, they had all died years ago.

'"...the sum of five thousand pounds outright to the Reverend Theophilus Fairweather, of the Parish of Great Massingham, in the County of Norfolk. This bequest I make in deep gratitude for his spiritual guidance, given so sincerely. Further, this bequest is made subject to the conditions laid down under separate cover and included with this Will and Testament..."'

In total disbelief, the cleric stopped sipping his tea, the cup glued to his lips which, almost immediately, began to tingle uncomfortably with the heat of the liquid.

'You are one of the beneficiaries of the late Mrs Catherine Bullerton,' said the senior partner, smiling, as he placed the sheets of paper on the blotter in front of him.

'Mrs Bullerton?' asked the cleric, replacing the cup in its saucer, which he still held in his left hand, 'but I cannot recall knowing a Mrs Bullerton.'

He found it necessary to soothe his burning lips by rubbing them with his tongue.

'Indeed?' replied the lawyer in his usual disconnected manner, which many years of experience in these matters had taught him. His task was to break the news to the relatives or inheritors – not to become involved in speculation as to why the deceased had made the decisions they had.

'I can assure you that in this particular instance, you *are* indeed the intended beneficiary of the deceased,' he said. 'We have made scrupulous checks.'

The cleric stared over the top of the cup and down to his highly polished shoes. Try as he might, he could not put a face to the name.

'And now, we must open and read the second document,' continued the senior partner, slicing open the top of a second, smaller envelope with his paper knife. On both sides of the single, large sheet of paper were several lines of very precise handwriting written in a cursive, flowing, and feminine hand.

' "Since the tragedy of the recent war in France and the loss of Andrew, my dear husband, and James and Peter, my darling boys, life for me had become an empty sham of an existence. I could not reconcile myself to any belief in a kindly, loving Creator God who could allow such carnage and who could take my family from me in such a violent way.

' "With the passing of the years, this emptiness grew more and more profound, driving me away from the life we had all known before the war. I sought solace in the anonymity of that suffering and loss, similar to my own, felt by so many others. The running of my affairs and properties, in which I increasingly had no interest, I left to others. I sought, instead, the comfort of loneliness and the solitude of the countryside. Perhaps, I thought, in the beauty of Nature, I might find the consolation I so desperately sought. I felt the need to start a new life, using my maiden name. I did this because the family and the former life that I had lost was so precious to me that I wished to keep it for myself as an imprisoned, much cherished memory, neither for public display nor for sharing with another living soul. I lived my new life in Great Massingham, which I had eventually reached after much wandering through the Home Counties, far away from my home and the painful memories it contained.

' "Gradually, I began to think that I saw the hand of God at work. It was through the sermons, guidance and example of the Reverend Theophilus Fairweather, rector of the parish of St Denys in Great Massingham that I slowly began to rediscover the belief that I had so cruelly lost. His talks on the Holy Land and the foundations of Christianity, the belief in which I had come so perilously close to losing, were also of great comfort to me. Over the six years during which I lived in the village, still very much under the cloak of anonymity of my maiden name, I slowly began to rebuild my Faith. I eventually felt spiritually strong enough to return to my home, leaving the village behind me with great sadness and gratitude, in equal measures.

' "Such people as the Reverend Fairweather, who work so diligently to uplift and to comfort, to consolidate the word of the Lord in our daily lives are, indeed, the conduits through which our blessings are sent to us.

' "Inspired by this saintly man, I had hoped to make a pilgrimage to the sites and places that were so eloquently described in the Reverend's talks and sermons. Sadly, it was not to be, as the Lord had decreed otherwise and I, myself, was to bear the final cross given to my family. Obviously, when you read this, I shall be dead, never having been able to make that pilgrimage.

' "I am leaving a bequest to the Reverend Fairweather, in order that he may use this sum to make that pilgrimage on my behalf. This is the only condition I attach, other than the hope that he prays for me, my dear husband and our boys, at the very sites at which our Faith began..." '

Samuel Burton looked up from the document. 'That is the only condition attached to the bequest. If you would be so kind as to advise me of the travel details of your proposed trip,' he said, 'I will make the necessary arrangements to have the funds released.'

Much later that same evening, back in the predictable comfort and security of the vicarage of Great Massingham, the Reverend Theophilus Fairweather was still in something approaching a state of mild shock. He sat in the familiar security of his study, absently pawing over one of his favourite volumes. It was a lengthy treatise on the subject of the exact location of Moses' Mount Sinai. Although he knew large sections of the book by heart, the cleric could not concentrate on the text and maps for more than a couple of seconds before his mind wandered back to the orderly, well-furnished offices of Burton, Burton & Rogers in Norwich. He still found the whole day's revelations somewhat unreal and was convinced that he would wake up in the comfort of his bed to find that he had overslept and that everything had simply been a tantalizing, improbable dream.

'Your supper is ready for you, Vicar,' called Mrs Brightwater, knocking politely on the architrave of the door. 'A nice rabbit stew ... with all the trimmings. The young lad from next door caught it this afternoon whilst you were in Norwich. He does well with his hunting, down in the woods,' she added, as she turned to walk back to the kitchen.

The Reverend Theophilus Fairweather suddenly froze, staring blankly at the open pages in front of him.

'Of course,' he said, suddenly looking up from his book. 'Mary Woods. Wasn't that what Mr Burton said her maiden name was?'

Mrs Brightwater, who had stopped in her tracks at the sound of his voice, now reappeared in the doorway. 'What was that you said, Vicar?'

He turned and looked at her, the excitement of recognition mingled with fond memories firing his usually placid face.

'Tell me, my good Mrs B., do you recall a Miss Mary Woods?' he asked.

After a few moments, the housekeeper's round, homely face broke into a warm smile.

'Oh yes. She was that kindly, quiet lady who always used to sit at the back of the church of a Sunday. And she used to come here to the vicarage for your Bible study classes ... Very quiet and retiring to the point of being near invisible, as I recall.' She paused, remembering. 'She always looked so sad, as if she'd lost a shilling and found a penny.'

'And she used to come to my talks in the church hall,'

the cleric added. 'We used to have the most interesting conversations. It always seemed as if she was looking for something, but I was never able to determine with any certainty what it was. These days there are so many looking for … for Heaven only knows what. I remember now … that sense of looking for something, which was so obviously displayed by the good Miss Woods upon her arrival in the village, gradually diminished with the passing of time. Perhaps, in her own way, she found what it was she was looking for…'

'And then one day, she says she has to go and off she went,' said Mrs Brightwater, who had advanced well into the hallowed space of his study – something which, apart from her cleaning duties, she very rarely did. 'Anyway, that was almost a year ago now, bless her,' she added, turning to retrace her steps to the study door. 'Don't forget your supper, Vicar … it's ready and on the table. We don't want it going cold now, do we?'

6

London

Whitehall – Friday, 24th October 1930

A highly detailed map of the Middle East was spread out on the large table that occupied a substantial space in the further reaches of the Uncle's large, well-appointed office. The table stood in a large pool of light cast not by the feeble daylight outside, which was growing noticeably weaker each day as winter approached, but by a row of strong electric lights suspended above it. The map, with its bright colours highlighting altitude and the contour of the landscape, occupied easily three-quarters of the table's surface; a strip of highly polished wood, about twelve inches wide, formed a frame between the edge of the stiff paper on which the map was printed and the rounded edge of the table itself. Arranged around the table were ten chairs, four on each long side and one each on the narrower sides. Resting on a leather blotter in front of each chair was a folder, tied closed with the best red tape the Civil Service could supply and stamped with 'Most Secret' in large letters. One folder lay open in front of the only chair with arms, which stood at the head of the table. Next to it, half on the map, half on the wood of the table, rested a large glass ashtray.

The Uncle was engrossed in studying a black-and-white photograph, about ten inches by eight, which showed a well-composed scene bathed in bright sunlight. It was of a stone doorway, through which could be seen a wide, open space, in the centre of which was a small statue of a faun standing in a sunken, tiled rectangle. Across the background ran a row of half-collapsed columns, some of which still supported what was left of a decorated lintel. In the distance Vesuvius rose up majestically with the smudged suggestions of white, wispy clouds, hovering above its summit. On the extreme right of the image, towards the back of the open space and in front of the columns, a small group of men were just entering the scene and were walking towards the camera. Several were wearing smart, dark suits; others, at the back of the little group, were wearing uniforms. They had emerged into the bright afternoon sunlight from what looked like a ruined doorway in a side wall.

The Uncle put the photograph to one side and took out a second one, of the same size as the first, but with its entire area filled with a greatly enlarged image of just the group of men. He looked at it intently for a minute or so before placing it on top of the first photograph. Then he started to reread the pages of the single-spaced typed report, which had been prepared to accompany the picture. In each of the other folders that lay neatly in front of the chairs was a duplicate of this second, much enlarged image, as well as copies of the typed documents.

The Uncle had almost reached the bottom of the second page when there was a knock on the stout office doors.

'Come!' he said, returning the typed sheets and the photograph to his folder and closing the front flap, which he left untied. The door opened and Collingwood, his private secretary, walked in.

'They are all here now, Sir,' he said.

'Good, show them in, would you?' replied the Uncle, pushing back his chair and getting up to cross towards the door.

A line of men entered one behind the other. Some wore smart Savile Row suits whilst the others were in uniform; two were in army uniform, one in a naval uniform and one in the blue of the Royal Air Force. These were the top brass of the Armed Forces, judging by the amount of heavy gold braid on the peaks of the caps tucked under their arms.

'Gentlemen ... come in, come in...' called the Uncle. As he reached the first man in the line, he extended his hand to take that of his visitor. He shook it warmly in friendly greeting. 'Julian, good to see you again ... and you, John ... Archibald ... George, how is your new grandson? ...' He continued in like vein, until all of the men had been welcomed and had made their way to their seats around the large table.

After everyone had settled themselves, the Uncle spoke. Though he had returned to his chair, he remained standing.

'Gentlemen,' he began, looking around the assembled faces, 'thank you for coming. I appreciate how difficult it is for us all to assemble at such short notice. I thought it best to call you all together again so soon after our last meeting, in view of some rather interesting information that has just come into my possession. As you might have deduced from the map in front of you, there could well be a strong connection between what I have to show you and the current situation in the Middle East ... to be specific, in Iraq...' he said, pointing down towards the map. 'Would you please open the folders in front of you and remove the photograph you will find inside,' he said before sitting down.

There was a subdued mumble of conversation, as the folders were opened and the photographs extracted. Then the Uncle continued. 'This is a very interesting photograph, gentlemen, but neither because of its location nor because of the historical context of the setting, which, by the way, is Pompeii in southern Italy. No, gentlemen, this is an interesting photograph because of the people who have been captured in it, completely by accident as the exposure was made. Jeremy, do you by any chance recognize the gentleman second from the left in the photo?'

In response to this question, Jeremy took out a small but powerful jeweller's magnifying glass from his inner pocket, opened it and proceeded to study the person mentioned very carefully.

Then, after a few seconds of silence, he replied. 'This is a rather good, very clear photograph, if I may say so ... of course, I mean in intelligence parlance rather than in a tourist context. I would say that chap is the Count Vittorio de Contini-Aosta, the Italian Minister for War.'

'I would agree with you,' replied the Uncle, 'but that august gentleman is not our *real* interest in the photograph. Look at the person to whom he seems to be talking ... the one with the sunglasses.'

They all returned their gaze to the photograph and to the men in it.

'Any ideas as to who *he* might be,' probed the Uncle with sudden seriousness.

'He looks dark-skinned, by comparison to everyone else,' offered one of the army men. 'An Indian ... or an Arab ... or possibly Jewish...?'

'Whoever he is, he merits an escort,' interrupted another. 'Those chaps in the background are Mussolini's Blackshirts ... his thugs. While the bunch on the left look like Carabinieri.'

'I can't be certain, not with those sunglasses,' said another man, looking up from the photograph and casting a glance around at the others, some of whom looked at him expectantly, whilst others remained with their heads down studying the photograph, 'but he does look like the cousin of King Faisal of Iraq; Prince Abdul Salaam Abd al-Allah, Iraq's Oil Minister.'

'Well done, George,' said the Uncle, beaming at his

colleague. 'That is precisely the same conclusion my people reached. The question is: what was he doing wandering around the ruins of Pompeii in the company of the Italian Minister for War?'

'Can we be absolutely certain that it is, indeed, he?' asked the man in the naval uniform.

'I would say we could be ninety-nine per cent certain,' replied the Uncle, 'enough for us to take very seriously the question of what he's doing there, and why he seems to be in the company of a significant Italian government minister. The Italians deny that the prince has made any visits to Italy recently... hardly surprising! We've had our chaps in Baghdad do some sniffing around, trying to find out if the prince was in Iraq at the time this photo was taken, which was about a fortnight ago. It seems his movements are unaccounted for leading up to and immediately after the date when this exposure was made. The Iraqi officials insist that he was in the country the whole time, but the Court diary makes no mention of him having carried out any official duties during the period in question. Also, over this same period, none of our people in Iraq actually saw him.' He paused briefly to allow the significance of this information to sink in. 'I do not need to remind you of the recent troubles in the region concerning the oil wells. You are all aware of the vital importance of oil to the Empire, including that which we both currently control and extract in Iraq.'

'Not to mention our interests in Persia,' added another.

'We should also not forget the significance of the location of those oil wells,' said the man in naval uniform, rubbing his forehead. The sleeve of his tunic, heavy with gold braid, caught the light as it moved and seemed to sparkle in reaction to this news. 'Apart from the oil itself, which is vital to keep the Fleet moving, there is also the matter of the security of the Suez Canal and our passage to India. Stability in the region is of paramount importance.'

'Thank you, Archibald. Indeed, stability in the region *is* of the utmost importance, perhaps more so than ever before, when we consider the question of the Arabs and the Jews in Palestine,' said the Uncle, waving in the direction of the map once again. 'Gentlemen, we only have to look at the map to see that we cannot tolerate another power trying to elbow in on what has traditionally been our sphere of influence. God knows, it's difficult enough fending off the French now that they have their claws into Syria ... and they are supposed to be our *allies*!' There was general, muttered agreement and the odd chuckle around the table. 'As far as the prince is concerned, the only thing we know for certain at the moment is that he is passionately interested in ancient history, which could explain *why* he was in Pompeii. In fact, he read history at Oxford and holds a degree in it – an upper second, I believe.'

'That's all well and good, but, if he decided that he wanted to visit the ruins of Pompeii, why was he being shown around by the Italian War Minister?' asked George. 'And why are the Italians denying that he was there in the first place?'

'We have quite a job on our hands as it is, trying to maintain order and protect our interests in the Middle East,' said the man in the RAF uniform. 'The oil fields are extensive and our resources are stretched quite thinly at times. We really could do with more aircraft.'

'Is there the chance that the Italians are up to something?' asked another of the army men, who had been absently tracing patterns around the gold braid on the peak of his cap with his finger. 'We already know that Mussolini has grandiose ideas of a new Roman Empire. Is it possible that they are trying to get in closely with the Iraqis behind our backs to ensure the supply of fuel needed to be able to set out on a programme of conquest?'

'I am afraid, Julian, that I am inclined to agree with your

suspicions. There is something else to all of this,' he continued, opening the typed pages. 'My chaps have put together scraps of information received, which seem to point to something of a power struggle behind the throne in Iraq and the central player would seem to be our Prince Abdul Salaam Abd al-Allah.'

'Has that any relevance to this photograph? Surely not?' asked one of the dark-suited men, looking at the Uncle over the top of his half-frame tortoiseshell spectacles. 'Do we know where this photograph came from? Can we trust the source? Unless we have the negative, we cannot tell if it is genuine. It could well have been touched up or altered.'

'A valid point, indeed,' replied the Uncle. 'In our profession it does not pay to be careless in any way, or to make assumptions without the basis of more than probable fact. In this instance, however, I can vouch for the origin and authenticity of the photograph. It is absolutely genuine, gentlemen, and it was taken on the date specified. Of that I can assure you ... and we have the negative.'

'If we consider the examples of the various political machinations that have gone on recently in the dangerous chaos which masquerades as the Soviet Union,' said the man at the end of the table, directly opposite the Uncle, 'I would venture to suggest that the prince could well be negotiating to trade Iraqi oil for Italian support ... if what you have told us about the power struggle behind the throne in Baghdad is true. It would not be the first time that one relation has removed another from high office and taken his place ... especially when an occupying power is about to withdraw. Our mandate in Iraq does not have much longer to run...'

'...And that would make a palace coup somewhat easier. Not to mention tearing up existing treaties and signing new ones, in the name of foreign support and recognition,' added the Uncle, his brow creased. He reached for his cigar, which, having rested in the glass ashtray since the arrival of the men was now cold and lifeless. 'There is a plan afoot, as some of you might already know through your departmental briefings, to build a pipeline from Mosul in the north of Iraq here, where the oil fields are...' he gestured with his finger towards a dot on the map, '... way across the desert and on to the Mediterranean coast terminating at Haifa in Palestine. I believe feasibility studies are already in hand. Naturally, as long as we have the mandate for Palestine and a controlling interest in Iraq, we can monitor and control the oil that flows through it, but we cannot easily control who buys it, or who might then decide to sell what they have purchased on to a third or fourth party.'

'Such as Italy?' asked one of the men in army uniform.

'It's very possible...' agreed the naval man, '... The distance from the present export terminal of Kuwait to the Italian mainland would be halved if there was a pipeline ... and they would not have to rely on passing through the Canal.'

'And then, of course, we must realize that the French will be in the market for oil as well and, again, we have the unanswered question: who would they be buying it for, if not for themselves?' added the man in the dark, pinstripe suit. 'It's a relatively short hop and skip from Haifa to Marseilles, and there are the ports of Taranto, Naples and Genoa en route. It would be easy enough to, shall we say, *lose* part of a shipment along the way.'

'The same could be said of any of the powers who are not particularly sympathetic towards us,' said the Uncle. 'But let us not jump to too many conclusions at this stage. After all, the pipeline is still only at the conceptual stage.'

The discussion around the large table continued in like manner for a further forty minutes.

'Gentlemen, time moves on apace,' declared the Uncle,

looking at the clock that stood on the mantelpiece. 'I suggest we set our various departments to work on this information. Let us see if we can find out if there *is* any truth in what we have been discussing here today. I would hope to receive the results of your investigations preferably sooner, rather than later. If there is, indeed, a situation building, then we might have to take steps to restore the status quo in our favour, and that could be somewhat complicated,' he concluded, as they all made ready to leave.

It was much later that same afternoon before the Hub of Empire slowly settled down in anticipation of the quiet of the weekend ahead. The labyrinth of administrative passageways – like the cardiovascular system of a body, the Body of the Empire – steadily drained itself of employees as the shadows of the late afternoon lengthened.

The Uncle sat alone in the spacious grandeur of his office, the lights over the large table and its map extinguished. He sat in his favourite leather armchair next to the fireplace, the empty brandy balloon on the little table beside him. The Treasury, on one of their never-ending economy drives, had decreed that there would be no fires in government offices until the first day of November. As he sat there, staring into the empty grate, he felt a chill. It was not a chill caused by the unseen cold seeping through the thick stone walls from the darkening streets outside and into the comparative warmth of his office; it was a chill of apprehension.

If Stephen and his friend hadn't taken the same photo from almost the same spot, just a couple of minutes apart, he ruminated, and if the dear boy hadn't had the foresight to keep his roll of film well out of harm's way, we'd have been none the wiser as to any of this. Perhaps fickle Dame Fortune has decided to smile on us, once again, by setting a figurative cat among the pigeons, as it were.

He got up from his chair and crossed back to his desk, switching on the tall, green-shaded lamp. The desk and surrounding floor were flooded with a warm, comforting light. It was Friday and he would travel down to the house for the weekend by the evening train. Donnington Castle, surrounded as it was by hundreds of acres of unspoiled woodland, was infinitely more preferable to his London club; but all the same he knew that he would not be able to leave the thoughts, which were moving round so persistently in his head, on his London desk that weekend.

7

London

14 Wellington Mansions, Westminster – Sunday, 28th December 1930

The urban sprawl that filled the dot marked *London* on the map sat gasping under a pall of thick, sulphur-rich fog. This particular day the sun had long since admitted defeat and given up its attempts to penetrate the thick, noxious soup, preferring instead to warm the purer air that filled the atmosphere above the cloying layer. With the festivities of Christmas behind them and the celebration of the New Year to look forward to, Londoners from all walks of life had been scurrying around the streets of the metropolis buying last-minute provisions for the parties to come. They were bent on using the event as an excuse to escape from the lingering effects of the recent economic collapse, which had spread across the world from New York's Wall Street. For a great many, the reality was that such an escape was little more than a pipe dream, but there were those who had fared better through the collapse of the financial markets and still had money to spend. The gloom cast by the pall of fog had not put them off; neither had the thought that this damp, cloying blanket, which annually claimed hundreds of lives in the capital, could well be a familiar visitor for the next couple of months until the arrival of spring.

Despite the all-subduing fog, the metropolis was still a

powerhouse of energy. Most importantly, the heartbeat of the vast Empire still thudded, soundlessly but reassuringly, within the boundaries of the city. Since the war it had been noted by some of those whose task it was to sustain it that the heart had, on occasions, been felt to beat with an irregular rhythm. It was as if the ravages and strain of the enormous responsibility that governing a quarter of the Earth's landmass entailed were finally beginning to show. There were also those who, whilst they would never dare to say so, had even began to wonder for how much longer the old, tired heart *would* still beat before fatigue and other equally unsavoury elements caused it to seriously falter, or stop altogether.

On this typical London December evening, in the lull between the frenetic celebration of Christmas and New Year, none of these issues concerned the occupants of number 14, Wellington Mansions. Rupert was crouched in front of the bedroom fireplace and, as he placed more coals on the fire, he became aware of Big Ben striking the hour. The tolling chimes of eleven o'clock, which echoed across the city, permeated this refuge from the outside world and were an audible reminder of passing time.

Propped up against the headboard of the bed, Stephen looked at the naked figure of his friend outlined against the orange glow of the fire. He watched as Rupert, satisfied that the fire was again burning happily, replaced the fireguard and made his way back to their bed.

You really are my Greek god, he thought as Rupert settled down next to him. 'That's just the ticket, old chap,' he murmured, as he put his arm around Rupert's shoulders, 'as snug as bugs in a rug, as some would say.'

They lay there, in a welter of happiness, cut off from the outside world, watching the flames dance and cavort.

'How is the stump?' enquired Rupert, after a lengthy pause of contented silence.

'Very well, thank you. Ask me again in a few minutes and

you might get quite a pleasant surprise,' answered Stephen, laughing.

'I meant your *leg*, actually,' replied Rupert, playfully slapping Stephen's chest.

The weather did not help the doctor's leg one iota. In fact, there had recently been days when he had found it almost impossible to walk or stand on it for more than a few minutes, before having to support his weight with the heavy black walking stick. Since their return from Pompeii he had reluctantly reached the conclusion that, possibly, he might benefit from the opinion of an expert and so had made the journey to Harley Street. The verdict had been that further investigation of the source of his discomfort was necessary, which would entail the taking of some X-rays, but this would only be done after the festive season had receded into memory and life, such as it was, had returned to normal.

'Not too goo—' He stopped himself. 'No ... let's be more positive about things. It could be better than it is ... and it could be worse.'

'Brave old soldier,' muttered Rupert, rubbing his friend's chest.

Stephen had found them the spacious flat in a grand Victorian block, not far from Westminster Cathedral. Although he never made an issue of it, nor flaunted it, money was not and never would be a problem for him. He had signed the lease in his name and on their first evening in their new London home they had sat on the floor in the middle of the empty, unfurnished sitting room. The furniture would only arrive with the New Year. A pair of candles had burned in the fireplace and they had eaten and drunk their way contentedly through the contents of the Fortnum & Mason hamper that had been delivered to their new address earlier that afternoon. Their happiness had been as boundless as the sky itself.

Now, in the glowing silence of the bedroom, neither spoke as the fire crackled in the grate. There was no need to speak; the intimacy of two naked bodies in such close proximity to each other said everything that needed to be said.

'Are you looking forward to the new decade, then?' asked Stephen eventually.

'I haven't really had the time to think about it, to be honest,' replied Rupert. 'There are plans to develop our tours beyond the present boundaries, which could be a good opportunity for advancement within the company. Since the end of the war there's been a growing interest in the Middle East and it's been suggested that a tour visiting the sights associated with Early Christianity might be started. Then there are plans for tours in the Jordan Valley and other parts of Trans-Jordan, including the old Crusader castles out in the desert, near Iraq. Someone even mentioned St Elijah's Monastery, way over in northern Iraq near a town called Mosul. Anyway, it all seems to be a bit up in the air at the moment, so I suppose anything can have happened by the time the new season gets into its stride.'

'Well, at least it will make a change from the same old slabs of carved Egyptian stonework,' said Stephen, a smile on his face, as he knew that his comment would elicit a mock rebuke from Rupert.

'Oh yes,' came the reply in feigned indignation, 'would those be the same old slabs that led me to a certain fellow, who has an uncle who is in the habit of using the name of a man who has been dead for four hundred years as a pseudonym? Those slabs of stone can't have been all *that* bad, so I won't hear a word against them.'

They both laughed.

'So, are we bound for Egypt again ... or is it to be something further afield?' asked Stephen, shifting the position of his left leg slightly.

'Well, I don't know,' replied Rupert. 'I'm quite clued up about Egypt, but I don't know too much about these other places in the Middle East. I had never even heard of this Mosul town, let alone St Elijah's Monastery, before it was discussed at the planning meetings. I had to look the place up in my copy of *The Times Atlas of the World*. Still, I suppose it could well be very rewarding to learn some new facts and figures and to see some new sights ... What do you think?'

'What do *I* think? I have no idea at all where this Mosul place is ... so lead on, McDuff, and your faithful retainer will follow,' declared Stephen, in a mock-theatrical fashion.

'You really are the limit, you know,' said Rupert, propping himself up on his left elbow and looking straight at his friend, a smile on his face. 'I ask for your opinion and all I get is unconditional support ... not even the faintest hint of an argument or discussion.'

'And isn't that what really matters?' answered Stephen warmly, as he reached up to put his arm back around Rupert's shoulders and draw him down to him once again. 'It doesn't matter where we go,' he said softly, 'as long as we go together.'

He had not forgotten the surge of panic and loss, of self-doubt and self-reproach, which he had felt when Rupert had disappeared in Pompeii. Neither did he ever want the trauma of experiencing the helplessness of that situation – of being the impotent prisoner of a bottle of cognac – ever again. He drew his friend even closer to him, but said nothing, preferring to hide his insecurities behind a show of affection. Their wordless embrace said it all.

Once again a comfortable silence descended upon them in their idyll of masculine contentment, as the room filled with the comforting smell of glowing embers. The smoke rose up the chimney and added to the fog blanket which shrouded the city. On the banks of the Thames, Big Ben struck eleven-thirty, the sound muffled yet still audible through the fog.

'I have to go down to my family's house in the country for New Year, I'm afraid. Would you like to come?' asked Stephen, inwardly wanting the answer to be positive, but at the same time still harbouring the lingering hope that it would be negative. He was a coward, he knew, but he still could not bear the thought of dragging the family name through the mud if this ever got out. Though was it really anyone else's business if he preferred the company of men – and of one man in particular – to that of women?

'And meet your uncle Cecil-Whatever-His-Name-Is?' replied Rupert, in a jovial way. 'Well, I'm sure I don't rightly know. I might not be up to the strain of the scrutiny,' he laughed. 'After all, attempting to match up to the outstanding standards of the nephew are already quite a tall order.'

'You'll do fine … We both will,' said Stephen seriously.

'Thanks for the invitation,' said Rupert, 'but I really ought to see the New Year in with Mother and my widowed aunt. They are both getting a bit forgetful these days and New Year, with all its memories, can be a lonely time for them. Mother and Aunt Claire are alike as two peas in a pod and seem to have developed a new way of having a conversation; they both speak at the same time, but neither of them has any idea of what it is the other one has said. And Mother has started to ask the same question several times. It's phrased in a different way each time, but it's the same thing she asks. Quite extraordinary, really,' he concluded, lapsing into silence at the thought of the passing years, and the toll they exerted on those who lived through them.

In the silence which once again settled contentedly over the warm room, Stephen found himself feeling disappointed at his friend's response. Although the excuse was a perfectly acceptable one, nevertheless Stephen felt a little hurt that the women in Rupert's family had been given precedence over him.

'I think I *will* put myself forward to expand the company's horizons,' said Rupert. Then in a voice which mimicked that of an announcer on the BBC wireless he added, 'beyond the marvels of ancient Egypt and the majesty of the river Nile, to new worlds, beyond the familiar limits of that which is already known...'

'In other words, my dear chap, you're prepared to swap one river for two,' said Stephen, smiling, his thoughts of a few moments before now banished, 'the Nile, for the Tigris and Euphrates.'

'I'm not sure if they plan to open up a route that far,' said Rupert earnestly, 'but, wherever they do decide to take tourists, it will be new territory for the mind, as much as for the body, wouldn't you say?'

'Amen to that, old chap,' said the doctor, as he reached across to his bedside table for his cigarette case and lighter. 'Fancy a last one before lights out?' he asked.

'Which could be considerably sooner than you think,' replied Rupert, as he turned to look at the fire, which had died down, 'I'd better give the fire one last stoking,' he said, as he slid out from under the covers.

As he went through the motions of adding more coal to the embers, prodding them with the iron poker that stood on the hearth with the other fire irons, a shower of sparks floated up from the coals and drifted up the chimney. As they did so, it seemed to Stephen, in his cloud of contentment, that they were a shower of stars wrapping his friend in an almost unearthly robe of beauty. He lay there, in the dim light of the room, admiring Rupert's physique, which was once again outlined by the glow from the dancing flames. As his friend turned and, smiling, once again crossed back towards the bed, Stephen reached out and replaced the cigarette case and lighter on the bedside table. There would be time for a final, relaxing smoke before sleep – but a little later.

8

Rome

Sala del Mappamondo, Palazzo Venezia – Thursday, 5th February 1931

Count Vittorio Contini-Aosta came from a long and very distinguished line of military men, whose roots were lost in the earliest trembling of the Italian Renaissance. Through a combination of sound political judgement and a good head for business and figures in general, the family had ingratiated itself first with the Medici and other wealthy citizens of Florence and then, by way of expansion, with the Sforzas, the rulers of Milan. The stakes had been high, both politically and financially and it had been a dangerous game to play, but the game had been handled with consummate skill by successive generations of Contini-Aostas. The count himself had emerged from the recent war battle-hardened and wounded, like so many of his men. His services had been rewarded with promotion to high rank and a chest full of medals.

With the coming of victory and the political instability that accompanied it, he had begun to wonder if his country would actually ever amount to anything, or even survive the birth of the so-called 'Brave New Europe' that followed the cataclysm of the war. In 1919, like many of his countrymen, he had been swept along by the charismatic wave unleashed by the leader of the Blackshirts, who promised to stop the country's slide into inertia and atrophy. Benito Mussolini – the one whom the people now deliriously called Il Duce, the Leader – had, in the count's opinion, begun to talk a lot of sense. However, since becoming the dictator of the Kingdom of Italy, Il Duce had banned organized political opposition to his own Fascist Party and moved swiftly towards repressing any expression of anti-Fascist feeling generally. Perhaps it was because of draconian measures such as these – the loss of far too many personal liberties – that the count had recently begun to consider his glittering decorations as little more than symbols of an oppressive nothingness. In Il Duce's modern Italy, such thoughts were extremely dangerous.

The count got out of his staff car and crossed the pavement. As he approached them, the sentries guarding the main entrance to the Palazzo Venezia snapped smartly to attention at the first sight of the Minister for War, who was immaculately turned out in the uniform of a general of the Italian army.

Once inside the building the count started to climb the marble staircase of the four hundred-year-old *palazzo*, which had once been the residence of the ambassador of the Venetian Republic. As he did so, he preferred not to dwell on the methods Il Duce had used to secure his dictatorship; neither did he wish to dwell on the numerous assassination attempts that had been made on the life of this beloved Leader of the Italian People. There were reports of increasing unrest amongst the left wing and pro-Soviet sections of Italian society, who were actively opposed to Il Duce and his theology and who, as a result, went in fear of the Fascist secret police, the OVRA.

History, the Minister for War mused as he continued to climb the steps, has taught us that states which rely on a secret police network for information do not, generally speaking, last too long. Why was he thinking like this? In this building, of all places! If the new Italy was what God wanted, why was there so much bickering over the Lateran Treaty? It was all so acrimonious and purely political. Where was the spirituality in it? In his opinion, the establishment of the Vatican State in the very centre of Rome had been as a result of the will of man, not God. And as for the growing legion of unemployed in this new Fascist state. He smiled to himself. Even a Fascist paradise is not exempt from the effects of the New York financial chaos. He preferred not to dwell on these things. He was, after all, first and foremost a soldier. Having ascended the staircase, he walked along the high-ceilinged corridor and finally reached the huge doors that led into the Sala di Mappamondo – the Room of the Map of the World – which was the opulent office from which Il Duce looked after the best interests of the Italian people.

A black-uniformed minion, seated behind a desk that was far too big for the few papers that rested upon it, caught sight of the count as he approached. In one fluid, well-practised movement he shot up and extended his hand in the Fascist salute, while staring straight ahead as he waited for the count's acknowledgement. It was very unwise not to be seen as totally supportive of the Party, so the count returned the salute in his own style, which was nowhere near as crisp as the minion's had been.

'Il Duce begs the count's indulgence. Il Duce must attend to some urgent matters. The delay caused to the day's proceedings is to be regretted,' the minion repeated parrot-fashion, before smartly lowering his hand. 'If the count would be so good as to sit down, it will be but a few minutes.'

'Very well,' replied the count, the heels of his jackboots clicking on the marble floor, as he crossed to a chair and sat down. *Now what could those urgent matters be?* he pondered, resting his slim leather briefcase on his knees. *Something simple, like trying to drain the Pontine Marshes? ... More dissatisfaction in the factories? ... What to do with the unemployed and the unemployable? Perhaps there is more trouble with the lira's shrinking purchasing power ... or is it something of an amorous nature... ?* The leader's reputation as a philanderer was well known. The count moved his position slightly. *So much responsibility for one man*, he thought, sarcastically. *There are flaws in Il Duce's paradise.* As he sat quietly on his chair, looking down at the intricate pattern of coloured marble on the floor, a wry smile twisted the corners of his mouth. Count Vittorio Contini-Aosta was thankful that he was just the Minister for War.

The left-hand door to the inner sanctum suddenly swung silently inwards and a uniformed secretary crossed smartly to where the count was sitting, lost in his own musings.

'Il Duce sends you his regrets for the delay. He will see you now,' said the secretary, standing rigidly to attention, his right arm extended in the salute.

'Thank you,' replied the count as he stood up, returned the salute and quickly smoothed out any creases in his uniform. The constant saluting, which seemed to accompany every movement or action in Il Duce's empire, had begun to irritate him. He found it wearisome. Even when recalling his years in the army, he could not remember so much saluting. It annoyed him so much that he forgot to take his cap with him and left it on the chair next to where he had been sitting. As he entered the *sala*, the secretary stood to one side and then silently closed the door, pulling it towards him from the outside.

The count made his way across the large, sparsely furnished room to where a desk stood in the far corner. The room was huge and the desk seemed minute. As he did so, Il Duce stood up and advanced a couple of paces into the vastness of the empty space to meet his Minister for War. Mussolini had been a journalist and knew the value of propaganda – and that included making his visitors feel dwarfed by the magnificence of his surroundings and making them walk across a large space to reach him. It was like the fly being drawn to the spider, as some of Il Duce's detractors had been heard to secretly mumble.

'Vittorio, how are you doing?' asked Il Duce, returning the count's salute and then embracing him in a bear-like hug, touching his own cheek to both of the count's in traditional greeting.

'I am well, thank you, Duce,' replied the count, noticing that Mussolini's face was heavily clouded. His warm, friendly greeting had done very little to hide whatever it was that was obviously still disturbing him greatly.

'What do you have for me today?' asked Mussolini, as he turned and walked slowly back to his desk. It was obvious that his mind was very firmly elsewhere.

The count cleared his throat.

'With regard to the navy, construction of our new ships has already commenced. Plans to convert the larger ships of our passenger fleet to troop transports, should that be necessary, are also nearing completion.'

The count paused and opened his briefcase, removed a few sheets of paper, and then placed the briefcase under his left arm, leaving his hands free to hold the sheets. Il Duce stood behind his desk, staring out of the window, his body in profile. Was he listening? It occurred to the count that the man was like a slab of marble – hard, un-giving and brutal. Contini-Aosta coughed gently. There was no response, so he carried on with his report.

'I am also happy to report that production of the prototype of our new bomber has already commenced. We anticipate the first test flight in April.' He shuffled the papers into a new order, then, after having quickly skimmed through the contents of the top one, he looked up and continued. 'The Office of Chemical Warfare has completed the order for mustard-gas bombs and a shipment is already on its way to

Eritrea. Artillery shells loaded with arsine gas have already arrived.'

Still there was no reaction from the statue behind the desk.

'Negotiations with our Iraqi friend concerning oil supplies are continuing. Since the British have moved more troops into the area around Mosul in the north of the country and also to Basra, on the Persian Gulf in the south, he seems to have become a little less enthusiastic about our proposals. Our ambassador in London has raised the issue of these troop movements with the British, who claim it is purely a matter of internal security, much like, they say, our recent deployment of another frigate and brigade to Tripoli and strengthening our forces in Eritrea...'

The count paused and stood looking at Mussolini, who had crossed his arms over his chest, but otherwise had not moved. The cavernous room had become filled with a massive, brooding silence that resembled a tropical storm that was about to break. By comparison, the sound of Contini-Aosta's voice seemed like an ineffectual wheeze. There was still no acknowledgement or comment from the man behind the desk, who continued to glare, menacingly, in the direction of the window.

'Utilizing all our options as you yourself have advised,' the count battled on, after what seemed like yet another endless pause, 'our negotiations with our French supporters are now well advanced, and there will be no problem in obtaining oil from them. Should our proposed territorial expansion be poorly received, or if an international incident should arise as a result, our ambassador thinks it highly unlikely that the British will sell us any oil. We will arrange continued oil purchases from French ships once they reach our ports. The British will never suspect that there are weak links within their French ally. Naturally, all of these arrang—'

'Why do I bother with any of this?' thundered Mussolini,

suddenly turning to face the count and crashing his fists into the thick leather jotter that covered a large part of the desk's surface. The assault caused the desk lamps to shake. 'After what I have done for the people, I still have to deal with traitors, malcontents and others who would undo what I have done in years, in a matter of seconds and at the sound of a single shot!'

The count, who had found it very difficult to disguise the sudden shock the outburst had given him, nearly dropped both his papers and briefcase on the floor. He stood rooted to the spot, as the marble statue suddenly burst into animated life.

'I am giving them schools, hospitals, homes ... I am giving them self-respect and I will give them pride in our new empire. Once again, they will be the envy of the world...' He was into his stride now. The pent-up anger which, a few short moments before had chiselled his face, now exploded into the room in a welter of words and hand gestures. '... As if it is not enough that I have to contend with those of my fellow Italians who are too stupid to realize that it is only I who have seen the true way for Italy to advance, I now have to deal with *foreigners* who share the same flawed outlook.'

He sat down, his angular face set in steel determination with his jaw thrust forward, in a gesture of defiance – or, as those who were less disposed to his theology would say, destructive, self-centred arrogance. 'And now, OVRA has an American; a mad man from New York!' He looked down at the jotter without either relaxing or moving his arms, which were still resting on the desk to either side of the jotter. 'Michele Schirru, an anarchist, who has come all this way to assassinate *me*! Is it not bad enough that we have our own traitors here in this country, without having to concern ourselves with those from beyond our borders?'

He glared at the count, as if searching the older man's

face for confirmation of his minister's unconditional support. For his part, the count, who had not dared to move, had been so taken aback by the outburst that he was at a loss for words. He also had no idea of what Il Duce was talking about. Contini-Aosta searched vainly for something appropriate to say, but, to his considerable relief, Mussolini thundered on before he could reply.

'And now, in addition to all the affairs of state that require my attention, not to mention the important military plans which we have to discuss and which I have entrusted to you...' He flung out his right hand in the count's direction, palm uppermost, and waved it about energetically, much as a conductor might direct the performance of a lively tarantella. '...I now also have to listen to the lies of the American ambassador.'

The count had started to feel very uneasy. He seemed to be bearing the brunt of Mussolini's considerable anger over something which, until the explosion of words, he had known nothing about. He had heard stories of those who displeased Il Duce, or who became the focus of his considerable desire for revenge. Now, standing in the path of a diatribe the cause of which, he felt, had absolutely nothing to do with him, he felt his palms start to sweat.

'I am told that they found this idiot American in one of our hotels two days ago, with a gun and two bombs,' ranted Mussolini, 'and now, today, I am told by the fool of an American ambassador that this man is an Italian! They claim that they have nothing to do with it and that this man was free to come and go, as he pleased. Ahhhh!' he raged, flinging both arms up in a gesture of exasperation and propelling himself back in his chair.

It seemed to Count Vittorio Contini-Aosta that his presence in the room had become a total irrelevance. Still, he stood rooted to the spot not daring to move.

'We have his passport,' continued Mussolini, brandishing

the document in the air, 'and still the Americans say it was nothing to do with them! The ambassador tells me, "This man is an anarchist and the United States Government does not support anarchists". And then the ambassador tells me, "This man was not born an American; he is only naturalized". Do they think I am a fool? Do they think I cannot see through their plan?'

He glared straight ahead, the lines of furious affront now slowly receding from the strong, square face. Suddenly, his head fell forwards, on to his uniform, where it stayed for several seconds. The count, still standing in front of the desk clutching his disorganized papers and slim briefcase, said nothing. With some trepidation, he waited for the next act in this alarmingly violent pantomime to begin. With a heavy sigh, Il Duce raised his head from his chest just as suddenly as it had collapsed, and once again looked straight ahead of him, out into the space of the *sala*. Most of the visible signs of his recent anger and outburst had disappeared, almost as suddenly as they had first exploded into the unsuspecting room. His view lighted upon his Minister for War.

'Vittorio, how are things going?' he asked.

Contini-Aosta had heard rumours about his leader's violent mood swings, but he had never actually been at the vortex of one – not until now. The rage and anger, which, at its height, could probably have been heard by passers-by in the street outside, had now almost totally vanished, to be replaced with a warmth and calmness completely at odds with what had gone before.

'What do you have to tell me today? What progress with the oil? What progress with our ships?'

Il Duce waved an arm in the air and leaned forward in his chair. The realization that his leader had heard absolutely nothing of what it was that he had reported on at the beginning of the audience suddenly dawned on the count.

Playing for time, he rearranged his papers in the correct order, the sweat on his hands complicating the task. For a split second he wondered if Il Duce had noticed his startled reaction to the outburst, or if he had even noticed how the immaculate sheets of paper had become badly mangled in his sweaty hands.

Sweet Mother of Jesus, he was not even aware of my presence, the count thought to himself in a moment of realization. He looked up from the creased sheets he held in his hand. *And I am certain he heard absolutely nothing of what I told him.* Thinking quickly, as Mussolini sat behind the desk and looked up expectantly at him, the count decided on the only course of action open to him.

'We continue to make good progress with our plans, Duce,' he began, trying to remember what he had said earlier. Contini-Aosta started his report from the beginning: 'The navy plans have almost been completed, the new ships will soon commence construction, and we have finalized...'

9

Palestine

The Golden Moon Nightclub, Haifa – Monday, 2nd March 1931

The jagged edge of the applause, such as it was, cut through the haze of stale cigarette smoke as Claudette Catzmann, *chanteuse* and cabaret star, flung her arms out in a grand gesture of finale, her mouth opened wide in a broad smile. She stood on the small, raised platform which served as a stage. Seated next to her on a tall stool, placed perilously close to the edge of platform, Morris Ginsberg, her husband and most avid supporter, sat savouring the glory of the moment. Like most of the clientele who frequented the nightclub he, too, had the smouldering remnant of a cigarette clamped loosely between his lips.

Claudette had just finished the last *chanson* of the second set of the evening – 'Mon homme'. She knew instinctively that Morris, her Moshie, would be beaming with pride and admiration over her performance as he pumped his accordion, sustaining the last wheezing chord of the song. A single, feeble spotlight fought its way through the stale smoke and illuminated her face, with its framing border of peroxide-blonde curls and its frighteningly wide-open mouth. She had first seen this style of finale used years before by her idol, Marie-Louise Damien, at the Concert Dania in Paris. It was the use of this simple, yet sophisticated lighting technique that had made Damien famous during the dark days of the war. At the Golden Moon in Haifa, the technical aspect of this technique was almost there, even if the illumination from the spotlight was a little dim, but there was something. Claudette's presentation lacked the panache – the savoir-faire – of her idol. Indeed, as some had been heard to say, the most important thing lacking in her act was talent!

As the sporadic clapping started to die away, she bowed from the neck, looking – as she thought – delicate, childlike and vulnerable. Then, unceremoniously, the single spotlight was abruptly choked into darkness. Once her eyes had adjusted to the reduced level of brightness she turned and, taking her Moshie's hand, she led them off the little platform and through the sparsely occupied tables until they reached the bar, which ran along almost the entire length of one of the side walls.

'We should be in a better place than this, Moshie,' she hissed indignantly. 'Did you see them just now? They didn't even turn around to say how good it was. *Schmucks*!' she whispered, vehemently, as she took a long sip from the ice-cold drink that the barman had prepared for her in anticipation of the end of her performance. He was just as indifferent to her singing talents as the rest of the clientele of the Golden Moon, but, through regular exposure to her performances, he had learned the timings of her act and when the breaks would be. Now, he was relieved that they would not have to listen to the singing again for another forty-five minutes. It was only a small mercy, but one for which he was, nevertheless, grateful.

'Did you see that one in the front? Over there...' she continued, her over-generous – some would say gauche – drop earrings swinging dangerously around her head as she turned to look in the offender's direction, '...He never stopped talking. Not for one moment did he stop!'

She turned back to look at Morris, 'and this set had some of my best songs in it. It's not every day that they get a singer like me in here, I can tell you!'

'Nuts?' interrupted the barman, as he pushed a small glass bowl of salted peanuts across the bar towards her. His expression was neutral, but his tone did nothing to hide the fact that he had taken her last statement at its face value. And she was quite right. He couldn't remember the last time the Golden Moon had hired such a dubious talent.

'Thanks, Avi,' answered Morris, smiling at the barman, 'can I have my beer now; nice and cold. It's hot, hard work up there.'

I'll bet it is hot, hard work pumping away with this one, no matter where you are, fantasized Avi, as he took a cold bottle from the ice chest under the counter. 'There you go. I'll put everything on the slate,' he muttered, as he wandered off to serve another customer.

'My talents are totally wasted here!' she continued, adjusting her voluminous blonde hair, which crowned an otherwise modest frame, 'we should go to Jerusalem, that's where the bright lights are, not here. Here ... is far too small ... and as for this lot,' she waved the glass around in the direction of the cloud of cigarette smoke, 'well, Moshie, what can a girl say? Eh?'

He was used to this. He felt genuine frustration that they had not made a bigger impression on the local entertainment industry since their arrival in Palestine.

'I know, Claudie,' he said soothingly, 'but we just have to keep trying and to be patient already. Give people time to realize what you can do.'

Avi, who had worked his way back up behind the bar to where they were standing, snorted in an attempt to suppress a laugh by covering it up with a couple of coughs. He quite liked Morris, but Claudette! He had quickly realized that, despite her repertoire of exclusively French *chansons* she was no more French than he was.

Claudette's earrings jangled as she swivelled around on the bar stool and drew one of the tin ashtrays across the bar towards her. 'Be an angel, my *bubalah*, and do me a gasper,' she said, as she put the glass on the bar. 'I'm fair dying for one.'

As he reached into the inside pocket of his rather creased jacket to retrieve his cigarettes – a luxury they sometimes found difficult to afford – a sparkle flashed into his eyes. Claudette was a tiger when she was aroused and now, with well over forty minutes to wait until their third and final set of the evening, they could go back to the storeroom out the back, their 'dressing room', as she liked to call it grandly. *Perhaps we could try...*

'That's the gasper I'd be dying for, Moshie,' she said sternly, 'nothing else, not with another set to perform. You know how it upsets your concentration afterwards and you start hitting the wrong buttons.' As quickly as she had spotted the gleam in Morris's eyes, she realized that what she had just said was a little harsh – perhaps even a little unkind, for he was a good man. She and Morris had been very happy with each other, but there had been the occasions lately when he had found it difficult to rise to the demand and satisfy her needs. It was the war. They had both been involved; she had helped in a hospital and he had worn a uniform, as had millions of others. He had been damaged – or, as he preferred to put it using his East End humour, dented a little. They both knew that sometimes things would malfunction below the belt, but they had learned to work around it – so far. She wiggled herself across the stool, a little closer to where he was leaning against the bar, looking adoringly at her.

'But you always manage to hit the right buttons with me,' she whispered seductively into his ear.

He beamed appreciatively at her, giving her arm an affectionate squeeze. It did not matter to him that people said she wore too much make-up and that her hair was far too luxurious at her age to be real. Others said that she sang flat and her diction was so bad that she could have been singing in any language under the sun *other* than French. She, however, had always been proud of her talent, from the days when, as a little child, she had sung and danced her way around her family's hearts, brightening their lives in the drab confines of the East End of London. Even during the war, when she had volunteered to go and help the wounded in the hospitals in France, she had kept singing. Given the crowded conditions of the wards in which she had helped, dancing was out of the question, but singing – well, that was always possible. She had once read an article in an old magazine about the therapeutic value of music, so Claudette reasoned that her singing would be her contribution to the war effort. Unfortunately, most of those she sang to were so physically and mentally scarred that her particular crooning was neither recognized nor appreciated.

They had been sitting at the bar for almost the entire forty minutes of break allowed them under the terms of the contract they had managed to wring out of the management. Now, shortly before eleven-thirty, it was almost time to start the final twenty-minute set of the evening.

'Are you ready, Claudie?' asked Morris, looking first at his watch and then up at the large clock, which was built into the wooden shelves lining the wall behind the bar. This was his set routine – a tradition which he had evolved over the almost two months they had been working there. When he had first noticed it, he had thought it a rather ridiculous place to put a clock: half hidden between the bottles and glasses. Now he realized that most of the clientele who frequented the Golden Moon were running away from time and would have little need to know or be reminded of its passing.

'Time to go,' he said, looking at his wristwatch, which was set to several minutes faster than the clock over the bar. 'Do you need to go places first?' he asked, helping Claudette down from the stool.

'No thanks, *bubalah*; I'm fine,' she replied, smiling as she adjusted her wig, which had slipped a little during the break. 'Come, Moshie,' she said with determination, 'I ask you one more time. Why am I wasting my talents in this place, already?'

10

London

Whitehall – Tuesday, 3rd March 1931

Stephen Hopkins was on his way to his uncle's office in Whitehall. He had been invited to have a little chat, as his uncle put it, and he was rather apprehensive as to what it was all about. Stephen knew only too well how fickle his family could be; he hadn't seen his Uncle Cecil since the house party at the country estate shortly before New Year. That time, he had stayed only for a couple of days and had made an excuse to return to London, amidst loudly voiced disappointment from everyone, so as to be back with Rupert as soon as possible.

In response to his uncle's summons, he had limped along Whitehall as quickly as he could, concerned that he may have offended his uncle either by not bringing Rupert with him on that occasion or by his own disappearance earlier than planned. But he had felt that he was not yet ready to subject his friend – the most precious possession he had – to the overbearing scrutiny of his family. The Hopkins-Donnington-Boughton family were used to the cut and thrust of Court and society life – but Rupert Winfield most certainly was not. Quite apart from any other consideration, Stephen could not bear the thought of putting his friend on display for familial approval like some prized exhibit in a case at the British Museum. He often thought he now fully understood what it was that Mr Wilde had meant when he referred to 'The Love that dare not speak its name'. Sometimes, he resented himself for being a coward by refusing to take that leap of faith that would acknowledge who and what he was. When the dull ache in his stump throbbed, he speculated if it was not some sort of metaphor for his lack of resolution to reveal himself and his friend to the world.

'Come in, my dear boy, come in,' said the Uncle, gesturing.

Looking closely at his nephew's face he was immediately concerned that the younger man had aged and looked strained. Behind the genuine smile there were lines around the mouth and on the brow, which had not been there before. 'It's good to see you again. How are you keeping?'

'Fine, thank you, Sir ... fine,' answered Stephen, as he crossed to the chair his uncle indicated. He walked stiffly, leaning on the heavy black cane, with its ornamental silver handle in the shape of a winged griffin with blood-red rubies for eyes. The Uncle couldn't help but notice; nevertheless, he thought better of asking about the state of Stephen's leg.

'There is someone I would like you to meet,' continued the Uncle. Stephen had become aware of another man who was seated in the chair opposite his. 'This is Professor James Longhurst of the British Museum. Professor, this is my nephew, Stephen Hopkins-Donnington-Boughton.'

'How do you do?' said the professor, from behind thick lenses. 'Pleased to meet you.'

'How do you do?' replied Stephen, unintentionally looking down on the professor, who could not have been more than five feet two inches in height. As they settled themselves into their chairs, with the Uncle taking up his usual position behind the desk, Stephen took the opportunity to look more closely at the other visitor. The wildly unkempt grey hair, the pallid wrinkled skin that had long been dried under a foreign sun and the thick spectacle lenses all indicated a lifetime's work of poring over old books, ancient manuscripts and exposed archaeological ruins. Such interests had placed this man, more often than not, into a world of his own, separated from the vast majority of his fellow beings. Now he sat upright in his chair, like a greyhound bracing itself for the starting gate to fly open and send it on its way. This little man was excited about something and it showed.

'Now, my boy, the professor has something rather interesting to tell us,' said the Uncle, reaching for a cigar and settling himself more comfortably into his chair. 'Professor...'

'Thank you so much ... er, yes ... quite where to begin?'

Stephen looked first at the professor, who was sorting through a small pocket notebook, and then quickly at his uncle. His gaze was returned with raised eyebrows from behind a curtain of cigar smoke.

'We have many, many items in the museum, you know,' began the professor, stating what, to his two listeners, was obvious, 'and it can sometimes take years before we have the opportunity to properly study something, which could possibly have been found as much as a century before. That is what has happened now ... with this tablet.' He paused and looked up from his notebook. 'And it is a most interesting find ... Really quite unique, I would say.'

Stephen smiled patiently, resting his hand on his walking stick.

'The tablet in question has been in the museum since 1882, when it was brought back from a field trip, which had been sent out to explore the region east of the Jordan River, including the so-called "rose-pink city" of Petra. It was really quite a dangerous thing to do, as the Ottoman Turks were not kindly disposed towards foreigners ... unbelievers ... being on their territory,' he said, as he adjusted his spectacles. 'However, the expedition returned safely, but we have only now had a chance to study some of the items they brought back with them...' He chuckled softly. '...Some fifty years later, I'm afraid.'

The other two men murmured quietly, in sympathetic encouragement.

'The inscription is unusual, in that it is incised into a marble tablet and not a clay tablet, as one would reasonably expect. It was found quite by accident by a Bedouin, according to the expedition's report, who then sold it to the expedition for a most paltry sum. Unfortunately, we have no idea exactly where it was found or even when. We cannot even be certain it originally came from Petra, although the style of the text could well place it at the time when Petra was a city of great significance to the Nabatean people. We understand Petra to have been the capital of their thriving empire, which was built on trade. This tablet could well have been a copy of something far older, possibly in another text or language, which was brought to Petra from somewhere else. If that is the case, then the original has most certainly long since been lost.'

As the professor paused once again to turn over a couple of pages of his notebook, as if looking for some specific information, Stephen suddenly had the thought that it would have been useful to have Rupert with him at this meeting – at least he had the academic background for this sort of thing.

'The tablet was obviously of great importance in antiquity, hence the use of marble. It is not so much the fact that we have the tablet that is the important thing; rather, it is what is inscribed upon it...'

'And that inscription is what, exactly, Professor?' prompted the Uncle, his cigar well and truly alight. Although he knew what was coming next, he was anxious to share this secret with Stephen.

'Well, it relates to a much earlier period than that of the golden age of Petra, which seems to have been around the first century BC,' continued the professor, 'so, it is quite possible that this tablet is a record of events that happened some considerable time before.'

He was looking very serious, in a scholarly manner, as he flicked through to the relevant page in his notebook.

'As far as we can ascertain, given our current understanding of the style and meaning of the writing used, this, in essence, is what the inscription says.'

He adjusted his spectacles once more, cleared his throat, and began to read in a quiet, yet authoritative voice:

' "... The Lord God gave commandment to Gershom to rise and conquer all before him who did not Covenant themselves to the Lord. This is to be the Commandment of Seir. Gershom, of Moses, is the Sword of the Lord, from the Land of Edom. From Seir shall the Law of the Lord rise up and go forth and the Sword shall be Gershom and his people shall be the true people of the Lord. They shall be the only chosen of the Lord, who will protect and nourish them in the lands of Edom and Canaan and beyond, until the..." '

The professor stopped reading and looked up at the other two men. He shifted his position as he turned the page in his notebook. He did not look at it, but stared instead into the space in front of him. 'The bottom right-hand corner of the tablet has been broken off,' he said, in a voice heavy with the regret he felt at the realization that the text was incomplete and that the missing piece of polished marble could well have held vital information. It was gone – for ever. 'We have more of the inscription, but it is quite fragmentary,' he continued, ' ".... And now the word of the Lord is safe ... where the rocks that burn are quenched by the eagle ... then will arise, at the coming of the Sword of the Lord ... the chosen ones and Gershom, of Moses ... the scroll of the Word of the Lord in safety ... for the time was not yet the Lord's ... those not of the Covenant..."'

Putting down his notebook, the professor heaved a sigh of regret. 'And that is the point at which we can decipher nothing further, I'm afraid. The rest of what is left of the inscription has been too badly damaged...'

The air in the office had grown very still, heavily laden with the words that a scribe had incised into the marble millennia before.

'That's very interesting,' remarked the Uncle. 'Do you think there is any truth in it? Does it relate to anything that can be linked with known historical events?'

'Well, I'm not an expert on the history of the Jewish people,' replied the professor, 'but I'd say that it could possibly refer back to something about which we have absolutely no knowledge, possibly even as far back as the time of Moses.'

'Moses ... indeed, as you mentioned earlier, Professor,' said the Uncle, who, because he had been listening with such rapt attention, had to relight his cigar, which had gone out.

'I have taken the liberty of asking some of my colleagues at the museum about this,' continued the professor, closing his notebook. 'Some of them are of the Jewish faith and are of the opinion that the Gershom referred to is possibly the son of Moses. There's ample proof of the existence of Moses' sons in the Old Testament, including one called Gershom. And there is a school of thought that places Mount Sinai and, of course, Moses in the Petra area rather than in the Sinai Peninsula. I would add that such references are faith-based and are not founded on quantifiable, historical fact. Nonetheless, it is a possible link.'

'Moses of the Commandments?' queried Stephen, who had sat quietly in his chair throughout the professor's speech, absorbing what was being said. 'But, surely, Professor, that would have been several centuries before the first century BC?'

'Very true, which is why we are inclined to say that this tablet is a record of something that was in the collective memory of the Jewish people, but that had happened centuries before the tablet was created. Possibly not even in or around the Petra area ... Such an event could have happened much further afield ...'

'What, exactly, is the meaning of the message?' asked Stephen, his brow slightly furrowed. 'I am not sure that I totally follow the gist of it. And as for "the rocks that burn" ... and "a quenching eagle" ... what is that all about? Presumably, it is intended to be a message of some sort ... if someone went to the trouble of creating the tablet using expensive marble, even if it *is* a copy of an earlier text?'

Once again, the professor looked deeply into the empty space in front of him, focusing on no one specifically, but rather on the considerable bank of knowledge he had amassed in his head over several decades of study and fieldwork. 'It contains a reference to the "Sword of the Lord", so, I would assume it to be warlike in nature: a call to arms to the people of what, today, we would call the Jewish Nation. This call would be for the region of ancient Edom and Canaan, more or less parts of modern Trans-Jordan and Palestine, to be cleansed of all non-believers: Gentiles, in other words. Once that has happened, then the Children of Israel would establish their kingdom, under the protection of God. At the moment, of course, all of this is educated speculation and is subject to further and more learned interpretation and discussion. We could possibly say that it is a call to arms to the Jewish Nation to establish itself, once and for all, under the divine aegis of the God of Israel,' concluded the professor.

'It could possibly even be an eleventh Commandment,' added the Uncle, his face a mask of seriousness now matching that of the diminutive professor.

'The eleventh Commandment?' repeated Stephen, laughing incredulously.

'Yes, the eleventh Commandment,' repeated the Uncle. ' "Thou shalt build a state for all Jewry in Israel", or Palestine, as we now call it.'

Once again the room fell silent, as the three men pondered what had just been said. Eventually, the professor sat back in his chair and slipped his notebook back into the pocket of his jacket. Then he sat perfectly still, thinking carefully before offering: 'I have no explanation for the "quenching eagle" and I cannot even acknowledge it to be a reference to Imperial Rome ... far too early.'

'As for "the rocks that burn",' said the Uncle, 'that could be a totally natural phenomena. We know that in certain geographical areas oil leeches out of certain rock formations and lies on the surface, where it is ignited by the sun. It can look as if the rocks are on fire and it will burn for centuries – as long as the oil keeps seeping through. I am reliably informed that there is an example of this near a mountain called Tall Salāh, out in the Trans-Jordanian desert and quite near to the Iraq border, though that's miles away from Petra.'

'Such phenomena were known to the Ancients, for example, by the Zoroastrians in Persia,' added the professor.

'But, if this tablet has been in the museum for almost fifty years, what is the significance attached to deciphering it now?' asked Stephen. 'Surely, at best, it's simply a flight of someone's fancy or, at worst, a call to arms that is several thousand years too late?'

'Not at all, my boy,' the Uncle replied, his cigar now a smouldering stub in the large glass ashtray that sat to his left on the desk. 'What do you know of the present Jewish

Question and our modern mandated territory of Palestine?' he asked softly.

A quarter of an hour passed, during which time the Uncle explained the British government's concerns over the increasing Zionist pressure for an independent Jewish homeland in Palestine. Their insistence was evenly matched by the growing wave of anti-Zionist resistance from the newly-founded Arab countries, which surrounded the territory that would become the proposed Jewish State, if such a thing were ever allowed to happen. A gentle knock sounded on the heavy office door.

'Let us pause there for a moment, if you please, gentlemen,' said the Uncle, as the door opened silently and a fourth person was shown into the room.

11

London

The Company Boardroom, Mayfair – Tuesday, 3rd March 1931

The monthly Board meeting had convened in the opulent surroundings of the newly acquired headquarters building in Mayfair, the once aristocratic area which had now become the centre of London society. The company's star was in the ascendant and the old headquarters in Ludgate Circus had become unfit for purpose and had simply outlived its usefulness. The move had been deemed as essential to the image of the company, but there were those of a more cautious disposition who thought that the company was in danger of overstepping the mark and spreading itself too thinly. They warned of dark days ahead, if there were to be a repeat of the recent financial disaster that had spread like wildfire from across the Atlantic, but these gloomy, over-cautious concerns found no nesting place in the mind of the Chairman. Far from it – he was particularly pleased with the present state of his company.

'Can we move on to the next item, gentlemen?' he said, shuffling a small pile of papers into a new order in front of him. 'To our proposed new destinations.' The Chairman turned to look at a young man who was sitting to his right. 'Kitchener, are we ready to launch our new destinations yet?'

Before speaking, the young man looked down at the papers on the blotter in front of him and, for a fleeting moment, it seemed that he was unsure of what to do next. This was the Chairman's nephew and something of an embarrassment – not that Augustus Halthwaite would ever admit it.

'We are very well advanced on all fronts, Sir,' the young man finally reported. Although he spoke with the tone of one accustomed to privilege, his voice had a puzzling undertow of uncertainty. 'I'm very pleased to say that the sporting tours and even the automobile tours of Europe are ready for the off. We have tied up almost all of the loose ends with our European colleagues and we can expect to launch the first of our new range of excursions within the next couple of weeks. Reggie's Art Department has already received some proofs back from the printers...' He indicated a short, balding man, considerably older than himself, who was sitting halfway up one side of the table. 'Perhaps you would do the honours?' he concluded, eager to pass the buck, whilst purposefully ignoring the other man's barely concealed look of resentment and disdain.

Folders containing the proofs of the new brochures, posters and other promotional literature were passed around the table to murmurs of general consent and congratulation.

'Your lot have really pulled out all the stops on this one, Reggie. Well done, old boy. I am almost tempted to sign up for one of these trips myself,' declared the Chairman to general laughter. 'And what about this one?' he added, as his gaze fell upon a brochure for the Holy Land and Petra. '... Is this Petra place *really* pink?'

'Pink and every other colour under the sun, apparently,' replied a retired diplomat at the far end of the boardroom table. 'I'm told it depends on the time of day and the height of the sun. Apparently, the colours range from pink to yellow, green to blood red and several other shades in between. Something to do with rich mineral deposits in the rock structure, I believe.'

'And are we actually ready to move on the "Holy Land and Petra Tour"?' asked the Chairman, reading the title from the proof in front of him.

'Not quite, the Trans-Jordanian government weren't too keen at first,' continued the retired diplomat, 'but they seem to be changing their mind ... now that they have finally grasped the fact that they stand to benefit financially from the undertaking ... as we will.'

There was more subdued murmuring and agreement from around the table. Kitchener Halthwaite cast a furtive glance at his uncle and then at the experienced faces around the table. He was only too aware that he did not occupy his seat because of his ability and knowledge.

'They are not as well developed in terms of accommodation and other facilities as, for example, Egypt is,' continued another member of the board. 'I even understand that there are Bedouin living amongst the ruins of Petra itself. It is because of the lack of facilities and, naturally, the question of the safety of our guests that we have had to do considerably more groundwork than would normally have been necessary. However, having said that, we have made considerable progress, as you can see from the initial reports and the proposed brochure. We will be ready to send our first intrepid group of travellers in the footsteps of Jesus within the next few weeks.'

There were some icy stares at this last, flippant remark. As forward thinking as the company was, there were still those on the Board who hankered back to the old days of decorum and respect – attributes they thought had been lost as a result of the war.

'We'll send Winfield with the first group,' the Chairman enthused. 'He's a reliable pair of hands and is one of our most senior representatives in the Middle East, particularly with our Egyptian operation. It'll be new ground for both the company and for him and I feel that his expertise in our business will be useful, should any changes to the proposed itinerary be either necessary or desirable.'

Kitchener smiled broadly, but kept his gaze lowered. This was good news. The area had a reputation for being lawless and, in parts, quite dangerous for travellers. Winfield might not come back. He was sick and tired of Winfield's name, which seemed to crop up in conversations far too often; it somehow highlighted his own inadequacy. Kitchener was conscious that the ability of the man, who was of his own age, might prove to be a hindrance to his own advancement in the years to come.

'Excellent, gentlemen,' boomed the Chairman, 'then let us aim to launch the sale of reservations for Petra by the end of this month.'

12

London

Whitehall – Tuesday, 3rd March 1931

'Rabbi Mosheowitz, Sir,' announced Collingwood, the Uncle's private secretary.

'Thank you, Collingwood. Could you organize some tea for us, please?' requested the Uncle, before dismissing his private secretary. 'Rabbi, thank you for joining us at such short notice,' continued the Uncle, who had come out from behind his desk and had drawn a third chair nearer to it, between the professor and Stephen. 'Please sit down,' he invited, indicating the newly-placed chair, before returning to his own behind the desk.

Rabbi Mosheowitz was stoutly built, and seemed to be even shorter than Professor Longhurst, or so it seemed to Stephen. From under his black waistcoat protruded the tassels of his prayer shawl; he made no movement to remove the plain black Homburg hat from his head.

The Uncle proceeded to tell the rabbi about the tablet and the message it possibly contained, but he said just sufficient to enable the man to have a realistic chance of answering the questions which were about to be put to him. The full content of the conversation that had taken place between the other three men before Rabbi Mosheowitz's arrival would, for the time being, remain between just the three of them.

'Yes, it is written that Moses had sons. The firstborn was named Gershom,' said the rabbi in heavy, carefully measured tones, 'and the Prophet Moses did receive the Law on Mount Sinai, following the Exodus. It is also written that there were those of Moses' family who were blessed of the Lord and received instruction and knowledge. Perhaps even Gershom, himself.' The rabbi shrugged slightly, as if to be absolved of the responsibility of such knowledge. He stroked his full, long grey beard as he spoke. 'It was a long time ago,' he added, with typical Jewish understatement.

Mindful of the possible political consequences should the professor's revelations become public knowledge, the Uncle then attempted to discreetly enquire into the reference to the "Sword of the Lord".

'Tell us, Rabbi, do you know of any writing which talks of an instruction, or a commandment even, that advocates the fight to establish a Jewish homeland in the Middle East?'

Sunk deep in thought, Mosheowitz stroked his beard before answering.

'Throughout our history of many thousands of years, we have always had to fight to exist. From ancient times, to our own King Edward I in the black year of 1290, to the pogroms in Russia under the Tsars and even today, we have to struggle to survive. It is possible that Gershom received wisdom from the Lord, calling him to lead a strong crusade to establish what was to become the Kingdom of David and of Solomon, but these events came about anyway, even if they did not endure. If such a command was given to Gershom from on high, it is not within my gift to say,' he concluded with a shrug, looking closely at the Uncle as he did so. He had begun to sense that there was more to this meeting than met the eye. 'There are many references to the delivery of the Children of Israel from those who would oppress them. In Numbers, it is written that "there shall step forth a star out of Jacob..."' He paused and sat looking down at his shoes, 'but this is only one reference of many.'

'What would be your interpretation of *this* particular passage, Rabbi?' asked the Uncle, before turning to Longhurst. 'Would you mind refreshing our minds with your translation of the second part of the inscription?'

Professor Longhurst once again withdrew the notebook from his pocket and set about searching for the relevant entry. As he did so, Stephen looked at the rabbi and was reminded of the steely determination of purpose that he had first recognized on the face of Simon Arling, on board the little Nile paddle steamer *Khufu*, several years before. Then, as now, he admired the single focus of faith, which had driven that race to survive through so many centuries of deprivation and suppression. For a fleeting moment he felt it was a determination for self-expression which he, himself, lacked in his own life, now that he had found a partner.

'I have it,' said the professor. 'Shall I...?'

'If you'd be so kind, Professor,' answered the Uncle.

Longhurst cleared his throat, once again, and began to read:

'"...And now the word of the Lord is safe... where the rocks that burn are quenched by the eagle... then will arise, at the coming of the Sword of the Lord... the chosen ones and Gershom, of Moses... the scroll of the Word of the Lord in safety... for the time was not yet the Lord's ... those not of the Covenant..."'

For a few moments nothing was said; the atmosphere became heavy with expectancy as all eyes turned to Mosheowitz, who seemed even deeper in thought than before. Eventually, he spoke.

'It is written in the Scriptures of how the struggle for survival of the Lord's favoured children was practically a never-ending one. We also read of this in our books of what you call the Old Testament,' he said slowly. 'If this is a record of any accuracy,' he continued, gesturing towards the professor, 'then, perhaps, such a writing does exist in its original form somewhere, waiting for Gershom or his modern-day counterpart to lead his people.' He paused, reflecting on what to say next, before continuing: 'I do not know where such a scroll would be kept ... or if it even exists.'

The Uncle threw a hasty, interested glance at Longhurst, who returned it with as much interest, as if alerted to some new, totally unexpected clue.

'Would this have been a *scroll?*' asked the Uncle. 'If, of course, it ever existed in the first place, as you say, Rabbi,' he added, by way of making his interest less obvious.

'There is a good possibility,' replied the rabbi. 'About forty years ago there was rumour that a very ancient copy of the Torah scroll had been found in the library of Bologna University. When it was requested, it could not be found ... It had simply vanished. That is why I advise caution; possibilities can often create false hopes,' he concluded, folding his hands in his lap and avoiding any further comment.

'Writings which were considered important enough were often recorded on velum scrolls, or sometimes even on thin sheets of metal – copper, for example – which were then made into scrolls,' offered the professor.

'So, if such a scroll still exists, then the original source of what you have translated from the Petra tablet, Professor, could possibly still be in the protection of Tall Salāh,' said the Uncle, who was fishing for information, 'where *the rocks burn.*'

The Uncle had emphasized the last few words of his sentence on purpose. As he waited for the hoped-for response he was to be disappointed, as the conversation sank into silence, the only sound being the steady ticking of the clock on the mantelpiece. At last the Uncle spoke. 'Is Tall Salāh perhaps known to you, Rabbi?'

There was a lengthy pause, before Rabbi Mosheowitz spoke with a carefully arranged expression of contrived ignorance on his face. 'It is the name of a person who is not known to me,' he stated. 'It also does not have the cadence of a Hebrew name.'

There was a knock on the door and Collingwood entered, bearing a large silver tray, with their tea.

They were well into their refreshment when Professor Longhurst suddenly put down his cup and turned to face the rabbi. 'Rabbi Mosheowitz, earlier on you made mention of the prophecy in Numbers ... Is that not the one referred to as the "Star Prophecy"?'

The question came as a warning shot across the bows to the rabbi, although he was very careful not to betray his surprise that this man – obviously a non-Jew – should even know about it.

'It is called so by some, but, as I have said, it is but one of many such prophecies. Our faith is built on such promises handed to us over the millennia by Yahweh.'

Professor Longhurst seemed about to add something further, but then sat back in his chair. He smiled at the rabbi and returned his attention to his cup of tea.

'If there is nothing else that I can help you with ... I have matters of some importance to attend to at the synagogue. We have the welfare of a great many of our members to concern ourselves with ... and time and tide wait for no man, as we English say.'

Stephen thought the emphasis placed on the word 'English' a little heavy, a fact that was not lost on the Uncle either.

'Of course ... of course, Rabbi. Please do not let me keep you from your flock. It was jolly good of you to find the time to come and see me at such short notice...' Rabbi

Mosheowitz had already started to rise from his chair without waiting for the Uncle's blessing to do so. 'Let me ask Collingwood to escort you...'

Once the door had closed behind Rabbi Mosheowitz, Professor Longhurst sat on the edge of his chair, a look of something between excitement and concern on his face.

'The good rabbi was somewhat evasive on the topic of the Star Prophecy,' he said, his voice low. 'I only happen to know about it because I have just finished reading a paper on the subject of the Bar Kokhba Revolt. I thought it might be of some significance to our present discussion'

The professor sat back a little, as if he expected his audience to make a comment on his pronouncement. Instead, he was met with a pair of totally blank faces.

'In Judea ... the revolt against the Romans that led to the establishment of a Jewish kingdom between AD 132 and 135. It was led by Simon bar Kokhba, who ruled the area as *Nasi*, or Prince. The rabbi did not mention that ... He was also somewhat selective in his quotation from Numbers, too.' The professor flipped through his notebook again. 'Yes, here it is ... I made some notes as I was reading ... really interesting stuff. This is what Numbers 24:17 actually has to say: "I shall see him, but not now: I shall behold him, but not nigh: there shall come a Star out of Jacob, and a Sceptre shall rise out of Israel, and shall smite the corners of Moab, and destroy all the children of Sheth."'

The Uncle's face had suddenly taken on a granite-like quality. He stared at the professor.

'The rabbi also omitted to mention that the revolt was crushed with the usual Roman thoroughness and perhaps half a million Jews paid for their experiment of freedom with their lives. The Jewish kingdom did not last.'

Not that particular one, but they had the drive and scriptural instruction to establish it in the first place, thought the Uncle, who suddenly saw the real danger of the inscription on the marble tablet. If it has happened before, it can happen again!

'How interesting,' said Stephen, putting his empty cup down, 'I had no idea about either this Jewish revolt, or of a Jewish kingdom during the Roman period.' Stephen had learned much about archaeology and ancient history since meeting Rupert. 'A remarkable achievement...'

The Uncle did not share his nephew's assessment of the professor's revelation. Instead, he looked gravely concerned.

'Indeed,' continued Longhurst, 'they even used their own coins ... Roman ones that they over-stamped and inscribed with their own message. One popular one reads, "For the Freedom of Israel".'

Once the professor had departed, the Uncle and his nephew stood next to the large table. Its surface was covered with a cloth, which hungrily absorbed the large pool of early-spring sunlight that fell through the tall windows lining the park side of the building.

'You've heard what the experts and the professor have to say about all of this,' said the Uncle, as he removed the white cloth from the table, 'now take a look at the map,' he continued, placing the crumpled cloth on a nearby chair.

On the table before them was spread the large-scale map of the Middle East. On it were the Kingdom of Egypt, the new Kingdom of Saudi Arabia, the Emirate of Trans-Jordan, the new Kingdom of Iraq and the French Protectorate of Syria and Lebanon.

'That is where the problem could lie,' said the Uncle, stabbing a finger down on the tiny strip of land between the Mediterranean and the river Jordan. 'Palestine. The state both Arab and Jew want to create for their own reasons, but which doesn't yet exist. The whole area is like a powder keg waiting to explode. Our French allies are busy with their mandate for Syria and this bit here ... Lebanon ...

and we're busy with just about everything else, including trying to keep control of the oil here.' He indicated the deserts of Iraq. 'And the people here,' he said, tapping his finger on the strip of land labelled *Palestine*. 'But, then again, you already know that there are others interested in the oil we extract from the region, don't you, my boy?'

Stephen looked at his uncle and smiled dismissively. He did not particularly wish to be reminded of Pompeii.

'In view of this business with the inscription and the scroll, that might now not be of such importance ... certainly not in the short term, anyway.'

Stephen nodded, but made no comment. Instead, he moved closer to the table for a better look at the detail of the map.

'I believe that the good rabbi knew a little more than he was happy to part with,' continued the Uncle. 'Tall Salāh is not a person at all, so it's hardly surprising that the name was not known to him as such; that much he inadvertently gave away. It is a mountain ... this one over here.' He pointed to the far north-eastern corner of Trans-Jordan. 'And of course it's not a Hebrew name; it's Arabic...'

'... And it wouldn't have been known to a scribe in Petra, two millennia ago,' added the nephew, 'as, presumably, it is a relatively modern name.'

'Exactly!' agreed the Uncle. 'If this scroll does still exist ... assuming it to be real ... and if word of Longhurst's tablet and its inscription gets out and falls into the wrong hands, it could act as the Holy Grail of Jewish statehood, and then we'd have an almighty struggle on our hands, trying to keep the peace.' He stared hard at the map. 'The whole region could go up in flames ... oil and all!' he declared. 'The Zionists have not forgiven us for the Balfour Declaration, back in '17. They are still waiting for us to deliver them the Jewish state we hinted at, but managed to avoid promising them.'

The Uncle fell silent. Stephen was studying the distance between Petra and Tall Salāh, trying to determine the scale of the terrain.

'Perhaps the trouble has already started,' said the Uncle softly, more to himself than to his nephew.

'How do you mean, Sir?' asked Stephen, looking up from the map.

'The more radical Arabs keep attacking the Jews. The more militant Jews have formed themselves into military-style groups, ostensibly to defend themselves ... and we British, who have been granted charge over Palestine through the League of Nations mandate ... well, we are caught in the middle, trying to keep the peace. Have you ever heard of *Haganah* or *Irgun*?' he asked, stressing the Hebrew words.

Stephen shook his head; he had heard of neither.

'If there is any truth in the professor's translation of this ancient tablet ... or if the rabbi is right about an ancient fairy tale being written down on a scroll...'

'I thought that he let that one slip, Sir,' said Stephen. 'He seemed to be a little less than his usual placid self after he had mentioned it.'

'He was playing his cards even closer to his chest than I thought I was,' added the Uncle. 'And don't be fooled for a second; he's a wily old bird, despite the placid exterior. I would be most surprised if he hasn't already passed on the gist of our meeting to his friends in the Zionist Council. That should get them excited. If there *is* a scroll and *if* it still exists ... the question of the Italians and their machinations over our Iraqi oil could well have been pushed into second place for the moment, wouldn't you say, my boy?'

For some time, neither man said anything, each concentrating their thoughts on the large map in front of them.

'Your friend, Winfield ... he still works for that travel

company, doesn't he?' asked the Uncle suddenly. 'Why don't you bring him around to the Club ... say on Thursday evening? Ask him if he knows anything about the Nabateans and Petra...'

13

Palestine

The Golden Moon Nightclub, Haifa – Wednesday, 18th March 1931

Morris Ginsberg was nursing the dregs of a beer at the bar during a break in the evening performance. As usual, Avi the barman was in attendance, polishing glasses, preparing drinks and listening to the woes of those patrons who were not too drunk to speak. Over the last few months he had enjoyed passing the time with Morris during the breaks between the three sets of music the performers were required to deliver each night. Often Claudette sat at the bar with her husband, twittering on about the injustice of life and how her talents were wasted in such a place. On those occasions Avi left the married couple to themselves; after all, he had to endure the woman singing every evening – why should he have to listen to her whingeing during the breaks as well?

Avi had seen and heard all of this before. The management only hired second-rate acts, as they were cheap and the artistes involved were only too keen to accept *any* contract, as they couldn't get any bookings elsewhere.

At the start of the break, Claudette had tottered off in a bad temper to, presumably, the dressing room she and Morris shared at the back of the nightclub. Whilst carrying out his intermittent duties behind the bar, Avi observed how deflated Morris was this evening. *Worn out from constantly bolstering up her ego, I shouldn't wonder,* he surmised.

'Is your wife not joining us tonight,' Avi queried, mustering up as much interest as he could.

'She will be back shortly ... She just had to attend to her appearance. Don't worry; my little *star* will be back in time for the next set.'

Avi grunted and moved away to serve another customer. He had his own views on Claudette's appearance and 'mutton dressed as lamb' came immediately to mind. Indeed, he had witnessed the incident during the last set, which now explained her absence from the bar. During the last number, Claudette had thrown both arms into the air in what Avi assumed to be some sort of amateurish plea or expression of anguish, when the cheap bracelet she was wearing around her wrist got caught in her wig. Unable to release the cluster of charms that were now entangled in the hair, and being the consummate performer she believed herself to be, Claudette carried on wailing about 'life in a slum in Paris', or whatever she was singing about, with one arm raised in what appeared to be a cross between a half-hearted military salute and a raised sign of benediction to the lost souls in the Golden Moon nightclub. To the few patrons who were cognizant or cared, this curious gesture had added a new dimension to the rendition of that particular *chanson,* and even when the singer staggered off the stage to retire to the dressing room in a curious crouched position, they would only have thought that the hand clamped to the side of her head indicated that she was overwhelmed by her own performance.

A few minutes later, just as he did every night, Morris first looked at his watch and then up at the large clock behind the bar. *Nearly time to go ... Where is my Claudie?* he thought.

Almost as if she had heard him, Claudette appeared on

cue. 'I'm here, Moshi. Did you think I wouldn't be here? My public need me ... my public ... oy *vey*! Look at my public ... are these s*chmucks* dead or alive? I ask you again. Why am I wasting my talents in this place, already? Something has to happen soon.'

'You and me both, my little *balibte*,' he answered, pausing to drain the last few drops of beer from the bottle before returning it to the bar.

'I tell you this for *nix*, one more week of this and I don't know what might happen,' she whispered angrily, straightening her dress. Once covered in sequins; it still managed to catch the light, even though it was moulting its sparkle on every outing. 'If I took this thing off, already, would it make any difference with this bunch of *klutzes*?'

Behind the bar, Avi was wiping down the counter top with a damp cloth, whilst holding the empty beer bottle in his other hand. For once he found himself able to agree with something Claudette had said, but thought it best to keep silent.

'And are we ever likely to get somewhere better?' she muttered, as they started to walk between the tables, back towards the raised platform, 'No, because where is the person who can make a difference and notice me? Eh?' She reached across and gave Morris's arm a pat. 'Apart from you, my *bubalah*.' She smiled. 'But, I mean, where is the agent?'

Halfway across the room, she stopped abruptly. 'Moshie, they aren't even looking at us,' she hissed, turning around and looking at the occupied tables. 'They haven't even *noticed me*.'

Turning back to face the stage, she bumped into a tall, well-built man, who seemed to have appeared from nowhere. He blocked their way.

'Hello,' he said in a voice which, to Claudette Catzmann, sounded like liquid velvet. 'Could we talk?'

She stopped dead in her tracks. Morris stumbled sideways to avoid her and knocked into one of the empty tables, which scraped across the floor with the impact. Again, nobody seemed to be interested in what had caused the noise. Nobody turned to investigate.

'And you are...?' she asked, trying to raise herself above her God-given five foot four inches, a coy smile creasing her over-wide mouth as she responded to the onslaught of male testosterone she sensed standing before her. It was no good – even balanced on her stiletto heels, she was short.

'A little of your time, that is all I ask,' replied the stranger, ignoring her question. 'It is an important matter, about the future.'

Without making it too obvious, she managed to turn and look at Morris, who had just straightened up after moving the table back to its original position. He eyed the stranger suspiciously. Haifa could be a dangerous place. He had read that only a short time before there had been trouble between the Arabs and the Jewish farmers, out on the outskirts of the town. Many had been killed. There was still tension between the Arabs and the Jews; there was also tension between the Arabs, the Jews and their British overlords. There was even tension between the Jews themselves. It was best not to get involved and to keep your head down – like it used to be in the trenches in the war.

'A-g-e-n-t?' she mouthed exaggeratedly.

Morris stared at the man, who was probably in his mid-twenties. He wondered what a young, healthy-looking man could be doing at this time of night in a run-down dive like the Golden Moon. He definitely did not look like a sailor; sailors with time on their hands often drifted in from the ships in the harbour. This man was different; he seemed to have a purpose about him. He looked educated and he looked sober.

Perhaps he's an agent; Claudie could be right ... Morris thought, looking at the man's face ... *or perhaps he was police, but why would the police want to talk to Claudette?*

'I have to perform,' Claudette purred, putting on her delicate, childlike, vulnerable appearance that, in reality, made her look more than just a little ridiculous, 'Perhaps later, after we have finished performing? In, say, twenty minutes?'

'I will sit at the back and wait,' said the young man, moving back between two tables, leaving their way clear to the raised platform.

'Good, Mr, er...?' questioned Claudette, but the young man simply turned and walked to a table right at the back of the nightclub, where he sat down and, so it seemed to both Morris and Claudette, melted invisibly into the background.

The chanteuse was convinced that at last her luck had changed. This strange man, who had quite literally walked into her life, *had* to be the theatrical agent she had been waiting for. It was he who would be her passport to stardom and success – well, both she *and* Morris, naturally. And so, for the following twenty minutes, Claudette Catzmann sang her heart out, largely incoherently, but with great conviction.

For the last time that evening, the single spotlight was once again extinguished. They waited for their eyes to adjust to the dingy light before climbing down from the little stage to look around for the young man. There was nobody waiting for them. In fact, apart from Avi and two of the regulars, both of whom were drunk and half asleep, the large smoke-soaked room was empty. Any clientele of the Golden Moon, who might possibly have still been possessed of a last vestige of self-respect, had already left.

'I tell you *bubalah*, this is too much; my nerves can't stand it,' she whispered, scanning the smoky shadows, vainly looking for the mysterious stranger. 'Come on, I need a drink.'

Within five minutes they had collected a drink from the bar and were walking silently down the narrow, dark corridor that led from the nightclub to the storeroom they used as a dressing room. As usual, she had removed her high heels – the only pair she had – for fear of breaking the heels in the dark on the uneven flagstones. They reached the door to the storeroom; Morris opened it, letting her in first.

'You do the light,' she instructed, as she crossed the threshold. 'I'm going to get changed.' She picked her way over to the rickety desk, on which her make-up was laid out. Hanging from a single six-inch nail was a mirror, its bottom edge balanced on the far end of the desk. The surface of the mirror was badly pitted in places, and the mercury coating on the back was flaking off – badly. Even its frame showed the signs of being very much the worse for wear. She stood there in the dark. The darkness in the room was barely challenged by the mere suggestion of the feeble light coming through the still-open door from the passageway outside. She sighed, as she reached up with both hands and carefully removed her wig. It was a sigh of resentful resignation. She was doing a lot of sighing these days.

'What has this girl ever done that is so bad that I should be treated like this, eh, *bubalah*?' she whined as, in the gloom, she felt amongst her make-up for the head form on which to sit the wig, 'I really thought our ship had come in with that...'

As Morris flicked the switch and the fly-spotted bulb flooded the little room with indifferent illumination, she let out a sudden strangled scream that, in truth, bore only a slight difference from her usual singing voice. The wig fell to the floor and, before she could stop herself, she stumbled forward and trod on it. With her heart pounding, she stared transfixed at the reflection that had suddenly appeared between the pits and blotches of the mirror as the light came on.

'Hello again,' said the tall, young man, 'I thought it best to be discreet. I let myself in. The lock doesn't seem to work...'

It took several minutes for Claudette Catzmann's heartbeat to return to normal and for her to regain her composure. She was not at all sure if it had been due to the shock she had received, or because of the twinge of excitement she fancied she had felt at the sight of so handsome a young man. Now, they were all seated on whatever they could find, she on the only chair in the room, the two men on upturned packing crates.

'What gave you the idea I might be a theatrical agent?' he asked, a faint smile creasing his tanned face. He was not like them – his complexion told of a whole lifetime in the sun of Palestine, not just a couple of years. 'I need to speak to you about something far more important than that,' he continued, without waiting for an answer and suddenly becoming serious. He ignored the look of disappointment on her face. 'We are in a struggle for survival, much as our forefathers were, since even before the days of Moses. If we do not resist the onslaught against us, we will not survive. It is as simple as that,' he said, staring intently at Morris. 'We know of your bravery in the war and now we need you to help *us*.'

For a brief moment, nothing further was said. The little room hung heavy with the air of expectation.

'What struggle?' asked Claudette. 'You make it sound as if there's a war still going on. What war? I didn't notice one on the way in here this evening,' she continued, flippantly, 'so, why should you want to involve my Moshie in a *war*? Eh? What are you up to ... and *who are* you?'

'There *is* a war going on, but not one that we are used

to. This one is not just bullets and bombs. There are other things involved, far more important things, like the very survival of an entire people. Not just one single country.'

Morris said nothing, but simply sat quietly listening to the stranger.

'This man could write a crossword puzzle, the way he talks in riddles,' she retorted, crossing her legs and folding her arms across her chest. She still had her own, short-cropped hair pinned up with hairgrips and they were beginning to irritate – almost as much as this man – handsome or not. As far as she was concerned, if he had no connection to the entertainment business, she wasn't interested.

'We know about Noyelle-sur-Escaut,' said their visitor, staring intently at Morris, who stared back, just as intently, 'and the medal you were given for the part you played.'

'So, he got a medal. My Moshie got a medal, but so did thousands of others,' Claudette exclaimed.

'But very few received the Victoria Cross,' answered the visitor, who was beginning to find her inane interruptions as irritating as her singing.

Morris shrugged, a little embarrassed at the memory of the fuss that had been made of him all those years ago.

In November 1917 the little French village of Noyelle-sur-Escaut, near the German Hindenburg Line, had been the scene of particularly ferocious fighting. It had been early dawn, with the smoke of the artillery barrage still heavy on the damp, gripping air. Together with several of his men, Sergeant Morris Ginsberg had taken refuge in a bombed-out house, grateful to have escaped the cloying winter rain and mud. They were on a forward reconnaissance patrol, always a dangerous undertaking. Suddenly, he had looked out from their hiding place and had been horrified to see a heavily guarded German machine-gun position, carefully camouflaged in the collapsed rubble of a neighbouring ruin on the other side of the street. It had been set up facing in the direction of what, as an NCO, he knew to be the route of advancement of a forward party of the 3rd Battalion of the Royal East Kent Regiment. He had checked that his rifle was fully loaded and had then collected three spare hand grenades from the rest of his men. Then, after whispering his orders to them, he had set off across the street, his rifle slung over his shoulder, dodging behind rubble for cover. As he ran, he had bowled his hand grenades as if he was playing cricket and then, from the shelter of another pile of rubble, he had picked off the surviving machine gun crew with his rifle, one at a time. Over his head, his men knitted a deadly blanket of supporting rapid fire. It had all seemed to happen in seconds – in a cold, rainy, smoky blur – and it had ended with the spectacular explosion of the grenade which, with its pin pulled out by a German soldier who was dead before he could throw it, had fallen and detonated amongst the ammunition belts that had been stacked out of the rain in readiness to feed the insatiable machine gun.

For his bravery, at the unhesitating risk of his own life, Morris Ginsberg had been awarded the Victoria Cross. Such tales of unselfish courage, even if the bravery in question was Jewish, did wonders to lift the dangerously disillusioned morale of a public back home; a public which had become thoroughly – and dangerously – war-weary.

The atmosphere in the tiny storeroom at the back of the Golden Moon nightclub had become charged with a mixture of urgency and seriousness underlined by barely disguised nationalism.

'At a time such as this, we need brave men of the Faith.

Men like you, Morris,' urged the visitor softly, 'men with the fire of Simon bar Kokhba in their souls.'

For the first time since the start of this conversation, Morris spoke. 'Who?'

'Simon bar Kokhba, the leader of our glorious revolt against the Romans and the man who established an independent Jewish state in our promised land.'

Morris Ginsberg had never heard of either the man or the fact that there had ever been a Jewish state free from the Roman yoke.

'We need our homeland,' replied their visitor, 'the land promised to us since ancient times. If we do not act, the Arabs will eventually drive us into the sea. We cannot trust the British; Balfour and his precious Declaration, is not worth the paper it is written on. We need to take control of our own destiny,' he continued, leaning closer to Morris, 'and now we have had news from London ... news of a sign that Palestine is truly ours.'

The young man focused his gaze on the war veteran. The intensity of the gaze made Morris feel a little uneasy. He was not at all sure what this man was talking about and he had no idea of who he was.

'What sign?' asked Morris softly.

Claudette had grown tired of the conversation. Retrieving her wig from the floor, she coaxed it back on to its form and attempted to prepare it for the next day's performance. Catching sight of her own reflection, she transferred her attentions to her own appearance. After all, there was a young man to impress.

'Do you know of Gershom?' asked the visitor.

'No, I know nobody by that name,' replied Morris, after a thoughtful pause during which he kept his visitor's gaze.

'No, not the name of a friend or an acquaintance,' replied the visitor patiently. 'You must think back to the olden

THE GERSHOM SCROLL

times, when our nation was still being formed. Moses...' he prompted.

'Didn't Moses have a son called Gershom?' Morris eventually recalled.

'Yes, he had two sons, but Gershom is the one who particularly interests us.'

Over the following fifteen minutes, the stranger talked of a scroll, reportedly containing divine revelation given to Gershom – a divine authority for the establishment of a homeland – a state – for all the People of Yahweh, the divine power of Israel. If it did exist and could be found, it would be the irrefutable evidence for the existence of a Jewish state.

'...Obviously, this is a very delicate matter. There are others interested in the existence of such a scroll, but for very different reasons than ours,' the young man continued. 'That is why this matter needs to be handled with the utmost care and discretion, by someone who seems to appear totally opposite to what and who he really is: someone who blends into the background, but who is still capable of acting decisively when the time demands it; someone like you, Morris.'

In the reflected light Claudette was doing what she could with her make-up. She turned her head in the mirror, lipstick in hand, to look at Morris. She was not quite sure how to react to the stranger's remark.

After the briefest of pauses, and without looking anywhere, other than at the oddly endearing reflection of his Claudie in the battered mirror, Morris spoke. 'If it is for the Faith and if I can help, then I will.'

'Hang on there a minute, Moshie,' said Claudette, her lipstick still opened in her hand, as she spun round to face the stranger, 'You still haven't told us who you are. I think you should, before you expect us to help you. What do you say, Moshie?'

The stranger smiled, as he stood up to leave. 'Who I am is of no consequence. But what I represent is vital to our survival,' he continued mysteriously. 'Do you know anything of Haganah?' he asked.

'"The Defence"?' asked Morris, translating the Hebrew literally.

'Hum,' said the visitor softly, 'the British are not going to look after us; neither are the Arabs going to welcome us into the Land of Our Fathers with open arms. So we are going to have to look after ourselves. Haganah has gone soft. So now we have Haganah Bet... the "Second Defence". We also call ourselves Irgun.

'Is this *really* necessary?' asked Morris quietly. 'All these names...?'

'Every Jew has the right to enter Palestine, not just the few the British allow to do so. If we are to overturn the events of recent months, our only course lies through active retaliation against the aggressor. It does not matter if they are Arab or British...' The visitor paused and, lowering his voice menacingly, added, '... or pacifist Jew. Only a Jewish force of arms will ensure the survival of a Jewish state.' By this time his voice was barely a whisper, but it had lost none of its steel-edged declaration of intent. 'That is why, if this scroll exists, we must take possession of it before the British lay their hands on it. It will be a rallying call to all Jewry to unite behind us.'

He had clasped Morris by the shoulder during the latter part of his speech as if to emphasize the point with brotherly contact, then he swiftly crossed to the doorway before turning back to add. 'You will have to go to Jerusalem. That is where we hope to learn more of this scroll. Do not attempt to contact us. We are everywhere and we will contact you. Say nothing about this. Our people have been murdered for saying far, far less.'

He crossed silently to the door, turned and, for the first time, spoke Hebrew:

לארשי לש שפוחל

For a moment his eyes met and firmly held Morris's own.

'What did he say?' asked Claudette, as her Hebrew was so shaky as to be almost non-existent.

'It means something like "For the Freedom of Israel", I think,' replied Morris, turning to look at his wife. When he turned back to the stranger in the doorway, he was no longer there and the dingy light out in the passageway glowed feebly once again. There was no sound of retreating footsteps out on the flagstones of the passageway floor. It was as if their visitor had simply vanished.

Morris turned and looked at his partner. 'Put your lipstick away, Claudie, he urged softly. 'It is time for us to go home.'

14

Palestine

Masada, close to the shores of the Dead Sea – Sunday, 31st May 1931

The early evening sun, about to disappear behind the massive outcrop of rock that lay to the north-east of the encampment, still coloured the white tents a warm shade of orange-crimson. The camp had appeared as if from nowhere during the latter part of the afternoon and would soon be ready for the tourists when they eventually arrived from Jerusalem, before the sun finally set.

Situated amongst the collection of accommodation tents were two large rectangular canvas structures, one housing the dining facilities and the other acting as a field kitchen. Outside this second tent an assortment of various pots and pans, containing the main constituents of the evening meal, simmered and bubbled over a fire of glowing coals. The smoke from the wood fire, together with the aroma of the cooking food, gently perfumed the entire campsite with a homely atmosphere in the otherwise barren landscape.

As he sat on a large rocky outcrop smoking a cigarette, Uri Ben Zeev glanced idly up at the mass of rock that formed a natural barrier hemming them in between the mountain and the Dead Sea, which lay a couple of miles further to the east.

Ben Zeev had been brought to Palestine as a young boy

of barely five years of age, when his parents had managed to escape the attentions of the Czar's minions and flee from the pogroms in Russia. They had landed in Haifa with precious little more than the worn and patched clothes they stood up in. Leaning on the rails of the steamship as she dropped anchor, the family had looked out at what was to become their new home. Although tired, they firmly believed that they stood on the threshold of a new life; the threadbare clothing they wore could not hide the fierce pride and determination they felt. That had been back in 1905. Since then, the particular brand of anti-Semitism meted out by the Czar had been swept away – as Czar Nicholas himself had been swept away – only to be replaced with other, more virulent forms of persecution. Uri and his family read the newspapers and listened to the talk of others who had arrived far more recently and were appalled, though not totally surprised, by the ominous reports of the systematic anti-Jewish policies that now seemed to be catching hold across Europe. The man, Stalin, was spoken of in very hushed tones, often with nervous, involuntary glances over the shoulder, even in the relative safety of Haifa. At least all those years ago they had escaped – and for that they were grateful.

Avram Ben Zeev had worked hard, taught his children the value of education and had prospered. Despite the tensions between Arab and Jew, which sometimes boiled over into violence, Palestine was a land where those who were not afraid of hard work could make a fortune, no matter how modest. Whilst they were naturally concerned at the plight of their fellow Jews throughout Europe, the Ben Zeev family considered they were fortunate in that they had health, wealth, several roofs over their heads and a bright future to look forward to. Uri, himself, was a case in point. He had decided that his future did not lie as his father's had done in the world of printing, but rather in the new and emerging world of tourism. Having weathered the storm of his father's vociferous disapproval, which his mother – his staunchest ally – had done much to diffuse, Uri had announced that he was going into the 'people business', as he called it. He had read an article about tourism in an old copy of an American magazine and it had fired his imagination.

'Are you mad in your head? Where have you put the common sense I drilled into it? Tell me that! Hhuum?' boomed his father, Avram, a well-built man of over six foot. His mother had gently put her hand on her husband's arm, but he had ignored it.

'But, Papa, you are the one who taught me to always accept a challenge and never to rest until I have conquered it!' Uri had replied, flicking a momentary glance in his mother's direction, acknowledging her support.

'Challenge, what challenge? What tourists, already?' continued his father, lapsing back into the Russian variation of Yiddish. Uri had grown more used to the Hebrew spoken by many in Palestine and sometimes found it quite difficult to follow his father's ranting.

'Papa, they will come. They will come to see the holy places, the castles and the Dead Sea ... Some will even come to see the railway lines blown up by Lawrence of Arabia and his Arabs in the war. They *will* come, Papa; trust me.'

'Oh yes,' boomed his father, 'and you are going to be the one to organize this flood of people when they get here? Eh? You are to do this? You and who else?'

'Just me and the skills you have taught me. I have as good a nose for business as you have. You have taught me well.'

His mother was about to say something, but stopped in mid-breath as her husband continued to rant and rave against the stupidity of his son's idea.

'Whoever heard of such a thing?' continued Avram, his bowl of chicken broth now quite cold on the starched white tablecloth before him. 'Who has the time to go and look at things like castles? I should be so lucky! Your grandfather Mordechai, may he rest in peace, would be turning in his grave at such a thought! And which people have the money to just travel around and *look*?'

'Your papa was the one who encouraged *you* to face the challenges of your youth, Avram,' said Uri's mother quietly. He turned and looked at her, but Uri spoke before he could answer.

'These days more and more people have the time and money to travel, Papa. There are even magazines that advertise trips and tours. It is a new industry which is growing fast ... and it *will* come here ... soon ... and I want to be ready when it does.'

His mother had put her hand back on her husband's arm and he seemed to be a little calmer than before, but still he questioned his eldest son.

'And why should these rich people with so little to do except stand and stare come to you to show them around?' asked his father, fixing him with the stern, unwavering gaze born of many years of experience of trying to keep his family under control.

'They will, Papa, because I will tell them that I am ready for them. I will start by calling myself "See Palestine" and I will organize their movements to the sites and their accommodation ... everything, in fact. Who knows in what direction such a business might grow? Someone will soon start doing this and there is no reason why it should not be the Ben Zeev family who gets in first.'

'And where do you expect the money to come from for this hare-brained scheme, if I were ever stupid enough to even consider it?' demanded his father, chewing on a piece of bread as he spoke.

Uri's mother got up silently and took her husband's bowl away to refill it with hot broth.

'You, naturally, Papa ... it would be a business deal. I will repay you every last shekel ... as soon as I can.'

Nothing had been said for some time, the only noises in the large dining room being those of cutlery against crockery. At last, when the meal was almost over, Avram rubbed his forehead with his hand and spoke, whilst fixing his gaze on the now empty bowl in front of him.

'So, "Mr People Business", how do you see this scheme of yours working, then?' Avram enquired quietly.

That had been a little over three years ago and now, in the shadow of the mountain which towered over both him and the campsite, Uri Ben Zeev smiled to himself. He looked up towards the top of the mountain and thought of his forebears. They had held out up there against the might of Imperial Rome in the firm belief of their own convictions. They had shown determined resistance and had defended their mountain-top fortress to the bitter end. Fired with the same zeal, Uri had defended his right to decide his own future. He was contented.

We are a tenacious people, he contemplated, *and we stick to our guns.* He had stuck to his, finally persuading his father to let him give his ideas a try. For his part, Uri had never entertained any notions of failure and he had been right. The early reverberations of the tourist boom had finally touched the shores of Palestine and 'the people with so little to do, except stand and stare', as his father had put it, had slowly started to invade the Holy Land like the harbingers of some twentieth-century crusade.

As he flung his cigarette away on to the barren earth he rose and, in the distance, saw the tell-tale clouds of dust thrown up by the wheels of the approaching cars. He looked at his watch. Not bad! They were more or less on time, after their ride from Beersheba. The campsite was ready and the food was well in hand. He had already met this Mr Rupert Winfield on a couple of occasions, during negotiations between the company and his own "See Palestine" Company. Uri thought him to be a very pleasant chap, who would be easy to work with: he was also looking forward to meeting the rest of this group of travellers for this, the inaugural tour. He estimated that they would arrive in about half an hour or so.

It was shortly before a quarter to eight when Rupert entered the large rectangular tent that served as the social centre of the tour group. Somewhat incongruously, given the barren nature of the surroundings, he had dressed formally and was keen to have a word with Uri before the rest of the party were summoned for the evening meal – the first of their "Journey of Exploration through Two Thousand Years of Civilization", as the promotional literature put it.

'Hello again,' he said, as he strode into the tent. Earlier, he and Uri had exchanged a few pleasantries as the cars arrived at the prepared campsite and disgorged both the travel-weary tourists and their luggage. 'This all looks quite splendid,' said Rupert, sweeping the air with his left arm to take in the table setting, which stood at one end of the tent, and the collection of wicker easy chairs, which stood close to it at the other end. 'Nice to see you again, Uri,' he added, extending his right hand, as Ben Zeev crossed the floor space to meet him.

'We always aim for the heights,' replied the tanned operator of "See Palestine", who was about the same age as Winfield. Uri was dressed in a dark suit and tie, which, he thought, was more practical than the formal evening wear he anticipated tradition had forced his guests to bring with them. 'It is good to see you again, too, Mr Winfield,' he added, flashing white teeth in a warm smile as he shook

Winfield's hand in a strong, yet gentle grip. 'We are ready for your party, now. As you can see, all is prepared.' He spoke excellent English, tinged almost imperceptibly with the occasional inflection of some foreign vowel.

'I'll say it is,' agreed Rupert, who was really impressed by the modest opulence that this man had seemingly conjured up out of the surrounding near-desert. 'And you have electric lights, too,' he added, pointing up at the string of glowing globes that was suspended down the apex of the tent's roof.

'All the latest conveniences,' said Uri, smiling. 'The guests' tents have gas lamps, but here we have a small generator ... a noisy little beast, but it serves its purpose well. It is on the perimeter of the campsite, so it should not disturb anyone. If you listen, you can just about hear it.'

He was right. Rupert listened for a few seconds and became aware of the steady throb of the little powerhouse somewhere out in the lengthening night. For a second his mind went back to a time some years before, to the throb of the engines on board *Khufu*. That had always been the comforting reminder that they were still part of civilization, even if they were in the middle of the Nile. The distant rumble of the generator and the glow of the light bulbs did the same now, in the shadow of the desert and of the massive mountain. The cooling waters of the river had been replaced with the burning rocks and sand of Palestine.

'Are you all right with the arrangements we discussed earlier, Uri?' asked Rupert, who would be the tour manager for this, the first of the Company's new Holy Land tours. He was more used to the role of archaeologist guide, but for this tour he would be the Company's Palestine answer to Mohammed, the efficient, gold-toothed little Egyptian, who had controlled *Khufu* with such efficiency.

'Absolutely,' replied Uri, 'my boys and I are fully prepared. I have the arrangements in place, as per our discussions, and I also have the printed itineraries and maps for you. I think you will be satisfied with what my father's print works has produced for you. Let me go and get them.'

Alone in the surprisingly spacious confines of the tent, Rupert made a quick circuit of the facilities to check everything for himself. As he reached the area where the wicker easy chairs were sited, he was pleasantly surprised to discover that there was a small bar, located against the wall of the tent.

Well, I never did! He smiled as he stood looking. So far so good. All the mod cons, as the Americans would say.

'Ready for the onslaught, old chap?' called a voice from behind him.

Rupert turned and his face lit up as he saw Stephen Hopkins entering the tent dressed as formally as he was.

'Ready as ever, I suppose,' he replied, crossing to the other man and taking his forearm in a gesture of affection. 'Any sign of them yet?'

'From the sound of it, there were a couple of them just about to burst forth upon the rude night air, but I hopped past the tent before they actually emerged. I think it was the mother and daughter duo...'

'Then just four more to complete the party,' said Rupert, smiling at his friend, 'there is a lot to be said for such a small group on our inaugural trip,' he added. 'Fancy a snifter before dinner?' he asked, gesturing towards the bar at the end of the tent.

No sooner had they negotiated the furniture and reached the small bar, than they were hailed by a voice from the entrance.

'Oh, good evening ... hello again,' said an elderly man, dressed like the other two in formal black, but this time the black of the Church, with a broad band of white encircling his thick neck. 'I do hope that I am not too early ... and that I am not interrupting anything.'

Stephen winked at Rupert, who tried, unsuccessfully, to avoid his friend's suggestive leer before turning to face the newcomer.

'Not at all,' said Rupert, crossing to greet the elderly vicar. 'Reverend Fairweather, if I remember correctly?'

All three men shook hands again, for the third time that day. Stephen had previously remarked on the elderly cleric's aura of peaceful tranquillity, which went with his almost beatific smile. In the confines of the tent he felt himself struck once again by that same aura. He had experienced it that morning when they had first met outside the hotel in Jerusalem. He had wondered then if it was possibly a spiritually induced state of grace, or perhaps knowledge of deep awareness generated by a liberal dose of some nasty substance, or whether the man was just slightly simple. Now, shaking the man's hand yet again, and staring into his eyes as he did so, he was still not really any the wiser, although he did fancy that he detected a deep sincerity behind the watery-edged pupils.

'Oh yes, indeed it is ...' replied the cleric, '... and doesn't this all look very grand?' he continued, turning his gaze on to the contents of the tent, 'I would not have thought it possible to get so much into a tent of this size and still be able to move around,' he said, laughing almost dismissively at his own observation. 'I'm afraid that I am more used to the tents of a Boy Scout camp, when I was a scout master, you know. Aah, such happy memories ... yes ... mmm.' For a second the vicar seemed to drift off to an earlier, younger time before suddenly returning to the large tent in the Palestinian desert. 'But these are splendid surroundings...' he continued, indicating the tent, '... and I even have my own sleeping tent ... Everything has come as a very pleasant surprise.'

Stephen smiled at him, but did not answer. His memories of large tents, filled with the stench of antiseptic and the sounds of death, were far less pleasant. He spent most of his time actively trying to forget them.

'Well, hello there, again,' came yet another voice from the entrance to the tent, but this time one with a heavy American accent. 'I hope that I'm not...' but he had to break off in mid-sentence, as he realized that there were two women behind him. He stood aside, showing them into the tent. 'Ladies, after you...' he said, smiling warmly at them as he did so. Stephen thought that the American smiled particularly warmly at the younger of the two women.

'Thank you, young man,' said the older one, as she walked past him and into the centre of the tent, the appliquéd ornamentation of her formal evening gown sparkling in the electric light as she did so.

'Hello, again...' whispered the woman's daughter as she walked behind her mother, smiling into the young man's open, honest-looking face. '...Joe,' she added, almost inaudibly.

'Good evening, Mrs Barnfield ... and Miss Barnfield,' said Rupert.

'Oh please, Mr Winfield, call me Mady,' replied the attractive young woman, who smiled bewitchingly and turned her head to flash it at the American.

'Humph ... any chance of a drink?' snorted Hester Barnfield.

Over the following few minutes the tent filled with the rumbling buzz of polite conversation. Drinks had been poured and the tourists had already settled into familiar conversation as they got to know each other better. They were all sitting in the wicker easy chairs at the far end of the tent.

'Excuse me for a moment, please,' said Rupert, standing up and moving as best he could towards the centre of the gathering. 'Our host informs me that our meal will shortly be ready for us. As we wait for Professor and Mrs Unsworth to join us, I would like to just fill you in on a couple of things. You've all met me and already know that I am your tour manager. I'm an archaeologist, actually, but on this trip I'll be keeping an eye on other things, which are far less ancient than what I am used to.'

There was a slight ripple of amusement at this. 'We are very lucky to have Professor Unsworth with us, as our archaeologist and guide. He is an expert on the Nabatean civilization of Petra and has extensive interest and knowledge of the Crusader period in this part of the world as well. He's a bit more up-to-date than I am ... With me, you'd be learning about Pharaohs and the Pyramids...' There were more chuckles, during which Rupert noticed that the man with the American accent and the younger of the two women were sitting very close to each other and seemed to have their eyes glued to each other's faces.

So soon into the trip and they've started already? Rupert thought, with an inward grin. 'Uri, our host, has prepared copies of our itinerary as well as maps of the area we will be exploring. I'll give you each a set before we retire for the night. There is absolutely no rush attached to your exploration of the sites we shall be visiting. We move more or less at our own speed and in our own time,' he continued. 'We start here, under the shadow of this mountain ... It's called Masada and is an important site in the history of the Jewish people and we'll end where you started, back at the airfield in Gaza, in about three weeks' time. You'll visit the Crusader castles of Karak and Shawbak, before travelling to the rose city of Petra. After that we'll follow the ancient King's Highway up around the Dead Sea and on to Jericho and Jerusalem. The fortress mountain of Masada itself', he said, gesturing out through the walls of the tent, in the direction of the looming mound of rock, 'is accessible only by a steep climb, so I'm not sure how practical...'

Rupert broke off, as a middle-aged woman entered the tent. On her arm she supported a man who looked much older than his years. He walked uneasily, although his countenance was cheery.

'Ah, Professor and Mrs Unsworth,' said Rupert, 'our little group is now complete,' he continued, crossing to greet the newly arrived couple.

Shortly after the Unsworth's arrival, the tourists were allocated their seats at the dining table and the meal commenced. Uri's cook had spared no effort in the preparation of what, considering the practicalities of their location, was a meal any of the leading hotels in Jerusalem would have been proud of. During the course of the meal the conversation ranged from details of the forthcoming trip, to speculation as to the state of the world's politics and the chances of the world's economy ever fully recovering from the recent financial turmoil. Stephen found this last point somewhat of a contradiction in terms. Formally dressed, in a large tent out in the middle of nowhere, surrounded by the Palestinian desert and hemmed in by the salt-laden air of the Dead Sea, it was as if these people – with the possible exception of the young American, Josiah Harrison, or plain Joe, as he preferred to be called – had not been touched in any way by the financial disaster that had crippled the rest of the world.

'When we reach Petra,' said Professor Unsworth, speaking through the haze of his after-dinner cigar, 'I hope to be able to introduce you to a Mr Hussein al Mohammed. He's the Trans-Jordan Assistant Director of Antiquities and is an expert on Petra, which is over the border in Trans-Jordan, you see. Hussein was one of my students during his studies at Oxford ... a very fine, clever chap. He'll be able to fill us in on what's been going on recently. They have a dig in progress there even as we speak and it is quite a daunting undertaking from what I've heard. It's a vast site and has hardly been touched by the hand of organized archaeology...'

Once the coffee cups had been cleared and the brandy drunk, the party began to break up and prepare for bed. Rupert offered to escort the Unsworths to their tent and to carry the promised itinerary and maps for them.

'If you don't mind, my dear,' said the professor, as they drew near their tent, 'I must answer a slight call ... Best now, rather than later. If you'll excuse me ... Thank you, Winfield; I'll see you in the morning, then.' And with that he disappeared into the night, towards the tent which had been erected for the tourists' convenience on the perimeter of the campsite.

As she watched him go, his wife sighed. It was unexpected and took Rupert a little by surprise.

'He's quite headstrong and knows exactly what he wants ... which is just as well I suppose ... I'm afraid he is not in the best of health.' She took the papers from Rupert with a smile. 'Anyway, thank you for these. We'll have a very good look at them,' she said, the cheeriness returning to her voice.

'We are fortunate, in that we have the services of a medical doctor on this trip,' Rupert said softly, yet with a barely subdued fierce pride, 'Dr Hopkins ... if he can be of any assistance ...'

'That's very kind, but I fear that my husband is approaching the time in his life when all the latest medical science in the world will be of little help to him ... or us. That is a hard thing to say, after nearly fifty years together.' She paused, looking down at the papers Rupert had just given her. 'But we cannot complain for an instant. Life has been kind to us both ... and we have each other. We do not have any regrets about the present ... We are reconciled,' she concluded, somewhat mysteriously.

Neither of them said anything for a few moments, Mrs Unsworth turning to look into the darkness in the direction taken by her husband.

'Cancer, I'm afraid,' she said, as she turned a smile of understanding and acceptance on the younger man. 'It is at quite an advanced stage, but is reasonably manageable; our man in Harley Street gives him six to nine months ... perhaps even as much as a year ... at most. It is incurable.' She turned away and spoke into the darkness of the night. 'Thank you for your concern, I appreciate it. I think my husband will enjoy talking to the Reverend Fairweather. They seem to have several common interests in the historical aspects of this area. Well, good night, Mr Winfield,' she said, and without looking at him, disappeared into her tent.

Back in the dining tent, Uri's boys had cleared away and had reset the table for breakfast. The Reverend Fairweather had already retired for the night and, despite her best efforts to remain in the tent, Mady Barnfield was about to be taken to her tent by her mother. Like Rupert, the girl's mother had noticed the close interest her daughter and this young American seemed to be taking in each other.

'Madeira and I will see you in the morning,' said Mrs Hester Barnfield aggressively, as Rupert re-entered the tent. She insisted on calling her daughter by her full name, which she been given in honour of the place where, in a moment of dizzy and unexpected passion, conception had occurred. 'Come along, Madeira, it's time for your beauty sleep,' and with that final instruction, she manhandled her daughter out of the tent.

Neither Rupert nor Stephen said anything. They simply smiled in Josiah Harrison's direction. They both remembered that several years before, on the Nile, they, too, had experienced the same electricity of attraction that had obviously flashed between Harrison and Mady Barnfield during the evening. For his part, Joe Harrison looked down at the floor in nervous embarrassment.

'So, Mr Harrison, what is your special interest in the

history of this region, then?' asked Stephen, offering him a cigarette.

'Photography,' replied the American, without hesitation, 'and please ... call me Joe. I don't wish to offend, but you British can be a bit heavy on the formal side.'

Stephen and Rupert glanced at each other: neither had failed to notice that Mr Harrison was not dressed in formal evening attire. Rather, he wore a dark suit and tie, of only a marginally better cut than the suit Uri had worn.

'I'm *really* hooked on photography,' he continued, 'that's what's in most of my luggage: cameras, lenses and such. In fact, that's just about *all* that's in my luggage,' he said, his face once again breaking into a genuinely warm smile. 'Just about all I got in the world went into that equipment. I'm aiming to make a splash with a photo assignment about Petra. I might have a chance with a couple of the European magazines ... They're quite hot on the idea in Germany. It's called photojournalism...'

The other two sat back in their wicker chairs, smiling patiently at him, but their faces showed that they had but scant knowledge of what it was that he was talking about.

'And what, exactly, *is* photojournalism?' asked Rupert.

'Well, you write an article about something. Maybe, a place, a person, anything you like, but you don't use words, you use pictures. They have to tell the story for you,' replied Harrison.

'Isn't that a bit like that American magazine with the yellow border on the cover,' asked Stephen. '*Geography* ... something, I think it's called.'

'*National Geographic*,' corrected Harrison. 'Yeah, that's the sort of thing, but they still run the copy alongside the pictures ... the pictures still only support the written text. Photojournalism turns the whole thing around on its head. The text, what little there is of it, supports the content of the pictures. There's this guy, Felix Man, he's done some great stuff ... He even managed to do an assignment on that Mussolini fellow in Italy. It's a bit like a fly on the wall ... watching a day in the life of the man. That's what I'm aiming to do, too ... eventually...' His voice trailed off.

Stephen suppressed his sense of devilment and resisted the urge to enquire of this very relaxed, yet seemingly earnest, young man, as to exactly why it was that he should have invested most of his capital in so much expensive equipment in order simply to impersonate a fly on a wall. Besides, it was getting late and he was starting to feel the absence of his lower left leg, as the stump nestled in the prosthesis and throbbed gently, but annoyingly. Despite that, he had not needed to use his cane.

'I find photography fascinating,' said Rupert, out of genuine interest. 'How the vast panorama of what you see can be twisted and shrunk on to a thin strip of film in a camera, and all as a negative image, too.'

'You should see how it works with colour film,' answered the American, warming to his pet subject very much as Rupert, at the drop of a hat, would warm to his passion for ancient Egypt. 'You've got these different layers on the film and each layer reacts only to a certain range of colours. It's complicated, but you process the film, project light through all the colours, expose it to colour photographic paper and whammo! You've got a colour positive print of your scene.'

'Do you process your own films, then ... Joe?' asked Stephen.

'Sure do ... well, leastwise, back home I do. I've got a darkroom in my apartment ... It's my bathroom actually,' he admitted, 'but I can make it light tight. And so far, the landlord hasn't complained about the smell of the chemicals,' he added, laughing.

'Can you process colour *and* black and white?' asked Rupert.

'Colour is mighty expensive, so I have to send my colour

film off ... you know the ad: "It's One Price from Film to Print and all in the Yellow Box..."'

'Er, no, sorry old man, you've got us there,' said Stephen, looking at Rupert, 'I'm afraid we don't know the er ... *ad* at all.'

'Sure y'do ... it's for Kodak.'

'Oh, well, of course we know *that* make, but we possibly don't have the same advertisements in Britain as you do in the United States,' said Stephen, smiling.

Later, in the small hours of the morning when the campsite was as quiet and still as the cold, long-dead coals of the kitchen fire, Rupert lay on his camp bed in the tent they shared, listening to the gentle snoring of Stephen on the bed next to his. In the few short years since they had met, he had noticed that his friend seemed to be having increasing trouble with the stump of what was left of his lower left leg. Stephen believed that it was eased by Rupert regularly massaging it with a soothing balm, which Rupert jokingly claimed was from an ancient recipe known only to Pharaoh's personal body servants, but which in reality was a concoction brewed up in the backstreets of Luxor. Whatever it contained was immaterial – it soothed the throbbing and for that Stephen was grateful.

As he listened to the gentle sound of Stephen's snores, and imagined the muscular, hairy chest rise and fall with each movement of the lungs, Rupert thought of Mrs Unsworth, who seemed to have resigned herself to the fact that her life's partner had had his cards issued and was on borrowed time. They, at least, had been together for nearly fifty years; he and Stephen for less than three. Sometimes, in the small hours of the night, when he thought about such things as the fleeting durability of life – as opposed to the massive immortality of carved monumental stone –

Rupert would reach out and tenderly take hold of the hand of this fellow being who had come to mean so much to him, and then wonder about the impermance of existence. *Fortuna Imperatrix Mundi,* he would think to himself. Fortune, Empress of the World would, like Khnum, the ram-headed ancient Egyptian potter-god, judge everyone's allotted span of happiness before handing down the predetermined sentence of that decision. Such thoughts once again filled his head in the tent next to Masada. Eventually, as he was finally sucked into the welcoming whirlpool of sleep, Rupert wondered whether Fortune and Khnum between them had already cast his own and Stephen's fates on the celestial wheel of existence, and would allow the two of them the same amount of time the Unsworths had been given.

15

Palestine

Masada – late afternoon, Tuesday, 2nd June 1931

There were only a few ice cubes remaining. Earlier the previous day a substantial supply of ice had been brought to their camp in a lead-lined chest from the freezer plant in nearby Beersheba, but the ice had not lasted long. The half-melted remnants of the supply now clinked against the sides of the frosted glasses, as the tourists sipped their various tipples. They were seated under the shade of several palm trees, which grew around a little spring a short walk from the tents of their campsite. They had completed the first real day of their tour, which had largely been taken up with a visit to nearby Engedi and a leisurely ramble around the foot of Masada itself. Now, as the early evening approached, they were enjoying their sundowners.

With his usual effortless efficiency, Uri had busied himself ensuring that none of his guests wanted for anything. The wicker chairs and tables had been removed from the dining tent and relocated here, under the shade of the palms. His 'boys', as he called his three-man team, were also fussing about, discreetly ensuring that everything was running smoothly.

'Is it not somewhat of a contradiction that we should be sitting here in the cool of this little oasis, when we are surrounded on all sides by the harsh, arid landscape of a near-desert?' asked the Reverend Theophilus Fairweather, as he put his frosted glass on the table in front of him. 'Is it not a metaphorical commentary on the struggle of the constant battle between good and evil, between comfort and discomfort ... between peaceful repose and unpleasant torment ... which we must all face?' He rested his arms on those of the chair, brought his fingers together in front of him and continued with a smile on his face. 'Are we not being sustained in the midst of nothing, so to speak?'

Professor Unsworth was looking as cheery as ever, despite the lethal battle raging within him. He turned his head to look at the cleric. 'Would that be in a biblical or a practical sense?' he asked.

In his turn, the cleric smiled at the professor. 'In either sense,' he replied, quietly, 'but, given our present location in the Holy Land, there could be the added argument that our nourishment, so ably provided here in this wilderness, could possibly have a parallel with a deeper, underlying biblical connotation ... in the sense that we are being provided for in the midst of nothing. Manna in the wilderness, as it would seem.'

'Well, it certainly is *in the midst of nothing*,' said Mrs Barnfield, lighting a cigarette with her gold Dunhill lighter. The others did not fail to notice that she waved her hand in such a way as to allow the fading sunlight to flash through the facets of the several large stones she wore in expensively tasteful settings on the fingers of her left hand. 'Everything is just so ... dry ... and so barren ... so God-forsaken ...,' she added.

The cleric looked at her in surprise. He had not assumed that she would say such a thing, but he kept his thoughts to himself and did not let his reaction to her outburst dissolve the contented smile he had on his face.

'Well, we must remember that we are in a place of almost unbelievable turmoil,' observed the professor, looking first at her and then gesturing off across the Dead Sea, towards the hills on the eastern horizon. 'This whole area sits on top of a great deal of turbulence in the Earth's crust. It is part of a massive fault line, which extends all the way down through Africa and up towards Turkey in the north. It's called the Great Rift and was formed over many, many millions of years. But it is important to remember that it wasn't always like this, or so the thinking goes.'

'In what respect was it different, Professor?' asked Mady Barnfield from her seat, which she had placed as close to Joe Harrison's as she dared without her mother being moved to say something by way of reproach.

'Excavations are going on all the time,' replied the professor, 'but it is possible that the vegetation around these parts has changed rather drastically over the millennia. It could all have been quite fertile once, before conditions changed. I have read one hypothesis which even claimed that the level of the Dead Sea was much higher than it is now and that, millennia ago, the waters lapped the shores of Jericho itself,' he said, raising his left arm and pointing vaguely north, in the direction of the distant town. 'When it comes to trying to decipher ancient texts and writings there is always the problem of sorting out the folklore and myth from reality. How much of what we can translate is based on hard fact, but how much is pure fiction? That is always the academic's problem,' he said, smiling at the assembly, 'always the academic's enduring conundrum.'

Stephen, who was resting against the sloping trunk of one of the palms, smoking, stared out ahead of him towards the distant hills. In response to the professor's remarks, he suddenly thought of how true the elderly academic's statement was, although, obviously, the man could not possibly know anything of the mysterious Scroll of Gershom and its encrypted meaning.

Fact or fiction, indeed, pondered Stephen, as his lungs

filled with cigarette smoke, and something which we are going to have to try and sort out.

The professor had a captive audience and was still talking. 'I am sure that Winfield is no stranger to the challenge of fact versus fiction,' he said, gesturing towards Rupert.

'Absolutely not,' he replied, 'as you say, Professor, the sources from which we draw our knowledge of the past can be extremely precise and we can prove their authenticity through cross-referencing to other, known details. At other times, however, things are not so easy and the written material reads like something written by the Brothers Grimm. We have a real problem with this in the study of ancient Egypt. Quite often, despite the improbable nature of the narrative, there *could* be truth in what was written, but we have no real way of proving it ... at least, not from our viewpoint of several thousand years after the originals were written.'

There was a lull in the conversation.

'I like your: *in the midst of nothing*, Mrs Barnfield,' said Harrison, who had just taken a photograph of the group with the palm fronds arching above them and the Dead Sea in the near distance. 'It would be swell as a title for my photo-essay ... if you have no objections to my using it, that is?' Harrison reasoned that, although it wasn't actually her quotation, giving it her ownership might be a useful ploy to get on the right side of her.

'Be my guest,' answered Mrs Barnfield, in her usual curt, matter-of-fact manner, 'they are only words.'

'There is so much of our past about us in this land,' said the professor mysteriously, 'so much of it almost unrecognizable from what it once was...'

'How do you mean, Professor?' asked Mady Barnfield, who was developing a genuine interest in what he was saying.

'Well, Miss Barnfield, think of what we saw today at Engedi ... several caves surrounded by quite a barren landscape, but in the midst of such desolation there was also the occasional spring. That could lead us to believe that in ages past, this area was not as barren as it now appears. I am reliably informed that there is an abundant supply of good, fresh water in the mountains surrounding us...'

The cleric suddenly quoted: '"My beloved is unto me as a cluster of henna flowers in the vineyards of Engedi".'

Everyone turned and looked at the Reverend Fairweather who sat, still with the beatific smile of contentment on his face, looking at the panorama that spread before him.

'Chapter 1, verse 14 of the Song of Songs, so you are probably quite correct, my dear Professor,' continued the cleric, waving his hand about him to encompass the rapidly darkening landscape.

Mrs Hester Barnfield had formed the opinion that Reverend Fairweather was far too pompous for his own good. She looked at him and was momentarily struck by the thought that his gesture resembled something akin to a final blessing.

'There must have been considerable agricultural activity in this area at the time when those words were written,' continued the churchman, his face confirming his conviction of the certainty that what had been written millennia ago was, quite literally, the gospel truth.

Uri suddenly appeared. Behind him one of his boys carried a small tray on which were several bowls of nuts and other assorted Arab sweets. 'I hope you are feeling restored after your exploring today,' he enquired. 'Please help yourself to some light snacks. They are all local specialities.'

'Uri,' said Rupert, 'can I ask you for your Jewish perspective?'

'But of course,' replied Uri, as he watched the bowls being distributed around the low folding tables. 'Er ... my Jewish perspective ... on what?'

'Do you think this area was always like this, or do you think that things have changed beyond all recognition here ... with the passing of time?' asked Rupert.

Uri thought briefly as he stared out at the landscape. 'The Reverend is quite correct, when he quotes from the Song of Songs,' he said, 'and who knows, perhaps in times to come new ways will be found to bring water here again and to develop agricultural settlements...'

'It seems such a contradiction in terms, to have so much water over *there*,' said Mrs Sarah Unsworth, speaking for the first time as she pointed to the Dead Sea, 'and yet not to be able to use it to grow things *here*.'

'That's because of the enormously high saline content of the water in the Dead Sea, my dear,' replied her husband patiently. 'It has something like thirty per cent salinity ... that's about ten times more than you find in the oceans. So, nothing grows and there are no fish, hence the name.'

'If I may add to that, Professor,' said Uri respectfully, 'in Hebrew, we call it "The Sea of Salt".'

'And a far more accurate name it is, too,' said the professor, smiling at him.

'I thought I noticed a lot of other caves in the cliffs ... this morning, when we were around Engedi,' said Harrison. 'Did anyone else notice them?'

'There are many caves in the cliffs around here,' answered Uri, 'and there are even more further north, towards the top end of the Dead Sea, around the ruins of an ancient, but unimportant settlement called Qumran. The Jewish people have always had to fight for survival, throughout history...' He paused. '... *This* area is of great significance to us.' Uri Ben Zeev twisted slightly and pointed upwards and away to their left, towards the towering bulk of the nearby, flat-topped mountain.

Hester Barnfield, who was already far advanced through her second, strong gin and minimal tonic, looked at the tanned, well-built young man and wondered if Moses had looked quite as handsome when he broke the news of the Commandments to his followers. She felt a certain spark of excitement shoot through her.

'We are sitting very close to the mountain we call Masada,' Uri continued. 'This outcrop of rock has great importance to the Jewish people since the time of the Great Revolt against the Romans hundreds of years ago.' He put his hand down and twisted back to once again face his guests. 'We also have the tradition that David hid from Saul in the caves of Ein Gedi,' he said, pronouncing the name as two distinct words, 'which means "Young Goat Spring" in our language.'

'"And David went up from thence, and dwelt in the strongholds of Engedi",' recalled the Reverend Fairweather, who, lost in a world of his own, seemed to have been oblivious to most of the preceding conversation. 'So it says in the First Book of Samuel, Chapter 24, verse 1.'

Mrs Barnfield turned and stared at the little cleric with a look somewhere between intolerance and loathing, but she said nothing. She had absolutely no time for the self-righteous. It was a category of her fellow beings into which she had long ago placed her loathsome husband, as she had come to regard him, and amongst whom she now unceremoniously included the Reverend Theophilus Fairweather.

'Could I have a refill?' she said, holding up her glass somewhat unsteadily in the air and swilling what was left of the ice cubes around in the bottom of it. She continued to fix the Reverend with her gaze of defensive distrust. She had also not failed to observe that her daughter and the American photographer were, in her opinion, once again sitting a little too close together for her liking. She had noted with rising concern, that the two had engaged in the occasional earnest conversation when they mistakenly thought that she would not notice. She would have to keep a careful eye on Madeira – a very careful eye. She was no stranger to having handsome young men traipsing along behind her attractively eligible and potentially extremely wealthy daughter. She had seen through every single one of them – even if her daughter had not. Yes, she would have to watch this young American very carefully, although, in a moment of reflection, she admitted to herself that this young man did seem to lack the usual professional gloss, which, from her own experiences, she knew to be one of the hallmarks of the professional gigolo. Instead, she fancied that he displayed a certain colonial roughness, which, in its own way, she found somewhat endearing. She allowed herself an inward smile of amusement at this reflection, but nonetheless determined to remain on her guard as far as Madeira and, more importantly, the family fortune was concerned.

'Tell me, Reverend,' said Stephen, 'these caves around here ... do you think they could be connected to Moses in any way?'

For a moment the little cleric seemed to be lost for words. He turned his head to look in Stephen's direction. 'Moses?' he repeated, more to himself than the assembled company. 'Well ... I should think it might be possible.'

'Moses or his son, Gershom,' continued Stephen, turning to look away, out across the landscape. 'Perhaps he could have been in these parts, too ... with his father?'

'I am sure that is possible as well. You are well informed as to the lineage of Moses, Mr Hopkins,' said the vicar. 'I am impressed.'

'It is just something you learn at Sunday school and never forget,' lied Stephen, looking down at the ground as he spoke. He had never heard of Gershom until his uncle and the professor from the British Museum had mentioned the name. 'I was just curious to discover if he might have been around these parts.'

'Speaking of Moses there is, of course, the question of Mount Sinai,' said the cleric, abruptly changing the subject. 'Now that is an interesting conundrum...' He seemed to lapse into a silent, private reverie, a contented smile creeping across his face as he once again lost himself in his own thoughts.

'It should also be noted that the Dead Sea is the lowest point on Earth,' said Rupert, starting the conversation again after a few moments of silence. 'The altitude here, where we are presently sitting, is slightly higher than that of the Dead Sea itself, but down there,' he said, pointing towards the expanse of water, 'it is something like fourteen hundred feet lower than the level of the oceans.' He had done his homework well.

A fresh G & T, complete with two clinking ice cubes, was duly deposited on Mrs Barnfield's table, whereupon it was snatched up by the be-ringed fingers.

'Are we in any danger of being flooded?' asked Mady Barnfield, involuntarily taking hold of Harrison's hand with the sudden shock that this revelation had caused her.

'None whatsoever, Miss Barnfield,' said the professor, laughing. 'There are far too many mountains and other areas of high ground between us and the ocean to allow that ... not unless the Earth decides to become very angry indeed and completely reshape itself again, but if that happens ... well, there won't be any need for any of us to think about anything, really.' He smiled at her again with that disarming, resigned smile that held acceptance and, at the same time, understanding.

'Well, everyone, time is moving on and perhaps we ought to think about starting to prepare for dinner,' said Rupert, looking at his watch.

Drinks were tossed back into hungry throats and the group rose from their comfortable wicker chairs, before strolling back to the campsite proper.

'Are you coming?' asked Rupert, as he stood next to Stephen, who was still leaning against the palm tree.

'I'll catch you up in a minute, old chap,' replied Stephen. 'I want to have a quick chat with Uri ... I won't be long.'

16

Rome

The Foreign Ministry – Tuesday, 2nd June 1931

Count Vittorio Contini-Aosta, Minister of State for War, sat behind the large desk in his office. He had spent the previous hour reading through several reports on the current progress of the test flights of the new aircraft he had authorized, as well as that of the naval building programme. Everything seemed to be going to plan: timetables had more or less been adhered to and there did not seem to be any reason to believe that everything would not be completed and delivered on time. But, completed and delivered on time for what? That was the question that had started to prey on his mind.

During recent weeks even his fellow ministers had begun to refer to the 'what' as being something of a mystery. But their conversations on the topic had been brief, discreet and whispered. Il Duce's ears were large – almost as large as his personal ego – and they missed nothing.

'You have it wrong, my friends,' Andrea Bardolongo, Minister for Propaganda, had said, 'we know precisely what the "what" is. Il Duce himself has often told us of his dream of a new Roman Empire. The people know of this as well. Rather, we must be thinking of "when" and that day draws ever closer, as our preparations are concluded. Vittorio, you can tell us more about this.'

Initially there had been no spoken response to this statement, only furtive glances exchanged at great speed, before anyone really noticed. Even the inner circle of Il Duce's government knew the folly of stepping out of line. The OVRA, the Fascist secret police, had spies everywhere.

'Following Il Duce's vision, we have strengthened our forces in Eritrea, but you all know this, it has been minuted for some time now.' Contini-Aosta was in the habit of saying very little that had not already been said or written down. He knew that to reveal original thoughts or details of something not already in general circulation could be very dangerous.

As he sat in his office behind his desk, reading the small pile of papers in front of him, he started to wonder whether they had any real chance of surviving a major international conflict. Mussolini's plan for colonial war with the Abyssinians, despite the friendship treaty signed back in 1928, was one thing. Having to fight a second or third front against the British, Americans, even the French, or all three together, would be quite a different matter. The count was a pragmatic realist: Il Duce's firebrand speeches, as inspirational and crowd-stirring as they often were, would not help at all if it came to a simple matter of logistical mathematics. Italy would have little or no chance of surviving if the superior military might of the Allies, as they called themselves, were to be unleashed against her in defence of poor, backward Abyssinia.

The French might be persuaded not to intervene, he reasoned, as he got up and crossed to the large French windows that overlooked the throbbing streets of the Eternal City. Our Fascist sympathizers are well placed in their government to possibly act as a break against them becoming involved. As for the other two ... He stared down absently, as the traffic surged about its business in the street below. The unanswered question is simply one of who is going to persuade Mussolini that we could well be stirring up a hornet's nest with these grandiose expansionist plans of his. It certainly will not be me! The memory of his leader's irrational outburst on the day the American anarchist had been arrested was still far too vivid in his memory.

A knock on the heavy panelled doors turned his attention away from the possibly unpatriotic thoughts he had been harbouring.

'Come!' he said.

A uniformed aide entered. He had only recently been transferred to the count's service. In his right hand he carried a small tray, on which sat a white ceramic cup and saucer.

'The Minister's coffee,' announced the aide, as he crossed to the edge of the desk, removed the steaming drink from his tray and placed it carefully next to the small pile of documents.

Contini-Aosta winced inwardly. He had forgotten to return the documents to their folder and had left them in a position where a skilled eye could rapidly scan through the typed lines of the topmost sheet, albeit upside down, and commit the contents to memory. Who was this lieutenant – this aide – anyway? Was he OVRA? These days it was difficult to tell who anyone was.

'Sir!' said the Lieutenant, springing smartly to attention.

Oh, not that bloody salute again, fumed the count inwardly, as he crossed back to behind his desk, but he need not have concerned himself. The aide did not salute.

'Will the Minister require anything further?' enquired the lieutenant, as he stood at the foot of the desk, the little silver tray clamped incongruously under his left arm, like some ornate helmet that had been squashed as flat as the proverbial pancake.

'No,' answered Contini-Aosta, returning the pile of documents to their protective wallet as he resumed his seat.

The aide turned smartly and walked out of the office, closing the door behind him with a soft click. To the count, that soft click reminded him of the action of the hammer being cocked, as a new bullet was pushed into the breech. He flung himself back into the chair.

What am I thinking of...? I am becoming paranoid! Sweet Mother of Jesus, get a grip man, he resolved, *you are a soldier and you have responsibilities. It is too late to be having second thoughts ... about anything. Besides which, all good soldiers obey orders. You have yours, so get on with it!* He was about to pick up his coffee, when the telephone on his desk jangled loudly. 'Yes?'

'Il Duce wishes to speak with the count,' said a masculine voice, as a couple of soft clicks were heard at the end of the message.

Probably OVRA listening into the call, Contini-Aosta surmised. He had heard rumours that such things were happening, even at the highest levels.

'Vittorio, my friend, how are you?' boomed a larger-than-life voice on the other end of the line.

'Duce, I am well, thank you. I trust Your Excellency is also in good health?' This was always the way such telephone conversations began.

'I am. Tell me, what progress is there with our aircraft?'

The count reported in some detail on the progress of the new aircraft's test flights, which seemed to put Mussolini in high spirits.

'That is excellent news, Vittorio. I knew I could count on you and I, too, have some excellent news for you. Our friends in France have confirmed that they are more than willing to act as our procurement agents, when the time comes for us to need more oil. They are also happy for us to go and look for oil in the Syrian deserts. Not that any of this is official or even true, if anyone outside of our circle wants to know.' Mussolini roared with laughter, which caused the count to move the handset away from his ear. 'They have made useful contacts with our friends in Iraq as well,' he continued. 'The prince is well disposed to our proposed plans and could be a useful ally against the British...'

He is in a happy mood. At least for the moment, Contini-Aosta decided, as he listened, dutifully. 'That is, indeed, very good news, Duce.'

'Good? Good? My dear Vittorio, it is *excellent* news. It means that when the time comes your avaricious little ships, tanks and aircraft will not go thirsty...'

The count was reminded of what Andrea Bardolongo, Minister for Propaganda, had said, about the question being "when" rather than "what".

Some minutes later, with the telephone handset once again resting securely in its cradle, Count Vittorio Contini-Aosta turned and looked at his cup of coffee. The steam had stopped rising in arabesques: the coffee was lukewarm. He reached out and pushed the untouched drink away. As he did so, he wondered if it was a sign of what lay ahead. Would the heated, steaming frenzy that had greeted Il Duce's rise to power end up as a lukewarm disappointment, which nobody wanted? He shivered slightly. He was a decorated soldier: a war hero and a patriot. He was used to facing the unknown, the impossible and the prospect of having to battle against overwhelming odds. He was used to all of this, but still he shivered slightly as he withdrew his hand from the cup.

17

Palestine

Masada – later that evening, Tuesday, 2nd June 1931

Most of the tourists had already passed out of earshot on their way to the campsite, as two of Uri's boys busied themselves with clearing away the remnants of the sundowners. Stephen, who had spent his time leaning against the palm tree, stood up and slowly walked over to where Uri was standing, folding the tablecloths and packing them away into a wicker hamper.

'You are well informed about the history of this place,' said Stephen, putting his empty glass down on the table next to the hamper.

'Thank you, Mr Hopkins; it is all part of my job.'

'And, if you will excuse me, I would say it is a good part of your belief, too...?' Stephen left the question open-ended.

Uri turned and smiled at him, at the same time continuing to fold the linen. 'Every Jew is aware of our ancient struggle to survive. It is part of our natural inheritance. Even some of our own kind have caused us many tears. That up there...,' he continued, gesturing towards the mountain with his chin, '...that is a symbol of Jewish tenacity and the desire for independence, no matter what the cost. Our people held out against Rome until the bitter end, so when the victorious legion finally breached the summit, they found only the bodies of the dead. Today, we regard it as almost a sacred place; a reminder of honour and the determination to be free...' He stopped talking and stood staring up at Masada. 'I am sorry. I did not wish to deliver a history lecture.'

Stephen waved the apology away with a smile.

'It *is* a powerful symbol of Jewish pride,' Uri continued, 'but it is also one of Jewish treachery.' He fixed Stephen with a resolute stare. 'The northern end was also the palace of King Herod ... Herod the Great, as he is called by some. Others would say that he was more Roman than Jew and persecuted his own people to curry favour with the occupying power in Rome. The feelings are still mixed after nearly two thousand years. Amongst my people, memories die very hard.'

Stephen said nothing, but waited with a questioning gaze that invited Uri to continue.

'And this land has seen much fighting. The People of Israel fought to survive in the time of King David and of Solomon the Wise. Then along came the Muslims, the Crusaders, the Turks and then, more recently during the war, the British, French, Americans, Australians, Indians ... I could include half the peoples of the world. Perhaps it is of little wonder that the Jewish faith is so strong amongst the People of Israel. No matter where we are in the world we have, quite literally, always had to link arms as brothers and fight to survive.'

'As did David when he hid in the caves over there, to escape Saul...' added Stephen.

'As you say, Mr Hopkins,' confirmed Uri, but without any anger or bitterness in his voice.

'Tell me, in your history do you have any ... how can I put this? ... any concrete instruction to establish a Jewish nation here, in Palestine ... Please, do not take offence at the question,' said Stephen hurriedly, realizing that he had risked shooting himself in the foot by asking the question so bluntly.

'No offence taken whatsoever...,' replied Uri, laughing gently, 'and you are correct, nationhood is very often a delicate subject. We Jews have the right to our own country, just as much as the Arabs have a right to theirs. The trouble is, unless we can devise some way of working things out together, there can be no possibility of there being two different countries both occupying the same geographical area. It is simply not possible.' He paused for a moment to clarify his thoughts. 'And then, of course, there is the small matter of you British ... Please, I do not want you to take offence,' he said, adroitly returning Stephen's earlier remark with a genuine smile of comradeship on his face.

'Point taken, old boy,' replied Stephen, 'but I was thinking back particularly to the ancient days ... to biblical times, actually. Has anything survived ... anything perhaps about the right of a Jewish nation to exist in its own sovereign territory?'

This time there was a considerable pause, during which nothing was said and during which Uri continued packing the hamper, before closing and fastening the lid. Just as Stephen was beginning to think that his line of questioning had been a dreadful blunder, Uri laughed, revealing his strong, white teeth.

'Are you asking if perhaps David might have left something up there ... hidden in a cave?'

'Or possibly even Gershom,' said Stephen.

'Gershom?' repeated Uri, surprised. 'Why Gershom? Surely it would have been Moses who would have been given things of value; things which might have needed to be hidden in a cave if there was danger ... not his son?'

Stephen sensed that Uri knew no more about the topic than he, himself, did. 'Gershom or Moses ... either/or? Do you think it *is* possible one of them might have hidden something around here in one of these caves...?'

'I will tell you the answer to that one, Mr Hopkins. Who

would know? Perhaps there is something up there ... or in any one of the caves which stretch from here to beyond Qumran in the north. Perhaps one day something will be found. Who knows? Perhaps there is something waiting to be found,' he repeated, shrugging his shoulders. 'I cannot say, as I have never heard of anything such. Perhaps, if there *was* something like that, we would have had a Jewish state already.' He smiled, as genuinely as before. 'But, then again, in that eventuality we would probably not be having this conversation, would we?' And he laughed again.

Stephen had drawn a blank. As far as the search for the mysterious Scroll of Gershom was concerned, he was none the wiser than he had been in his uncle's Whitehall office, months before. He tried one last, possibly very stupid, approach. 'But you are lucky to have your ancient scrolls; the Torah and the Talmud. They have survived the ravages of time and battle. And you have the Law and the Prophecies of Moses and of Gershom...' Stephen watched very carefully, but Uri did not show any reaction to this last remark.

'Aaron. You should talk to *him* about prophecies and politics...'

Stephen was taken aback by Uri's answer. 'Pardon me? Who is Aaron?'

'I have two brothers and Aaron is the middle one. He is only slightly younger than myself and is very much the man of action. Papa has very heated debates with him, as to the rights and wrongs of using force to achieve political ends.' He stopped and turned his head, looking up at the mountain fortress, which was already starting to blur into the gloaming. 'Even after all these years Papa is still not used to a concept of statehood and democracy, having grown up under the control of the Czar and his officials. Aaron is studying Economics at the University of Haifa. Papa is happy to pay the fees for such a worthwhile course of study; it will be of benefit to our family's business interests...' Then he broke off and chuckled loudly. '... What poor Papa did not expect was the extra course in politics, in which my brother has enrolled. You should hear the arguments they have.'

'Yes,' replied Stephen, grateful that his last, clumsy line of questioning had neither caused offence, nor soured the positive relationship that had already started to develop between himself, Rupert and this highly affable and obviously extremely competent Jew. 'Politics can very often divide a family right down the middle.'

'And now, if you will excuse me, Mr Hopkins, I must turn my attention from the mountain and our interesting conversation to the kitchen tent. Tomorrow we cross into Trans-Jordan and make our way to Ar Rabbah and the King's Highway. It will be a busy day and we should make an early start. And I still have the evening meal to supervise.'

As he walked slowly back towards the tents, Stephen reflected on his two attempts to glean information on this Gershom Scroll, neither of which had produced any kind of positive response. He began to think that Professor Longhurst, working as he did in the bowels of the British Museum, might have made a mistake over the mysterious marble tablet from Petra with its potentially explosive inscription.

Perhaps the professor should get out into the fresh air a little more, he ruminated.

18

Jerusalem

Mid-afternoon, Saturday, 6th June 1931

'Oh, look ... isn't she the sweetest thing, ever?' cooed Claudette Catzmann, as she smiled broadly at the little girl who was standing with her parents on the opposite side of the walkway. 'Moshie ... *bubalah,*' she said, drawing out the sounds, 'doesn't she make you wish to have one of your own?'

Morris Ginsberg, decorated war hero and avid supporter of his wife's singing talents, did not answer. No. In truth, even as pretty a little girl as this one, did not make him long for one of his own. Neither did he like it much when Claudie started to brood and make such silly conversation. It was all they could do to feed themselves: where did she suppose the money to feed another mouth would come from? It would have to be the proverbial manna from a beneficent heaven! The little girl, who was carrying a small bunch of flowers, beamed back at Claudette.

'Oh, what a sweetie...' she said, clutching Moshie's arm tightly, as she continued to smile at the little child.

'Claudie ... enough, already,' he whispered emphatically out of the corner of his mouth. 'You'll have people looking at us ... and we don't want any trouble, remember!'

He had been in this awkward place before. Sometimes, despite trying very hard, he just could not rise to the occasional, exceptional demands of his wife's seemingly insatiable desire to fulfil her maternal instincts. He had to admit, in all fairness, that she was very understanding, and never made too much of a fuss about his inability to perform at his peak. She never took a firm stand on his shortcomings. In fact, her stand was no more firm than was his, under the circumstances. So, at least in that respect, they again had something in common. But he would always feel bad afterwards, as he felt that he had let her down and that was something he tried very hard not to do. In his opinion, she simply deserved the best and there were times, especially when she became broody, when he began to wonder if she could do better for herself than Morris Ginsberg, VC.

'Oh ... Moshie,' she sighed, clasping his arm very tightly.

But Morris was thinking. He realized that Claudette was becoming more and more broody of late. Each time she would ask him if he would like a child of his own and it was becoming more and more difficult for him to deflect these advances. The simple truth was that he did not want to be a parent: he had never been overly fond of children in the first place and, secondly, he was blissfully happy with what just the two of them had in life.

'Hello, sweetheart ... Oh, how pretty that is...'

Oy vey, here we go again, Morris realized, as he heard Claudie's voice coming from the bench close to him. She was bending forward and talking to the little girl, who, with her parents, had crossed the paved walkway and now stood in front of her holding out one of the flowers for Claudie to take.

'Is that for me ... it's really beautiful ... just like you are,' said Claudette, taking the flower and holding it to her nose to smell it. It was some sort of common daisy, and so had no smell, but that didn't deter her in any way. The mere fact that something so tender and precious, so fragile and yet so full of life, was offering her something as simple as a single flower was almost too much for her to bear. Of course, her Moshie was always buying her beautiful flowers; at least, he did when they had the money. This child's gift was symbolic. The simple action of this innocent little girl had sent a message to her and that message was simply that she, too, should have one of these, one of her very own, before it was too late.

'Thank you so very much...,' she said to the little girl, who smiled back in a confident, yet diffident way. '...And thank you, too, for letting her come over to present it to me,' she said to the two parents.

'It was no trouble,' replied the girl's father, who nonetheless kept himself very close to his daughter.

'Her name is Naomi,' said the mother, smiling.

'Thank you, Naomi, for my beautiful flower,' responded Claudette, overwhelmed by the maternal emotion which this encounter had provoked.

'Do you know that my name means "enjoyment"? I am now five and a half years old,' said the child, quite fluently and in a matter-of-fact way. 'How old are you?'

Her father gave her shoulder a slight prod, by way of correction, but the question had been asked in total innocence, as one human being to another.

'Do you have any...?' asked the mother, in an attempt to lighten the embarrassment she felt her daughter had just caused.

'Not yet,' interrupted Morris, squeezing his wife's hand gently, 'but we hope to ... one day.' Even he felt that his reply had been just a little too enthusiastically positive to be convincing.

They chatted amicably for a short while longer, during which time they exchanged comments about the weather, the cost of living and about Naomi's two brothers, both of whom had gone off into the mountains with their grandfather for the weekend. Morris had even managed to get in the fact, seemingly quite casually, that Claudette was the singing star of the entertainment currently being provided by the Petra Hotel on King David Street, next to the Jaffa Gate in the Old City.

Later, as they sat and watched the small family group walk away in the direction of the nearby lake, which stood at the western end of the park, they both knew perfectly well that they would not see either of the parents in the audience.

'I'm sorry, Claudie,' pleaded Morris. 'I really do love you...'

'Hush, *bubalah*... I know you do... you precious thing... shush,' came the whispered reply as she snuggled her head on to his shoulder, but tilted it in such a way that she could still just see the two parents and their little girl disappear as they mingled with the rest of the afternoon crowd.

'*Oy, yoy, yoy! Bubalah*... what are we doing with ourselves? Are we actually doing *anything*?' she asked, her voice quivering slightly.

'Of course we are... and you know that. You've done well to get the show at the hotel. It is a much better venue than the Golden Moon in Haifa... At least you have to admit that. And we have the chance to do something positive for our people, if and when anything ever happens. Who knows? It could be far worse.' Then, never having been particularly blessed with a strong command of language, Morris continued in his clumsy way to try to lift the mood. 'Things could be far worse. You could be a prostitute and I could be dead.'

In the silence that followed, Morris could feel Claudie stiffen at his side. Eventually, she raised her head and looked straight at him; his strong profile was already reddening. She continued to sit and stare at his hot, red face, neither moving nor speaking. For his part, he continued to look straight ahead, desperately trying to stretch his eyeballs around enough to see if she was going to explode or not.

Suddenly, she broke into a hearty laugh, which was so loud in its intensity that it caused several passing strollers to turn and look. '*Bubalah* ... y'know, you are right ... as always, my love,' she said, perking up perceptibly, 'and who knows ... today Jerusalem, tomorrow, the world!'

Morris laughed, too, relieved beyond measure that his gaff, so lovingly and so well meant, had not been thrown back into his face.

It was late afternoon by the time they had walked back through the narrow cobbled streets and up through the Old City, almost back to their lodgings on Mishmerot Ha-Kehuna in the Jewish Quarter. The accommodation was very basic, but comfortable enough. In the short time they had been there Claudie had done wonders turning it into their home and the best part of it all was they did not pay the rent – that had been taken care of by *them*. Since leaving Haifa, they had been contacted only a few times, but without any instructions being issued. Morris had wondered if they were being dragged into something perhaps a little too shady, but Claudie seemed to have let all such concerns go over her head – perhaps she had not fully understood the implications of their involvement in the undercover organization. Still, he reflected, their decision to go along with what they had been offered was better than staying in Haifa. His Claudie would never be discovered in Haifa. At least here, amongst the bright lights of Jerusalem and the Petra Hotel in particular, she stood a far better chance of success. And the new King David Hotel was just about to open – if they could get to perform *there* ... well, who was to say it might not actually happen?

They kept walking until they reached Hurva Square, the busy hub of the Jewish Quarter, and were almost home when Claudette, taking Morris by the arm, impulsively announced that they should buy a bagel each from the little Spanish shop on the corner. Then they could sit on the nearby bench and eat them, soaking up the warmth of the afternoon sun.

'Humm … that's good, hey, *bubalah*,' said Claudette a little while later, through a mouthful of bagel and cream cheese.

'Shalom …, enjoy your food, but take care that nobody takes too much notice,' said a deep, musical male voice from behind her. 'It is dangerous for all if your face is remembered by too many.'

Morris froze, his teeth clamped into the soft texture of the fresh bagel he held in his hand. He shot a sideways glance at his wife, who had already started to turn her head to look behind her at the owner of the voice.

'Do not turn around!' hissed the voice severely. The tone was one of somebody in control; of somebody used to giving orders and having them obeyed – instantly. 'Have you had an enjoyable afternoon? The weather has been very pleasant; do you still have your little flower?'

Claudette stopped munching and put the remainder of her bagel down. For some inexplicable reason Morris relaxed. It was *them* again and, as in the past, it was a voice he did not recognize.

'We have nothing for you at the moment. The operation, which you were briefed on before you left Haifa, is still active, but we are awaiting developments. At the moment, we have nothing for you to help us with.'

Neither Claudette nor Morris said anything. Both of them had learned through their earlier meetings that they should not speak unless asked to do so.

'So … in the meantime I will leave my copy of today's *Haaretz* on the bench here for you to read. Pay particular attention to pages 9 and 10, where you will find something to help you pass the time. We are not a bottomless pit, so I suggest you count each *shekel* wisely before you decide to part with it.'

There was a pause during which the distant, muted sounds of Jerusalem floated around the bench and mingled with those of the little square.

'Is there anything you wish to report, or to ask me?' said the voice.

'No, nothing that we can think of,' whispered Morris, so as not to appear to be talking.

'Very well, then. We will be in contact again once we receive any information concerning your operation. In the meantime we expect you to act normally and to keep your eyes and ears open.' There was the sound of a newspaper being folded. 'Do not be late for your performances this evening. There are some important guests in the hotel at the moment. Who knows, they might have useful information. We can never tell...'

At that moment, quite unexpectedly, the muezzin of the nearby al-Aqsa mosque started his call to the faithful to attend Asr – the afternoon prayers in the Muslim cycle of daily devotions. Claudette and Morris sat on the bench, she with her half-eaten bagel in her hand and he, with his teeth-marked, but otherwise untouched, one in his, listening to the call as it echoed from the nearby Temple Mount.

'Do you know how long we will be at the Petra Hotel?' asked Morris, for lack of anything better to say. But there was no reply, only the call to prayer and the distant rumble of the ancient city.

After another few seconds of silence, Morris slowly swung his eyes around, until he could just see the space behind his wife's head, from where the voice had come. There was no one there. Only a copy of *Haaretz*, its name easily visible at the top of the folded page, lay abandoned on the bench. As casually as he could, Morris reached across the back of their bench and picked it up; careful to keep it folded closed as he did so.

Once they were safely back in their lodgings, with the door firmly bolted against the outside world, they gingerly opened the newspaper to pages 9 and 10 and had their breath taken away by what they found. Money – not a great amount – but, at least, when measured against the standards to which they had grown accustomed over the last couple of years, enough to get by on, and modestly comfortably, too.

'You were right again, *bubalah*,' said Claudette, taking his hand in hers. 'We are going places at last. And we still have the money from the hotel to come. Things have really started to move for us ... Hey, my *bubalah*?' as she took his head in both of her hands and smothered his mouth with hers.

Later, as Claudette was getting ready to leave for the Petra Hotel, Morris Ginsberg sat quietly at the little table in their kitchen area. The copy of *Haaretz* had been folded into neat quarters and pushed to the far corner. As he sat looking across at the newspaper, he reflected on what it was that worried him the most. Well, no – not *worried* exactly; *concerned* might be nearer the truth. After all, he was an old soldier and quite used to the unexpected and the dangerous. He had his medal to remind him of that. At a very early age, when he had been growing up in the East End of London, he had learned that for people of his station there was no such thing as a free meal. This money that they were being given, including the rent for these lodgings, was going to have to be repaid in some way or other. Quite how and when, he had no idea.

As Claudette swept into the kitchen area, looking as radiant as she possibly could, he picked up his accordion, which stood in its case next to the door, and smiled approvingly at his wife. He had no concerns for himself; he could still count on his military training to get him out of an unexpected scrape, but it was for the future welfare of his beloved Claudie – the precious, diminutive little flower that he worshiped – that he harboured a distant, nagging fear.

19

Rome

Office of the Minister for War – noon, Friday, 5th June 1931

'My dear Louis ... how good to see you again,' said Count Vittorio Contini-Aosta, as he and his visitor took their seats, 'and how are Marie and the children?'

The two men exchanged pleasantries as the footsteps of the count's aide echoed across the marble-floored office to the door, before the smart young lieutenant disappeared through it.

'We are all in good spirits, thank you,' continued the visitor, as he put a leather briefcase on the highly polished floor. 'I hope you are also in good health?'

The count made an all-encompassing gesture by way of acknowledgement. 'Tell me then, Louis, what brings you to Rome? It is barely two months since you were here last.' He had an idea of what it was that had brought this visitor back to his desk so soon, but in matters of diplomacy it did not pay to rush the expected niceties of protocol – especially with the French. They could easily feel cheated out of what they saw as their due as representatives of the Third Republic, and they had been known to become petulantly obstructive as a result. 'Has there been progress since our last meeting?'

Louis de Saint-Etienne Monteschalle, Under Minister for

War in the government of Pierre Laval, smiled as he opened his briefcase and removed a small folder.

'That depends on exactly where you might expect the progress to have been made,' he replied enigmatically, placing the folder on the edge of the count's desk.

The count smiled back politely, watching the visitor take a pair of pince-nez from his inside pocket and anchor them firmly on his nose. Contini-Aosta was a military man, first and foremost. He was used to receiving direct orders and then carrying them out as quickly and as successfully as possible. He was still not accustomed to the cat-and-mouse nature of the game of diplomatic machinations. He doubted whether he ever would be.

'Firstly, my dear Count, let us discuss the matter of the proposed combined military manoeuvres. I am pleased to report that the Prime Minister is absolutely in agreement over the question of our two fleets staging joint exercises in the Mediterranean.' This was something the two men had discussed during Saint-Etienne's previous visit. 'It will send a message to the world that we are united in our bonds of solidarity and friendship,' he continued, looking up from the paper he had removed from the folder. 'It will also show the British that they do not have the exclusive right to the high seas.'

Contini-Aosta sat forward in his chair and rested his elbows on the desk. 'Il Duce will be very pleased at the news. He is of the opinion that we peoples of the Mediterranean should take back our ancient right to control passage through *our* waters, without having to ask someone else's permission before doing so. And what of our proposals for joint land exercises?'

Saint-Etienne smiled again, removing his pince-nez as he did so. 'That is still a possibility and it is open to further negotiation. We will set a precedent by holding our joint naval exercises, which will mean that further joint military undertakings will be easier to announce to the world. Whether they like the news or not will be of little relevance.'

'Il Duce will also be pleased at that news. It will be foolish to rush into anything which could be perceived as provocative, which, of course, joint land manoeuvres could well be,' the count added. He was aware that they were playing a dangerous game. 'The planning is considerable and we must be absolutely certain that our united front will withstand the objections of others ... the British and the Americans, for example.'

'The British are not the power they once fancied themselves to be. Their empire was exhausted after the war and even now, when most economies seem to have recovered somewhat, they are not in a position to mount as splendid a spectacle as our grand Colonial Exposition in Paris. We have already had over three and a half million visitors.' The Frenchman replaced his pince-nez and continued, 'And as for the Americans ... pha! They thought they were going to win the war for us, but their arrogance cost them dearly in casualties, which did not go down at all well back home. Our people report that there is general disquiet and dissatisfaction over there. The economic crisis has damaged them and their foreign policy seems without direction. It would seem that they have returned to the inward-looking policies of their President Lincoln ... Besides which, they are on the other side of the Atlantic.'

That's as good as maybe, ruminated the count, *but it did not stop that foolish American from coming all the way from New York to attempt to kill Il Duce.* He wondered if Saint-Etienne had heard of the recent assassination attempt, so narrowly foiled by OVRA. 'Still, it would be foolish of us not to prepare thoroughly,' replied Contini-Aosta, thoughtfully, 'and there is also the question of what Germany might think of our plans.'

Saint-Etienne did not respond immediately. Instead, he

rose from his chair and crossed to a large-scale map of the world that hung on the far wall of the count's office, directly opposite the desk. He stood and studied it for a few seconds.

'This map is of good quality; it has a fine detail about it. Why do you suggest that we hold our joint land exercises down in our colony of Somaliland? Does Il Duce not think that any future peril to our interests will probably come from the north ... from our old enemies in Europe?'

He had clasped his hands behind his back and turned his body to look at the count, the tails of his frock coat flapping like a spaniel's drooping ears as he did so.

For a moment, Contini-Aosta was taken by surprise at the bluntness of the question, but he was no fool and structured his reply accordingly: 'That would be for Il Duce himself to decide.' Despite the clandestine negotiations, the protestations of secret friendship and the declared intention of standing firm against the adverse opinion of the rest of the world's major powers, he knew full well that each of the two players in this dangerous game was looking out for their own best interests. Besides, who apart from the man himself actually knew what was going on in Il Duce's mind? 'Il Duce has informed us that the army should be prepared for action in all climatic conditions and geographic locations. We are all used to our conditions here in Europe. It is Il Duce's opinion that our troops need more practical experience in the hotter, more arid conditions of Africa. After all, who is to say from whence any future aggression may originate?'

Saint-Etienne turned back to the map for a brief moment, then looked back at the count and nodded. 'There is some practical sense in that thought. After all is said and done, we have our French Foreign Legion.' He returned to his seat in front of the desk. 'Now to move on to the second topic of our recent discussions ... We are starting to become concerned over the possibility that Germany might emerge once again as a threat to French security,' he said. 'We were alarmed by the recent proposed customs pact between Germany and Austria. That would have damaged French economic interests, so we had to take steps to prevent it.'

Contini-Aosta knew that the French had called in loans to Austria in an attempt to sabotage the proposed pact, but he said nothing, preferring to keep an expression of detached unawareness on his face. 'We have not failed to appreciate the fact that Germany is steadily rebuilding itself,' muttered the count, *and they have used several of our Fascist ideas in the process,* he added to himself.

Naturally, as a minister of the state, the count was aware of Il Duce's interest in the fledgling Nazi Party, but he said nothing further.

'I am instructed to inform Il Duce that the Prime Minister would not be averse to discussing future military co-operation between our two great nations being on a, shall we say, more *protective* and mutually beneficial footing...' The visitor looked long and hard through his lenses at the count, who had sat back in his chair, the fingers of his hands touching each other across his chest.

'My dear Louis, I am not quite sure I totally follow you,' replied the count. 'Is your Prime Minister proposing ... an alliance of some sort?'

It was Saint-Etienne's turn to offer an acknowledging shrug. '... If an agreement between our two countries were to be mutually beneficial, then why not? I can assure you, my dear Count, that we have no wish to be invaded and occupied for a third time. If such an undesirable situation were to suddenly arise, we would greatly value Italy's support ... if such support could be, shall we say, *negotiated* beforehand, on mutually favourable terms ... naturally.'

Saint-Etienne returned the papers to his briefcase, secured the flap and sat back in his chair, a look of quiet satisfaction on his face. He had managed to deliver his message without it sounding like an ultimatum. He removed his pince-nez and proceeded to clean the lenses on a large white handkerchief. 'Perhaps Il Duce has plans which involve North Africa ... After all, it is not for us to know *what* great leaders are truly thinking. We each have territory in that region ... territories which, if our discussion is to bear fruit, would become lands of *potential* allies...' The Frenchman left the statement unfinished, but both men understood perfectly what had been implied.

'*If* such a thing were to be part of the greater plan, a great deal of fuel would be needed ... you understand? Of course, my dear Louis, I speak purely in hypothetical terms.'

Saint-Etienne smiled knowingly in the short pause which followed, as he returned his pince-nez to his inner pocket.

'Would one ally be able to assist another in that regard?' the count persevered.

'The British think that they control the oil in Iraq, even though their mandate there cannot last much longer. We have hopes of finding oil in our Syrian province, near the Iraqi border. And there is also the open oil market. He who purchases the crude oil is not necessarily the same one who finally uses it, for whatever ends. So yes, my dear Count, I can see no reason why such assistance would not be possible and forthcoming – *if* such an alliance were ever to arise, of course.'

Some while later the Count Vittorio Contini-Aosta sat comfortably in his padded chair staring across his desk at the large wall map opposite. As he looked at the French possessions marked in north-west Africa and the Middle East, he felt quite pleased with himself. The day's meetings had gone well – that with Louis Saint-Etienne de Monteschalle far better than the rest. He picked up his fountain pen and returned his gaze to the sheet of paper on which he was writing an official report. It would reflect the successful outcome of the recent negotiations with the French to hold joint naval manoeuvres in the Mediterranean. What it would not record was the beginning of highly secret negotiations towards forging a strong military alliance with Paris. In the morning, the count would ask for a meeting at the Palazzo Venezia and would tell Il Duce about that himself. For the moment, it was better for those negotiations, embryonic as they were, never to have officially taken place.

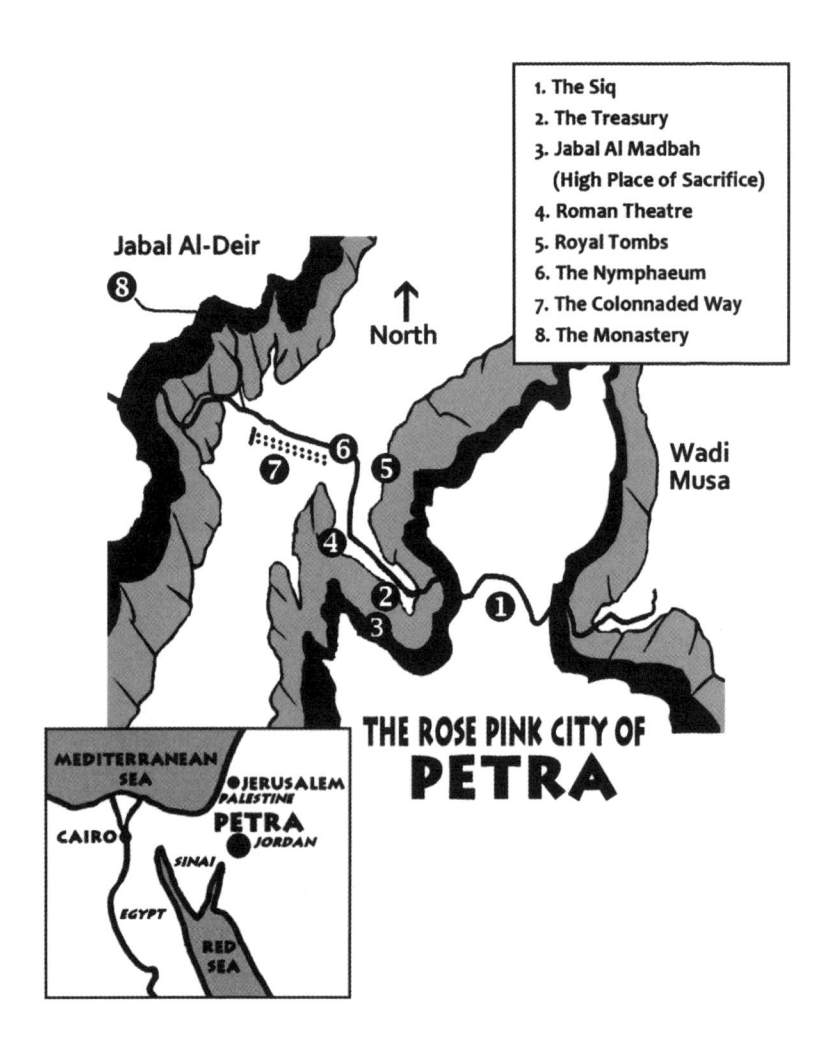

THE ROSE PINK CITY OF PETRA

1. The Siq
2. The Treasury
3. Jabal Al Madbah (High Place of Sacrifice)
4. Roman Theatre
5. Royal Tombs
6. The Nymphaeum
7. The Colonnaded Way
8. The Monastery

Jabal Al-Deir

Wadi Musa

North

20

Petra

The campsite – evening, Tuesday, 9th June 1931

The tour group had been made very comfortable in a little collection of tents pitched in the open space directly to the left of the Siq – the long, very high fissure in the rocks that was the only access to the rose-pink city of Petra.

A few days before, the group had left the small town of Wadi Musa and, on a bedraggled assortment of donkeys that had been hired for the purpose, travelled through the mile-long narrow gorge to reach the ruins. It had been a truly memorable journey. The animated chatter that had accompanied their departure lapsed into silence as each member fell under the spell and mysticism of Petra. The steady noise of the donkeys' breathing and the sounds of creaking saddle leather echoing off the surrounding rocks heightened the anticipation felt by each member. They were about to have their first view of a place that had been 'lost' for centuries until it had been rediscovered in 1812.

The first sighting of ornately carved rock on a monumental scale, basking in the late-afternoon sunshine, had not disappointed Rupert or his group's expectations. And now they were actually camped in Petra. To the right of the encampment lay the Siq and to the left rose the stupendous enormity of the so-called Treasury, a monumental façade carved, like so many of Petra's other wondrous monuments, into the living multicoloured rock. Ahead of them, protected between towering cliffs, lay the road to the rest of what was known of ancient Petra.

Uri Ben Zeev and his boys had established the camp in the heart of the Petra gorge, amongst the remnants of a long-vanished civilization and the dwellings of numerous present-day Bedouin families, who looked upon this invasion of their home with general good humour. Uri had even used the massive triclinium of the Treasury as a dining room, although, like almost all of the monuments in Petra, it was actually a tomb. Collapsible tables and chairs had been neatly arranged on the floor of compacted sand.

During the days since their arrival the tourists had had the ruins largely to themselves, sharing the massive space with the occasional group of Bedouin and a small party of archaeologists from the newly established Trans-Jordan Ministry of National Heritage and Antiquities. Despite looking tired, Professor Unsworth had revived considerably when they reached the area of the dig and even more so when the chief archaeologist had stepped forward to greet them. Hussein al Mohammed had studied history at Oxford, where, in the first year of his course, he had been one of the professor's students. Over the days since their arrival in the gorge, the tourists had all benefited from al Mohammed's vast store of knowledge of the Nabatean civilization and he and the professor were often to be seen engaged in lengthy discussions over the progress of the excavations, which were dotted around the ancient city.

It had been a busy three days. Now, as the desert stars blazed and twinkled high above the gorge, the little encampment had fallen silent. Uri's boys had finished their work for the day; Hussein al Mohammed and his archaeologists, who had been invited to join the tourists for dinner, had gone back to their encampment, and the rest of the group had retired to their respective tents for a night of restorative sleep.

But not everyone was quite ready for bed. In the Unsworths' tent, the professor had fallen into a fitful sleep. Sarah Unsworth was seated at a small, square collapsible table, which, together with the Tilley lamp, she had moved into the far corner of the tent so as to put her husband's camp bed in as much shadow as possible. She turned and looked over her shoulder at the sleeping form in the far corner. The breathing was regular, but troubled; the occasional soft, unintelligible moan escaped the dry lips. Turning back to the table, she opened her journal at June 9th and picked up her pen.

> *It has been a very exciting, but tiring day for George, who has been a little uncomfortable since we arrived in the heat of the Holy Land – not that he admits it. He tries valiantly to carry on as if nothing is wrong, but I fear that the disease has really started on its path to claim him as its own. We will, however, both be pleased that he can reach the end of his pilgrimage whilst he still has reasonably good control of his faculties. I am also very grateful that he has been given the opportunity of being the archaeologist guide on this trip, as it has taken his mind off things and has – unexpectedly – offered him the chance to fulfil his pilgrimage. I hope that we will have collected enough to enable him to set out on that journey when the time comes...*

She stopped writing and looked up, staring absently at the coarse weave of the canvas tent. In the dimly lit interior, from her position inside the cocoon of light cast by the Tilley lamp, the warp and weft seemed to be performing a confusing, intertwined dance in front of her eyes. For a moment, she fancied that the fabric strands took on the shape of arms, waving and beckoning. Sarah Unsworth rubbed her eyes gently. She was tired and she had accepted the inevitable outcome of the diagnosis of her husband's fatal illness; they had both done so – together. It was not the unstoppable progress towards what they both knew would be the finale of her husband's affliction that she found tiring and so sapping of her considerable reserves of tenacity and acceptance. It was not even the possible repercussions of the course of action she and her husband had decided upon. Rather, it was the sense of finality that sometimes threatened to engulf her and bury her in a cloud of blackness. She had accepted their position; what she found hard was accepting what was to follow. She returned her gaze to the neatly written lines of writing in her journal.

> ... I am suddenly reminded of the war. I felt a momentary flash of memory and saw myself once again sitting at my desk, in a tent not too dissimilar to this one, surrounded by the broken and damaged bodies of so many young souls, whilst writing up the ward log for the evening. What odd tricks our memory can play on us at times.
>
> Mr Winfield is proving to be a very competent manager of our tour. He is very pleasant and has gone out of his way to help George, but, thoughtfully, without making it too obvious that he knows how ill George is. Everyone on the staff is most kind and thoughtful. What a blessing to have the Reverend Fairweather with us, too. That really was an unexpected bonus. George has found his company invaluable – not so much for any spiritual consolation, as much as for the wealth of knowledge the man has about the Nabateans and the sites of the Holy Land. How refreshing to find a vicar who has the ability to think beyond the Scriptures! They are of one mind on several issues regarding the Holy Sites – or, more particularly, the High Place, here in Petra. Darling George and he have had many pleasant discussions, for which I am grateful. Tomorrow, George is looking forward to spending

the day with Mr al Mohammed and his archaeologists. That has been another great stroke of good luck, having one of his former students out here! I hope the day doesn't tire him too much. I suppose that we do have to face up to the reality that our time, in many respects, is limited. My greatest fear is that...

Professor Unsworth suddenly moaned and turned his head towards the light. Sarah got up and crossed over to his camp bed, a look of concern on her face.

'I'm here, my darling', she said, stroking the furrowed forehead and taking his hand in hers. It was clammy and warm to the touch. 'Rest gently, I will mop your brow ... it will make you feel a little cooler.'

Despite the cold of the desert night, which had already started to advance down the Siq and into the ravine where the tents were pitched, George Unsworth was quite hot – almost feverish. His wife poured a little water on her handkerchief and proceeded to mop her husband's brow.

'There we are ... is that better?' she asked when she had finished.

For some weeks now, the professor had been on a course of diamorphine – small doses which, they both knew, would have to increase considerably as the cancer headed towards its ultimate triumph. Now, the diamorphine in his system was having its own dream-like conversation with the professor and, although he had heard what she had said quite clearly, he found himself too tired to answer.

She gave his hand another squeeze, patted his brow with the cooling water one more time and then returned to her journal.

... I hope that I will be able to successfully complete George's wishes on my own in this rather hostile landscape. How fortunate that the Reverend Fairweather is here to help. There

is also Mr Hopkins – or Dr Hopkins, as I suppose I should say, although he has never shown any inclination to be addressed as such. After Mr Winfield told me that Mr Hopkins is a doctor, I did notice that he has a doctor's bag. That might prove useful, but I hope not necessarily so. Still, it is comforting to know that it might well be part of the solution.

She stopped writing to stifle a yawn. It was late – almost midnight – and she suddenly felt very sleepy. The past few days had been rather daunting and the prospect of the days ahead was even more so.

We both know that the conclusion to our journey and to George's pilgrimage cannot be far off now...

She let the ink dry and then closed the journal with a sigh. It was not a sigh of hopelessness, but rather one of resigned gratitude.

So far, so good, she reasoned, *that's probably the best way of looking at things. It's what George would want, too.*

21

London

Whitehall – mid-morning, Wednesday, 10th June 1931

Stephen Hopkins's uncle held a Waterman fountain pen, its cap pushed over the end of the barrel. Clasped between the well-manicured, but nicotine-stained fingers of his other hand a cigar smouldered, comfortingly. He was engrossed in a report into the current position regarding the future of the British mandate over Iraq and the likely short-term effects the transfer of power to a sovereign Kingdom of Iraq might have upon British interests in the Iraqi oil fields. It was always thus these days. There was always something, somewhere, which posed a potential threat to the well-being of the Empire. There were external threats: economic, military and political. There were also internal threats. India was restive again and there were even vague whispers of ideas of nationalism emerging from the African continent. The Uncle knew that most of what he was being fed was just that – whispers and innuendos – but he could not afford to be blasé or indifferent to any of it. Buried somewhere in the middle of it all there could well be a time bomb of truth. Where the Empire was concerned, he simply could not take the chance of ignoring anything. Nearer to home there was also the question of exactly who was allied to whom these days. How reliable were the Empire's traditional European allies? And what of the vexing question of the

United States? Sometimes it was difficult to ascertain exactly where *she* stood on certain points of foreign policy.

He tapped his cigar on the rim of the large ashtray that stood on the desk. He had no need to do so, because he had been so absorbed in the contents of the report that the end of his cigar had burned, smouldered and cooled and the ash had fallen off on to the blotter. He glanced up from the report and noticed the marble bust of Wellington which he kept on his desk; was he imagining things or had the face of the Iron Duke taken on a sternness that had not been discernible on the marble features before?

There was a soft knock on the highly polished mahogany door and the Uncle's private secretary entered, closing the door quietly behind him.

'Yes, Collingwood?'

'I am sorry to disturb you, Sir,' the secretary said as he held out a folder stamped with red lettering indicating it was urgent.

'What's this, then?'

'It has just been decoded, Sir. It is from the Embassy in Rome. Our people report that there is unusual activity in the naval bases at La Spezia and Taranto. It would appear that the Italian navy is up to something.' Collingwood stood silently in front of the desk, respectfully waiting for his superior to finish reading the contents of the folder. 'This concurs with what we received last week from the Consulate in Toulon.'

The Uncle took off his glasses and took a long draw on what was left of his cigar. It had gone out, so he reached for his matches and relit it. 'So what game are they playing, then, Collingwood, eh? Why would the French and the Italians start unusual naval activity at the same time? And why would they make it so easy for us to find out about it, I wonder?'

'Sir, you might recall that our people in Rome also

reported that Monsieur de Saint-Etienne Monteschalle was in Rome last week ... for the second time in as many months. We also know that he had a meeting with Count Contini-Aosta...'

'... And those two couldn't possibly be up to any good, could they?' the Uncle interjected. 'After all, we have the *Entente Cordiale* with Paris...' There was a pause in the conversation. 'On the other hand, Collingwood, perhaps that in itself is a perfectly good reason to be suspicious.' The Uncle closed the folder and handed it back. 'Best keep our eyes and ears open, just to be safe. Usual procedure and inform our people in the appropriate places. Thank you ... that will be all.'

'Sir,' said Collingwood, as he took the folder.

'One other thing,' continued the Uncle, stopping his secretary in mid-turn, 'have we had anything in from Palestine?'

'We have only received the usual reports, Sir ... on-going troubles between the Jews and the Arabs. There has been nothing yet concerning the other matter.'

'I see. Thank you, Collingwood.'

22

Petra

Morning, Thursday, 11th June 1931

The tourists had settled comfortably into a daily routine since their arrival in the rose-pink city. The mornings were given over to an early breakfast in the shade of the triclinium within the Treasury tomb. The options open to them for the day were then outlined by Rupert and it only remained for them to make the decision as to which of the day's offered activities appealed to them the most.

There were, however, those of the party who seemed to find it difficult to find anything which interested them. Mrs Hester Barnfield, the wife of an extremely wealthy manufacturer of radio valves, was an example of this: she found very little to arrest her attention other than the seemingly never-ending task of keeping Josiah Harrison away from her daughter.

As on previous mornings, Rupert rose from his place at the table. 'Ladies and gentlemen ... if I could have your attention, please.'

The gentle murmur of conversation subsided, leaving only the echoes of what had been said to float high up into the furthest recesses of the large room.

'Today I am pleased to say that we can offer you a choice of two expeditions. The first one will spend most of the day with Mr al Mohammed at his excavation and, indeed, it will be he, himself, who will be your guide for the experience...'

'More sand and stones... moved from here to there, but still more sand and stones...' muttered Hester Barnfield. She was not one to keep her opinions to herself.

Madeira glared at her mother disapprovingly. Only another couple of months and she would come into the money from her trust fund. She would then be extremely wealthy in her own right, which would mean not only financial freedom for life, but also that she could finally escape from the dominance of her mother. She turned her gaze on the fresh-faced young American photographer and smiled. Madeira liked him – even if her mother did not.

Rupert noted Mrs Barnfield's interjection, but he paid it little heed. Over the years he had learned to ignore all but the most blatant of interruptions. 'Mr al Mohammed has been excavating the main highway through the old city and has done extensive work on the complex of buildings at the far end of what he calls the ceremonial way. He will show you his work in detail, as well as some of the finds made thus far. There is a spectacular temple as well... it's called Qasr el-Bint and was dedicated to the two main Nabatean deities, Dusahara and al-Uzza...'

Stephen coughed, softly. Rupert was getting carried away with his enthusiasm again.

'That sounds like quite an effort. What's the second choice for today?' Hester Barnfield asked, in an even more disinterested manner.

'To explore the Theatre and then the Royal Tombs... literally just around the corner... I shall be leading that exploration,' replied Rupert, turning to look at her.

'I'm definitely opting for Hussein's offering,' enthused Professor Unsworth. 'No reflection on you, Winfield.'

His wife smiled at him encouragingly and by taking her

husband's hand she confirmed that she would accompany him.

For his part, Professor Unsworth now gave the outward appearance of being several years younger: his face had taken on an expression of inner calm, fused with controlled excitement. Sarah Unsworth ascribed this almost miraculous transformation in her husband down to the interest that had been rekindled by Hussein al Mohammed and his association with the extensive archaeological dig the Trans-Jordan government had sanctioned at Petra.

'I fancy that I shall be accompanying Mr Winfield to the Theatre and thence to the Royal Tombs,' said the Reverend Fairweather in his unintentionally pompous manner. 'I have read a little about the mixture of architectural styles to be seen amongst the tombs. I particularly want to see the Urn Tomb, which I believe was used as a church by the Greeks in the fifth century...'

'Joe, what interests you today?' asked Rupert, turning to look at the young American photographer.

'I've a mind to just tag along behind and then possibly go off and just do my own thing with my cameras ... if that's okay with you?'

'Of course,' replied Rupert, 'as you wish. Just make sure you have plenty of water and that you tell someone where you're off to.'

Harrison smiled his agreement.

'Mrs Barnfield...?' continued Rupert, turning his attention back to her.

'When you've seen one pile of ruins, you've seen them all. I'm afraid that I do not find speculation over the reason for a forest of columns having been broken off at their bases or toppled over on to their sides that much of a talking point' she said, with indifference. 'I'll opt for the one involving the least effort. We *both* will,' she added, turning to stare at her daughter.

'I want to go and see the main street and the temple. Even if *you're* too tired today, Mother, I'm full of beans and can't wait to get started.'

'Good ... then that's everyone settled,' said Rupert, cutting in before Mrs Barnfield could turn the conversation into an argument. 'We have donkey carts laid on, as well as a couple of camels for the more intrepid amongst us. Be warned, though, they are cantankerous beasts at the best of times. Let us say thirty minutes to get ourselves together and then we'll all meet on the steps outside the Treasury, *here.*' He gestured out through the high, massive doorway.

The party began to break up, as they made their individual ways back to their tents to prepare themselves for the day ahead. The echoes of Mrs Barnfield's voice and that of her equally headstrong daughter, both enmeshed in a raised battle of wills, reverberated in the spacious confines of the triclinium long after they had crossed the threshold and melted into the early-morning heat beyond.

'There's one on every tour,' said Stephen, as he brushed up against Rupert. 'If you don't mind, my dear chap, I'll do Hussein's offering as the land's a bit flatter and I'm not sure that scampering along the rocks amongst the Royal Tombs would do the old stump much good.'

Rupert smiled and took his friend by the arm. 'You can always stay in camp or go off with Uri in the cart, if you'd rather. He's a resourceful chap and says he's found out that someone in Wadi Musa has a small refrigeration unit that can produce ice. So he's off up there to get some.'

'What? And miss out on "The Adventure that is the Rose-Pink City"?' replied Stephen, quoting from the Company's promotional brochure with mock seriousness, 'not to mention the heat and the flies ... the bad-tempered English woman with the headstrong daughter ... and the professor, who is on his way out,' he added, dropping his voice to barely a whisper. 'Always station yourself where your help might be needed the most, eh?' As he spoke, he tapped the side of his nose with the ornate silver handle of his black walking stick.

'As you wish, my ... er, *our* guardian angel,' said Rupert, resisting the impulse to create a scandal by hugging his friend in public. 'I had best check with Uri to make sure he has the water and food organized,' he continued, trying to relinquish the vivid fantasy that had been evolving in his mind's eye.

'I think I'll have a quiet smoke back in the tent,' replied Stephen, as he turned to leave the cool of the triclinium. 'It will take the weight off the stump for a bit and I'll have a better chance at managing the rest of the day's exertions,' he added, smiling broadly and winking. Then, with increasing frustration in his voice, he continued, 'I also need to think about how we are going to try and track down our mysterious Scroll of Gershom. We've been here a few days now and not one person we've spoken to seems to know anything about it. So, maybe old Professor Longhurst at the British Museum got everything wrong, stirred up a hornet's nest and got us involved in a wild goose chase in the process.'

'I must say that I didn't expect that we'd find the thing just lying about when we got here,' suggested Rupert, 'but I have to admit that I'm also beginning to wonder if it exists at all. Apart from the locals around here, the Reverend Fairweather and friend Uri don't seem to have anything to say on the topic either.'

'Not a promising start, I do agree,' said Stephen, as he moved towards the doorway, 'but we'll just have to keep at it, I suppose. Someone, somewhere might know something ... You never can tell.'

The sun had commenced its decline to the horizon. Those tourists who had opted for the more strenuous expedition to the colonnaded main street of the ancient city and the nearby temple complex of Qasr el-Bint swayed rhythmically in the donkey cart on their return journey. The cart bumped and rattled its way down the once-magnificent avenue and back towards the campsite outside the Treasury, several miles away at the mouth of the Siq.

'Hussein is doing a fine job,' remarked Professor Unsworth, from under the ineffectual shade of the canvas awning that had been rigged up over the donkey cart. 'He is reasonably certain that what we are looking at today is just the tip of the iceberg in relation to what there is still to be found and excavated.' He took a swig of water from the canteen that his wife offered him. 'Do you know he also has a theory that there may even be influences from the Early Christian era as well? After all, for hundreds of years this was the major trading route from modern Turkey to the Near East and beyond. Goods, civilizations and faiths all flowed backwards and forwards, from the sea at Aqaba to Petra and then to Palmyra and beyond.' The professor's eyes were glinting with an intensity which matched that of the sun. Despite this animated conversation, he was beginning to look tired again.

'Do you know if Hussein has found anything of interest beyond where we were today?' asked Stephen. 'Surely there must be caves around these parts, what with all these cliffs...'

'Oh yes, he has,' replied the professor. 'He hasn't mentioned anything about any caves though, but he has recorded and photographed a rather splendid carved tomb behind us, through the cliffs over there...' He turned in his seat to indicate the receding cliffs behind them. 'It's called el-Deir, or the Monastery. He says it is like the Treasury, where our campsite is, only it's on a much larger and grander scale. Apparently it was originally a royal tomb, but it was later used as a church in the Byzantine period. Perhaps that's why it is now called the Monastery.'

'Professor, I thought Mr al Mohammed said that, given time, any of those Christian influences would be discovered,' said Madeira Barnfield, from behind dark glasses. Although she had a complexion and inner glow which almost outshone that of the professor and the sun combined, she also appeared tired and seemed a little downhearted.

'He hopes to find an *original* church one day,' replied the professor, 'one that was purpose-built for the new religion, unlike the older buildings that were just reused for Christian worship.'

The professor smiled at Madeira. He enjoyed her company and found her interest in the sites they had visited quite refreshing. He had also ascertained that it was at her insistence that she and her disagreeable mother had come on the tour in the first place. Her youthful enthusiasm had restored, somewhat, his confidence in the future of Britain's youth, large sections of which, he believed, seemed to be demoralized, demotivated, dispirited and generally uninterested in just about everything.

She smiled back, but her expression had a look of melancholy about it. 'They do say that everything should have its purpose,' she replied, turning to look ahead of them, up the steep winding path to where the Royal Tombs were cut into the huge edifice of the living cliffs themselves.

Sitting next to the tailgate of the cart, Dr Stephen Hopkins had also begun to consider what exactly Miss Madeira Barnfield's purpose had been that day. She had driven up the track with them and had spent the first part of the morning dutifully following along behind everyone else, as Hussein al Mohammed showed, explained and speculated amidst the heaps of excavated blocks, sand, statuary and carved stone. She had been there for the luncheon they had all shared, seated in the shade of a little clump of gnarled olive trees. After that, Stephen had no recall of seeing her again until almost the time they had started back to the campsite. Now she sat glowing and smiling in the swaying cart, the faint mockery of the first early-afternoon breezes playing around her hair and face.

Now then: has Madeira had a touch too much sun today ... why is she a little flushed? Or, I wonder, is she experiencing a moment of post-coital tristesse ... she certainly has a look of fulfilment about her, almost of graduation to the adult world, but she appears anxious; or, on the other hand ... has she, perhaps, been experimenting with narcotics and the effects of cocaine or morphine are wearing off ... pity I can't see the pupils of her eyes, Stephen speculated. *I shall have to keep my eye on that young lady!*

Just as the cart was making its way through the ruins of the triumphal arch that had once spanned the ceremonial way, they were hailed by Joe Harrison, who seemed to suddenly step out of the very rocks themselves.

'How do?' he said, in his usual cheery voice, 'Okay if I catch a lift with you guys?'

'We don't mind at all, provided the driver thinks that the donkey can cope with the extra load,' replied the professor.

Before anyone else could say anything, the Bedouin driver of the little cart appeared at Harrison's elbow and eagerly helped him and his heavy rucksack of equipment into the cart.

'Steady on there, fella, there's some mighty expensive equipment in that bag,' Harrison said, as the cumbersome rucksack was manhandled over the side of the cart.

'I've got it, Joe,' said Madeira, as the American settled himself into the space next to her.

'Well, thank you, Ma'am,' he replied, flashing his white teeth in a disarming, though genuine smile.

The little cart moved off down the track, the tired donkey finding the extra load manageable, as the terrain at that end of the track, nearest the Siq, was relatively flat.

'What brings you out here on your own?' asked Stephen

casually. As he spoke the penny dropped and he suddenly knew where Madeira Barnfield had disappeared to that afternoon. And, more pointedly, with whom she had spent her time. He smiled at the thought: something between a smirk and a knowing leer. *You don't have to be a medical doctor to make that diagnosis!*

'I got some swell shots of the Royal Tombs ... that one of the Urn, with all those arches. Then I told Mr Winfield that I wanted to go off and do my own thing. After all, I don't want all of my photographs to be the same,' he said, laughing, 'but everywhere you look in this place is worth a photograph. Early yesterday morning I was up on top of that hill up there before dawn,' he continued excitedly, gesturing up to the towering crags of a nearby mountain.

'That mountain is called Jabal al-Madhbah ... Mount Seir ... or the High Place of Sacrifice. There is even a belief that it is the real Mount Sinai in the Bible,' explained the professor. 'It is a very ancient site.'

'Gee, the High Place of Sacrifice,' repeated the American, who seemed more in awe of the name than of the looming bulk of the mountain. 'Well, you wouldn't believe the fantastic views from up there ... and the brilliant colours on the cliffs on the other side as the sun comes up. They change from grey to blood red to pale pink. I got some swell shots ... in colour.'

'And did you find anything else of interest?' asked Professor Unsworth.

If you can call an attractive young woman like Miss Barnfield 'something of interest', then yes, Professor, our young American certainly did make a find this afternoon, deduced Stephen.

'Sure did, there are some great ruins down there ... on the right ... near to where I guess you folks were,' Harrison said, pointing lazily back down the track in the direction from which they had travelled.

'I think you're very clever to be taking all these pictures,' said Madeira Barnfield, brushing some dust off his shoulder. 'I can't wait to see them.'

There was something in the way in which she spoke and in the gesture she made that confirmed Stephen's suspicions. As the little cart continued to sway during the final few minutes of its journey back to the campsite, he gave serious consideration to the fact that there was a lot more going on between these two than would meet with the mother's approval.

At the same time as Stephen Hopkins sat swaying in the donkey cart speculating as to Madeira Barnfield's whereabouts during that afternoon and where Joe Harrison had sprung from, Rupert was shepherding his sole remaining charge back down the steep incline to the sandy track that ran along the natural fissure in the rocks below the soaring façades of the Royal Tombs.

'Splendid ... quite splendid,' said the Reverend Fairweather, as he removed his panama and mopped his perspiring brow. 'The Urn Tomb is truly magnificent ... and what engineering ability they must have had to be able to construct all of those arches, one above the other. And we think we are so clever to be able to build a structure of several storeys with *flat* floors!' He replaced his hat and waddled off down the path, towards the waiting donkey cart.

None of the tourists had felt either brave or stupid enough to have even contemplated a camel ride.

'What a pity Mrs Barnfield felt unwell and had to return to camp so soon,' continued the vicar, as Rupert caught up with him. 'She didn't really have the opportunity to see much at all ... what a pity!'

'She decided it was for the best,' added Rupert non-committally. He had had plenty of experience with his more difficult guests suddenly becoming 'unwell' when it suited them. This arrogant and sometimes bad-tempered woman – who, he correctly assumed, was still in a fit of pique over her daughter's wilful display of opposition to her parental authority – was no exception. He had been glad to consign her into the care of one of Uri's boys, with instructions to take her back to camp.

In fact, once the dampening influence of Mrs Barnfield had disappeared up the winding path, past the impressive ruins of the Theatre, Rupert's small group – the vicar and the photographer – had spent a pleasant hour or so exploring the Urn Tomb. Rupert had just suggested moving on to the next tomb, the so-called Silk Tomb, when Joe Harrison announced that he would go off and take some more photographs further up the valley – towards the ceremonial way.

'My film's limited, y'see, and I've got some really swell exposures of this tomb. I don't want to end up with all my photographs of the same thing.'

Rupert squinted off in the direction in which Harrison was pointing and decided that the American was probably quite correct. The other tombs, which were cut into the cliff face and which extended off to their right, did seem to be all rather similar.

'As you wish, Joe, but where are you going exactly? And are you sure that you have enough water?'

The American patted his canteen. 'Sure have. I've had three mouthfuls since we left camp, so there's plenty left. I reckon I'll wander off over in that direction,' he said, pointing vaguely in the direction of Qasr El-Bint and the stumps of the columns which still lined the ceremonial way. 'I remember that Hussein told us of a new discovery they've made near there. "The Camp", I think he called it the other evening at dinner. He thinks it could be the commander's quarters of the legion that was stationed here around the time of Jesus. Now that's something to take a photograph of, yes siree. And don't you fret yourself about me. I'll make my own way back to camp.'

As Rupert watched him stroll off towards the distant horizon, he had no recall whatsoever of Hussein al Mohammed having mentioned anything at all about a recent find in Petra of something he thought could possibly be connected with the legions. *I must ask Hussein about that, the next time I see him.*

By three o'clock the donkey cart from Rupert's outing was just about to reach the box-canyon in which the campsite had been pitched. The promise of a cooling breeze had whispered down the Siq and had temptingly suggested itself to the air around the tents. Cut into the cliffs and towering above them stood the Treasury. The cliff face, like a chameleon, had started its daily routine of changing colour as the sun began to decline; this simple action determined the different levels of reflected light that permeated the canyon. There, sunset would happen long before the sun itself finally dipped below the horizon for the day.

Some fifteen minutes later the other donkey cart carrying the party that had ventured to the archaeological dig arrived back at camp. As the passengers stepped down from the cart and made their tired, hot and dusty ways back to their respective tents, Stephen walked back to the turn in the track to where a group of Bedouin were selling some curios – he suddenly felt the urge to see if they had anything interesting for sale and to, maybe, find a clue to help find this elusive Gershom Scroll.

Having made a satisfactory purchase, he too returned to the dark shadows of the tent he shared with Rupert and flopped down in a chair to take the weight off his aching stump. Swinging his left leg up onto a stool, he reached for his cigarette case, as he reflected further on the day's developments.

Suddenly, his attention was drawn to some whispering outside in the walkway between the tents. He cocked his ear to try and hear what was being said.

'... the other way. She won't know because...'

The voice dropped to a whisper, too soft to be audible.

'... don't care. Another few weeks and then I...' A second voice, a woman's, joined the conversation.

'... but I don't want to cause any...' said the first voice, the male, but this time with something that sounded like urgency borne of sincerity.

'... hell! She's coming this way...' cut in the female voice suddenly.

'I'll get rid of her,' replied the male voice, with considerable urgency, this time identifying itself as American by his accent.

As Stephen continued to stare at the opening of the tent, the flaps were thrust aside and the figure of Madeira Barnfield backed in, drawing the flaps closed in front of her. In the process, she knocked over a small camp table, upon which rested Stephen's black medical bag. She did not see Stephen sitting in the corner.

'Mr Harrison,' boomed another female voice from outside, 'where is Madeira?' The voice was angry and barely civil.

'Mrs Barnfield, how are y' doing?'

'That is of no consequence!' snapped back the other voice. 'Where is Madeira?'

'She was not in our group ... as you know, Mrs Barnfield, but she did come back with Professor Unsworth's party ... a couple of minutes ago.' He made no reference to his having caught a lift with them. 'Perhaps she has gone off to look for an iced drink. Mr Winfield did say there might be some ice in camp this afternoon. I fancy a cold drink myself. Shall we go over to the Treasury and see if we can find something?'

The voices moved off becoming indistinct and then inaudible.

Holding the flaps of the tent closed in her hands, Madeira Barnfield let out a long sigh and dropped her shoulders with relief. Then she turned slightly and picked up the table and the medical bag, the catch of which had sprung open in the act of falling off the table. Still bending and with the open bag in her hand, she turned around to pick up the couple of items that had fallen out of it. As she did so, the rest of the interior of the tent came into view.

'Oh, my God!' she exclaimed, as she spotted Stephen sitting in the far corner of the tent.

'Miss Barnfield,' said Stephen softly, 'perhaps it would be best to keep your voice down. The last thing I imagine you need at this moment is for your mother to join us here, in the confines of this tent.'

'What? Er ... yes, of course ... and no ... thank you ... I wouldn't,' she responded, following his sensible advice and calming down visibly.

Any more than I would imagine that you would have liked her to be with you when you and Harrison were up to whatever it was you were up to this afternoon, he thought, a smile spreading across his face, as he imagined the possibility of young Madeira and Harrison making passionate love in the desert sands. *Would Rupert and I have succumbed to such an opportunity if it had ever presented itself?*

'I'm sorry to have disturbed you ... I have to go now,' she continued, putting the medical bag back on to the small table. She opened the tent flaps and, after carefully checking that the alleyway outside was empty, she made as if to exit. Halfway through the tent entrance, she suddenly stopped and turned to look at Stephen again. It was almost as if she intended to say something. Stephen raised his eyebrows, inviting her to do so, but, as suddenly as she had turned to speak, she was gone.

That's interesting, thought Stephen, as he finally lit his cigarette. *A very attractive firebrand. I wonder if it is she who sees something in Mr Harrison, or if it is Mr Harrison who sees something in her?*

23

Petra

Early evening, Thursday 11th June 1931

'I say, is that ice?' exclaimed Madeira Barnfield, as she entered the triclinium for the evening meal.

'And we have something special from the ice box for desert this evening,' added Uri, as he offered her a tall glass of her favourite tipple, the outside of which was covered with rivulets of condensation.

'How exciting,' she answered, as she walked over to her allotted space at the large table that had been set up in the middle of the cavernous room. 'Good evening, everyone,' she called, taking in the faces of those already gathered at the table. 'Sorry if I'm a bit late. Oh, Joe seems to be late, too,' she added, with a slight chuckle.

And I have a pretty shrewd idea why that might be, thought Stephen, as he stood next to the entrance, glass in hand, finishing off the last of his cigarette. She had said nothing further on the subject of her sudden intrusion into the tent earlier that afternoon.

'I think today really took its toll on some of us,' offered the professor, who was still illuminated by the inner glow of satisfied achievement. 'Sarah will be along shortly.'

'Are you better this evening, Mother?' continued Madeira. 'I do hope the sun was not too strong for you.'

Mrs Barnfield turned the colour of the pink stone which

encased them. Her daughter continued without waiting for her mother's reply.

'I hope you remembered to drink a lot of water during your expedition ... One always needs to avoid dehydration in these very hot climes, as Mr Winfield is always telling us.' She flashed a disarming smile at Rupert, turning the back of her head to where her mother was sitting.

Hester Barnfield's anger at such blatant provocation was barely concealed behind her flushed cheeks.

'Indeed one does, Miss Barn ... Mady,' answered Rupert. He, too, had sensed the antagonism between mother and daughter. He cast a furtive glance at Stephen, who was taking his place at the table.

'Mrs Unsworth, good evening,' said Uri Ben Zeev, as the professor's wife entered. She looked a little flushed, but whether from the exertion of the day or something else more recent, it was impossible to say.

'Good evening,' she said, 'I hope I haven't delayed things.'

'Not at all, dear lady,' said the Reverend Fairweather, as he gallantly rose to his feet and held back the chair for her to sit down. 'I trust everything is satisfactory?' he continued softly over her shoulder, as she settled herself.

She did not answer, but merely smiled before opening her napkin and smoothing it on to her lap. She cast a quick glance at her husband, who smiled back, and then sat staring through the high entrance doorway at the darkness outside. 'Oh, here's Mr al Mohammed,' she said, almost involuntarily as the pleasant Jordanian strode in.

'And Joe,' added Madeira, 'the table is now complete.'

The evening meal had lived up handsomely to the exacting standards set by Uri Ben Zeev and it was past ten o'clock before the campsite started to settle down for the night. The professor and the Reverend Fairweather were left absorbed in conversation in the triclinium as Joe Harrison strolled off, whistling, to his tent and the Barnfields made their way to theirs, daggers drawn, saying nothing to each other. Sarah Unsworth disappeared to their tent, with the parting comment to her husband that he should take all the time he needed chatting to the vicar.

'Tomorrow will be a day for further exploration,' Hussein al Mohammed said, as he stood on the threshold of the entrance, waiting for his camel to be brought. 'We will journey beyond the ceremonial way and the Temple of Qasr El-Bint, up into the higher hills to the Monastery, as it is called by some. We call it El-Deir. You will have your breath taken away by the sheer size of the structure and the beauty of the architecture. It is the largest building found so far here in Petra. And who knows,' he continued, mounting his camel and smiling broadly at Stephen, 'we might even discover a cave up there in the hills, along our route.'

He bade everyone a safe night's rest, before plodding off down the path with his two Bedouin guards, towards his own campsite.

Stephen laughed good-naturedly at the friendly Jordanian's quip, as he and Rupert waved them good night from the top of the steps. However, they silently contemplated the lack of any progress concerning the Scroll of Gershom and its likely hiding place, if it even existed at all. Re-entering the triclinium, Stephen took a small piece of marble from his trouser pocket and crossed to the table.

'Excuse me, gentlemen,' interrupted Stephen, as he and Rupert sat down across the table from the other two men. 'I appreciate the lateness of the hour, but I was wondering if I could call upon your expertise...'

'But of course, Hopkins... We are entirely at your disposal,' responded the professor.

'I have, shall we say, *acquired* this from one of the Bedouin this afternoon ... and I wonder if you would be able to translate the inscription ... it may be of interest...' added Stephen, placing a small square of marble in front of the professor.

'My field of expertise is Egypt and Egyptian hieroglyphics,' apologized Rupert. 'I'm afraid I'm not much help here in Petra.'

The professor and the vicar both laughed softly, as if to brush Rupert's protestation away as completely unnecessary.

'As, indeed, I would be if this were Thebes or Memphis,' responded the professor generously. 'Now ... let us see what we have here. You say that you obtained this from a Bedouin?' asked the professor, as he studied the marble fragment. 'I would not have thought of you as a collector of souvenirs, Hopkins.'

'And you would be quite correct in that assumption,' said Stephen, 'but one has the interests of historical research in mind. I have a relative who works at the British Museum, who once showed me something which looked very similar,' he lied convincingly. 'It turned out to be an inscription of the utmost significance.' He chuckled as if to make light of the statement.

'Are you collecting likely artefacts for the museum?' the vicar asked. Then, recalling previous conversations Stephen had embarked upon during this trip, he added, 'That might explain your interest in caves in this area...?'

'Possibly...'

The triclinium fell silent, as the professor studied the incised characters on the piece of marble. A minute or so later, he looked up and smiled broadly. 'Gentlemen,' he said, a twinkle flashing from his eyes, 'this is a most extraordinary piece. It has got to be a fine example of the art...'

A flash of excited expectation surged around the table.

'What does it say, Professor?' asked the vicar, before anyone else had the chance to ask the same question.

'What I meant to say is that it is a fine example of the art of the *forger*,' continued Unsworth. 'It looks genuine, but I am afraid that it is not. This has been made to trap the unwary tourist ... No reflection on your good self,' added the professor, smiling at Stephen. 'I would suggest that someone has cleverly tried to copy parts of a genuine inscription from somewhere, on to a piece of marble, but they have made a total hash of it in the process.' He looked at Stephen with something bordering sincere regret. 'I really am most awfully sorry; this is simply a piece of worthless nonsense.'

24

Bury St Edmunds, Suffolk

Hawkhurst Aeronautics – late afternoon, Thursday, 11th June 1931

The offices and assembly hangars of Hawkhurst Aeronautics were a hive of activity. The company had an almost full order book following the owners' recent trip to the United States. In the planning department, sketches for the new Avenger machine, with its promise of record-breaking speeds, had long since been transformed into production blueprints and the assembly lines had already carefully followed these instructions to produce several of the revolutionary, lightweight aluminium craft. The first three of the American orders had been completed and delivered; in their turn, they had generated yet further orders. The mood of quiet, yet barely restrained, optimism that pervaded all corners of the offices of Hawkhurst Aeronautics was matched outside by the brilliant sunshine of a midsummer's day. The telephone on Richard Stirling's desk rang. He answered it.

'Yes?' he said absently, as he studied the latest set of sales projections in front of him.

'I'm sorry to disturb you, Mr Stirling, but there is a gentleman on the line who has asked to speak to Miss Alexandra or Mr Lawrence. As both of them are in London today, should I put him through to you?'

'Er ... yes, very well, Miss Lewis, put him through.'

Richard Stirling was a distant cousin on the Hawkhursts' mother's side. He had joined the company because it was felt that, in the absence of any children from their uncle, the brother and sister would benefit from their older cousin's expertise with business and figures. It was also a way of keeping things in the family, as their father used to say.

'I have the gentleman for you, Mr Stirling,' said the pert voice on the other end of the line.

'Good afternoon, can I speak to Mr Stirling?' demanded a deep, well-educated voice.

'Hello ... er, yes ... indeed, it is he who is speaking. How can I help you?'

'I had hoped to be able to have a short, preliminary discussion with either Miss Alexandra or Mr Lawrence Hawkhurst, in connection with your Avenger machines.'

Richard Stirling was not very good with people – figures were his speciality. He had found them to be honest and reliable, which, from his experience, was more than could be said for most humans. 'I am afraid that they are both out of the office today ... but maybe I can assist you, if you have an enquiry.' He felt it unnecessary to tell the stranger that they had gone to London to try and convince the 'dinosaurs' of the Air Ministry, as Lawrence called them, that the days of the cavalry were now well and truly over and that the future lay in the skies – preferably in skies full of powerful, lightweight aluminium Hawkhurst fighter machines.

'I represent a very influential client, who has expressed an interest in the Avenger. I should like to make an appointment to visit your offices and discuss the matter further. Could that be done?'

'Most certainly it could, but I have to just mention that our order book is extremely full at the moment and that there is a considerable waiting list...'

'That is most certainly good news for your company,'

continued the deep voice, 'and, quite naturally, I am sure you appreciate that, at this early stage, I would prefer neither to discuss the nature of my enquiry in any substantial detail, nor the person whom I represent. I can, nevertheless, assure you that my client is a person of considerable importance and influence. My instructions are to discuss the delivery of a single Avenger but with the understanding that, should my client be happy that the aircraft comes up to expectation, there will be orders for others ... perhaps as many as ten or twelve...'

Richard Stirling took off his glasses and rubbed the bridge of his nose. 'That is most interesting,' he said, 'and, of course, your client would receive our most urgent attention. Am I correct in assuming that such an order would be from a...'

'Mr Stirling, I am sure that you will appreciate that this is a delicate matter and certainly not one to be discussed over the telephone wires. I will be able to answer any questions when we meet,' continued the caller, cutting across Richard Stirling's question.

'Of course ... just as you wish.'

Richard Stirling had been about to redirect the call back to his secretary for her to make the necessary appointment, but now he had second thoughts. This man, whoever he was, sounded earnest in what he said and, with the promise of a further substantial order, he needed to be handled with kid gloves. 'Let me just consult the appointments diary a moment, Mr, er...'

'Greening, Jerome Greening.'

'Thank you, Mr Greening. If I could ask you to hold the line for a few moments, I need to consult our diary?'

Stirling held the receiver tightly to his chest, where the fabric of his waistcoat deadened the sound of his voice.

'Miss Lewis!'

Almost immediately, his office door opened and a smartly

dressed, pretty blonde woman filled the doorway, an enquiring expression on her face.

'Would you bring in the appointments diary ... as quick as you can please.'

Some minutes later, Stirling had resumed his perusal of the figures on the desk in front of him and Miss Lewis had replaced the appointments diary on her desk in the outer office.

Well, that will please Alex when she gets back, he speculated. He had long ago realized that she was the driving force and Lawrence, capable as he was, was the force who had to be driven. What he could not have known, however, was that a single telephone call, as intoxicatingly exciting as it seemed at the time, was to have far-reaching consequences – consequences of which, even in the wildest excesses of a fertile imagination, could not possibly have been conceived of.

25

Petra

Approaching midnight, Thursday, 11th June 1931

Despite the lateness of the hour, the campsite was far from still.

'I cannot express my gratitude to you, my dear fellow, for all the spiritual support you have given me since we started the expedition and for the support you are still to give.' George Unsworth looked tired and his features, lit by the shadowy light cast by the Tilley lamps on the table were, for the first time, drawn into a ghastly mask of what was to eventually befall him.

Grotesque shadows, out of all proportion, were cast upon the high, multicoloured rock walls, as if to recall the frenzy of a bizarre witches' Sabbath or lost religious rite of the ancient Nabatean civilization. It was only in the immediate area where the clergyman and the professor-historian sat that an aura of calm tranquillity prevailed.

The professor continued: 'And how fortunate that I should have found someone of your undoubted academic ability, who is as well versed in the same theories about the ancient sites as I am. Is it not a strange coincidence?'

'I am pleased to have been the instrument of such help,' replied the vicar. 'God moves in mysterious ways...'

'...And men in ways even more mystifying!' added the professor, laughing. He removed a handkerchief from his pocket and wiped his face with it. He was finding the evening close and the air in the confines of the triclinium humid.

'Are you certain in your own mind that the time is now?' asked the vicar.

'I ... *we* are,' replied the professor. 'I came here as a result of a whim of Fate, which has allowed me pleasantly and unexpectedly to pursue my own pilgrimage ... following my own Via Dolorosa, if you like, although I must say that I am at peace and have found it anything but sad. To be honest, there were times recently when I could not see how this was to be accomplished, but, nevertheless, here we are and I am more than fortunate to have had Sarah's support.'

'And you have reconciled yourself to ... shall we say, being at odds with the teachings of the Church on the matter?'

'My dear fellow, I believe that to *have* faith is one thing, but the important thing is what one *does* with it. Belief in a faith for its own sake is the rocky path to hypocrisy.'

The vicar smiled and spread his hands in a noncommittal gesture of neutrality. They had had similar conversations before. 'At least we agree on the question of Mount Sinai,' he said, inclining his head slightly.

'We do,' replied the professor, who was enjoying their conversation enormously. 'Mount Seir ... Jabal al-Madhbah ... the real mountain of Moses, not the one in the Sinai Peninsula, but here in Petra, the ancient Land of Edom.'

'"God calleth me out of Seir", Isaiah, Chapter 21, Verse 11,' said the vicar, 'and also "Set Thy face against Mount Seir", Ezekiel, Chapter 35, Verse 2.'

'Not to mention "The Lord came from Sinai and rose up from Seir unto them", Deuteronomy, Chapter 33, Verse 2,' added the professor.

'Indeed,' nodded the vicar, 'there are a great many references to Mount Seir in the Scriptures ... mainly the Old Testament, naturally.'

'Naturally ... somewhat convincing I would say, even allowing for translation from the original.'

'But what do you think about Mount Paran? That is also said to be in Sinai,' asked the vicar, a mischievous twinkle in his eye, 'and there are many references to that, too.'

'Who is to say, my dear fellow?' interjected the professor. 'That is the beauty of faith ... personal interpretation rather than absolute obedience to an established doctrine ... No offence meant to your good self.'

'And none whatsoever taken, I can assure you,' replied the vicar. 'As long as you are convinced that this is the time and the place ... and that you have made up your own mind...' There was a slight pause, as the vicar fixed the professor with his gaze, '... All I can do is to advise...'

For a moment the professor said nothing, before looking the Reverend Fairweather straight in the face. 'I have been told by the experts in Harley Street that I have perhaps another six months at the very most. To be honest, I have started to feel the approach of the inevitable.' He smiled and raised his eyebrows. 'The offer of this trip was too good an opportunity to miss ... one could almost be forgiven for thinking it was divinely inspired.'

The vicar said nothing, but repeated his gesture of neutrality.

'Even if it is before the predicted time, there could not possibly be a *better* time than the present. I have no desire to fade gradually, as does a dying fire. On that point both Sarah and I are in full agreement. I am very fortunate in having her total support in this.' The professor had grown very serious. 'She is fully aware of the circumstances and has long ago accepted them. She is also fully aware of the possibility of repercussions.' His voice dropped to barely a whisper, before abruptly changing the subject. 'If truth be told, my dear fellow, we are all of the Jewish family, as was Moses. Jesus was a Jew, as were His Apostles. It is only what man has done with belief

'... with *faith*, if you will, that has separated us from one another since those distant days. I believe that Moses received instruction from God ... right here, on top of Jabal al-Madhbah ... Mount Seir ... and I can think of no better place from which to return to ... wherever.' He chuckled softly, as if to lighten the topic of conversation. 'You might like to think of it as the alpha and omega of a journey.'

'The site is, indeed, a very ancient one. It is believed to pre-date the Nabateans by a considerable time,' offered the vicar. 'It is more than possible that the mountain was sacred at the time of Moses. And the town out there could also be a clue – Wadi Musa ... the Valley of Moses.'

The two men sat silently for a few minutes, each lost in their own thoughts.

'Perhaps that was why I was destined to embark on this tour of the Holy Land,' said the vicar eventually, 'to act as a sort of Good Samaritan to a fellow traveller.'

On the other side of the campsite any thoughts of the Good Samaritan were the last thing on the troubled mind of Hester Barnfield. She had finally drifted off into a fitful, troubled sleep, in which the unwelcome vision of Josiah Harrison persistently refused to go away. In her anger-shrouded, frustrated mind she had even reached the point of asking herself if there was any point in continuing to protect her ungrateful, wayward daughter from speculators who would be after the considerable fortune the young woman was about to inherit.

In many ways, Hester Barnfield was reluctantly looking forward to her daughter's independence and the transfer of any responsibility from her own tired and frustrated shoulders to those of her daughter. Once that happened there would be nothing she could legally do to prevent her daughter doing anything she wanted.

In the camp bed next to her mother, Madeira Barnfield's thoughts couldn't have been more different. In *her* mind, she had drifted off to relive an erotic memory of that afternoon, in which Joe Harrison had featured so prominently, but in a totally different role from that in which her mother had cast him.

Madeira felt again the thrill of meeting the handsome American behind the secure cover of a grove of olive trees, incongruously growing from amidst the tumbled ruins of a former temple in the ancient city. The olive trees themselves were the product of carelessly scattered seed, spat out centuries before by Bedouin or by the drivers of a passing camel train. That afternoon, seed had again been spilled.

In her memory, Madeira felt again the soft sand of the secluded grove of trees on her back, as she reached up and undid the buttons on Joe Harrison's shirt and he, in turn, undid her blouse. She felt again the dappled coolness of the overhanging branches on her exposed skin, as he squatted over her, opening his own cloth barrier and revealing the urgency of his own desire. Then she felt the shape of his chest, as he gently covered her, allowing his hands to find their way to her unprotesting breasts, each capped with an expectant, aroused nipple, like the bastion of some Crusader castle. In her sleep, she remembered his movements, fluid and regular, like the motion of the olive trees above them, swaying gently in the caress of the early afternoon breeze. A smile crossed her sleeping face, as she remembered the ecstasy of climax, and she gave an involuntary, low moan. Her hand went to the empty valley between her breasts, where Joe Harrison's perspiring face had been buried, as the rest of his young body shuddered with spasms of release.

As she had strolled contentedly back to where she knew the others would be assembling for the cart ride back to the campsite, she had tried to rationalize the situation. She had fallen for a young photographer who had nothing to offer her other than himself. In fact, she realized that she loved him and that thought was only exceeded in its pleasantness by the extreme irritation that same recognition would cause her mother, once she found out. Joe Harrison had not been her first lover, but this time she felt strangely attracted to this man in a way not previously experienced. He was honest and straightforward, not like the others that her mother had introduced her to; they had all tried to be something other than what they were. Madeira Barnfield had long ago decided to distance herself from the artificial world of the social standing in which her wealth and background placed her. This American was different. He really did seem to be the person he appeared to be. She liked that. She also liked the faint smell of peppermint on his breath. He always seemed to be chewing. Perhaps she, too, would start buying packets of the same chewing gum he always had in his shirt pocket.

In their tent, Rupert and Stephen were also preparing themselves for their night's rest.

'Sorry about your souvenir. Even if it is a fake, it's still a good memento of our trip.'

'Oh, don't worry about it, old chap, the locals have to make a living somehow and besides, it was rather over optimistic of me to even think that it might give us a clue to where the rocks burn.'

As they undressed they continued to review the day's activities.

'I'll tell you what I found most extraordinary,' said Stephen. 'Miss Barnfield burst in here like a frightened faun and then wreaked havoc with the furniture. Then, when she finally saw me sitting over there looking at her, she nearly passed out with the shock.'

'But why was she hiding?' asked Rupert, as he removed his dinner jacket. 'And from whom?'

'The dreaded mother, from the sounds of what I could hear,' whispered Stephen, sitting on the edge of his camp bed, the artificial lower part of his left leg propped up neatly against the folding chair. 'There was also the distinct vibration of an American "twang" in the air, so I should imagine that Mr Harrison featured largely in the script. Did you notice the way they were mooning at each other during dinner?'

'I did, but they've been all over each other since we started this tour,' added Rupert, as he hung up the coat hanger holding his dinner jacket next to Stephen's. 'It would seem that I was well and truly hoodwinked by Joe Harrison this afternoon. During our visit to the Royal Tombs, he said that he wanted to go off on his own to photograph a new site that he had heard about ... something about Hussein's discovery of what might be the commander's quarters of the legion that was stationed here around the time of Christ. I was made to feel a complete fool when I later asked Hussein about his exciting discovery.'

'And was Hussein enthusiastic about the discovery of this site?' Stephen quipped, suspecting what Hussein's reply would be.

'Hardly! He looked at me in a rather odd way and made it perfectly clear that he didn't seem to know what I was talking about. He said that he has found no such thing as a Roman site ... and he was at great pains to politely tell me that my timeline is completely wrong. It would appear that Harrison was talking pure nonsense.'

'No flies on our Mr Harrison,' said Stephen, laughing, 'and you're quite right: he and the lovely Madeira *have* been all over each other.' He then recounted his deductions concerning the whereabouts of Madeira Barnfield during the afternoon and why Joe Harrison had detached himself so covertly from Rupert's group. 'They're up to a bit of rumpy-pumpy, I'd say,' he added. 'No wonder the mother is incandescent. From what we've seen of her attitude to her daughter's ... shall we say *fulfilment* ... it's no wonder that in her eyes our Mr Harrison is definitely *persona non grata.*'

'And I suppose her money would be a big help towards Harrison's career,' added Rupert, as he started to secure the tent flaps for the night, his naked, muscular shape outlined tantalizingly on the coarse canvas of the tent. 'I like him. He seems a decent sort of chap to me. I wouldn't have thought of him as a gold digger, though. He's never given even the vaguest hint that he has aspirations in that direction. Ready?' he asked smiling, as he turned around.

'Ready, willing and able, as always,' replied Stephen, 'but before pleasure I must work. I'm neglecting my professional calling. Hand me my bag, if you would, my dear chap. Our friend Miss Barnfield knocked the whole thing flying this afternoon and I still haven't put things back in Bristol fashion. It wouldn't do to be called to an emergency with one's tools of the trade in disarray.'

Stephen carefully emptied the bag, spreading the contents on the camp bed in front of him. Then he packed everything away again, but before he closed the bag he held up a small glass ampoule, containing a fine white powder, and turned to look at Rupert.

'I say, my dear chap, would you mind having a ferret around on the floor ... over at the entrance, where the table was knocked over. See if you can find a couple of these ...'

Rupert did as he was asked, but, after the most careful of inspections, he found nothing. 'Nothing on this part of the floor,' he said, standing up again. 'What is it?'

'It is a miracle drug, which relieves pain and suffering,' said Stephen softly and purposefully. 'It is also highly addictive and quite dangerous.'

'What is it?' asked Rupert, as he sat down next to the doctor.

'Diamorphine...' replied Stephen, returning the ampoule to his bag before securing the clasp, '...and there are two ampoules missing.'

26

Petra

Very early morning, Friday, 12th June 1931

The relaxed daily routine of the tourists had suddenly and abruptly been thrown into disarray almost before it had even properly commenced.

The topic of conversation had unexpectedly veered from what was archaeologically on offer for the day to what could be done with a dead body. For the moment it had been packed with what little ice remained in Uri's stock and then wrapped in several layers of heavy tent canvas.

It now lay, reverently covered with yet more canvas, in the furthest corner of the triclinium – by far the coolest place available. Despite this, there were the first signs of puddles of melted ice appearing from underneath it. The men of the party sat around the table.

'This is unfortunate, to put it mildly,' said Rupert, by way of understatement. 'I'm not sure that there's much that we can do, stuck out here...'

A little before six forty-five, not long after the smouldering disc of the sun had first appeared in the clear blue sky above the crowns of the surrounding hills, the campsite was dragged from its slumbers by the agitated sounds of one of their number who had risen earlier that morning.

Looking extremely distressed, the Reverend Fairweather shuffled his way through the structured order of the pitched tents, moving at what, for him, was a considerable pace. He was sweating heavily with the exertion. It was also quite obvious that his sombre, black ecclesiastical suit had been thrown on in some considerable haste. For the first time in years, the Reverend had appeared in public looking as if he had been drawn through a hedge backwards.

'Mr Winfield ... Mr Winfield,' he wheezed, as he shuffled towards Rupert's tent. 'Mr Winfield ... please ... oh dear ... what a to-do!'

'Reverend Fairweather, what on earth is the matter?' Rupert called from the top of the steps leading up to the triclinium. He had risen with the dawn and had been busy with the paperwork necessary to keep head office fully informed of the tour's progress. He had no way of knowing that, on that day, one of his reports would be highly unusual and quite unexpected.

'Oh, there you are ... thank God,' the vicar continued, as he changed direction and plodded towards the foot of the steps. 'I fear there is need of assistance ... up there ... on Mount Seir...' He swayed unsteadily and, raising his right arm, pointed back down the track and away from the campsite, towards the nearby outcrop of Jabal al-Madhbah, the High Place of Sacrifice.

'What assistance? ... What's happened?' Rupert asked, replacing the cap on his fountain pen and anchoring it in his shirt pocket as he quickly descended the steps.

The commotion had brought several of the other members of the group out of their tents, in various stages of dress.

'Oh, this is most unfortunate...' the vicar gasped. 'I fear it could already be too late ... Perhaps I should have spoken earlier ... but I felt it would be betraying a confidence ... and it was not really my place to do so ... Oh, how complicated life can be at times...' It was the most animated the Reverend Fairweather had been in years. 'Look!' he said, thrusting a sheet of crumpled paper in Rupert's direction. 'I found this on the floor, just inside my tent. I had risen and was about to attend to a call of nature, when I noticed it ... Please ... do read it...'

Rupert smoothed out the crumpled note and read it silently to himself:

> My dear fellow, I would not like to miss the opportunity of thanking you for your company once again, and for the numerous, most interesting conversations we have recently enjoyed. The time for the omega of my pilgrimage is upon both Sarah and me. We both face it with stoicism and acceptance and ask that you understand why I am settled on a course of action which might have been somewhat at odds with your own thinking. I hope that you will be as good a companion to dear Sarah as you have been to me, in the difficult time which lies ahead for her.
>
> With my very warmest best wishes,
> Your fellow pilgrim,
> George Unsworth.

'What does this mean?' Rupert asked, bemused.

'It means that the professor is going to leave us,' the flustered cleric replied, suddenly very serious, but now a little calmer and not quite so out of breath. 'Hurry ... we must go up to the top of the mountain. Perhaps there is still something we can do...'

Turning around again, he seemed suddenly fired by an inner strength, and was about to start down the track that led to Jabal al-Madhbah, when he caught sight of Stephen. 'Doctor ... please ... come quickly,' the vicar implored, as he shuffled past Stephen and the rest of the assembled group, 'although I fear it could already be far too late...'

'Take this,' said Rupert, handing the note to his friend, 'read it as we run ... Come on.'

'I am very sorry, Mrs Unsworth, but the professor has gone,' Stephen said, as he removed the stethoscope from his ears. He had felt for a pulse at the professor's wrist and neck, but there had been none. 'It could possibly have been his heart ... There are no outward signs of distress.'

'It is an early release, with which he was totally contented,' Sarah Unsworth replied, not taking her eyes of the composed and peaceful features of her husband. He looked as if he was sleeping.

'I am truly sorry that I could not summon assistance in time, dear lady,' mumbled the vicar, as he mopped his brow with a large white handkerchief.

It was not yet half past seven and already the heat was starting its daily conquest of the ancient city. Reverend Theophilus Fairweather was more used to a gentle bicycle ride to the home of one of his recently departed parishioners, than to a frantic climb up a high mountain.

They had all rushed up the steep pathway, treading the steps trodden by thousands of feet before them and, on the plateau-like top of Mount Seir, had hastily crossed to the recumbent form of the professor. Now, for the first time since they had reached her, Sarah Unsworth took her eyes off the still, unmoving body of her husband. She smiled and looked straight into the open, honest face of the cleric.

'Please do not blame yourself,' she said very calmly. 'George knew what he wanted and you were of inestimable assistance to him ... to both of us. You, more than anyone else, generously contributed to what George felt to be necessary. I thank you most sincerely for that.'

As he put his stethoscope back into his medical bag, Stephen paused momentarily, pretending to study the bag's contents. It seemed odd that the newly widowed Mrs Unsworth was so remarkably calm, considering the loss she had just sustained. There was something strange in what she had just said, as it had sounded as if it was a code of some sort; a secret cipher known only to her and the vicar. The other thing that worried him was the tiny pinprick of blood in the region of the elbow, which he had noticed on the left arm of the professor's white shirt.

'Perhaps you would like to go back to the campsite now, Mrs Unsworth,' said Stephen gently. 'Mr Harrison could accompany you.' It was more of an instruction than a question. 'There is nothing more to be done here, I'm afraid. I have to carry out one or two simple procedures, which are a legal requirement; in order that I might accurately certify the cause of ... the professor's passing.' He paused, so as to study her facial expression for any sign of emotion.

'If you think that is for the best, then of course ... You *will* look after George, won't you, Doctor?' she said, squeezing his arm and looking straight into his eyes.

Again, Stephen had cause to consider her remark and the manner in which she had made it – emphatically, very matter of fact and with no sign of distress – unusual for someone so very recently bereaved.

'Of course,' he replied, smiling comfortingly.

Joe Harrison helped Sarah Unsworth down the path and back towards the campsite. A second procession followed a short while later. Uri and his boys carried the body between them on a makeshift stretcher and the Reverend Fairweather, who seemed to be mumbling prayers as he walked, brought up the rear of the cortège. Behind them, walking some distance further back and out of earshot, walked Stephen and Rupert.

'This is not quite what it seems. Or, more clearly put, it's not as some would like it to appear to us,' said Stephen softly, as he and Rupert finished the descent from Jabal al-

Madhbah and reached the track. 'His heart did stop, but I very much think it was not due to the onset of his cancer.'

'What do you mean?'

'Think of it, my dear chap. We knew he was on borrowed time. Surely the first question is why were the two of them on top of the mountain at such an early hour in the morning? Given his condition, they must have risen well before dawn to allow them time to get up here. It was obviously something they had thought through and planned...'

'You mean that the professor was going to...'

'What other reason can there have been for being up there?' replied Stephen, keeping his voice low. 'The second question I have, is about the note the good vicar discovered in his tent.'

In response to Rupert's blank expression, Stephen reminded him of the contents of the professor's note, as they continued to make their way along the track leading to the campsite. 'The good Reverend seemed truly agitated at its discovery, but was that because of the imminent departure of a soul, or because he could well find himself implicated as an accessory to suicide, which is in itself a crime?'

'Well, Professor Unsworth and Reverend Fairweather used to have those marathon discussions in the evenings after most of us had gone to bed. I overheard something on one occasion about the significance of Mount Sinai and that place up there,' Rupert said, turning slightly to point back up to Jabal al-Madhbah.

'Yes ... I also heard the professor talking about his conviction that this is the real Mount Sinai and not the one down in Sinai itself,' Stephen added.

'Perhaps the effort of getting up there was too much for him,' whispered Rupert, as they rounded the final bend in the track. 'He was ill, after all.'

'He was indeed,' answered Stephen, 'but not *that* ill ...

yet! We have no knowledge of what condition his heart was in. We only know at this stage that he had a form of terminal cancer and had only a few months to live. Although there were no traumatic signs of a heart attack – vomiting, et cetera – it is still possible that he could have died quite peacefully from a heart attack and that is the way it looks. If his heart was weak, the exertion of the climb would probably have made him feel light-headed and he may have fainted prior to his heart stopping beating. And so we arrive at my final conclusion and in my humble opinion it is certainly a more likely answer to our problem. Question three is simply why did the professor's otherwise immaculate white shirt have a tiny pinprick of blood over his left elbow joint? If what I think has happened, then it still fits in with the visual evidence we have seen already Anyway, I had a look at the professor's arm after the apparently un-grieving widow had been assisted away. There were *two* tiny puncture marks in the skin, over the vein in the antecubital fossa region. He had been injected by someone and by someone who knew precisely what they were doing. I would venture to conclude that the punctures were far too accurate and neat for him to have done them himself. I would further suggest that he had been sent peacefully on his way with an overdose of diamorphine!'

'How do you know that?' asked Rupert. He had stopped in his tracks with an expression of incredulous surprise on his face.

'I had a look behind those peacefully closed eyelids. The pupils were totally contracted ... the size of tiny pinpricks, actually. Atropine would have countered that, but we're not dealing with cold-blooded killers, who would have taken steps to cover their tracks...'

'So, hang on a minute, Sherlock Holmes ... Was it suicide ... or not?' whispered Rupert.

'You are on the right track, my dear chap. The poor man

knew he was on borrowed time and had started to feel the beginnings of the discomfort of what was to come. But I would be inclined to say no, not suicide and not murder either. Rather, let us say an act of humanity. When one who has been sentenced to a life beyond all help is allowed to escape from the merciless shackles of this earthly coil and proceed to the next step of their journey ... with a gentle push ... it's called assisted euthanasia ... it is an act of compassion ... and it is also illegal...' He let the sentence hang on the early-morning air.

'But is that *really* a crime?' Rupert asked, as they resumed their slow progress to the campsite ahead.

'It depends how you look at it, my dear chap. Ethics, you see. That sort of thing happened quite frequently back in the war. What was the point of lingering on when there was absolutely no hope and the levels of suffering were unbearable? To do so really served no purpose. And it is quite one thing for someone to pontificate from a pulpit or the King's Bench and quite another thing to work with and experience it, I can tell you.'

They walked on in silence; each considering what had been said. Then Rupert asked a question. 'You said something about having an answer for an existing enigma?'

'I did, my dear chap, and I think I do. I fear I have done the charming Miss Barnfield a dastardly wrong by initially thinking that she, like most of her over-wealthy sort, derives pleasure from the use of nasty narcotics. I had originally thought that it was *she* who had taken the missing ampoules of diamorphine, to support her in her folly as a pleasure-seeking drug-taker. I am now more inclined to think it was the good Sarah Unsworth...' He turned and looked at Rupert. '...Do you remember that she was very late for dinner last evening?'

Rupert nodded.

'She must have been looking for some more diamorphine

to augment the supply she and her husband had acquired from God knows where, to help him on his way. I would think at this stage he had the drug in pill form for his pain relief. Remember that she mentioned her nursing work during the war ... so she would know her way around a syringe. I would think that she could well have experience in mixing and administering the powdered form of the drug. Furthermore, I would say that she only had a small syringe with her and had to give the professor two injections to achieve the fatal overdose level. That was why there were two puncture marks in the skin.'

'You mean...' Rupert exclaimed, taken aback.

'Yes, my dear chap, I do.'

'Mrs Unsworth sent her husband on his way?' continued Rupert, his face a mask of disbelief.

'Only because that was what he wanted and only because she had decided that such a course of action was for the best ... all things considered,' surmised Stephen.

'I find it hard to believe that Mrs Unsworth would have actually pushed the plunger and killed him, though,' said Rupert innocently. 'I thought that she loved him. How can anyone kill the person they love?'

'Perhaps we should think in terms of putting to sleep, rather than killing in this instance. Whichever way you prefer to think of it, it must be the greatest act of love there is,' replied Stephen solemnly, 'to knowingly create the impassable void of separation between two linked souls for the benefit and release of just one of them.'

They walked on for a while in silence, as the sun continued to rise higher and the rocks started to warm themselves.

'Well,' said Rupert eventually, 'at least he chose a picturesque location for his departure ... and one of such biblical significance. Did you notice those magnificent cliffs on the opposite side of the valley? What a backdrop...'

But Stephen was not listening to his friend's observations;

he was deep in thought fighting with his professional ethics and the instincts he upheld from his war experiences.

It was mid-morning and Mrs Sarah Unsworth, widow, was lying down in her tent. Despite her protestations, Stephen had promised to call in on her and Madeira Barnfield had volunteered to sit with her until then. Hester Barnfield had said nothing, other than to offer her mumbled condolences, before walking off to sit on the topmost of the triclinium steps to smoke a cigarette. Inside, the men of the tour were sitting around the table talking about their next step.

'This is unfortunate, to put it mildly,' repeated Rupert. 'Uri has sent one of his boys into Wadi Musa to call the police ... Apparently there *is* a solitary policeman stationed in the town. That is correct, isn't it Uri?'

'Yes,' answered Uri, 'but he will not be here for a couple of hours at least.'

'The other pressing question, of course, is what to do with the professor's body once...'

Hussein al Mohammed suddenly strode into the room, cutting across what Rupert was saying.

'Is this dreadful thing true?' he enquired, genuine concern and sadness clouding his usually jovial features. 'I came as soon as I received the news...'

News certainly travels fast in these parts, thought Stephen. 'Yes, I am afraid so,' he responded before Rupert could answer. 'A most regrettable outcome caused, most probably, by the condition of the professor's health.'

'I did not realize he was ill,' said al Mohammed. 'He seemed to me to be as robust and as healthy as ever...' His voice died away in the vastness of the room.

'Regrettably, that was not the case,' said Stephen softly. 'The professor was suffering from the early stages of a terminal illness. As you know, I am a medical doctor and I can say that it was a fatal heart attack that carried him off,' he lied, 'but at least Mrs Unsworth was fortunate enough to have been with him at the end.'

He indicated the body shape, covered in canvas, in the far corner of the room. The puddles were now larger and more obvious than before. Hussein crossed the cavernous room slowly and stood for some minutes next to the professor's body, offering prayers to his friend and mentor.

'Perhaps we could find a carpenter who could make us a coffin,' said the Reverend Fairweather eventually, 'and then perhaps we could pack the body with a lot of ice and take it back to Jerusalem ... or Amman?'

'You would need a lead-lined coffin that is airtight to stand any chance of the ice not melting within a couple of hours in this climate,' said Uri Ben Zeev, 'and I do not think there is enough lead for that in Wadi Musa.'

'That is why we bury our dead very quickly out here,' the Jordanian archaeologist contributed. 'It will take you far too long to get to Jerusalem and even longer to get to Amman. It is best to bury the professor in Wadi Musa, rather than to try and transport him somewhere else.'

'Could we bury him here ... or somewhere in Petra? It seems appropriate to me,' suggested Joe Harrison.

'We can make arrangements for the dead in a little while. I think our first priority should be with the living,' said Stephen, looking towards the body. 'If you'll excuse me, I must go see how Mrs Unsworth is doing.'

As Stephen crossed the campsite towards the Unsworth's tent, he was struck once again by the serene calmness Sarah Unsworth had shown as she had knelt next to the dead body of her husband. Reaching the tent he drew back the flap and entered.

'Hello, Miss Barnfield. How is Mrs Unsworth doing?' he whispered.

Sarah Unsworth was lying on her camp bed; her eyes were closed and she had a look of deep contentment on her face.

'She's asleep,' replied Madeira Barnfield, as she turned and looked at the recumbent figure.

'I think it best if I give her a quick check-up,' whispered Stephen. 'Shock is bad enough, but delayed shock can be even worse.'

Madeira nodded her understanding.

'Would you mind giving me a few minutes with her? Then I'm sure that she'd appreciate your company once again.' He smiled at the young woman.

'Of course,' she said, 'shall I see if I can find her a cup of tea?'

'An excellent idea,' agreed the doctor, 'with two spoons of sugar.'

'Really ... I am perfectly all right, I assure you. Please ... there is no need for any fuss,' said Sarah Unsworth, opening her eyes as the tent flap swung closed behind the retreating younger woman.

'It doesn't hurt to be cautious,' replied Stephen softly, as he crossed to the bed and put his medical bag on the low table next to it, 'and you've had to contend with a very severe shock.'

'Not at all,' replied Sarah Unsworth. 'It was what we both wanted and we are both very happy with ... things.' She turned to face him, a smile gently caressing her face.

Stephen had removed his stethoscope from the bag, but it now hung suspended in mid-air, held loosely in his hand.

'Things?' he repeated, looking a little mystified. 'You mean...'

'I mean over half a lifetime spent with the only other human on this planet who made me totally happy,' she replied. 'Are you married, Doctor?'

The question caused a momentary hiatus in Stephen's response. He had found his life's partner, but not one that society would readily accept. 'Er ... no,' he replied, momentarily hating himself for lacking the courage to speak the truth.

'You will, when the time is ripe,' she said. 'George and I found each other ... that was way back when the old queen was still on the throne.' Her smile broadened as she went deeper into her place of fond memories. 'And now, through the kindness of Dame Fortune, we have reached the end of our joint pilgrimage ... here, where George said he wanted to do so. Who would have thought that possible? Certainly not all those years ago, when two souls were first united in a common love and everything was rosy. As for tomorrow...' she paused, '... well, tomorrow is so far away it doesn't really exist. We never gave a thought to the path we would travel together ... or even how long or short it might be. You don't when you're young and in love, do you?'

Stephen nodded. He understood her completely. She could just as well have been talking about Rupert and himself, although their joint pilgrimage had thus far been a short one by comparison to the Unsworths' journey.

'When you set out as a couple, you have no idea of the highs and lows of life through which you will pass ... You just start walking and keep going, don't you?'

The tent was suddenly filled with the silence of mutual understanding, Stephen's hand holding the unused stethoscope still suspended over the opened medical bag.

'You are very kind, Doctor,' she continued, propping herself up on her elbow and putting her hand on Stephen's forearm, 'and I truly appreciate your understanding of how we both wished George's journey to end and, believe me, I am perfectly all right, I assure you.'

Stephen put his stethoscope back into the bag quietly. He would have no need of it ... not for this patient.

'There are two things I would ask of your kindness and generosity,' she continued.

'Of course,' replied Stephen, smiling at her. What had been said within the canvas confessional of the tent had forged a silent bond of understanding between the two.

'Firstly, George asked me to give you a letter. You'll find it in my journal, which is on that table over there. Please take it and read it.'

Stephen turned his head in the direction of the table. Then he turned back to Sarah Unsworth. 'And the second thing?' he asked, softly.

'Let George go on his way with the hope that, once you find your soulmate, you may have as many happy years together as we were given.'

Stephen gently put his free hand over hers, which still rested on his forearm. Nothing was said ... nothing needed to be said.

'I think you had better get some rest,' he said, once again the doctor, 'so I'm going to give you a mild sleeping draught. Miss Barnfield is going to bring you a comforting cup of tea and then, once you have drunk it, take this powder. She has offered to continue sitting with you whilst you sleep.'

'How kind you all are. Thank you so much,' she said, lying back down on the bed. 'I must confess that I do feel a little tired now.'

Five minutes later, Stephen had re-joined the others in the triclinium.

'When I went to see if she needed anything, Mrs Unsworth gave me this,' he said, removing an envelope from his jacket pocket. 'It's a letter from the professor to us all. I won't read everything ... I'll leave it on the table and you can do that for yourselves later ... but I will first read part of the last paragraph.'

He opened the single sheet of paper and there in the Treasury, a tomb dedicated to a soul from a bygone age, Stephen started to read to those who, by accident, had been the fellow pilgrims on the professor's last journey.

> ...my intention, should I die on our tour, is most certainly not to cause any trouble. I would only ask that you offer the same support to my darling Sarah as you have done to me. My final wish would be to be buried somewhere in Petra, if my dear colleague Hussein would permit such a thing. Should this eventuality...

Nothing was said in the room for several seconds, as the echoes of Stephen's voice drifted away to eternity against the high ceiling.

'There are certain formalities which have to be observed and with which I am perfectly happy to comply as a medical man,' said Stephen, as he placed the unfolded letter on the table, 'including the completion of a death certificate stating the cause of death to have been cardiac arrest, as a result of physical over-exertion.'

Rupert looked at his friend and smiled. He nodded his head in agreement, slightly and almost imperceptibly, but enough for Stephen to recognize his friend's tacit agreement. He would tell Rupert about his conversation with Sarah Unsworth later.

'I should imagine that the police involvement will probably be purely a formality,' said the vicar, looking somewhat relieved, 'given the evidence we can present to them.'

'And we have the Reverend to say the Committal Service for us,' added Rupert.

'I am certain that such a burial within the area of an archaeological site is forbidden,' said Hussein softly. 'I could ask Amman for special permission given the professor's status and his support for our work...'

'During the war many, many people were buried in places where they should not have been. It was a practical necessity,' said Stephen, raising his eyebrows as he lit a cigarette, 'and nobody really objected at the time. How many days would it be before you receive Amman's response to your enquiry?' he asked through the smoke.

'Yes ... that is, of course, the problem ... It would take many days at the very least,' said Hussein, 'and that is time we do not have, as you have correctly said. Perhaps such a thing could be permitted ... as a practical necessity.'

27

London

Whitehall – Monday, 29th June 1931

'I thought you needed to know. When I saw him this morning, the PM was none too pleased about this, but he's not one to be seen to take decisive action to stop a hiccup becoming a severe case of whooping cough ... if you follow me,' said Stephen's uncle, as he placed another piece of beef into his mouth. He stared at the person opposite him and did not notice that two spots of gravy had dribbled off his own poised fork, as he had been speaking, and had fallen on to the white tablecloth.

'Not being a medical man myself, old boy, I can't see the connection in a clinical sense, but I think I follow you,' said the other man, as he stuck his fork into a roast potato.

'Well, then...?' continued the Uncle.

'Well, what?' echoed the other man.

'For goodness' sake, Sebastian,' replied the Uncle earnestly, resting his knife and fork on his plate, 'what are you going to do ... or should I rather say, what are you going to tell the PM to do? You are the Foreign Secretary, after all...' He picked up his cutlery and continued his luncheon.

'I've read through all the papers you've been forwarding to me. How serious a threat to us do you think this business with the French and the Italians is?'

'I would say *very* serious, with the distinct possibility that it could become even more so ... eventually,' replied the Uncle, reaching for his glass and taking a sip of wine.

'This latest business you've just told me about ... these ships near Malta ... it could have been purely coincidental.'

'Oh come now, my dear Sebastian. When you send a gunboat somewhere you hardly do so to collect the mail! You do so as a *warning*. I am convinced that that is what we are supposed to make of this latest provocation. You know as well as I that Laval is only interested in what's best for France and Mussolini fancies himself as the new Julius Caesar ... and you know how conquest-hungry *he* was!'

The Foreign Secretary looked fixedly at the Uncle, who was not known to make a mountain out of a molehill.

'Three of our ships threatened with menaces in less than forty-eight hours! I would hardly call that a coincidence. Anyone can hold joint exercises on the high seas, but that doesn't give them the right to interfere with the free passage of shipping. You know as well as I that there are laws to prevent that sort of thing in international waters.'

'But these ships of ours were not actually *stopped*, were they?' asked the Foreign Secretary.

'No, but two of them had Italian destroyers sailing around them in ever-decreasing circles for nearly twenty minutes and the third, which, you might recall, was miles away on the *other side* of Malta, suffered a similar gruelling from different destroyers and was then subjected to the spectacle of the French heavy cruiser *Dordogne* nearly capsizing it in its wake, as it rushed by at top speed. Can you imagine the public outcry if this sort of thing happened to one of our passenger ships? The weight of public opinion could well force us into some sort of belated action we would later come to regret.'

'You know as well as I that the PM will want concrete proof before he decides on anything,' replied the Foreign Secretary.

'Very well, old boy, then let us consider the common

factors in each of these three incidents. Firstly, all three ships were British and we have had no reports of similar incidents involving any other nationalities. Secondly, these ships were on their way to and from Malta ... our bastion in the middle of the Med.' The Uncle leaned in closer. 'Of course it is a gunboat message,' he continued, dropping his voice to a whisper. Even the Members' Dining Room in the Palace of Westminster was known to have ears. 'Our principal sea route to India goes straight through the Med to the Canal, and Malta is the key to that route. Laval and Mussolini between them obviously think that a little sabre rattling around the shores of our little jewel will do their cause the world of good.'

'Really ... what is your assessment of their *cause*, then?' the Foreign Secretary asked.

'My dear chap, I would have thought that *you* were far better placed to tell *me* the answer to that one,' hissed the Uncle, with a pained expression on his face, which did little to mask the frustration he was beginning to feel at everyone else's seeming reluctance to act.

'Hardly, old boy,' replied the other man slowly. 'With all the fingers you seem to have poked into the most unlikely pies, I should imagine that there is absolutely nothing you do not know about or could not tell the rest of *us* about!'

'You are too kind and generous with your praise,' replied the Uncle, but the mood passed like lightning and suddenly he was serious. 'Their *cause* is simply one of territorial expansion ... at least, that's what Mussolini is up to. They've both had grandiose ideas of empire ever since they were old enough to cast covetous eyes on ours. To be honest, though, I'm not at all clear what game Laval fancies he's playing. Do you have any ideas?'

'I have information which could suggest that he's simply looking for allies, in the event of German rearmament ... The French are terrified of another German invasion, so it's a case of once bitten twice shy with them. You know that already ... I forwarded the report to you.'

'Indeed you did, indeed you did...' replied the Uncle, 'but we were all on the same side in the last war and it does not necessarily follow that we will all be on the same side in the next one. Things have changed, old boy, and the pieces of the jigsaw don't fit quite as snugly as they did before 1914.'

'Oh, come now ... I hardly think so...' replied the Foreign Secretary. 'I really can't see the French trying to enter into an alliance with Mussolini. They are *our* allies, besides which we have the *Entente Cordiale*.'

'That's as may be,' replied the Uncle, 'but if you want some advice from my department, I would suggest that you have the French and Italian ambassadors in for a chat and ask them what the hell is going on!'

A waiter appeared and took the dirty plates away. As he did so, a second waiter wheeled a dessert trolley up to the table. The two diners made their selection and were soon alone again.

'I'm seeing Archibald and some of his Naval Intelligence chaps at the Admiralty later this afternoon. They're going to want to know what we propose to do about things. I need hardly tell you that the White Ensign is stretched far too thinly in the Med. Things could become a little too tricky to handle, if we're not careful...' He left the sentence unfinished, staring at the Foreign Secretary with raised eyebrows.

Sometime later the Uncle was back behind the desk in his office. His luncheon had been acceptably passable, if not quite up to the standard of that served by his club, but necessity had dictated that his meeting with the Foreign Secretary take place in the Parliament buildings next to the Thames. He was replete but, as he prepared his notes for the forthcoming meeting at the Admiralty, he was aware of the struggle of his digestive system in coping with the richness of the meal.

His concentration was broken by a knock on the door.

'Yes, Collingwood?' said the Uncle, glancing up momentarily from the papers in front of him.

'I'm sorry to disturb you, Sir, but this has just been deciphered. It's from the High Commission in Jerusalem, via the Embassy in Cairo...'

The Uncle looked up again and reached out to take the folder from Collingwood.

'Perhaps we have some news from my nephew at last,' he said. 'I was beginning to wonder if he had forgotten about us.' He opened the folder and took out the typed sheet it contained. The message was rather formal and to the point, devoid of any pleasantries.

```
Petra Hotel, Jerusalem, 26th June 1931
We have returned to Jerusalem safely, having
completed the first of the Company's new tour
successfully. Regret to inform you that
Professor George Unsworth suffered a heart
attack at Petra and died...
```

'Professor Unsworth?' said the Uncle out loud, as he looked up, puzzled. 'Collingwood, do we know anything about a Professor Unsworth?'

'I am not familiar with that name, Sir. I can make some enquiries...'

'Good man,' muttered the Uncle, 'then do so,' and he returned to the typed sheets.

```
Unfortunately, there is nothing much to report
on the other matter, other than to say that
nothing was discovered through our enquiries
```

during the tour, nor through our investigations during our time in Petra itself. We did, however, hear something of significance. Hussein al Mohammed, the archaeologist in Petra, confirmed the instances of surface oil seepage near the Iraq border, around a mountain called Tall Salāh. I remember that you had mentioned these phenomena during our meeting with Rabbi Mosheowitz; that once the oil is ignited by the sun, it appears as if the rocks are on fire. I believe that this site should now be investigated, although the military command in Jerusalem does not seem too supportive of the idea. Access is best achieved by aircraft, using the Imperial Airways service from Cairo to Baghdad, via the depot at Rutbah Wells, which is over the Iraq border. We will need a military escort, I am told, as the region is almost totally deserted, except for the occasional Bedouin group and others who would intentionally lose themselves in that wilderness. Law and order are two concepts almost totally unknown in the region. An escort can easily be provided from the garrison based at the Wells. Perhaps you could apply a little pressure in the relevant places?
  S.

The Uncle rose from his chair and crossed to the table, on which was spread the highly detailed map of Palestine, Trans-Jordan, Iraq and the French Protectorate of Syria.

'Will there be a reply, Sir?' asked Collingwood, who was still standing at the foot of the desk.

The Uncle studied the map and easily found the little

dot next to the name Rutbah Wells. He also located the mountain called Tall Salāh. 'No answer, Collingwood,' he said softly, 'not just yet.' Still looking at the map he declared hopefully, 'Perhaps our quest for this scroll will now lead us to the place called Tall Salāh.'

28

Jerusalem

The Old City – early afternoon, Friday, 3rd July 1931

Hurva Square, the busy hub of the Jewish Quarter of the Old City, was full of people, some strolling leisurely and some about the serious business of purchasing the necessary foodstuff for the forthcoming Shabbat. The little Spanish shop on the corner was particularly busy, the queue of shoppers almost spilling out and filling the pavement.

On a nearby bench, on the opposite side of the square, Morris Ginsberg and his wife Claudette sat watching the passing parade. She was busy munching her way noisily through a crisp, juicy apple, her drop earrings jangling with each movement of her jaw. He was smoking and now held the cigarette in his fingers as he stared ahead of himself.

'How do you mean *the burning rocks*,' asked the voice from behind them.

'That was what they said. They were going to see if there was anything out where the rocks burn. One of them said something like: ... *the burning rocks could be a clue to its location* ... and then the other one said: ... *that's all we have to go on? Perhaps it doesn't exist, after all* ... That's as much as was heard.'

'Are you sure of this?' asked the voice. 'We do not take kindly to being made fools of...' There was more than just a hint of a threat in the way the man had spoken.

'I'm telling you, that is more or less what was overheard.'
'This is what you heard?'
'No ... not us. We were performing. It was Mordechai the waiter who overheard the conversation. He overheard these two Englishmen talking at the hotel after dinner.' Morris took a long draw on his cigarette and exhaled the smoke slowly.

'And is this Mordechai to be trusted?' asked the voice sternly. 'Mordechai who? We do not have anyone of that name in this unit. He is not one of ours.'

'You do not have to be *one of yours* to be a true Jew and a patriot,' argued Morris softly. 'He is in sympathy with us and wants to see our own state established. He just doesn't want to get involved in any nasty business or trouble, that's all.'

'And why did he think this information might be significant? Was he trying to sell it to you? You have not told him you are with us, I hope?' The man's voice sank down to a deadly whisper, heavy with the menace of retribution and punishment.

'Of course not!' snapped back Morris, who was beginning to get more than just a little fed up with the cloak-and-dagger existence *these* people seemed to lead. If he was to encounter an enemy, Morris Ginsberg preferred to do so face to face – as it had been in the war. At least he knew where he stood when he could see his foe. *Their* suspicion and mistrust were not part of his character and he did not much care for it. For a few seconds, silence reigned across the two benches.

'So how *did* you find this out from Mordechai, then? And what made him think that you might be interested in burning rocks? Only mad people think that rocks can burn....' The voice had now taken on the faintest hint of laughter, almost mocking.

'We were just chatting in the lounge bar after Claudie's

last set of the evening, that's all. We often have a drink there when we've finished work. Mordechai had cleared the tables away and was behind the bar. Most of the guests had gone to their rooms. It was getting late. His family live in Haifa and he gets lonely. He knows nobody in Jerusalem. There is only...'

'I feel for him,' said the voice, cutting across Morris in a sneering tone, 'but I have to tell you that I am not interested in his personal life. So I ask you again, why would he have thought you would be interested in what he had to say? Were you not suspicious?'

'Why would we be suspicious?' Morris retaliated.

Claudie had finished her apple and was wiping her sticky hand on her handkerchief. She took Morris's arm and squeezed it. She knew the signs, which warned of his growing anger and impatience. The last thing they wanted was a scene in public and in broad daylight.

'He thought it eccentric and typically English that these two men would be going wherever to look at burning rocks. He mentioned it in our conversation because he found it unusual and more than just a little amusing. And I am telling you this, because you told me to tell you if I came across anything unusual and out of the ordinary. I would think that burning rocks qualify, wouldn't you? But I cannot see any significance in it at all.'

Another silence settled over the benches as they sat staring ahead of them, the sounds of the life of the Old City echoing around and about them. In the silence, the other man was thinking. Morris could not see the significance of what Mordechai had overheard, but he fancied that possibly his contact could. *They* knew about the scroll and the rocks that burn and the eagle which would quench the flames. The Zionist Agency had passed all of this on to them almost as soon as Rabbi Mosheowitz had told them of his interview with Stephen's uncle in his Whitehall office. Anything that might help establish a Jewish state was of inestimable value, both politically and morally. Everyone knew that the British would not stay in Palestine for ever. If anything was to be feared when the British left, it would be that there would be an Arab takeover. The Jews of Palestine had to be ready to establish their new Kingdom of David the moment the Union Flag descended the flagpole for the last time. Otherwise, it might be too late. Unlike Morris Ginsberg, this other man knew all about the rumours of the existence of the Scroll of Gershom and of its enormous political significance. The more radical elements in the Jewish Agency in London had made certain that Rabbi Mosheowitz's report had been disseminated throughout the Diaspora almost as soon as the Uncle's office door had been closed on the rabbi's retreating back.

The questioning continued.

'And did this Mordechai happen to overhear where these two eccentric Englishmen were hoping to find these rocks that burn?' asked the other man, his voice once again normal and deeply rounded.

'He thought he heard one of them say something about "... at the wells". And also that someone called Cecil would arrange the escort and a flight. That was all he could hear. Isn't that so, Claudie?'

She said nothing – she found these meetings rather frightening and preferred to leave the talking to her Moshie. Instead, she nodded her head slowly.

'Cecil?' repeated the voice softly. 'Who is this Cecil?'

'You're asking me as if I should know?' muttered Morris.

'And you're certain he overheard "wells" and "flight"?' asked the other man.

'That was what Mordechai said he had heard, yes,' answered Morris, as he flicked his butt end on to the cobblestones and stamped it out under the sole of his shoe. 'I am only repeating to you what it was that was told to us. If you can make something out of it, then it will have been worth the effort.'

For the third time during the conversation, a silence descended over the benches. Eventually, Morris spoke. 'Is there anything else? The time is getting on and we still have our own preparations to make before Shabbat.'

The sounds of Jerusalem, both the old and the new, mingled about them in the pleasant afternoon air.

'Well, is there? Or is that all for this afternoon?'

Again, the only response was the sound of the ancient city. Carefully, Morris turned his head, imperceptibly, until he could just see over his shoulder out of the corner of his eye. The bench behind them was empty.

'Well, thank you for talking to us,' said Claudie, in a half-mocking tone, as she, too, turned her head to look at the empty bench behind them. 'Really, I don't know at times! How much longer is this going on already, *bubalah*?' she asked, looking at Morris.

He took her hand and kissed it gently.

'Possibly for a good, long while yet, my sweetie,' he said slowly, 'for a good long while yet. Come, let's be on our way.'

29

Rutbah Wells

Monday, 6th July 1931

The afternoon was well past its hottest as preparations were being made to receive the Imperial Airways scheduled flight to Baghdad. The ground crew were busy filling their single bowser with aviation fuel, whilst on the other side of the flat, compacted expanse of hard desert earth that served as the runway the fire crew lounged around in the shade of their bowser, which contained precious water. They usually had nothing to do, other than follow the prescribed arrival and departure procedure and wait. Set back from the runway was Rutbah Fort, its high, solid walls standing out in stark contrast to the flat, arid landscape of the hard, stony desert of north-western Iraq. Rising above the level of the walls stood a wooden tower, topped by a tall radio mast. The tower's lattice cross-beams supported a small hut, which was surrounded on all four sides by a narrow walkway. The air-traffic controllers served their time atop this tower rather as Saint Simeon had done on top of a pillar in nearby Syria during the fifth century. Unlike the saint, who was reputed to have lived on his pillar for thirty-seven years, the traffic controllers could descend once they had safely overseen any aircraft arriving at, or departing from the airstrip. Clustered around the western end of the fort was a collection of Bedouin tents, the ancient way of life of these nomadic people rubbing shoulders with the latest technology of the twentieth century in seemingly perfect coexistence and harmony.

'And now they want me to let these two go off into the desert with an armed escort! Do they think we have an entire brigade out here and that we can afford to send half of it off to protect the whims and fancies of a couple of archaeologists?' The captain sat behind his desk in his small office, which functioned as the fort's command centre. He was staring at the message he had just been handed.

'No, Sir,' said the lieutenant, who had just brought the message in from the radio room. 'Unfortunately, we have a couple of the Rolls armoured vehicles in the motor pool for repair at the moment, too. So we are a bit short in the old transport department.'

A degree of informality existed between the two men. Being based out on the fringes of civilization and of the Empire sometimes afforded the opportunity to relax the rigidly formal and long-established structures of administration, which were usually encountered in the Civil Service and the military.

'Well, Peter, I don't know what things are coming to. We don't seem to have progressed much beyond the days of Johnny Turk, if you ask me. What are we actually doing out here, do you think? Keeping the Bedouin happy? Maintaining the *Pax Britannica*? Propping up that lot in Baghdad? They would just as soon see the back of us as not.' He put the radio message on his desk and sighed heavily.

The lieutenant did not answer. He was used to the outward signs of disillusionment of his commanding officer and knew when it was best to keep his own counsel. The captain had been in the Middle East since before the war. During that conflict, he had come into contact with the Arabs during the Great Arab Revolt and had, on one occasion, even met T.E. Lawrence. 'Keeping the link between Cairo and Baghdad is an important task, Sir,' said the lieutenant softly. 'We have to guard the airfield and the fuel.'

'I suppose that you are right, Peter,' answered the commanding officer, looking at him. 'At least we're not too badly off heat-wise, are we?' he asked, a weary smile trying to creep across his wrinkled face.

Rutbah Wells lay on a high plateau, roughly halfway on the route to Baghdad. It was cooler than the surrounding, flatter desert and even had a modest rainfall of nearly five inches in a good year. Several miles away from the fort and airfield lay the town of Ar Rutbah. It was a sizeable settlement, almost totally devoid of European inhabitants. It was also generally peaceful.

'So ... these two are arriving this afternoon, are they?' said the captain, drumming his fingers on the desk as he looked down at the radio message again.

'Yes, Sir ... in about forty minutes,' replied the lieutenant, looking at his watch.

'Right, then, we'd better sort out some sort of a welcoming party for them and see who we can spare to take them off on their flight of fancy.'

'I can check with Johnstone down in the motor pool, Sir. He should be able to tell me how many of the Rolls he'll have operational by tomorrow. The Airways have confirmed their accommodation for the night ... I checked on the way in here.'

The flight to Baghdad was a long one and necessitated a refuelling stop at the Wells. Night flying was out of the question, as the pilots had to follow a wide furrow that had been ploughed into the hard desert ground back in 1922 and which was only visible from the air during daylight hours. This was the only direction-finding equipment they possessed and without it they would soon be lost and way off course, flying over terrain in which one square mile looked identical to the next. An overnight stop at the Wells was, therefore, necessary and unavoidable. The accommodation offered by Imperial Airways was adequate, although rather cold during the freezing desert nights at that altitude. In fact, the climate of Rutbah and its environs was almost a contradiction in terms, as the desert temperatures varied wildly from one extreme to the other between day and night.

'Right you are, Peter,' said the captain, handing back the radio message. 'I suppose you'd best get ready to receive them.'

Some thirty-five minutes later, the Handley Page aircraft had descended gracefully from the clear blue skies, its four Bristol Jupiter engines growling in restrained unison as they spun the propellers. It had taxied to a halt, the ladders had been securely attached in position and the passengers had started to disembark. All around them, the ground crew had started their well-practised routine of refuelling and maintenance and the fire crew had begun to sense, once again, that their services would probably not be required. The aircraft, which was carrying a full load of passengers, was almost new and had flown the route for the first time the previous month.

'Welcome to Rutbah Wells, gentlemen,' said the lieutenant, as he saluted and then extended his hand first to Stephen and then to Rupert as they walked across the hard earth to where he was standing waiting for them. 'Mind the wing. Let's get out of the way,' he said, as he ushered them away from the activity which surrounded the aircraft. 'Captain Strang would like to see you in his office. I'll get someone to take your overnight bags to your quarters ... if you would like to step this way.'

'I have received this radio message from Jerusalem, gentlemen, requesting that I provide you with transport and an escort for a journey ... out into the desert?' The captain turned the statement into a question with an upward inflection of his voice. He sat and stared at his two visitors, as if encouraging an answer and some clarification.

'That's most kind of you, Captain,' said Stephen, smiling. 'We would not be able to accomplish our purpose without your support.'

An uneasy silence descended on the little office. The lieutenant stood behind the chairs placed in front of the commanding officer's desk and which were now occupied by Stephen and Rupert.

'And what, exactly, *is* your purpose?' asked Strang eventually. If these two wanted to disappear into the unforgiving void of the desert, that was their prerogative. For his part, he certainly did not want to lose any of his own valuable men and vehicles in the process.

'We have been charged by the Trans-Jordan Department of Antiquities to investigate the ruins of a Crusader castle in the region of a mountain called Tall Salāh.' That was the agreed smokescreen to be used to cover the real reason for their trip. 'Do you perhaps know anything of the region, Captain?' asked Stephen, disarmingly.

Strang had never even heard of Tall Salāh and had no idea where it was. 'I can't say that I have, gentlemen ... no,' he said, getting up and turning around to face a large, detailed map, which hung on the wall behind him. It was a smaller version of that which resided on a large table several thousand miles away in the Whitehall office of Stephen's uncle. Captain Strang studied the map for a few seconds. 'Where did you say this place was?' he asked.

'Allow me to show you,' said Rupert, as he joined the captain in front of the map and pointed to the position.

'So that's just over the border in Trans-Jordan, then?' he said, turning to look at Rupert. 'Would it not be more appropriate for the Trans-Jordan Desert Patrol to have assisted you in this?'

'Normally, yes, Captain Strang,' said Stephen, butting in before anything further could be said, 'but we have severe time constraints to contend with, I'm afraid, and it would simply have taken too long to reach our destination and then return, if we depended solely upon camel power ... as reliable as that no doubt is,' he added, chuckling.

'I see,' said Strang, resuming his seat, 'there is some truth in that. The old "ship of the desert" is dependable and very reliable, but it can travel frustratingly slowly at times.' He allowed himself a chuckle, too, at the thought of past campaigns during which he had spent many days swaying backwards and forwards as his humped 'ship' made its stately progress across the burning sands of Egypt and Arabia – over fine talcum powder-like sand; not the hard, compacted sand of Rutbah Wells.

Nothing was said for a few moments, during which Stephen cast a confident glance at Rupert and the captain lingered in his memories of what, for him, had seemed happier days.

The lieutenant stood respectfully at the back of the office waiting until eventually, he coughed softly and broke the silence. 'I have checked with Johnstone, Sir. He reports that he'll have three of the Rolls operational by the morning, excluding the two which are currently out on patrol.'

'There you are, then, gentlemen, we should be able to spare one of them for you. What about an escort?' Strang asked, looking over his visitors' heads to his subordinate.

'I suggest Sergeant Ferris with Potts and Woods, Sir,' replied the lieutenant.

'Humm ... and how long will your expedition take?' asked Strang, looking in turn at both of his visitors. 'Remembering that our primary reason for being here is to guard the airfield and fort...' He raised his eyebrows enquiringly.

'You are far better placed than we are to estimate travelling time from here to Tall Salāh,' replied Stephen. 'You know the terrain far better than we do.'

Captain Strang nodded his tacit agreement. At least in that respect he felt himself to be far better informed than were his visitors.

'Once we arrive at our destination, I would estimate no more than two days to complete our survey, possibly even less if we do not find what it is we are supposed to record. It is a very isolated spot and there have been hardly any visitors there since the Crusaders left,' Stephen added, carefully avoiding any reference to the oil seepage and the burning rocks.

'Very well, then ... if you set off tomorrow, it should take you no more than two days to reach the mountain ... plus your own estimate of no more than two days at the site once you get there and then the two days to return here ... you should be back here late on Sunday. Wouldn't you agree, Peter?'

The lieutenant nodded his agreement.

Later that evening, after the passengers had enjoyed a pre-dinner drink, the atmosphere had been quite genial, if a little embarrassed and stilted, which was the result of people who had very little in common with each other finding themselves in the position of having to make polite conversation in order to satisfy the accepted norms of civilized society.

As coffee was being served, the lieutenant made conversation about the clarity of the night sky over the desert. 'After dinner I suggest you climb the stairs to the walkway along the walls and look at the stars. The night sky is very clear and the stars are breath-taking ... millions of them sparkling away up there. It's actually very romantic,' he had added, smiling at Stephen and then at Rupert, as if to say *we* can relate to such beauty, can't we?

'Phew! Look at all those stars,' said Rupert a few minutes

later, as they stood on the walkway, looking up in awe. 'Our friendly lieutenant didn't exaggerate. It's breath-taking.'

They had detached themselves from the assembly after dinner and had climbed the circular stone staircase to the roof of the fort. They walked further along the dark walkway, as they smoked their cigarettes in companionable silence, pausing every now and then to look up at the sky and pass an appropriate comment. Eventually, they found themselves standing in the shadow of the bulk of one of the fort's towers. They were quite alone.

'He was, indeed, quite right ... It is breath-taking ... and also very romantic,' Stephen added, as he reached for and then squeezed Rupert's hand in his.

30

Iraq

High above Mosul – Friday, 10th July 1931

The air was sharp, crisp and hot – as sharp and crisp as the thoughts that filled the mind of the solitary occupant of the aircraft's tiny cockpit. He was quite used to flying – he had totally embraced the new technology of powered flight almost as soon as he had arrived in Oxford to begin his studies. That had been before the war. Despite the privileged position his birth had brought him, Prince Abdul Salaam Abd al-Allah had been brought up by a very practically minded father, who had eagerly seized every opportunity to drag his sons out of the relatively obscure bubble of isolated luxury they enjoyed in Medina.

The prince's father had been driven by aspiration and determination – characteristics which had been inherited by his sons. The father had also harboured an ambitious desire to spread his influence and power over a far larger canvas than that of the burning sands of Arabia. Steely determination would make him succeed in this, even if he had to always walk in the shadow of his elder brother, the prince's uncle, for an accident of birth had decreed that the prince's uncle would be the one to whom the British would talk; they had promised him the title and recognition of King of Arabia, in return for his extended family's support in the struggle against the Ottoman Turks. Once the planned

Great Arab Revolt had seen off the hated and despised Ottomans, the Land of the Prophet would be free. The prince's uncle, if the British could be trusted, would be the new ruler. In a short time the Arabs had, indeed, seen off the Turks, but the British had reneged on their promise. This thoughtless action had left the prince's uncle an embittered man in Aqaba, tolerated as an embarrassment by the British. The prince's uncle had suddenly become a spent force as the powerful Saudi family had emerged as the new powerbrokers of the desert, rising from the confusion and chaos of the Ottoman collapse to stamp their authority on the land and establish the new, independent Kingdom of Saudi Arabia.

The prince's cousins had fared better than his uncle. Cousin Abdullah had been made Emir of Trans-Jordan, the desert wasteland between Palestine and Iraq. The British had been a little embarrassed over what to do with him, following the end of the war. They had denied his father and so had thought it prudent to appease the son, for fear of igniting another Great Arab Revolt, but this time against themselves.

Cousin Faisal, whom they had only recently installed as the King of Syria, was expelled by the French, following the granting in their favour of a mandate to administer Syria. Being ruled by a king, even a virtually powerless one, did not sit easily with their republican ideals. In consolation, the British then made Faisal the King of Iraq, which had been somewhat of an empty gesture on their part, as they held the League of Nations' mandate to administer the territory and did so vigorously. His kingdom, too, was largely an arid wasteland, except for the highly fertile area around the two great rivers.

At the time and with more than just a touch of irony, Prince Abdul Salaam Abd al-Allah had joked that the British defence of his cousin's problems with the French had been deafening in its silence. Needless to say, the remark had not gone down at all well with the British authorities. The prince had good reason to despise and distrust the British and the French in equal measure. Events such as those which had befallen both his uncle and cousins had taught him not to rely on or even trust anybody but himself. As a result, he had the utmost confidence and belief in his own ability and ultimate destiny. This belief in his own abilities had been part of his psyche for as long as he could remember.

As the wind whistled through the double wings of his Tiger Moth, he remembered with an almost sexual excitement the exhilaration he had felt when he had quickly mastered the controls and had been allowed, finally, to fly solo for the first time at the university flying club. That first feeling of power – of total control over the alien environment which surrounded him up in the air – had never left him; he felt himself to be very much the child of destiny. He had also become consummately adept at playing the extremely dangerous game of power politics, unlike his cousin Faisal whom, if truth be told, he despised for his indecisiveness and malleability.

During his years at Oxford, Prince Abd al-Allah had also learned a great deal about the British psyche; about the arrogance of the so-called social elite, as well as that of his fellow students, many of whom were his social inferiors. His carefully calculated charm allowed him to mix freely across the social barrier of class. It had not, however, shielded him from colliding head on with the bias and social snobbery of the British class system. Despite being the son of minor royalty, he had always been viewed by his peers first as *one of those Arab fellows* and as a *royal chap* second. Now, in the cockpit, as the aircraft clawed its way through the warm air high above the arid desert, he smiled to himself. He thought it quite amusing that these same peers – his fellow students – had generally never realized or even registered the fact that this particular *Arab fellow* was extremely ambitious and, in his own discreet way, ruthless. For his part, he had learned a great deal from observing his fellow students and, as a result, had become fired by an even greater ambition, which would be satisfied – and even then only partly – when Faisal's crown sat on his own head.

Up in the clouds, in the middle of the vacuous nothingness and with the wind rushing past him, he was supreme and it was up here, surrounded by the solitude, that he did his clearest thinking. It had been in this same companionable solitude of rarefied air that he had first decided that it would be his boundless ambition that would drive him to take firm hold of his own destiny. If needs be, he would have to take Faisal's crown by force. It had also been up here, from where the landscape of the desert far below appeared endless and the occasional rocky outcrop looked to be no more than just a collection of small pebbles, that he had reached another important decision. He had reasoned that the Italian leader's vision and ambition matched his own; as a result, the prince had decided on the Italians as potential allies. He would need strong allies once he had the crown and the British had left.

He glanced down through his goggles at the compass and made an adjustment to his course. Another forty minutes or so and he would start his descent towards Mosul. With its recently discovered deposits of oil, Mosul had become the unexpectedly important bargaining tool Fate had presented to him. It had come out of the blue – *his* blue, like the sky which surrounded him.

With very little difficulty, Prince Abdul Salaam Abd al-Allah had persuaded Faisal to make him Oil Minister. The huge deposits of oil had changed Iraq almost overnight from a sleepy, archaeologically rich nothingness to a developing power with the ability to influence or even control world events through its black gold. It would take a firm hand to control the country's new destiny and who better to do so than himself? He smiled again, but this time with a sense of self-congratulation, as he automatically followed his routine of regularly casting his eyes over the structure of his aircraft.

Far below him, off to his left, he noticed a caravan laboriously plodding its way across the unforgiving sands, like an extended necklace of black pearls. He looked at the tiny dots and suddenly thought how bizarre the true nature of life was. He was flying above the Earth, surrounded by the reality of his own plans and ambition, cocooned in a wonder of the modern technological age, speeding to his distant destination with relative ease. Far below him was the reality of the old world, a relic from a much earlier time. Following the ancient and uncharted trade route at a snail's pace, the caravan plodded slowly and sedately across the vast expanse of uncharted sands like a column of worker ants. This last thought he found particularly apt, as ants could be easily crushed. In time to come, he would have to treat his opponents like annoying ants and would have to crush them. If this new Hawkhurst Avenger aircraft was as good as he had been told it was, then his new air force, equipped with perhaps a dozen of these machines, would soon crush all opposition to his rule. He had watched and learned from the activities of the British and their Royal Air Force – how their bombs had soon silenced the dissenters out in the desert and other parts of the country. If the aircraft were that effective, they might even prove useful in the cities. He had watched, learned and been very impressed.

In fact, he had been almost as impressed by the use of controlling air power as he had been by the expansionist rhetoric of Benito Mussolini. The prince had known almost instinctively that they could do business together – they were kindred spirits, whose ambitions were seemingly boundless. With the benefit of modern technology, Mussolini wanted to build a new Roman Empire that would be even more splendid than the magnificence of the ancient one. For his own part, he would build an Empire of Iraq to rival that established in the name of the Prophet Mohammed himself, but this new empire would not be built on faith. Rather, it would be built on the proceeds derived from the new oil wealth. His concept was almost childlike in its simplicity: his Iraqi oil would fuel the ships, aircraft and tanks of Mussolini's expansionist plans, in exchange for Italian support for an independent Iraq – one free from the constricting, meddlesome control of the British. Il Duce had been positively enthusiastic about this proposal during the prince's recent visit to Rome, a visit which had proved to be highly successful and had delivered the desired results. The prince had obtained the hoped-for statement of intent to proceed to a formalized agreement from Mussolini himself. Although Il Duce had seemed somewhat reluctant to commit himself to the project in writing, the prince had been assured that this would follow at a later date. Apart from the meetings in the Palazzo Venezia, there had also been the opportunity to visit Pompeii. His two burning passions – the pursuit of power and the history of ancient Rome – had both been satisfied on the same trip.

All he had to do now was to be patient. It couldn't be more than a matter of some sixteen months before the British mandate over Iraq would expire and the British would be gone. Iraq would be his. Cousin Faisal wouldn't last five minutes without the hand of the British to hold him up – the taking of the crown and real power would be a relatively easy matter. Just to ensure the smooth transition of power to his own hands, Prince Abd al-Allah had been careful to recruit sympathizers and to plant loyal supporters throughout the administration. As for the arrogance of the British – well, did they *really* think that they would be allowed to retain control of the oil once their precious mandate had expired? Independent Iraq was not going to become a second Persia, where the British still controlled the oil. No – in the new Iraq he would see to it that they most certainly did not!

A couple of minutes later, he made a further minor adjustment to his course and then pushed the control stick gently forwards. The Tiger Moth slowly dipped by the head in response to his command and the reassuring throb of the single engine eased a little, as if to rest, as gravity began to draw the little craft back down towards the hard earth. Below him, the caravan had long since been left far behind below the distant, shimmering horizon. He had begun his descent towards Mosul.

31

Iraq

The desert – mid-morning, Friday, 10th July 1931

At about the same time that Prince Abdul Salaam Abd al-Allah was enjoying the contemplation of his ambition in the solitary confines of his Tiger Moth's cockpit, a sand-coloured Rolls-Royce armoured car – a relic from the war – was making its way across the compacted sand of the desert floor. Several hours behind it, to the north-west, lay Tall Salāh.

'I really don't know how you make head or tail of those piles of rocks and rubble, Sir,' said Sergeant Ferris over his shoulder. 'It all just looks like a jumbled muddle to me.' He had to raise his voice considerably to be heard over the noise of the protesting engine. Confined within the protection of the steel framework of the vehicle, the noise was amplified, which made their general discomfort all the worse.

Stephen smiled and raised his own voice to match that of the sergeant.

'It does take a considerable amount of practice and experience,' he lied, looking earnestly honest. Like the sergeant, Stephen had very little idea of how an archaeologist was able to differentiate a genuine ruin from a pile of nondescript, jumbled and uneven-looking stones. 'Even with years of experience we can't always be certain that we've correctly interpreted what we've seen.' He cast a knowing glance at Rupert, who was looking decidedly uncomfortable in the swaying, hot, cramped confines of the lurching vehicle. It might have been made by Rolls-Royce, but the military vehicle had certainly not been designed with the occupants' comfort in mind.

'Sometimes we don't even know what it is that we are looking for … until we've actually found it,' continued Stephen, warming to his role.

'Have you two gents been archaeologists for long, then?' asked the sergeant.

Rupert stared at him, trying to decide if this was simply polite conversation, curiosity or something, perhaps, more sinister. Although nothing was said, Stephen did not share his friend's concerns. To him, it was obvious that this man was simply showing some sociable interest to pass the time.

'It has been some years now, since we first worked together in Egypt,' he shouted back at the sergeant, only half-lying this time, 'but things down there are often a lot easier to work out.'

Sergeant Ferris nodded his understanding and turned in his seat to peer out of the open letterbox slit in front of him. What Stephen had said about the object of a search was at least partly true in archaeology generally. In this particular quest, the reality was that they had only the vaguest idea of what it was they were searching for. They had found absolutely nothing at Tall Salāh – no scroll, no clues and certainly no ruins of a non-existent Crusader castle! They had, however, found a small cluster of outcropping rock, in the depressions of which there seemed to be traces of what looked like oil. Once, centuries ago, the porous nature of the rock must have allowed enough oil to force its way to the surface to collect and be ignited by the merciless heat of the sun. So the stories told by al Mohammed about 'the rocks which burn at Tall Salāh' had been partly correct, but now there was no oil and no burning. There had been nothing else of any interest and certainly nowhere to hide anything. If these few extinguished puddles in the rocks were the direction markers to the location of the Scroll of Gershom, then the hiding place to which they pointed had long since disappeared – if it had ever existed in the first place.

After a few minutes the sergeant swivelled around in his seat once again. 'Excuse me asking, Sir, but I am a bit curious. Don't you archaeologists have to make sketches and take measurements and that sort of thing?' He had found it a little strange that two archaeologists had seemingly set forth on an expedition without so much as a tape measure or ruler between them.

'Well ... yes, as a matter of fact we do, actually,' answered Rupert, 'but that is only when we actually discover something that needs to be accurately recorded...'

There was a pause, amply filled by the loud growling of the engine, but during which nothing seemed to happen.

'And this time, unfortunately, there was nothing worth recording,' interrupted Stephen, sensing that Rupert was struggling to think of something more convincing to say. 'That's the way it goes. Better luck next time, eh?' he added, smiling his most disarming and charming grin.

'Sarge,' said Private Woods, mercifully putting an end to the conversation, 'we've got a problem.'

'What's up, Woods?' asked the sergeant, turning his full attention to the driver and suddenly ignoring the other occupants in the rear of the vehicle.

'Listen, Sarge ... that doesn't sound too right...'

They listened as the engine continued to fill the confined space with its comforting growl, but there was something different in the tone – something menacing.

'It's the bloody water again!' muttered Woods. 'I thought they'd had a go at it the last time and fixed it!' Steam started to billow out from under the bonnet and escape into the arid desert air. 'She must be losing water again.'

'Is that serious?' asked Stephen.

'Not as long as we've got enough water to keep filling her up,' replied Ferris, 'and we've got plenty, so we'll still make it back to the fort. It just means that we'll have to stop every now and then to let things cool down before refilling the radiator. It's a damn nuisance, but she *is* getting on a bit.' He turned his head and grinned at the others. 'She should have been retired some time back. We've got another couple that were left over after the war ... we just about manage to keep them going, too.'

The armoured car crested a sand ridge and drove on to a flat plateau, where the ground was much firmer. Woods slowed down and finally came to a standstill, switching off the engine. The steady, comforting growl was abruptly replaced by the windless silence of the desert, the stillness of which was broken only by the steady hissing of the escaping steam.

'It'll be a while now, Sarge. She's got to cool down a bit first, before I can do anything,' said Woods, as he opened the driver's door and got out.

The blast of hot air that greeted his exit and filled the already hot interior of the vehicle took Rupert's breath away. He was used to the heat of Egypt, but this heat was quite different – all-embracing and sapping. They had been driving with all the hatches open, but what little air had been sucked in had made little difference to the discomfort of the passengers, although the soldiers seemed to be more used to it than were Stephen and Rupert.

'Water all round, I think,' said the sergeant, as he opened his door and got out.

It was a full thirty minutes before Woods and Potts managed to unscrew the radiator cap. Even then, once the seal had been broken, wispy tendrils of steam swirled seductively past their gloved hands, causing them to step away.

'You've done this before,' Stephen called out. He was fanning himself with his hat whilst sitting on the running board on the shaded side of the vehicle.

'Once or twice, Sir,' replied Potts, without taking his eyes off what he was busily doing with the water can and the radiator.

Rupert had wandered off a little way from the party to empty his bladder and was now walking back to them. 'What's that ... over there?' he asked, half-turning to point towards the distant horizon behind him.

For a few seconds Sergeant Ferris shielded his eyes from the glare and stared off in the direction in which Rupert was pointing.

'Bugger it!' he exclaimed, as he clambered into the vehicle, only to emerge seconds later carrying a pair of binoculars. 'It's a bloody sandstorm ... and a big bastard at that!'

'Can we outrun it?' asked Stephen. He had read about the intensity of desert sand storms.

'Not in this old girl,' replied the sergeant, half smiling, half smirking in a gesture of resigned acceptance. 'They can blow for days and if we try to keep moving we can easily get lost into the bargain.' There was a brief pause, as he once again looked through the binoculars. 'And that could be a fatal mistake,' he added, under his breath.

On the far horizon the dense cloud of sand, which had started out as barely a thin smudge, had thickened slightly as it drew ever nearer.

'Only one thing for it,' said Ferris, ever the practical soldier, 'we'll have to stay put and just batten down the hatches ... literally. Sand stations, lads!' he shouted to Woods and Potts. He lowered the binoculars on to the sweat-stained front of his shirt. 'We'll turn round and park rear-on to the storm ... over there, in the lee of this plateau...' He indicated the far side of the flat expanse in front of them. '... Then we'll cover the bonnet and engine with tarpaulins and just wait. That's what the Bedouin do ... camels and all!' he added, trying to make light of this sudden, unexpected element of their predicament. 'Woods, we need to move her ... over there,' he concluded, pointing.

'May I have a look through the binoculars, Sergeant?' asked Stephen.

Ferris handed them to him and walked off to supervise the moving of the armoured car to his satisfaction.

'Sergeant Ferris! Why don't we make a dash for that oasis ... over there,' Stephen said, lowering the binoculars and pointing.

Ferris turned from what he was doing. 'What oasis, Sir? There aren't any around these parts.'

'Then what's that tall black thing over there,' asked Stephen, still pointing. He handed the binoculars back to the sergeant. 'It could be a mirage, of course...'

The sergeant looked through the lenses in the direction indicated by Stephen's outstretched arm. After a few moments, Ferris spoke, but without taking his gaze from the distance.

'That's not a mirage, but I'm not convinced it's a palm tree either. There's nothing like that marked on our map for miles around,' he continued, adjusting the focus slightly. 'Damn it! These things aren't powerful enough. But there *is* something out there which could offer us some cover ... which is more than we've got here. Woods! Come and take a butcher's at this. What do you think? Can we cover the distance to that over there, before the sand catches up with us?'

The three soldiers were all very experienced in the ways of the desert. Woods took a look through the eyepieces before he answered.

'If we get a move on, Sarge. Are you done yet, Potts?' he shouted across to the parked vehicle.

'Full to the brim and cap secured,' replied Potts.

'Right then, let's be having you,' shouted Sergeant Ferris. 'Everyone back inside ... and let's hope that the old girl doesn't get too thirsty before we get there...'

32

London

Whitehall – early evening, Friday, 10th July 1931

The Uncle winced over his consommé as his dinner guest blew his nose yet again into a large, starched white handkerchief. 'That doesn't sound too positive, old man,' he said, disguising his irritation.

'It isn't, I'm afraid,' replied the other man through blocked nasal passages. The end of his nose had already begun to glow an angry red from the sustained use of his handkerchief. He wiped it gingerly and then replaced the damp square of cotton in his pocket. 'It rained cats and dogs during the parade down at Dartmouth last week … I got as wet as a drowned rat. All the braid didn't make any difference, either! I just had to stand there, saluting.' For a moment, it looked as if he might need the cotton square again, but the threatened dribble didn't materialize. 'So … what is it that's so vitally important that you wanted to talk over this particular evening? Your phrase "there is something important" is, more often than not, an understatement that usually has very serious underlying reasons for concern.'

During the break in the conversation, necessitated by his guest's nasal discomfort, the Uncle had finished his soup and had cast his eye around the other occupants of the dining room. They were in probably one of the safest places in London, but having learned that caution was always the best policy – even in the hallowed confines of a location as reliable as his club, he lowered his voice to ask. 'You already know about the provocative behaviour of the Italians and our so-called allies, the French ... with their ships in the Med?'

The other man nodded. Despite his grey hair he was several years younger than his host and his tanned skin bore evidence of a lifetime at sea – years of experience of practical seamanship – before the arms of his dress tunic became weighed down with the thick layers of heavy gold braid. 'I have been briefed,' he said, 'and I would agree. They seem to be up to something.'

'They most certainly are,' replied the Uncle. 'The only trouble is that we can't quite work out what it is ... yet. And that worries me considerably. They've flexed a joint muscle with these naval manoeuvres ... and then there was that business with...'

His voice trailed off into anonymous silence as an elderly waiter approached the table and removed the Uncle's empty soup plate. The other man waved his plate away with most of its contents untouched.

'... Then there was that business with our ships off Malta,' continued the Uncle as the waiter disappeared towards the kitchens. 'I'm grateful to you for your response to my memo. You say that *Lysander* and *Middlesex*, together with a couple of destroyers, will be on station in Valletta by the end of the week. That'll either put a stop to their little game or simply pump up the tension ... We'll just have to wait and see.'

The other man nodded in agreement.

It occurred to the Uncle that his guest's facial expression betrayed his unspoken wish to be tucked up in bed with a restorative hot toddy inside him.

'What really concerns us is that...'

Once again the Uncle broke off in mid-sentence, as the waiter returned to serve the fish course.

As soon as the fish dishes had been served, the Uncle resumed the thread of his conversation. 'What really concerns us is that there seems to be a naval arms race in full swing and we are being left way behind the starting line!'

The other man nodded in response.

'There are far too many politicians and do-gooders who are overly concerned with the amount of public finance being allocated disproportionately, in their misguided opinion, to the defence of the Realm and to the Royal Navy in particular,' snorted the Uncle contemptuously. 'We make the assessments and produce the requirement submissions, or at least we make the suggestions and your chaps at the Admiralty fill in the procurement documents and that's as far as it goes! That lot in Westminster just keep blocking our major naval building plans on the grounds of cost!'

'I know,' replied the other man, who had managed a mouthful of his Dover sole between attending to his dribbles. 'Some of our capital ships go back to before the war and they are falling to pieces ... literally. Then there are others that wouldn't stand a chance against what's coming out of the Italian and French shipyards, not to mention the production from the German yards, which could yet prove to be the biggest concern. You'd hardly think that they'd lost the war at all.' He paused and attempted a smile, before continuing, 'But then again, my dear fellow, I suppose that you are already aware of all of this?'

The Uncle raised his eyebrows and smiled benignly, much as a parent would do to acknowledge that what their child had just said was perfectly true. 'Although Germany was pulverized in the war, the country is now preparing for the next one and they're doing that by cleverly getting round or simply ignoring the rearmament restrictions placed on them at Versailles. They're turning out new warships and a great deal else besides ... almost as soon as the ink has dried on the planner's drawings!'

The room suddenly seemed to fall deadly silent.

'Mark my words, they *are* getting ready for another war,' the Uncle concluded ominously, before cutting into his poached fish with as much ease as the Kaiser's shells had sliced through the Royal Navy's armour-plated hulls at Jutland fifteen years before. Technology had moved on considerably since then – even if Britain's warship-building programme had not.

'What do you want me to do?' asked the other man. 'Not that I think there is much I can do, other than what we are already doing.'

'Keep up the pressure,' replied the Uncle. 'You have influential friends, just as I do. If that hopeless bunch of politicians down at Westminster can't see what is coming ... can't see the wood for the trees, as it were ... then it is up to us to force the issue and get things moving – before it is too late. When the shooting starts we can't be at all sure as to who will be shooting at whom. We can't fool ourselves into a sense of false security by relying on old alliances like last time, either. It really could boil down to us against...' He paused to mop his mouth with his table napkin. '... Shall we say, possibly everyone else?'

It was as if a heavy weight had suddenly descended on to the shoulders of the other man, as if the worst possible option had suddenly become the only one which Fate had left on the table. 'But what about the Americans,' he said nasally. 'There are always the Americans ... aren't there?'

'I need hardly remind you of the staggering speed with which they came to our aid during the last war,' replied the Uncle, a suggestion of annoyance in his voice. 'If it hadn't been for the German submarines sinking their ships willy-nilly outside their own ports, they'd have arrived here just in time for the victory parade ... and that could well have been in Berlin rather than London!'

'I say, old friend,' said the other man, as he reached once

again for his handkerchief, 'would you mind awfully if I call off the rest of our evening. My head is throbbing and I'm really not being much help in all of this...'

'My dear fellow ... of course,' replied the Uncle. How callous of me not to have noticed,' he lied, but nonetheless voicing a genuine concern. 'Let me get Richard to organize a taxi for you.'

'Much appreciated,' answered the other man, making ready to get unsteadily to his feet. 'Rest assured that you may tell your people that the Admiralty has received and understood the signal and will stand to, to help in whichever way it can.'

The Uncle continued to eat the rest of his meal alone, his mind turning over again and again the possible reasons for this unexpected naval activity on the part of the French and Italians. By the time he was served with his dessert, he had reached the stage of pondering on the truth that, in diplomacy as well as politics, there *were* no real allies – only self-interest. He picked up the heavy spoon and tapped the caramelized topping of his crème brûlée. It took two good taps before the surface fractured and gave way. As he sat and ate, he wondered if this present vexing situation would be any easier to crack.

33

Iraq

Early evening, Friday, 10th July 1931

'You have absolutely no right to keep us here! What you have done is highly provocative and is an act of open aggression!' thundered Sergeant Ferris, through the bars of the padlocked door.

It flashed through Rupert's mind that Ferris was not a man to cross or anger. Despite his easy-going and very affable nature, Reginald Ferris had a temper that could be easily prodded into flaming life. That prod had been delivered several hours before. All five of them had been ordered into the far end of a corrugated iron hut at bayonet point. Now imprisoned behind bars, they sat wherever they could – between the piles of spare drilling machinery and tins of machine oil – and tried to reason through the odd twist of events that had placed them unexpectedly in this situation.

Earlier that day, the Rolls-Royce had been making good progress across the sands towards the promise of protection that the mysterious, tall black object in the desert offered. Just as they approached this building, visibility had been reduced dramatically as the sun was blotted out by the swirling advance guard of the sandstorm. As the five occupants of the armoured vehicle had flung open the doors to clamber out of the vehicle and brave the angry elements in order to seek cover, they were surrounded by a well-armed group of uniformed men, muffled against the sand, brandishing rifles with fixed bayonets. Engulfed and disoriented by the beginnings of the sandstorm, the prisoners had not had the time to take in what was happening. They had simply been ordered to move forward, through what seemed to be a compound of some sort, before being herded into a small iron hut that was covered in several layers of thick, sand-coloured camouflage netting. Everything happened in a matter of minutes.

In the confusion and in competition with the rising wind, Stephen had heard several loud voices in a mixed chorus of enquiry and instruction; voices that had been shouting at each other in what sounded like French and Italian. Suddenly, they had found themselves alone in this small hut, locked behind a barred door and with the settling remnants of the billowing sand that had blown in as an accompaniment to their unceremonious entry into the hut, settling on the rough floorboards. Outside, the wind had howled angrily and clouds of whipped-up sand had been flicked violently into the air.

Some hours later, the sounds of the sandstorm died down. Ferris had been proved wrong in his assertion that the desert sandstorm might last for days. It had lasted a matter of only a few hours.

Confined as they were behind bars at the far end of the hut, Sergeant Ferris' temper had risen with their increasing discomfort. It was hot and stuffy.

Stephen Hopkins had been trying to rationalize the situation and was wondering, quite how his Uncle Cecil could intervene, when the door to the hut suddenly opened and a tall man, together with three other soldiers, squeezed in. The space had not been designed for so many bodies.

'What authority do you have to keep us here like this?' demanded Ferris.

'Your actions could well provoke a major international

incident,' interrupted Stephen, his voice somewhat more calm and conciliatory than the sergeant's. 'I do hope that you are fully aware of the consequences which will result from what you have done,' he continued, addressing the tall man who seemed to be in charge.

'That is your opinion, to which you are perfectly entitled...' replied the tall man in perfect, accent-free English. From his insignia, it appeared that he held the rank of captain. '...But it is not for me to decide what must happen next. That is for my superiors to do so, in Damascus.'

Ferris opened his mouth, but the man continued before the sergeant had a chance to say anything. 'In the meantime, gentlemen, given your demeanour and the fact that you arrived in a military vehicle and most of you seem to be in uniform, I have no option other than to detain you like this for the present.'

'Detain us on what grounds?' asked Rupert, who had joined the others crushed against the bars of the locked door.

'Given *your* appearance,' added the captain, pointing to Stephen and then to Rupert, 'I could shoot you for being spies. You are obviously not in uniform, therefore, I would be quite within my rights to do so, given the present situation.'

'What present situation?' asked Stephen, who was starting to feel his own anger rise. 'Has a war broken out about which we know nothing?'

The captain removed his sweat-stained kepi and was wiping the rivulets of sweat and congealed sand from the back of his neck with his hand. Behind him, crammed into the small hut, stood the three heavily-armed troopers, bayonets now returned to their scabbards, but their rifles held at the ready.

'How dare you keep us here like this!' snarled Sergeant Ferris, resuming his tirade more or less where he had left off, as if he were ordering a company around a square.

'It is really no good whatsoever shouting at me like that,

Sergeant,' said the captain, replacing the kepi on his head. 'You have been caught inside French territory and can offer no plausible reason as to why you should be here in the first place. You must now answer to my superiors in Damascus. There is nothing I can do.'

'We was nowhere near the Syrian border!' said Private Potts, glaring defiantly at the four armed men. 'It's you what's in the wrong place, *mate*!' He emphasized the last word. 'It's you what's inside British Iraq and it's you what should come back with us to Rutbah Wells to explain why.'

'My friend has a valid point,' said Stephen, lowering his voice. 'You know perfectly well that we are nowhere near the Syrian border. What is it that you're up to? Judging from this hut full of machinery and machine oil, it must be something to do with machines ... drilling machines ... ?' He left the sentence an open question, but the captain's face remained expressionless.

The atmosphere inside the hut was made worse by a distant, regular low whine. They had become aware of the noise, which was now irritating, as the sound of the storm died down. It suggested that some sort of heavy machinery was operating nearby.

'Why are the French and Italians drilling for oil inside Iraq ... inside British mandated territory?' asked Stephen suddenly, fixing his glare on the tall French officer.

'I have no idea what you are talking about,' snapped the captain, folding his arms across his chest. 'You are in French territory. It is you who should be offering explanations.'

'Oh, I think that you have a very good idea of what it is that I am talking about,' replied Stephen, who had managed to push his way past Sergeant Ferris. He grasped two of the iron bars of the door in his hands as he continued. 'All of this is just a little excessive to be drilling a borehole for water,' he continued, gesturing over his shoulder with his chin towards the stacked machinery behind him.

Once again, the captain did not answer, but simply glared at his inquisitor.

Stephen suddenly noticed the cap badge on the officer's kepi: 'And why would the Foreign Legion be inside British Iraq, perhaps drilling for British oil?'

The captain seemed to be unsure of what to say next.

'We had some of your chaps with us on the Western Front during the war. I was a doctor then, with the Royal Army Medical Corps. Were you involved...?' enquired Stephen, in a charmingly disarming manner, which was in sharp contrast to Sergeant Ferris's bluster.

For several seconds nothing was said and the hut was filled with nothing other than the irritatingly regular throb of the working machinery outside in the compound Eventually, the captain spoke proudly, 'Verdun ... I was at Verdun.'

'Then what are you doing out here in the desert ... on the wrong side of the border ... drilling for oil ...?' continued Stephen.

The captain did not answer immediately, but seemed to be weighing up what his response might be. He opened his mouth to speak – slightly, almost imperceptibly – but then thought better of it and shut it again. 'Your fate is for others to decide,' he admitted, after a pause for consideration. 'It is not for me to do so. I simply do what I am told.'

'There is going to be a lot of trouble over this,' said Sergeant Ferris, who had calmed down a little during the previous exchange between Stephen and the Foreign Legion captain.

The Frenchman did not respond, but rather turned his back on his prisoners and spoke softly to the three troopers. Their conversation was too soft for the prisoners to hear what was said, but the three troopers nodded their understanding of the orders they had been given and then left the hut. The captain watched them go and then turned back to face his prisoners.

'Gentlemen, I have no argument with you whatsoever. I wish to make that perfectly clear. We are brothers in arms,' he said, looking at Ferris and the two privates, 'and you two gentlemen, I regret to say, are definitely not the material from which spies are made!' At this last pronouncement, his face creased slightly into the beginnings of a grin. 'I knew of many comrades who were helped and saved by your Royal Army Medical Corps during the war. But that was then. Now, unfortunately, I have my orders and so that is that. We will leave for Damascus in the early hours of tomorrow morning. That will allow us to travel much of the way before the heat becomes too much. Then we will rest.'

Speaking rapidly and clearly, he appeared to be more relaxed than before. It was, however, also plainly obvious that he was used to giving orders. 'Luckily, you have provided your own transport, which we will use. It will be very cramped, but I am afraid to say that there is no alternative. The sand does not seem to have done any damage to the engine. One of my men has checked it ... He was a mechanic before joining the Legion.'

'What the hell made him do that?' asked Woods.

The captain glared at this lower order of the British Army, the icy determination returning once again to his chiselled features, wiping away the earlier hints of a softer side to the man's nature. 'We do not enquire into a man's past in the Legion,' he said coldly, misinterpreting Wood's question. 'Your vehicle is ready for our departure. We leave shortly after midnight. You will be given something to eat and drink before we set off.' Once again, he looked at the five prisoners, hemmed in behind the iron bars, and then turned on his heel to leave. As he reached the door he paused and half-turned to face them once again. 'Oh ... and one other thing, gentlemen ... you will be bound, I am afraid. I do not want any heroics or attempts at escape during our journey.' Then he was gone and the door to the hut was slammed closed. They were alone.

The rest of the evening seemed to drag by interminably. As evening became night, their surroundings cooled and the fetid silence was broken only by their soft conversation and by the steady throb of the machinery outside, which increased the tension within the hut as the sound became as a hammer beating against each of their skulls. In their discussions, whispered in case they were overheard, they reached agreement that any escape would be impossible once they were bound and crammed together with their guards in the confines of the Rolls-Royce.

Eventually, Private Woods suggested their course of action. 'When they bring in the food ... just before we go ... that's when we should get the bastards. Pottie here can give out like he's in agony and the rest of us can act all concerned and hysterical. Then, when they get the bars open, we 'ave a go at 'em ... wiv this,' he said, producing a fine, knotted string from around his waist, where it had been hidden under his regulation issue belt. 'I learned how to use this in India ... dangerous place, if you're not careful,' he added, smiling, 'but, if you knows what yer doin', it's very quiet ... and quick!'

Shortly before one o'clock the following morning, they were alerted by the sound of the bolt on the outside of the door to the hut being drawn back. Private Potts lay down on the floor and started moaning and twisting about, clutching his stomach in feigned agony. Seconds later, the door opened to reveal two of the troopers, the first of whom carried the promised provisions and a large can of water. Behind him came the second trooper, rifle slung over his shoulder and a hurricane lamp in one hand. They entered the hut, the light of the lamp casting weird, fantastical shadows across the walls.

'Help us!' said Ferris, making his voice sound desperate and pleading, but careful not to make too much noise. Outside, in the cold darkness of the compound, the tall black drilling gantry whined on, the noise of its labours filling the little hut and almost drowning out the hissing of the hurricane lamp. 'He is ill, help us!' repeated Ferris, pointing to the writhing Potts and gesturing towards his own stomach.

'Huh?' said the first trooper, not understanding what Ferris had said. The second trooper put the lamp down on the floor and unslung his rifle.

'*S'il vous plaît, monsieur, assistez-nous. Malade...*' said Stephen, pointing to Potts and trying to remember his schoolboy French.

To emphasize the point, Potts squirmed with greater energy and let out another low, sustained moan as he clutched his stomach with renewed vigour.

The first trooper put down what he was carrying and fumbled with the key in the large padlock that secured the barred door to their prison. What happened next seemed to do so in even less time than had the events of their arrival at the compound the previous day. The first trooper had just cleared the threshold of the door, when Woods turned on him and had the cord around his neck in a flash. The trooper's arms flailed the air, but the man was dead before he could make any noise. As the human shapes danced across the walls, mixing with the shadows cast by the lamp, the second trooper started to swing his rifle round to face the mêlée in the cell. He did not notice Ferris, who had nipped behind Woods and shot out of the door in a single, fluid movement. In his hand he held a heavy steel gearwheel which he had taken off one of the shelves. The sergeant darted at the surprised second trooper, bringing himself up to his full height as he did so. He swung his arm upwards, smashing the heavy gear into the trooper's face, causing him to reel backwards and collapse on to the floor. Ferris maintained his forward motion and fell forward, landing on top of the unconscious man. Suddenly, the apparent chaos that had filled the hut moments before evaporated, leaving Ferris, Potts and Woods panting for breath, but victorious. There were no obvious signs of alarm out in the compound and everything remained silent, apart from the hiss of the lamp and the unending throb from the machinery of the drilling rig.

'I'll put this down, then,' said Stephen quietly, as he replaced a large, heavy spanner on the shelf. 'Glad I didn't have to use it, after all.'

'Well done, men,' Rupert said, putting his own weapon, a length of heavy steel pipe, down on the floor, 'What now, Ferris?'

'Kill the lamp and let's get out to the car ... Potts, you take the rifles. Follow me ... and not a sound ... I want to hear the flies shitting ... all right? Any trouble and you two leave the fighting to us.'

It was a cloudless, cold night and the moon gave off sufficient light for them to be able to gingerly pick their way across the compound, using the huts as cover. The Rolls-Royce was parked almost where they had left it when they arrived, on the far side of the compound. To get to it they would have to pass close to the drilling rig, making sure to keep to the shadows and avoid being seen in the light reflected from the masked working lamps on the rig itself.

'Listen,' whispered Rupert in Stephen's ear, as they passed close to the rig. There were people working in the light, servicing the demands of the machinery. 'They're speaking Italian ... It's like being back in Pompeii...'

'... And we don't want to be reminded too closely of that experience, do we...?' muttered Stephen, cutting across Rupert's sentence. 'Come on ... almost there,' he said, as

Potts beckoned to them to follow him across the last part of their escape route.

Ferris had already carved his way through the moonlit compound and was silently prising open the door on the passenger side of the armoured car, on the side furthest away from the huts. Like a line of well-trained ants, they were inside the Rolls-Royce almost as soon as they reached it.

'So far, so good,' whispered Ferris, once they were all inside and the door had been silently and carefully closed again. 'Right you are, Potts ... Reckon you can get her going in one go?'

'Easy as falling off a log, Sarge,' replied the Private. 'You just try and stop...'

There was a sudden thump from the back of the vehicle – a sound of metal falling against metal. For a split second, it seemed to fill the still desert air with a deafening cacophony of unwelcome sound. It was followed by an equally sudden stillness. All five of them held their breath. If it came to it, they had their own rifles, the Webley revolver and plenty of ammunition – that was all still in its place – and they would have the benefit of being encased in steel plating for cover, even if it meant that they were sitting ducks. The seconds ticked by and there was nothing, save for the sound of the rig.

'Sorry,' whispered Rupert from the rear of the armoured car, 'that was me. I knocked over this can ... didn't see it in the gloom.'

In their haste to outrun the sandstorm, Potts and Woods had put the water can they had used to refill the radiator in the back of the Rolls-Royce with the passengers, instead of securing it in its proper storage position. In the dark, Rupert had accidentally knocked it over.

'If anyone heard it, they probably thought it was something to do with the workings over there,' whispered Ferris, stabbing the air in the general direction of the rig. 'No damage done. Right, Potts ... let's go!'

The Foreign Legion captain had been quite right in his praise for his legionnaire-mechanic. The old ironclad of the desert sprang into life at the first attempt. It was as if she had been resting and now, in answer to the summons to be on her way, was champing at the bit to do so.

'Good girl!' wheezed Potts, as he let out the clutch and swung the wheel around, sending the vehicle into a wide arc away from the compound. In the blackness of the night, even allowing for the moonlight, he couldn't see much in front of him through his driver's slit. He remembered that their approach, despite the swirling sand, had been almost perfectly flat, so he drove on with renewed confidence. He pressed the accelerator hard to the floor and the Rolls-Royce shot forward with even greater energy, into the safety of the desert night. As the lights on the drilling rig receded, to become as small and distant as the other twinkling lights in the sky, Woods said that he thought he heard shots, but the general consensus was that he must have been mistaken. The comforting growl of the revitalized engine had masked any such sound.

'Tell you what, Sarge,' said Potts, 'that Froggie mechanic seems to know his stuff. Listen to her ... She's fair purring along.'

The sergeant had more pressing thoughts on his mind. 'This is going to take a lot of believing when we report back,' said Ferris, over his shoulder from the front seat, where he was sitting next to Potts.

'I'm not sure if that's such a good idea, actually,' said Stephen, as he bounced and bumped around in the darkness. 'There could be the most frightful stink if this got any further than the few of us,' he said.

'But ... Sir ... surely we have to report the French for being in the wrong place?' asked Ferris incredulously.

'Ordinarily, yes, but perhaps not this time. You know what red tape is like ... Anything you report will have to be passed on, higher and higher ... until ...' Stephen paused, '... well, let's say that there could be some really messy repercussions.'

'But they were going to take us to Damascus ... I suppose they could have imprisoned us,' said Rupert, somewhat alarmed at what his friend was proposing, 'just like they tried to do in Pompeii, when...'

'Exactly,' cut in Stephen, 'you and I both know what happened in Pompeii, but the official Government version will make it look as if your internment by the Blackshirts was just a misunderstanding and that no harm was intended. We know that everyone is lying through their diplomatic teeth to cover everything up. It'll be exactly the same here.'

'I'm not sure that I follow you, Sir,' said Ferris, who had no idea what the references to Pompeii meant.

'That drilling camp will be long gone by the time any of our chaps go looking for it. It was all very temporary and wasn't meant to be discovered in the first place ... hence all the camouflage. Any accusations we make against the French will be hotly denied, as will any protests about them being within our territory. Without the physical presence of the drilling camp, we can prove nothing. Even if we did accuse them of what *we* know they were doing, without any hard evidence to present on our part, they would simply beat their diplomatic chest with typical Gallic overreaction and go out of their way to make the British out to be the aggressors. All things considered, it would be us who would look stupid and end up with mud on our faces...'

There was a lengthy period of silence, during which everyone was lost in their own thoughts.

'... In any case, we will still arrive back at the fort tomorrow night as anticipated. Although we stayed only the one day at Tall Salāh, the time we gained there by leaving a day early was effectively lost by being locked up by the Foreign Legion. Despite that, to all intents and purposes our expedition will appear to have gone to plan,' Stephen summated.

'So you mean that French lot will get off scot-free,' said Sergeant Ferris, eventually.

'Not exactly, Sergeant,' replied Stephen. 'Our friendly captain is going to have to explain how one of his chaps was killed and another had his face smashed in and, as if that's isn't enough, he's also probably going to have to explain how he could be so careless as to let us escape, leading to the entire drilling camp having to be spirited away, as quickly and as mysteriously as it got there in the first place. No, I wouldn't say that they'll get off scot-free at all. And, most importantly, we're all still in one piece.'

Some hours later, outside the still-speeding vehicle and barely visible through the driver's slit, the first pale fingers of dawn could be seen clawing their way up the eastern horizon. The general mood had also brightened, since the tension earlier in the night. Sitting in the darkness at the back of the Rolls-Royce, Stephen sat tracing patterns on Rupert's back. The illicit nature of such an expression of their relationship brought a thrill to his being and diverted his attention from his throbbing stump. What also occupied his mind was the question of why the French had been so far over the border in the first place and why they seemed to have been in such close co-operation with the Italians. They might not have found the hiding place of the Scroll of Gershom, but they had certainly found something else, potentially just as politically explosive. Even if no official report were to be lodged once they reached the Wells, Stephen knew that his uncle would have to be told.

As the dawn advanced further and the desert began to brighten up, it occurred to Sergeant Reginald Ferris that the intensifying dawn was very much like the thought he had been harbouring in his head since Stephen had proposed the idea of not reporting what they had seen and experienced. Like the blossoming dawn, Ferris's idea had grown until the obviousness of it all had almost struck him physically between the eyes. This man – this passenger in the back – was no more an archaeologist than he was. Neither, for that matter, was his companion. He had everything far too well worked out to be simply a digger after the past. Everything was always far too logically explained and far too well reasoned through to have been done by someone who wasn't used to dealing with similar situations. For his part, Ferris would never have thought of half the things this chap had put forward as sound reasons to keep the incident quiet. And this mystery man also seemed to know a lot about politics and diplomacy – too much to simply be an interested outsider. As the sun blazed its arrival across the desert, Sergeant Ferris confined his thoughts to pondering over one simple question: if this man wasn't an archaeologist, then who – and more importantly, *what* – was he?

34

Jerusalem

The Old City – afternoon, Thursday, 16th July 1931

Hurva Square was bathed in the warmth of the afternoon sun. As people went about their business there was the subdued hum of conversation and commerce in the air.

Morris Ginsberg sat on one of the benches eating an apple. He had seen the fruit displayed on the pavement outside the little Spanish delicatessen across the square and had given in to the temptation to buy one. It was crisp and juicy. He thought he'd buy one for Claudie – she particularly enjoyed a firm, crispy apple. She would relish the surprise and it would be easy enough to do, because he would have to pass the shop again on his way back home. He didn't actually know why he was sitting on the bench – he had no specific reason to go to the square that afternoon. It had been a gut reaction to a premonition. He felt sure that *they* would contact him that very afternoon. It irked him that *they* would always contact *him*. It was never the other way around. *They* would never allow it to be. And this time, for a change, Morris actually had something to pass on.

He had been sitting on the bench for nearly an hour and had long since finished picking the remaining shards of the apple out of his teeth. In the time that he had been sitting there, he had started drawing imaginary patterns on the cobbles with his foot and had finally decided that the bench was actually quite uncomfortable. Perhaps the day was not to be a contact day after all. He sighed, resignedly, and made to get up. Claudie would be waiting for him back at the house.

I hope Claudie's headache is better by now. The apple will cheer her up, he thought.

'Shalom...' said a deep, musical, male voice from behind him. '... Sit down.'

'Shalom ... I thought that I might hear from you today,' said Morris, doing as he was told and settling himself back on to the uncomfortable bench.

'Why? What made you think that?' asked the voice, immediately suspicious and on the defensive.

'Nothing ... no reason ... I just thought I might hear from you today. I can hardly say "I thought I'd *see* you today," can I?' said Morris, who as ever found the cloak-and-dagger nature of his contacts irritating. There was no reaction from the voice. Morris had decided some time ago that the owner of the deep voice did not possess a sense of humour. 'It's just that today I have something to tell you,' continued Morris.

'Indeed?'

'Something Mordechai overheard ... at the hotel.'

There was a silence, during which the contented sounds of the square floated around them.

'Well?' demanded the voice. 'What was it that Mordechai heard?'

'It was in the hotel. You remember that Mordechai waits on the tables in the lounges?'

There was a further pause. 'Go on,' said the voice.

'The two Englishmen came back to the hotel on Tuesday ... the same men that I told you about two weeks ago. Even I remember them from before ... They liked Claudie's singing and applauded politely ... So, anyway, they left the hotel after a few days ... and now they're back to stay again.'

'Is this what you have to tell me?' asked the voice, sounding impatiently disappointed.

'If you'll let me continue,' said Morris, feeling that he held the upper hand for a change. It was a new feeling for him in these meetings and it was a feeling he enjoyed enormously. Although careful not to let his new sense of superiority show through his voice, he added, 'They came back from Rutbah Wells ... That's over in Iraq. They had been out in the desert ... or something like that. Anyway, they were back in the hotel and one of them had been handed an envelope from the reception desk. When they opened it, they took out some photographs and a letter. One of them read out the letter. Mordechai was careful to walk around the tables slowly, so that he could hear properly. He's a sly one, that Mordechai...' Morris chuckled. 'Anyway, the note said something about the photographs being some copies of what had been taken at Petra ... also something about there being a colour photograph as well. Apparently the writer also apologized for there being only a single colour picture, as they were expensive to produce.' Morris subsided into another pause. He was beginning to enjoy this particular encounter with his minder.

'And...?' demanded the voice, displaying distinct signs of impatient annoyance.

'One of them picked up the colour picture and looked at it for a few seconds. Then he said something about how they'd been running around on a wild-goose chase ... off into the desert. The other one got excited too, but when they realized that they were attracting attention from the other residents in the lounge, they then became very conspiratorial. Mordechai's got a good pair of ears on him ... He could still hear what they were saying: *So it's in Petra, after all.* Then the other replied something about: *The rocks that burn ... it's the rising sun that turns them red and makes them look as if they're burning ... nothing to do with oil or Tall Salāh at all!*'

'You're sure that is what was said?' asked the voice, suddenly very interested. 'Was anything else mentioned?'

'They both got very excited when one of them pointed to an outcrop of rock, which cast a shadow on the cliffs. It must have looked like a bird ... Mordechai thought one of them said: *The eagle's a stone one!* And then the other one said: *Maybe the bird's beak points to a cave in the cliff.* By that stage they were laughing and seemed to be very excited and they started to whisper ... very fast. Then one of them said that they would have to tell someone called Cecil about it and the other one replied that they could investigate it during the next tour.'

'What next tour?'

'Mordechai says that one of them works for a tour company and that the other one is a medical doctor. He has ways of finding the answers to such questions already, does Mordechai.'

'A tour company?' repeated the voice. 'A tour company, which operates a tour to Petra. That could be of great importance. Are they still in the hotel?'

'No. They have booked out and have gone to Cairo and Alexandria, but they have made another reservation at the hotel for the end of September.'

'I will report our conversation. You have done well. Perhaps you should hold yourself ready to leave Jerusalem at very short notice. We may have something for you to do, at last,' said the voice.

Once again there was a lull in the conversation. A group of small children were shepherded across the square and disappeared down one of the side streets. Two women stood in animated conversation on the far pavement. A young lad was pushing a cart of freshly harvested vegetables towards the delicatessen. It was a pleasant afternoon to be sitting in the sunshine.

'Do you have any idea when that might be?' asked Morris

eventually. 'I mean, when it might be that we will have to leave Jerusalem. Claudie still has performances to give...'

There was no answer. Morris waited a short while and then carefully turned to look over his shoulder. The bench behind him was empty, save for a folded copy of that day's *Haaretz* newspaper.

Oh ... all right then, we must just be ready, Morris realized. He got to his feet and walked around to the other bench. He picked up the paper and carefully peered into the folded pages. There was the money, as usual. *Oy!* he thought, as he folded the paper on itself again and slipped the money into his pocket, before walking off across the square towards the little Spanish delicatessen.

An apple for my Claudie and ... perhaps, another one for myself.

35

London

Pall Mall – noon, Thursday, 13th August 1931

The lingering aroma of cigar smoke and pipe tobacco filled the members' smoking room with a strangely comforting feeling of permanence. Around the large room there were several members of the club, seated comfortably in the richly upholstered armchairs that were dotted around the wood-panelled room. It was a masculine retreat from the hurly-burley world of London and the Empire on the other side of the tall, brocade-draped windows. Painted images of those former club members who were now numbered amongst the great and the good of the nation gazed down complacently from the walls. From a couple of plinths stared the marble busts of the very select few considered even greater and better than their peers who hung on the walls. Over the preceding two centuries much British foreign policy had been conceived and thrashed out within these hallowed precincts, often with results that reverberated loudly around the globe. This was a strange contradiction in terms, as, within the confines of the club, it was considered impolite to speak in anything much above a gentle, barely audible whisper.

'Another one?' asked the Uncle, nodding towards the two glasses on the small round table that stood between their chairs.

'Thanks, rather a good one, that,' Stephen said, draining the last remaining mouthful from his glass before replacing it on the table.

As if by magic, a waiter appeared at his uncle's elbow.

'The same again please, Gerald.'

The empty glasses were removed and the waiter disappeared once again into the deceptively peaceful lethargy that was the club.

'That was a stroke of luck ... your American photographer sending you some of his handiwork,' said the Uncle, picking up the buff folder from the table and resting it in his lap.

'Of course, it could be exactly that, Sir,' replied Stephen, 'but it's all we have managed to find out ... perhaps it might lead us to this scroll ... if it exists at all.'

Stephen stretched his left leg out in front of him; the stump was beginning to throb again. Since returning to London, he had found that it was much more sensitive and he had to rely on the heavy black cane more and more. Rupert had tried to make light of it by suggesting that the stump might well be allergic to the English climate. Stephen had been inclined to agree – in the heat of the Middle East his stump worried him far less. These days it throbbed almost continuously. He moved his position in the chair again, resting his left hand on the ornate silver handle of the cane – the symbolic phoenix, with its ruby-red eyes.

'As I reported to you, the people we spoke to seemed to have not the vaguest idea that such a document might exist ... in folklore or otherwise,' said Stephen, 'and the only pointer we thought we had ... the burning rocks ... was a white elephant. There was absolutely nothing out at Tall Salāh, except for the Foreign Legion, the Italians and a drilling rig.'

'I had a word about that with some of the people in the know,' said the Uncle, smiling. 'The French were running around diplomatically like the Keystone Cops at the cinema, denying that any of their people would even dream of crossing an ally's border without permission. The Italians made little comment, other than to say that there must have been some sort of a mistake, as they were not in the habit of sending their people into someone else's territory without asking permission first. It all sounded as if they were singing two translations of the same verse from the same hymn sheet...'

The waiter silently reappeared and placed the two glasses of scotch on the table.

When they were alone again, the Uncle continued, '... And, of course, officially none of it ever happened. But they have been caught with their trousers down, nonetheless, and had to do some pretty quick thinking to squirm out of the mess they had got themselves into. Thanks to you ... cheers,' he continued, picking up his glass. 'Here's to the next embarrassment you cause them...'

'Winfield and I, Uncle,' corrected Stephen, replacing his glass on the table. 'I thought that we had an *Entente Cordiale* with the French. Aren't they supposed to be our staunch allies?'

'Indeed we do, and yes ... of course they are, dear boy ... but only when it suits them. At the moment, it would seem that they are sniffing around looking for new partners. The old alliances have worn very thin, so when the next war comes...'

Stephen cut across his uncle. 'Please excuse the interruption, Sir,' he said, sitting more erect in his chair. 'Do you think that there is going to be another one ... after the mess of the last one? Surely, we cannot let that nightmare repeat itself ... can we?'

For a moment, the Uncle stared hard at his nephew, his face a mask of utter seriousness. 'The Government will go to endless lengths to try and avoid another one, but I'm afraid there isn't much we *can* do to avoid it, my dear boy.

The Russian Bear to the north is totally unstable, the Italians are bent on creating a new Roman Empire somewhere ... starting most likely in Africa ... and the French, well they are very much under a question mark. We also have our own problems. India is rife with nationalist fervour and there is trouble in some of our African colonies and even labour unrest on a small island like Mauritius. Then there is the threat from the Far East. Japan was with us last time, but the next time...' He paused, looking even more serious than before. '... They have flexed their expansionist muscles already and they obviously like the feeling of the power that brings. There's going to be trouble over China, too. Japan needs raw materials to fuel her war machine, so she's casting covetous eyes to the Chinese mainland, where such materials are to be found in abundance. I fear they will soon emerge as an enemy rather than as an ally, so we can't count on them for support in the Far East.'

Stephen had relaxed slightly into his chair and had again moved the position of his left leg. 'Which means a threat to Singapore and Hong Kong?' he said seriously.

The Uncle nodded and took a sip from his glass.

'Do we actually *have* to rely on anyone else?' continued Stephen. 'After all, we have our cousins across the Atlantic.'

The Uncle smiled, but it was the smile of a cynic. 'I would predict that the only way they will voluntarily enter the conflict will be as a result of Germany bombing New York or the Japanese invading Hawaii ... or both. They are generally rather unreliable, I'm afraid,' he said, 'and they are far too concerned with their own good. It's the legacy of the inward-looking foreign policy which hasn't changed much since the days of President Lincoln. Remember Wilson at Versailles? He saw himself as the arbiter of the delegations to the Peace Conference, but it was very much a case of him telling everyone else what to do and Congress in Washington telling him not to get too involved in Europe. It's all a bit of a contradiction, actually. The annoying thing is that we *will* need them when the balloon goes up. Their production capacity makes ours look like a run-down cottage industry!'

The waiter appeared once again. 'Your table will be ready for you in a quarter of an hour, Sir. Perhaps you would care to peruse the luncheon menu...?'

After they had done so and ordered their meal, the Uncle picked up the buff folder from his lap. 'That is quite enough about the approaching chaos on the international stage,' he said, taking his horn-rimmed spectacles from his suit pocket. 'It goes without saying that there are plenty of problems for us to address within the Empire, not least of which is the Palestine question.' He opened the folder and removed a colour photograph. 'So, your American chap took this, did he?'

'Yes, Sir,' answered Stephen, who had had the image duplicated photographically before giving it to the Uncle. 'He said that he had gone up to the top of the mountain called the High Place of Sacrifice well before dawn, so that he could set up his equipment in time for the sunrise. That photograph is the result.'

'And this could well be the hiding place Professor Longhurst referred to in his translation of the tablet in the British Museum?'

'It is possible – yes, Sir,' replied Stephen. 'At that particular moment, when Harrison pressed his button and took the photograph, the scene he captured does seem to match the details of the professor's translation somewhat.'

The Uncle looked again at the photograph with its broad expanse of majestic cliffs, flaming red as the sun rose on them. Spread across part of the cliffs, like a projected image, was a pale shadow in the shape of a large bird, its wings outstretched and its beak turned to one side. It must have been cast by an innocuous-looking outcrop of rock on the other side of the valley, from the bed of which rose the massive bulk of Jabal al-Madhbah, the High Place of Sacrifice. Across the cliff face there were several shadows indicating the presence of caves.

Stephen pointed to these shadows and suggested that perhaps at a certain time during sunrise, the bird's beak would line up exactly with one of those shadows. 'We have to go back and watch the effect of the sunrise on that cliff face to determine which cave we must explore.'

'And to think that you were that close to it,' said the Uncle, barely concealing his excitement.

'Indeed, and to think that we missed it,' added Stephen, 'but the light plays strange tricks out there, Sir. The colours it creates, because of the minerals in the rocks, can change literally from minute to minute as the sun rises or sets. When we were up there with Professor Unsworth it was quite early, but already too late in the day for us to be presented with the same image Harrison had captured when he was up there at dawn.'

The Uncle continued to study the photograph in silence. 'I've had Rabbi Mosheowitz back for another chat ... I didn't say anything about this, of course. He still claims that he doesn't know anything about a Scroll of Gershom, but I am convinced that he is being very economical with the truth. We've also been keeping an eye on the Jewish Agency recently and they seem to know that something is in the air. The Jewish nationalist movements in Palestine also seem to have been more active of late, so I'd suggest that they are all in the know about the scroll. At least we're one step ahead of them. Does anyone else know about this?' he asked, holding up the photograph.

'No,' replied Stephen, 'although I have had a copy made ... for future use. I can't begin to tell you how excited we were once we had deciphered the colour photograph Harrison had left behind for us.'

That was very true. Back at the Petra Hotel in the Old

City of Jerusalem, when they realized what the photograph was showing them, Stephen and Rupert had been so excited that they had not noticed the waiter, who was hovering amongst the tables in the background.

'Good,' replied the Uncle, 'you must go back ... to Petra ... and finish this business once and for all. How's Winfield doing?'

'Very well, thank you, Uncle. He asks to be remembered to you.'

'Pity he couldn't join us here today,' replied the Uncle affably.

'Indeed, but unfortunately he has several meetings to attend at his company's headquarters. The first tour of the Holy Land was really quite a success ... apart from the unfortunate incident with Professor Unsworth...'

'Ah yes,' interjected the Uncle, 'the good professor...', but nothing further was said on that subject.

'Winfield has several suggestions to make with a view to improving the next tour when it sets out towards the middle of September. He and I should be back in Jerusalem by then.'

The Uncle nodded his understanding.

'What do we do if things get nasty, assuming we find something when we get back to Petra? Whom do we turn to ... in Trans-Jordan? There is a solitary policeman in Wadi Musa, but that's two hours away from the ruins.'

'I hope that there will be no need for anything like that,' replied the Uncle, 'but we'll put a contingency plan in place to cover any such eventuality, never fear.'

Stephen should have felt comforted by that, but somewhere deep down in his stomach he felt a twinge of apprehension. He had the memory of the time his uncle had "put a plan in place" to protect them when they had become embroiled in diamond smuggling in Egypt. He would have preferred to have had something more concrete by way of reassurance.

'Sir,' said Stephen, resting both hands on the handle of his cane, 'can I ask you why it is *we* who have been charged with this task and not one of your agencies ... Military Intelligence, for example?'

'You know about the volatile nature of things in Palestine. Too many people running around looking for this scroll would be counterproductive. There would be too many people who would have to be in the know and, besides, the red tape you have to wade through when you work with some of these departments is truly restrictive ... Even my powers and contacts have a limit.'

There was the sound of a soft clearing of the throat. 'Excuse me, Sir, but your table is ready for you now.' Gerald had once again appeared from the very ether. 'If you would like to follow me...'

36

Bury St Edmunds, Suffolk

Hawkhurst Aeronautics – afternoon, Thursday, 13th August 1931

At the same time as the Uncle and his nephew were enjoying their luncheon, Alexandra stood watching a silver Avenger aircraft taxi to a standstill at the end of the runway attached to the factory of Hawkhurst Aviation. Chocks were placed against the two wheels and the mechanics climbed up on to the broad wings to release the cockpit canopy.

'She handles like a dream,' said Lawrence, as he jumped down on to the grass, his flying helmet in his hand. 'I prophesy that His Highness will be very pleased.'

Brother and sister turned and walked across the expanse of grass that separated the aircraft stand from the main office block. Once inside, they climbed the stairs to Alexandra's office, which overlooked the runway, and sat down.

'Flying her is a piece of cake,' he repeated, taking a cigarette and lighting it, before lounging back in the chair and resting his feet on the edge of her desk.

Alexandra had long ago given up trying to correct what she saw as her brother's errant ways.

'There was talk of him ordering more...' he said, smiling through the smoke. 'Well, after he's had a spin in her, I'd say that a further order is just a formality.'

'That's your opinion,' she said, 'but it doesn't pay to count your chickens...'

'... Before they've hatched. I know, I know,' he said, good-naturedly, 'as you are always reminding me. Still, I'd say it's in the bag.'

They were interrupted by the telephone ringing on the desk. The conversation did not last long before Alexandra replaced the handset.

'And now, I'm going to hold you to your promise, made on the water so long ago ... I bet you thought that I'd forgotten about it,' he said, looking boyish with excitement.

Alexandra looked at him with patient tolerance on her face. 'As if I would ever bring myself to even think of such a thing,' she said in mocking reproach.

'Of course, you wouldn't,' he said, smiling, 'so I've thought of a way of mixing business with pleasure. That should please you.'

'I'm really so excited, I can hardly contain myself, Law, dear,' she answered, in a maternal way, as a mother might tolerantly talk to an exasperating child. 'Am I to be a party to this idea of yours?'

'Rather,' he replied, swinging his feet off the edge of the desk and sitting upright. 'We fly the Avenger out to Iraq and deliver it to HRH ourselves ... I'll fly his and you fly a second one ... the one I tested yesterday. We'll drop his off in Baghdad and then fly back to Jerusalem and go off on our tour. Look at this...' He thrust his hand into his pocket and took out a folded and crumpled piece of paper. 'This was in the *Daily Telegraph* this morning. It's an advertisement for a tour of the Holy Land and Petra, including Jerusalem. I can go and pick up a brochure and we can book ourselves on to it. If we get ourselves out there before we join it, they might even give us a discount on the fares we won't require.' Lawrence Hawkhurst was a strapping young man, well-built and muscular, but now he was rambling on, without pausing for breath, like a schoolboy let loose in a sweetshop. 'Then, after we've done the tour and seen the sights, we'll fly ourselves back home in your Avenger. She's a two-seater and there's plenty of room for a suitcase or two. What do you think? You promised,' he added, losing nothing of his boyish excitement.

37

Jerusalem

The Old City – afternoon, Thursday, 13th August 1931

The third thing happening that day in the web that was being spun by Fate occurred thousands of miles away in Hurva Square in the atmospheric Jewish Quarter of the Old City of Jerusalem.

Earlier that day, Morris Ginsberg had been approached by Mordechai and told to go to the square. That could only mean one thing – *they* must have recruited the waiter to their cause as well. He felt a spasm of disquiet course through his veins as he considered the twin, disturbing thoughts that currently occupied him the most. First, he wondered just how far *they* could reach within the society of Palestine without anyone becoming any the wiser; second, and even more alarming, was the possibility that he had allowed himself – no, he *and* his beloved Claudie – to be drawn into something which was obviously far beyond the little organization he had originally thought it to be, back in the seemingly distant days of the Golden Moon nightclub in Haifa. What had originally appeared to be a passport to better things – a way forward – had now developed into something exceedingly ominous which, he worried, might have a very high price tag attached to it. If push came to shove, did he really want the two of them to find themselves in the position of having to pay that high price? What concerned him greatly was an awareness that they might no longer have the luxury of being able to make such a choice. When the piper played his tune, they would have to dance.

He sat on the bench in the corner of the square and waited with his mind full of these unpleasant thoughts. For nearly an hour he sat there, waiting.

'Shalom,' said a deep voice behind him.

'Shalom,' mumbled Morris in reply.

'We have a task for you ... at last,' said the voice. 'We are very pleased with your work ... the report you made concerning the doctor and the tour manager.'

It flashed through Morris's mind that he hadn't actually *done* anything for *them* worthy of commendation. He had simply passed on something that had been overheard.

'And your contact Mordechai has done equally well. His information is what we have been waiting for.'

So, thought Morris, *you've been talking to Mordechai as well, have you? How wide does your net spread?*

'I thought that his information might be of use to you...' Morris lied convincingly. He had no idea as to the deeper meaning of what Mordechai had overheard in the hotel, any more than did Mordechai himself. '... To *us*', he added, after a pause. He was starting to sweat and he fancied that he had detected the first, faintest whiff of lurking danger. He thought it best to smother any outward signs of anything which could be misinterpreted as disloyalty or nervousness.

'There is something which could be vital to our people and give them divine authority to exist. It is a scroll ... an ancient scroll.'

'A scroll?' repeated Morris, in disbelief, wondering if he had heard the deep voice correctly 'How can a scroll be important to the people. Which people...?'

'The People of David,' answered the voice, full of serious intent and tinged with a little menace. 'It is the Scroll of

Gershom, son of Moses and the one chosen to lead the people to the promised state of Israel.'

'And a scroll is going to accomplish this thing?' asked Morris, disbelief creeping dangerously into his voice. He had to fight to hide the suggestion of humour in his voice that this man's last remark had provoked.

'The scroll is going to give us and the world the proof that we have the divine right to exist in the Land of David.'

'I see,' answered Morris, but he was not that convinced that he actually did. 'And where is this wondrous scroll?'

'That is where you come in,' said the voice. 'We need you to go and bring it back to us.'

'Go where?' asked Morris, resisting the temptation to turn around and finally look the voice squarely in the face.

'Petra.'

'Where is this place Petra?' asked Morris. He had never heard of the name before Mordechai had mentioned overhearing it in the hotel.

'It is an ancient city in Trans-Jordan,' replied the voice in a very matter-of-fact manner. 'Your friend Mordechai overheard the two Englishmen foolishly announce to the world that they had finally found the scroll's hiding place ... when they looked at the photographs in the hotel.'

Morris was beginning to lose the thread of the conversation. 'I still do not see how a scroll ... even an ancient one ... is going to do what you say.' As there was no reply, he started to worry. For a second he felt the hint of fear in his stomach turn into reality. Had he gone too far with his questioning? Was the voice behind him still there? He did not dare to turn around and look.

'Shalom, Morris,' said another voice behind him, after what seemed like several minutes, but which in reality had only been a matter of seconds. 'We want you to do this for us. You have the military training and you have the courage.' This voice was far more soothing, more coaxing.

'Do you not have younger men ... fighters ... that you could send instead?'

'Not level-headed men with your experience,' replied the soothing voice. 'You will have to make judgements on your own and then act upon them without hesitation. It is essential that the scroll be returned to us. There will be others looking for it.'

There was a slight pause, during which Morris suddenly noticed the singing of a little bird, perched on a nearby bush. It reminded him of his Claudie's singing. She was his little bird and now he felt as if he had dragged her – both of them – into a cage from which there might not be any escape.

'Do you understand me, Morris? It must be returned to *us.*'

'Is there someone else who wants it then?' asked Morris lamely. Almost before he had finished uttering the words, he had realized how feeble the question must have sounded.

'I have already said so. There are several others who would be pleased to have the scroll, in order to destroy it and deprive us of our very right to exist,' answered the voice, which had lost some of its soothing timbre and had taken on a hard-edged steely quality. 'That is why we must find it and take it before they do.'

'And it is in this Petra place?' repeated Morris.

'According to the photograph the two Englishmen in the hotel were given, yes,' replied the voice, 'and we were told of the clues as to the scroll's location by our contacts in London. Of course, our people have known of it since the time of Moses, but we have not known where to find it. Now, possibly, we do.'

'In Petra, which is in Trans-Jordan,' repeated Morris.

'Which is a British Protectorate,' added the soothing voice, now fully restored to its persuasive charm, 'which is why we are sending you and your wife. You will be British tourists on an organized tour, visiting several places of historical importance, including Petra. *If* you get into trouble and it emerges that you have anything to do with us there will be serious complications, which could put our cause back centuries ... or even destroy it altogether. That is how serious this matter is,' concluded the voice dramatically.

'And when is this to commence?' asked Morris, 'and how am I to know what to look for?'

'It will be towards the end of September, if not before. You must hold yourself in readiness. We will brief you nearer the time and tell you everything that you need to know. If you do not have your own weapon, we will supply you with one. Then it will be up to you and your own initiative. That is why we have selected you.'

'Am I to have any help, should I need it?' asked Morris. 'What if I need someone to support me ... if things do not go according to plan.' *Whatever the hell the plan might be!* he thought.

'I have given this operation a code name. It is Ehyrling. Should you need anything from our people, give the code name and they will help you. There will be no questions asked ... the code name is authority enough,' continued the voice, 'but once your tour group has crossed the border, there *can* be no help. We dare not risk the embarrassment of discovery over the border on British-protected territory.'

Morris thought for a few moments and then spoke; giving voice to the sickening realization he had just reached within his head. 'So that means that in Petra I am left to my own devices ... I will be on my own. There will be no one to give this code word to if I need help?'

'Once you cross the border you will be on your own. There could possibly be a single contact within reach, should there be a case of the direst emergency ... but that we still have to arrange...'

'And who will that contact be?'

'You do not need to know. They will contact *you*, should it become obvious that it is necessary to do so.'

'So ... I will be on my own, then,' repeated Morris, more to himself than for the benefit of the soothing voice.

'As you were when you had to make the sudden decisions which gave you your Victoria Cross,' suggested the voice.

Morris Ginsberg had no taste for the shadowy, undercover world of spies and intrigue. He felt sucked even further into *their* world, without the option of escape. As he sat thinking, he noticed that the little bird was still sitting on the bush, singing. That made him smile.

'And when do we set off? Can I tell Claudie any of this yet?'

There was no reply. He asked his questions again. Still there was no reply.

Suddenly, he realized that he was alone on his bench. Without hesitation and chancing the consequences, he turned around. He had been quite correct – the bench behind him was empty, save for a folded copy of that day's *Haaretz*.

38

Palestine

Masada – evening, Monday, 28th September 1931

'So there you have it ...' Peter Olivier puffed, floating in a sea of self-importance. '... There was a chronic need to stop the further decline in family values in our modern British society, so I stepped in and, with God's guidance, I set up CAFFVIS.' He paused and took a mouthful of his wine before continuing. 'We've made such a mark already that His Holiness has recognized my efforts and was gracious enough to grant me an audience during our recent stay in Rome.' He mopped his mouth, whilst a smirk of pompous self-righteousness covered his face.

'CAFFVIS?' repeated Lawrence Hawkhurst before Olivier could continue with his paean of self-praise. 'I'm afraid I've never heard of it.'

Alexandra, who was seated on the opposite side of the dining table from her brother, smiled. She had a genuine admiration for her brother's mastery of a jibe. *That stopped the pompous ass*, she thought, as she continued to eat.

But it would take more than Lawrence Hawkhurst's interruption to derail Peter Olivier. 'You've never heard of CAFFVIS?' he echoed, glaring at Lawrence in something approaching disbelief.

'No, sorry ... can't say that I ever have,' replied Hawkhurst, popping a piece of fresh buttered roll into his mouth.

For a second it looked as if Peter Olivier was about to either explode or suffer some sort of an arrest. Jane Olivier, his wife, smiled vacuously at the rest of the table as if to apologize for her husband's imminent eruption, but said nothing. In fact, during the twenty-three years she had been married to this man, she had been allowed to express very little in the way of original thought, as she had been systematically suppressed and dominated by him.

'My dear chap,' began her husband, 'I am the founder and chairman of the Catholic Foundation for Family Values In Society. I do an enormous amount of work to bring about a return to the true values of family life, which were lost during and after the war.'

'Really?' interrupted Lawrence, an innocent expression on his face. 'I had no idea...'

For the second time that evening, Peter Olivier had been stopped in his tracks.

'And His Holiness has even acknowledged the work Peter has done,' chirruped Jane Olivier, repeating what her husband had already said, in an attempt to calm his ruffled feathers.

'Indeed,' replied Lawrence, looking straight into her husband's face, 'as you have already told us.' He smiled his most disarming smile.

Alexandra kicked him gently under the table in acknowledgement that he had, once again, got the better of the likes of this odious man.

'Is this family society for everyone?' enquired Morris Ginsberg, from the far end of the table, where he and Claudette were seated.

'Yes,' replied Olivier, 'I set up the Foundation to help all true believers who feel they are in need of moral support.'

'But, surely, that depends on what is understood by the term *true believer*, said Stephen Hopkins, as he placed his knife and fork together on his plate. 'A Muslim considers himself to be a true believer. Do you welcome people of all faiths to your Foundation?'

'There is only one true faith,' replied Peter Olivier icily, his malevolent glare alternating between Stephen Hopkins and Lawrence Hawkhurst. 'Anyone of that faith is welcome to come to us for help,' he continued, the heated rage in his voice at odds with the icy expression on his face.

'It is a pity, then, that your good work is not available to all,' said Morris Ginsberg softly. 'Think of how much better your Foundation could do, if it were...' He left the statement unfinished, as his gaze focused on the glass in front of him.

'Peter believes that the family is the most important asset we have left. Its value is inestimable. Something we cannot feel or touch, but which is nevertheless the glue which holds the Nation and Empire together,' said Jane Olivier, suddenly becoming animated again.

She's learned that off by heart until she's word perfect, thought Stephen, *and probably been beaten black and blue in the process, either physically or mentally, by that overbearing bully.* He looked over the top of his glass at Rupert Winfield, who was seated opposite him. *Well, my dear chap, you are right again. You always say that there is one on every trip ... and this one looks like he's the one!* He smiled suddenly at the thought.

Rupert, who had not been party to his friend's thought process, looked enquiringly at him, wondering why his friend was smiling behind his glass.

Uri Ben Zeev's men entered the tent and began to clear the dirty dishes away and to prepare the table for the next course.

'I hope that everything was to your satisfaction?' asked a well-tanned young man, who had only just joined the hospitality team. There was a general murmur of approval from around the table.

'Excellent, as usual, Aaron,' Rupert chuckled, 'and we eagerly await the next course.'

'I will tell Uri,' the young man replied, as clean plates were laid in front of the tourists. He smiled as he spoke, but Rupert couldn't help but feel that it was a smile of convenience and a little forced in execution. Perhaps this younger brother of Uri Ben Zeev was still learning his big brother's skills.

Rupert watched as the next course was duly served and the diners set to with a will. He recognized that the presence of the Oliviers caused an immediate tension within the group and this had been apparent right from the start of the tour; the dynamics between the husband and wife were certainly unusual. Winfield found that he was always on the alert to defuse any situation that looked as if it was likely to get out of control.

Sitting opposite the Ginsbergs were the other two members of the tour. The younger man, Collins St Anthony, sat in sullen silence and, as usual, was unwilling to engage in conversation with the rest of the group. But the older of the two men was far more sociable and now enquired, 'Masada has played an extremely important role in the founding of the Jewish Nation, has it not?'

'Indeed it has, Mr Barrington,' replied Rupert, turning to look at the man.

'Indeed, the history of this entire region has played a crucial role in the formation of our modern Western society and faiths,' added Stephen, 'not least, Christianity.'

Peter Olivier stared at Stephen with ill-concealed disdain.

'But, then again,' continued Stephen, 'I need hardly remind you of that fact, do I, Barrington?'

'No, I suppose not,' replied Barrington smiling broadly, a faint hint of a Scots accent in his voice, 'although I should say that my area of real interest and expertise is the Byzantine period. Still, at the British Museum, they do expect us to be not only a thorough expert in *something*, but also to have more than just a passing knowledge in several other things as well.'

'Do you know about the sites of the Holy Land, then?' enquired Jane Olivier, hurriedly looking towards her husband for what appeared to be reassurance and permission to speak.

'Oh yes,' replied Barrington, 'Petra was a very important site to many civilizations, not just to the Nabateans and the Romans. The Byzantines, in their turn, also had more than a passing interest in the city, because of trade and their desire for empire. That was quite a bit later on, of course.'

'Oh ... yes ... of course,' replied Jane Olivier. After so many years in the dark, depressing repression of her husband's shadow, she found conversation on topics other than her husband's obsessive Foundation trying and difficult. Archaeology was not her strong point. She suddenly felt herself way out of her depth.

'Anyway, I was owed some leave by the museum, so when I saw your brochure,' he said, nodding towards Rupert, 'I thought *why not?* I could take the opportunity to do a bit of personal research and intellectual improvement, whilst enjoying a bit of a holiday. Two birds with one stone, all wrapped up neatly in a single historical scroll, as it were.'

Stephen shot a hurried, questioning glance at Rupert.

Catching Stephen's eye movement, Rupert leaned forward so that he could see Barrington at the far end of the table. It had been a welcome surprise for him to find another archaeologist on the tour, as they would have many shared interests. 'So, they've actually let you come all this way without an ulterior motive?' Rupert asked innocently.

'None whatsoever,' replied Barrington. 'I'm here purely on a holiday ... fair and square.'

'You must know a lot about children and families,' said Claudette Ginsberg, looking at Jane Olivier as she spoke.

'How many children do you have?' Although she had to be content with merely hoping for one of her own one day, she always felt a compulsion to talk about other people's families.

For a second Jane Olivier seemed to be at a loss for words. In the pause that followed, her eyes seemed to cloud over as she disappeared into some inner recess of her mind, before recoiling from the horror that was there. She stared ahead of her for a moment. 'I beg your pardon?' she asked, somewhat distracted, 'I didn't quite hear your question.'

'Children,' repeated Claudette, 'how many do you have?'

'The Lord has seen fit not to bless us with the gift of children,' replied Peter Olivier quickly. 'It is His will that we bear this burden ... that Jane has to bear her cross for both of us.' There was not the slightest trace of warmth or compassion towards his wife in the words he had just spoken.

'Oh, but I thought that *he* was...' Morris took Claudette's hand and squeezed it before she could finish. Claudette shrank back in confusion: she had assumed that the younger of the two men sitting opposite her was their son; the bridge of his nose and the set of his eyes were very similar to those of Jane Olivier. Claudette had noticed this early on in the tour, but as neither Mrs Olivier nor this last member of the group were particularly easy to draw into conversation, she had not had the opportunity to enquire further – until now. All she could do now was to mumble, 'Er ... well, we are still hoping for a child.'

'And what about you, then Mr St Anthony?' asked Morris, releasing Claudette's hand and looking straight into the face of the young man opposite him. 'Are you an archaeologist, too?'

For a moment the man, who was only in his early twenties, seemed to resent the impertinence of the question. Then he returned Morris's smiling, enquiring look. 'No, I'm not an archaeologist; I've come here to learn.'

'Are you with the museum as well?' enquired Jane Olivier.

The young man did not answer immediately, just remained staring at her with a look that resembled barely disguised, smouldering hatred.

'No, I am not with any museum. My family make fine porcelain ware and we are *By Appointment.* We have held the Royal Warrant since the time of Queen Victoria.' His voice was quite flat, as if it was heavily under control and devoid of any real interest in imparting what it was saying. All the while, Collins St Anthony kept his gaze firmly on Jane Olivier. 'I have an interest in personal ethics ... in the rights and wrongs of things.'

'You should consider the Foundation,' interjected Peter Olivier. 'We also strive to sort out the difference between right and wrong. You and I must discuss matters over the next couple of weeks; perhaps we have something in common in that regard.'

As Collins St Anthony slowly switched his gaze from Jane Olivier's face to that of her husband, Rupert caught sight of his expression and almost reeled with shock, for it was filled with absolute venom.

39

Palestine

Masada – late afternoon, Wednesday, 30th September 1931

'Was that you I heard singing?' asked Jane Olivier, as she sat down in the chair next to Claudie's. '... A little earlier, when we were having our rest...'

'Yes ... yes, it was,' replied Claudie, smiling her awkward smile, which emphasized her over-wide mouth. 'I hope that I did not disturb you?'

'No, not in the least,' replied the other. 'It was lovely ... in fact it sounded foreign, not an English song ... if you know what I mean. I'm afraid that I'm not in the least bit musical. What with Peter's responsibilities at the Foundation and our Church work ... well, we don't seem to have the time for anything else.' She seemed to have suddenly deflated into herself. Her face still held the warm, almost meaningless smile it always wore, but her eyes had suddenly clouded and she had gone to another place and another time, somewhere deep within her memory.

Claudie had not noticed; someone had asked her about her singing and to her that was the most important thing. 'It is a French *chanson*,' she replied. 'In fact, I have been singing two; one was very slow and ponderous, while the other was much livelier. What did it sound like to you? I can tell you about it, if you like.' There was a childlike sincerity in her voice, her mouth still hovering over her white teeth in its arching smile.

For what seemed like an age Jane Olivier did not answer but sat in the looming shadow of the outcrop of Masada, staring out across the arid landscape towards the flat expanse of the Dead Sea in the distance.

'Can you remember what it sounds like?' repeated Claudie, eager not to let this opportunity to talk about her ruling passion slip from her grasp.

'Yes ... I suppose it was,' muttered Jane Olivier, as the cloud of remembering lifted from her eyes. She turned her head to face Claudie. 'Yes,' she repeated.

'Yes ... ?' repeated Claudie, confused, 'Yes, what? Of course, if we were back at the Petra Hotel in Jerusalem, my Moshie would have his accordion and he would be playing for me ... We perform together, you see. We are professional musicians. So was it ... ?'

'Oh yes, you were singing. Well, now ... let me think. I think it sounded sad.'

'In that case, I know exactly which *chanson* it was,' replied Claudie, sitting on the edge of her seat, like a puppy straining its powers of obedience waiting for the command to retrieve the stick or ball. 'It really is a song full of sadness,' she continued, her voice low and intense. 'It's about a mother, who lo—'

'Hello,' said Alexandra Hawkhurst brightly, as she sat in the vacant chair next to Claudie. 'Wasn't it an interesting day?' she declared, unintentionally interrupting the conversation.

Lawrence had followed his sister from the campsite and seeing that she sought female company had continued onwards to join Morris Ginsberg, who was in conversation with Uri Ben Zeev.

A short way away from where the three women sat talking, Gordon Barrington sat facing the little collection of chairs.

He had perched himself on the toppled trunk of a palm tree that lay to one side of the little pool of water that was the surface proof of the existence of a spring below. He was dressed formally, ready for dinner. His lounging posture on the palm, with a burning cigarette clamped firmly between his fingers, made him look a little incongruous.

'Hello, Barrington,' said Stephen cheerily, as he walked up from behind him, 'mind if I join you?' Without waiting for the answer he climbed over the fallen palm tree and sat down.

'Oh good evening ... I say, did you hear singing earlier on?'

'Indeed ... I believe it would have been Mrs Ginsberg. Rupert seems to think that we heard her in a cabaret at our hotel in Jerusalem. Personally, I can't recall that, although I admit that the voice is quite ... distinctive.'

Barrington let out a knowing chuckle.

'So, what did you think of the caves and springs of Engedi?' Stephen continued, lighting a cigarette of his own. 'Do you believe that this arid wasteland could once have been a fertile field of abundance?'

'Quite possibly it was,' replied Barrington. 'Weather patterns change over time. What we see today doesn't necessarily have to have been there for ever ... since the dawn of time, as it were. I've even read a hypothesis that the area around the Pyramids of Giza and the Sphinx was once green and fertile. Someone even suggested that there are signs of water erosion on some of the rocks ... That's hard to imagine, looking at that blistering desert now.' He chuckled again at this thought.

'I know of others who hold similar views,' said Stephen, thinking back to what Professor Unsworth and the Reverend Fairweather had said on an earlier trip. 'And what does your professional opinion have to say about the historical implications of *this* place?'

'I wouldn't mind having a look around up there,' said Barrington, as he pointed up, cigarette in hand, at the towering bulk of Masada, which seemed to loom ominously over them in the evening light, 'but Winfield tells me that we don't have the time.'

'Besides which, it's one hell of a climb,' added Stephen, laughing.

'Winfield tells me that our next port of call is probably more up my street, anyway,' continued Barrington, good naturedly. 'The Crusader castle at Kerak. Have you been there before?'

'No, it's the first time it's been included in the tour,' replied Stephen, 'so it will be something new to all of us.'

They sat smoking in silence for a while, during which time they noticed Peter Olivier strolling slowly towards them across the short distance between the campsite and the spring.

'Isn't it amazing how some people can be so pompous all of the time?' murmured Barrington, more by way of statement than question.

'Particularly when it comes to the eternally vexatious question of religion,' added Stephen, exhaling a plume of white cigarette smoke. 'No offence meant, if you're a religious soul.'

'Lapsed soul would be more accurate,' replied Barrington, turning and smiling at Stephen, 'so no offence caused. You are, however, quite correct: our Mr Olivier is a prime example of an over-opinionated bigot. Just like the ones we used to have in the service, whose thinking hadn't moved on much from the days of the Scarlet Pimpernel and the magnifying glass!'

'That sounds intriguing. Were you in the police?' asked Stephen, as he flicked the butt end of his cigarette down on to the wet sand around the little pool, where it hissed and went out.

'No... not the police,' replied Barrington, without looking at Stephen, 'Military Intelligence, or what passed for it ... during the war. They thought it might be a good idea to try and work out what the other side was thinking and planning.'

'Then you went into archaeology and started at the British Museum ... when it was all over, I mean,' prompted Stephen.

'No, not really,' answered Barrington, laughing and making a dismissive gesture in the air with his hand. 'I went up to Oxford at the tender age of seventeen and, in due course, came out with a degree in History ... specializing in the Byzantine period. Then I went to work in the museum. When the war started I eventually found myself with the Military Intelligence lot I've just told you about, which is something I suppose I should not have mentioned. Anyway, my people have connections ... they have certain strings, which they like to pull. All quite beneficial to me you understand, but it goes against the grain sometimes ... the, er ... *them and us* sort of thing...'

'Oh, I don't know, old chap,' replied Stephen, 'in our brave new, equal world it could be of use to be able to say that one is a little *more* equal than the majority ... A perfectly level playing field isn't the easiest thing to cross without a little help ... every now and then. What do you think about the new *equality* in Russia?'

Before he answered, Barrington seemed to shiver for a second in the pleasant warmth of the setting sun. 'Brutal,' was all he said.

As that reply sunk in, the two men enjoyed a companionable silence and watched the campsite going about its business at this time of the evening. They each observed how Jane Olivier stiffened noticeably when her husband joined the group of women and sat in the chair facing hers. They had also noticed Morris Ginsberg, who remained talking to Uri as young Lawrence Hawkhurst walked away from them and back to the campsite. Further on, the boys could be seen, busy putting the finishing touches to the evening meal; nearby Aaron Ben Zeev was busy painstakingly straightening the unoccupied chairs near Peter Olivier and the small group of ladies.

'Everyone seems to be present and correct,' said Stephen absently.

'All except for the intriguingly silent and reticent Mr St Anthony,' replied Barrington, without taking his gaze off the scene in front of him. 'No sign of him.'

'Well observed...' replied Stephen. '... No sign of him ... yet.'

'What about you?' asked Barrington, changing the subject abruptly. 'Excuse me for saying, but I notice you walk with a slight limp. Were you in the war ... perhaps in the infantry?'

'In a manner of speaking, I suppose I was in the infantry.' Stephen laughed. 'I was surrounded by them, bodies and bits in all directions.'

Barrington turned and looked at him quizzically.

'I was in the Royal Army Medical Corps,' continued Stephen. 'I spent my time trying to piece the infantry back together again...'

'Ahhhh, because the dinosaurs in my lot couldn't manage to get their information correct,' cut in Barrington, 'like that farce around Ypres. They grandly call it "The Third Battle of Ypres" now, but it was awful. The left hand didn't seem to know that the right had even existed, let alone what it was up to. And that was just on our side!' He had started shaking again, with more than just the hint of a sob in his voice; a sob mixed with emotion and a generous amount of anger.

'Steady on, old chap,' said Stephen, recognizing the distress of a fellow veteran. He put a comforting hand on Barrington's arm. 'It was a damn unpleasant business and it affected all of us, but you can't possibly blame yourself for any of it. You are no more responsible that I am. We were all simply cogs in the greater machine and we did what we had to do. Cut and dried. Have another fag.'

Some twenty minutes later, as the long shadows cast by the mountain turned from deep violet to almost inky black, the gong announced that the evening meal was ready. The hungry members of the tour group started to converge on the dining tent. The party had almost reached the entrance to the tent when Jane Olivier suddenly stopped.

'Oh dear,' she said, half turning to look back in the direction of where the chairs had stood, close by the little spring. 'Peter, I've left my bag over there, where I was sitting.'

Almost without losing his stride her husband called to her over his shoulder in a voice that held more menace than tenderness. 'Then you had best go back and get it.'

Jane Olivier was halfway to the spring when, as if by magic, Collins St Anthony appeared at her elbow: wraith-like, out of the darkness.

'Are you looking for this?' he asked in a low voice, his eyes fixed firmly on her face. Owing to the rapidly fading light, she couldn't make out his features very well. What she could see, though, was the reflection of the distant campsite torches in his eyes – eyes which were as hard as the marble that decorated the remains of Herod's palace atop Masada and which were as unforgiving as the desert heat at midday.

'Oh! You gave me such a fright!' There was no one else to hear her. The rest of the tourists had already entered the dining tent. 'Er ... yes ... thank you ever so much. How forgetful of me,' she stammered, fear suddenly rising within her. A fear greater than the simple shock she had suddenly experienced at St Anthony's unexpected appearance. It was a much deeper, irrational fear, almost a base instinct for which she could find no logical reason. She clasped her hand to her neck, as the fear slowly rose from her legs upwards, towards her breast and face. It grew as St Anthony continued speaking:

'Allow me to escort you back to the camp. Do you believe in putting right what is wrong?' he asked, as they started walking back towards the dining tent, his courteous politeness barely concealing the iciness in his voice.

For a few seconds she was nonplussed at the question. 'Peter has always said that wrongs are evil and *must* be put right,' she mumbled. Because of the darkness, she had been obliged to take his arm for support over the uneven terrain. This close proximity to the young man made her instincts all the more disturbing.

'Yes, but what do *you* think?' insisted the young man.

'Well, I really don't kn— what I mean to say is ... well, of course wrongs must be put right and...'

'And this would be irrespective of what the cost might be?'

'Well, I sup— Peter would always ... Why ... are you asking me this?' she asked, becoming even more flustered.

'It is an interesting concept, wouldn't you say? Particularly with your husband's involvement in his Foundation; preserving the Catholic family values of a damaged society and all of that. I am most interested to know how you feel about those who have suffered wrong; those innocents who have suffered at the hands of others.'

Jane Olivier was feeling weak and light-headed. As they reached the dining tent, she stumbled and nearly fell, as her foot caught in some loose gravel.

'Don't worry, I've got you now,' said Collins St Anthony soothingly, as he reached out and held her in a vice-like grip that was of little comfort. 'And I won't let you go,' he whispered in a voice that was cold and ruthless.

40

Rome

Villa Biranconi – evening, Friday, 2nd October 1931

High in the hills outside Rome the lights were ablaze in the Villa Biranconi, the complex of buildings which was the ancestral home of the Contini-Aosta family. There had been a villa on the site since late Roman times. Since then, over the centuries, the villa had been constantly added to – as funds permitted and as needs dictated – until there was practically nothing of the original Roman buildings left. Vast formal gardens sloped away from the villa and down towards the twinkling lights of the Eternal City, visible between the branches of the tall trees that demarcated the formal Baroque garden. It had been laid out in the mid-eighteenth century and was still a talking point amongst the horticulturalists in modern society.

In the formal grandeur of the main reception room Count Vittorio Contini-Aosta, the last of his long and very distinguished line, was entertaining his guests. The meal had been served in the opulent dining hall, with its cut-crystal chandeliers and tapestry wall hangings, and now the count and his guests were enjoying a strong cup of coffee and a glass of Tuscan Vin Santo.

'Do try one of the chocolates,' said the count. 'I have them sent especially from Brussels. I'm afraid it is an extravagant habit I acquired just after the war, when I spent some time there in the Embassy as military attaché.' He smiled and made a slight gesture of excused apology, as he settled himself down in one of the comfortable chairs that were grouped around a large, ornate open fireplace. It could get very cold up in the hills around Rome during the winter nights. 'So, my dear Gian, tell me of your recent successes.'

'We are very happy with our posting to the Embassy in Rio de Janeiro,' answered Gian. 'The climate is good and the people, with all their different colours, seem to be friendly enough. We also have the prospect of building better trading relations with the Brazilians. Cheaper rubber, timber and, possibly, even oil...' He paused, took up his coffee cup and raised it from its saucer. '... Not to mention cheaper coffee!' He laughed, revealing perfect white teeth before he put the cup to his lips to drink. 'We will be sorry to return to Rio next week; despite producing mountains of coffee beans, they are unable to make a decent espresso!'

Gian Galeazzo Ciano, 2nd Count of Cortellazzo and Buccari, was tall, well-built and handsome. He was also Il Duce's son-in-law.

'Your father would have been very proud of what his son has achieved,' said Count Vittorio Contini-Aosta, a look of wistful memory about his face. 'I remember the days when you were small enough to be bounced on my knee and how you used to play at sea battles with your little battleships, before your *papà* went off to fight the real war in his much larger, iron ones. We were of the same generation, your father and I. He conquered the sea and I the land,' continued Contini-Aosta, his face suddenly bursting into a warm, genuine smile as he laughed. 'But that was long ago. Where do you think your next posting might be when your tour of duty in Brazil comes to an end?' he concluded, reaching for another of his chocolates.

'There was talk of a post in the cabinet here in Rome,'

replied Ciano. 'Apparently it was thought that my legal background might prove useful to the Ministry of Foreign Affairs, but quite how that could be so escapes me, I'm afraid. Then again, these appointments are made by persons greater than us. I know a posting back to Rome would please Edda enormously,' he said, turning to his wife, taking her hand and raising it to his mouth to kiss it, 'but I don't feel quite ready for that yet. I want to acquire some more experience first. The prospect of representing our interests on the international stage is quite daunting at present.'

'Very commendable,' said Contini-Aosta, 'we could well have the need for countrymen with such experience.'

'How do you mean?'

'We must be prepared for all eventualities, given that our destiny is to once again create an empire, this time on an even more massive scale than the ancient Roman one. Skill on the diplomatic front could well be a highly desirable asset in the future. We cannot assume, for one moment that the rest of the world will stand by and silently admire us as we create this new empire. Diplomacy will always have its place in the volatile world of international relations, even if used purely as a stalling tactic. But I'm sure that I do not need to tell you of such things.' The count smiled and waved a hand in the air dismissively. 'Il Duce will guide us to our brighter future, when he is ready, then the expansion of the territories we already possess will commence in earnest. We already have Libya and Eritrea,' he concluded.

Contini-Aosta had always treated Ciano as the son he had never had. In fact, Contini-Aosta was Ciano's godfather – his *padrino*. But he had never fully trusted Ciano's wife, Edda Mussolini. She had always been very open and friendly in his company, ever since the days when his godson had first started courting her and, although she seemed a warm, companionable sort of woman, she was, after all, her father's daughter. Who was to say what she might repeat back to her father in the course of conversation – innocently or maliciously – in passing or intentionally? Contini-Aosta had decided from the outset to watch what he said in her presence, but that decision had disturbed him greatly. By not entering wholeheartedly and without reserve into Ciano's happiness at the prospect of love and partnership with his new wife, the count had come to regard himself as a traitor to his own godson. He fancied that he was becoming more paranoid with each passing day. It had certainly not been like that in the old days.

'I hear that you have made outstanding progress on the question of our French allies supplying us with oil,' said Ciano. 'Their Minister for War had a recent meeting with you, which, I am reliably told, went very well. What's his name ... De Saint-Etienne Monteschalle?'

For a split second Contini-Aosta saw a red warning light flash in his head. How did his godson, normally posted on the other side of the Atlantic in Brazil, know that?

'Indeed, as you have said, my boy,' replied Contini-Aosta, in a noncommittal way.

'Do you think this talk of the French Prime Minister visiting us here in Rome will come to anything?' asked Ciano, warming to the subject. 'Pierre Laval could well be an advantageous ally for us, particularly if the British think that he is *their* ally. The acquisition of some of France's Somalia colony would be of inestimable help in our planning of the new empire in Africa.'

For a moment, the room was filled with the silence of the tomb. Even the chirruping of the cicadas outside in the expanse of the gardens seemed to have stopped.

In the vacuum which had been created by Ciano's remarks, Contini-Aosta suddenly became aware of the pounding of his own heart. *This is totally ridiculous! I am becoming obsessed to the point of sheer stupidity*, he admonished himself. *He cannot know anything that is not known either by me, or by*

Mussolini. Whatever is said on the subject cannot possibly be compromising in any way. Do not be so foolish!

'I think that we are all extremely fortunate to be living at such a time as this,' said Edda suddenly, in a level, soothing voice. 'Think of how proud it will make us to be able to tell our children that we were all part of the building of the new empire.' She smiled at Contini-Aosta.

Ciano once again took her hand and kissed it. Turning to his godfather he proffered: 'We will soon take back our ownership of the Mediterranean with our new warships. That should give the British something to think about, although we should never underestimate them. Slow they might be, but stupid they are not. Would you not agree?'

'It is as you say, my dear,' said the count, inclining his head towards Edda. 'We live in very exciting times, of which all Italians can be justly proud. However, I might be excused for thinking that these same times are, perhaps, moving just a little too fast for those of us who are of an earlier generation.'

'What on earth do you mean?' asked Ciano, a smile on his handsome face.

'It is not that I am too old, you understand,' lied Contini-Aosta, 'it is just that sometimes I begin to wonder if a younger pair of hands, perhaps more experienced in the modern ways of war and of politics, should assume the helm. After all, I am a soldier by profession ... I am not really a politician...'

He had been feeling the advance of the years more and more of late and had even begun to look forward to the time when he could dispense with the uniforms and endless saluting and spend his days in his vineyard, high up on the slopes above the villa, where the purple grapes caught every single ray the generous sun threw down upon them.

'You are doing a splendid job as both politician and soldier,' retorted Ciano. 'I am certain that you would not want to retire now, after all the hard work you have put in. You deserve to take your rightful place in the reviewing box on the day the new empire is formally declared and our victorious forces march triumphantly through Rome.'

It suddenly crossed Contini-Aosta's mind that his godson had never once called his father-in-law by his name – Christian or political. In fact, he had spoken about everything almost as if Il Duce didn't really exist at all. That occurred to him as somewhat strange. Did he perhaps feel awkward flaunting that connection, or was he privately uncomfortable with such a close link to Il Duce and all that he stood for?

'No, of course not, my boy, and you are quite right. We must all work with total commitment towards that glorious day.' Contini-Aosta inwardly winced, as he heard himself once again sprouting the approved Party line. For some considerable time he had wondered just how glorious that day would be, particularly if the parade were more of a rout through the shattered remains of the Eternal City with the furious and vengeful Allies in hot pursuit demanding reparations for war damage. He had seen something similar happen after the previous conflict, when everyone wanted their share of what was left of the deposed Kaiser's empire. He did not want that to happen to Italy.

It was just before midnight. His guests had long since left and Contini-Aosta stood on the rear balcony of the villa, looking up at the sky. It was a clear night and the stars sparkled and glinted above the Eternal City. For a moment, he thought that they appeared to be more like artillery flashes than twinkling stars. He sighed and lowered his gaze to the hillside above the villa – to his beloved vineyard. There was a feeble moon that cast very little light, certainly not enough to make out the terrain. It was of no consequence, as he knew every inch of his land like the back of his hand.

Somewhere off in the distance, perhaps on the neighbouring hillside, an owl hooted once. Then it hooted again before giving in to the silence of the night. Still keeping his gaze on his vineyard – up there in the darkness – Contini-Aosta was reminded of his favourite play by William Shakespeare. How the hooting of the owl, a bird of ill-omen in popular folklore, was the harbinger of death – the death of the Scottish king. He stood and listened, but there was no third hoot, no third comforting hoot of the Trinity, the divine number that would offer protection and salvation. There was only the darkness and the silence of Nature at rest.

As he turned and entered the villa, closing the French windows behind him, he wondered if he had been wise to have hinted at his intentions in front of potentially so dangerous a pair of ears as those of his godson's wife. And yet he had no evidence that Edda's ears *were* dangerous.

It is too late to consider such ill-advised folly now, he thought, as he turned and slowly walked through the reception room, towards his bedroom and what he hoped would be the blissful release of sleep.

41

Trans-Jordan

Kerak Castle, on the King's Highway – Saturday, 3rd October 1931

'Just look at that view!' said Lawrence Hawkhurst, as he walked out on to the battlements of Kerak Castle. 'Spectacular!'

He had been the first to emerge into the sunshine from the top of the long flight of stairs, just ahead of Gordon Barrington and Peter Olivier. The rest of the party were strung out a short distance behind them, still trudging up the seemingly endless flight of worn stone steps that led enticingly from the castle's large, dusty courtyard, up through the solid bulk of the massive stone walls to the bright blue sky atop the battlements. Jane Olivier had said that she was feeling under the weather, and so had stayed with the drivers and the vehicles outside the castle. Claudie had contemplated giving up when she was only halfway up the stairs, but she had been encouraged to continue by Alexandra Hawkhurst, who didn't seem to be bothered by either the steps or the heat. Rupert had remained at the back, where he said he would be better able to assist and encourage, as necessary. His real reason had been to help Stephen, whose artificial leg made clambering over ruins and up steps as steep as these somewhat difficult at the best of times. In the cloying, sapping heat generated within the stone-enclosed confines of the stairway it became even more difficult. Collins St Anthony had gone just ahead of Rupert and Stephen, seemingly ignoring everyone else.

'This really is something. It would take a thousand words to describe,' said Barrington, as he crossed the wide stone walkway and leaned on one of the tall stone crenulations that formed the battlements. 'Just think of it,' he continued, gesturing away down the valley, through which snaked the dusty ribbon of the King's Highway, 'you'd be wearing your heavy protective armour, standing up here in the heat, shielding your eyes from the glare of the sun, watching for trouble coming up that road and all the time believing that God was on *your* side.'

He had spoken without thinking, guided simply by his imagination and the palpable atmosphere generated by the massive bulk of the Crusader castle, perched atop its vantage point high above the valley.

'God is *always* on our side,' said Peter Olivier dryly and very curtly, mopping his forehead with a large white handkerchief. Following the exertion of climbing the stairs, his breathing had almost returned to normal. For a man of his age, he seemed to be in very good physical condition. 'How can anyone even doubt that God is on our side,' he droned on, as if warming up to deliver a diatribe in front of one of his Foundation meetings.

Even the appearance of the rest of the group on the battlements, emerging like a bedraggled caravan of weary camels from the low archway that led to the dark stairway, did little to stop him.

'I say ... well, that certainly makes the climb up here worth the effort,' said Alexandra Hawkhurst, as she fanned herself with her straw hat and crossed to join Barrington at the battlements. 'That really is breathtaking,' she said, smiling at him.

'If it were not for the conviction the Crusaders held that

God and right were, indeed, on their side, they would not have been able to accomplish any of this.' Peter Olivier had resumed his sermon and waved his arm through the air in an expansive gesture that embraced the castle.

'Listen everyone, Mr Olivier maintains the proposition that God is always on our side,' said Lawrence Hawkhurst, addressing the rest of the group and, in so doing, barely attempting to hide the smirk on his face. He regarded this pompous and thoroughly boring man as hardly worth his attention. After all, he had got the better of him at least twice back at Masada. 'Our friend Barrington was just painting a very good word picture for us of what life up here must have been like for a Crusader knight and Mr Olivier has somehow sanctified their position, when really they were little better than money-grabbing bandits invading someone else's territory.'

'Meaning no disrespect, but surely Mr Olivier's point of view is a very subjective one, is it not?' asked Morris. 'Does it follow that, if the Crusaders always thought that God was on *their* side, then surely the Saracens coming up the valley to attack and hopefully kill the invading Crusader knights up here, also believed they had God on *their* side?'

Peter Olivier did not even bother to turn and face Morris. The man was a Jew – the Jews had crucified Jesus Christ, therefore he was beneath contempt and hardly worth answering. 'God is always with the righteous,' he said, his jaw almost clenched closed, as he gazed down into the valley far below.

Barrington who had been listening with quiet interest added his voice to the discussion. 'The Great Saladin was a brave leader and a man of considerable chivalry for the period, which is more than can be said of the Crusaders generally. They persistently broke treaties with the Saracens who, one must not forget, were defending their land against unwelcome invasions of Christian knights, most of whom were simply out for what they could make ... or simply take.'

Morris had his arm around Claudie's shoulders and she, in turn, was clinging tightly to him. She had a fear of heights. Had she realized that the aspect gave the feeling that the viewer was actually in flight, like a soaring bird, she, too, would have stayed down with Uri, the vehicles, Aaron and Jane Olivier – safely on solid ground.

'This Highway is a very ancient one, you know,' said Barrington abruptly. He had sensed the tension in the air and attempted to break it. 'It could possibly go back to 5000 BC ... There's something about it in the Bible. Moses is supposed to have led his people up it.'

'Perhaps with his son, who was carrying the actual Scroll of Gershom,' said Stephen quietly, watching for some sign of reaction on Barrington's face.

There was none.

Although the conversation had lost its way somewhat, it had successfully silenced Peter Olivier, who remained leaning on the battlements, his face clouded with the lines of suppressed anger.

'It was the main route from Aqaba in the south up to Palmyra in Syria in the north. As you go along it you're passing through centuries of history ... from ancient times to Roman, Byzantine, Islamic ... You name it and you'll find it here. From where we're standing, perched up here like eagles,' Barrington continued, 'you'll find a Roman legionary fortress out there to the east.' He turned as he spoke. 'Up north is an early Byzantine church complex, to the south is the site of the first clash between Islam and Byzantium ... that was in AD 632 ... and here we are in the centre of it all, standing on the topmost battlements of a castle built in around 1140.'

There was a general rumble of conversation, and then the tourists wandered off to individually explore the broad expanse of the stone battlements.

'You obviously know your stuff very well,' said Rupert, as he stood with Stephen and Barrington in the shade of the towering keep.

'I've always been interested in this part of the world,' Barrington replied. 'In fact, during the war I had a posting out here; a secondment to Allenby's staff, fighting Johnny Turk. I didn't get much of a chance to see anything, though.'

Stephen offered cigarettes all round.

'Was that in Military Intelligence?' queried Rupert. Stephen had briefed him on the conversation he and Barrington had had at the spring.

'Humm,' replied Barrington, as he drew in a lungful of warm smoke.

A few feet away, Peter Olivier was still standing at the battlements, his eyes fixed across the valley on to the far horizon. His reverie was broken by an intense, softly spoken voice at his elbow.

'What would you say to someone who had knowingly done something so wrong that it caused another person to spend years in the darkness of uncertainty, before the light of understanding shone before them?'

Peter Olivier was unaware of Collins St Anthony, who had approached him on the side furthest away from everyone else. Hidden behind Olivier, he stood patiently waiting for an answer to his question.

'In what sense *the darkness of uncertainty*?' asked Olivier, turning his head to face St Anthony.

'Just what it means ... If someone's foolishness causes another to suffer the anguish of years of not knowing ... is that right or wrong?'

Olivier faced his inquisitor. It was the first time since the start of the trip that Peter Olivier had exchanged more than the polite niceties of good manners with this man. And now he was being asked a question which, at best, was of ambiguous opaqueness or, at worst, was provocative and could lead to a prolonged debate on ethics. Neither aspect appealed to him, as he had no real wish to talk to this rather ineffectual young man in the first place. 'All wrongs must be set right in the sight of the Lord,' said Olivier, looking somewhat annoyed at being addressed in such a forthright manner.

'Irrespective of whom it is that has done this wrong?' asked St Anthony, turning his head away from Olivier and staring out across the valley.

'A wrong is a wrong in the eyes of God and must be put right,' muttered Olivier. He had become irritated by the conversation, which seemed to him to be largely pointless. What was this silly ass getting at? Olivier had often seen people like this at the Foundation meetings: fragile, damaged and broken souls in search of some sort of healing miracle or kind word. This one was similar, but somehow different; this one seemed to have a backbone and a determined air about him. 'Why are you obsessed with this question?'

'Good,' said St Anthony, completely ignoring the question, 'that is what I needed to hear you say.'

Olivier was taken aback by the remark, but before he could say anything further, St Anthony walked away in the direction of the others, who were slowly making their way back towards the entrance to the stairway.

'I think that we had best be getting back down to the vehicles,' called out Rupert, waving towards the stairs. 'We've seen an awful lot of what there is to see today and Mrs Olivier must be getting lonely, waiting down there on her own.'

Peter Olivier gave a slight grimace of annoyance. He did not like it when his wife embarrassed him, as she had done by refusing to explore the castle with the rest of the group. To him it represented unacceptable weakness and he did not like it when the fissures in the façade of their solid, married life were laid bare. 'My wife will be perfectly all right,' he said, as he reached the dark cavern which was the entrance to the steps. 'She has her breviary to read for inspiration and to keep her company.'

Lawrence Hawkhurst rolled his eyes heavenwards at the remark; an action which was not lost on most of the rest of the tourists. 'I'm also quite fond of a good book to keep me company,' he said laughingly, 'especially a good crime story.'

The group entered the dark mouth of the stairs with Barrington in the lead. Behind him came Peter Olivier and behind him Collins St Anthony. Barrington was seven steps down before Alexandra and Lawrence Hawkhurst started to descend, followed by Rupert and Stephen.

'Make sure that your eyes have accustomed themselves to the light, or lack of it, before you start climbing down,' said Rupert from the rear of the line. 'There's not much light in here and some of these steps are very worn and uneven.'

There was a moderate level of conversation and a little laughter, as the group made its way slowly down the steps, using the rough-hewn sides of the passageway as support in the more treacherous sections.

'You can imagine what it must have been like going up and down in here with armour on,' called out Barrington from the front of the line, 'and it would have been even worse in a closed helmet, with just two narrow slits for you to look through. It must have been a bit like driving a tank, actually!'

Rupert looked at Stephen and, in the gloom he could just make out the other's smile. They each silently acknowledged their recent experience of travelling in an armoured car and so had some sympathy with the Crusader knights.

'And then there would have been the weapons...' continued Barrington, who had started to turn the upper part of his body to face back up the several steps which separated him from the rest of the group, '... cumbersome and heavy. Not to mention the shields and...'

Suddenly there was a stifled shout and Peter Olivier seemed to pitch forward. In the poor light he seemed to hang above the step like a cloud of ill omen, before tilting slowly forward in a gentle arc, first his head and then his body falling gradually forwards, until he was almost horizontal.

'Look out!' a high-pitched voice shouted from behind.

Amid the noisy confusion, which had suddenly erupted as if from nowhere and now echoed and re-echoed up and down the steep stairway, Barrington, who had half-turned to face up the steps, was suddenly aware that a large shape had almost blotted out the bright sunlight at the top of the staircase. It descended towards him at speed and at a crazy, unnatural angle. Instinctively, he turned at right angles to the walls and wedged himself across the width of the stairway, his feet firmly on the step on the left-hand side, his shoulders wedged against the wall on the right-hand side. He felt the rough wall bite into his shoulders as he braced himself against the oncoming bulk. Like a projectile hurled in silence by an unknown force, Peter Olivier collided with Gordon Barrington halfway down the steep stone steps. Barrington let out a moan, as he felt the rough wall gauge across his shoulders as Olivier's bulk crashed into him. The force of the impact caused Barrington to sag, making him lose his balance and his grip on the walls. Involuntarily, he staggered down a couple of steps. As he did so, he swung his body around and reached out, blindly, for the wall. The whole action was over in a matter of seconds and he ended up bruised, winded and sprawled across the steps. A couple of steps above him the figure of Peter Olivier sat in an undignified heap. His downward progress on the stairs had been halted by Barrington's quick-thinking and selfless action.

'What's happened down there?' called out Lawrence Hawkhurst.

'Olivier's tripped,' shouted the same high-pitched voice as before.

'Oh, my God!' exclaimed Alexandra Hawkhurst, supporting herself against the wall.

Lawrence was about to pass a suitable amusing repost, but then, given the possible seriousness of the implications of what had just happened, thought better of it and instead offered, 'Is everyone all right?' He made his way past his sister, to see for himself, and reached the step where Olivier was sitting.

Rupert was hot on his tail. 'Is anything broken?' he called out, praying that, if anything had been, it would be the least of any damage caused during this incident. In the confined semi-darkness he couldn't see what had actually happened.

'I'm fine,' shouted Barrington. 'Just winded, that's all ... and a bit scuffed around the shoulders. Nothing's broken. How's Olivier?'

'By the grace of God delivered,' said Olivier, slowly pulling himself upright and sitting straight on the step, his feet on the second step down.

Alexandra Hawkhurst, who had made her way to the step immediately above her brother, sensed his intake of breath and prodded him in the back before he could say anything.

'Well done, Barrington,' shouted Stephen, the dull ache in his stump forgotten for the moment. 'You avoided a really nasty accident with your quick thinking. What exactly happened, Olivier?'

'I must assume that my foot caught on part of a rough step...'

Forty minutes later, the group had emerged through the

main entrance to the castle and were once again gathered around the parked vehicles from where they had begun their exploration of the castle earlier in the day. Jane Olivier had emerged from the car the moment she had seen her husband approaching with his clothes badly scuffed and the left sleeve of his jacket torn.

'It was an accident. He tripped,' said Collins St Anthony, before anyone else could say anything.

'And Barrington here had the quick wits to use himself to break his fall,' added Stephen, who had noticed that Jane Olivier, upon seeing St Anthony, seemed to have shrunk back into herself, much as a cat would do at the approach of a dog.

'It was divine intervention,' muttered Olivier, as his wife helped him into the vehicle. 'I was saved by the Grace of God.'

'It was the intervention of this gentleman here that saved your husband from falling to the bottom of the steps. To him you should say *mazel tov*,' said Morris in a very matter-of-fact way.

'I'll have a look at you once we return to the guest house in Kerak village,' said Stephen, talking to Peter Olivier through the window. 'It's probably just a few bruises and a couple of scratches, but it never hurts to be doubly sure.'

Peter Olivier made no reply, other than to grunt something through semi-closed lips, which was unintelligible to Stephen. The Hawkhursts climbed into the vehicle, together with Jane Olivier, Morris and Claudette. Then, with Aaron in the driver's seat, the vehicle headed off down the dusty track towards the nearby village.

The others stood around the second vehicle, watching the other one drive off.

'Are you ready to depart?' asked Uri.

'Not quite,' replied Rupert. 'Barrington fancied a quick smoke first.'

'Would you like one?' asked Stephen, holding out a packet in Uri's direction.

'Thank you,' replied Uri, taking one.

'Well, that really takes the biscuit,' said Rupert to Barrington. 'You probably saved his life back there and he didn't even say thank you for your efforts!'

'Poor man is lost in a delusional world of his own denial. I shouldn't worry about it at all,' said Barrington good-naturedly, as he blew a large smoke ring. 'It certainly won't bother me.'

'I'll give you the once-over as well when we get back,' said Stephen. 'Those abrasions across your shoulders don't look too good and you need to be careful about those cuts and scratches on your hands. Best not eat anything until I've had the chance to clean them up.' For the first time that he could remember, Stephen had set out on that morning's expedition without his medical bag. The one occasion when his precautions would have paid dividends, he had left his precious bag and its soothing contents behind.

'Yes, I know. Risk of infection in these hot, polluted climes,' said Barrington, chuckling softly. 'I well remember that advice from my time out here with Allenby.'

'Where's St Anthony?' asked Rupert suddenly. 'Did he go off with the others?'

'Not a chance in hell, old chap,' replied Stephen, 'not in the confines of the same transport as the wee timorous Mrs Olivier. I don't think her nerves would stand it.'

'So you've noticed that, too, have you?' asked Barrington. 'I don't remember her being that jumpy when we first set out on this trip. It seems to be a condition that has developed since then. Would you not agree, Doctor?' he concluded, smiling warmly at Stephen.

'I would, indeed,' Stephen agreed, with mock solemnity, 'and it would seem as if her condition is influenced in some way by the proximity of the now absent St Anthony.'

'I have seen such a thing before,' said Uri, who had remained in the circle of the conversation.

'Oh?' said Stephen. 'What do you mean, Uri?'

'One of my uncles had a friend who married a very young wife. It had been arranged by the broker. It was very traditional. Very soon after the wedding, people noticed that she had become very nervous sometimes when she was with her husband and there was an important function going on in their house. She was terrified of him, because he used to beat her if she did something wrong or brought disgrace, as he saw it, on their household. This we only learned of much later.'

'That can hardly be the case with our St Anthony and the timid Mrs Olivier, though. Can it?' said Barrington.

'I am simply saying that the wife of my uncle's friend was scared of something which people, for years, knew nothing about. Only she knew that her husband beat her. That was why she was always so scared. No one else knew of it for many years. Perhaps it is the same with Mrs Olivier. Perhaps there is something which troubles her and she keeps it hidden ... Who can say?'

'I say ... you don't think ... No, that's absurd...' said Barrington.

'What is?' asked Rupert, who had been looking around where they were parked, trying to find Collins St Anthony. He turned back to face Barrington.

'Did you see that St Anthony and Olivier were locked in what looked like a very serious conversation up there, when we were all on the battlements?'

'And who was on the step above Olivier when we were coming down?' added Rupert.

'The missing St Anthony,' replied Stephen, 'but, if you think you can somehow connect Mrs Olivier with St Anthony, the husband with St Anthony and St Anthony with Olivier's fall down the steps, I'd have to ask you for the reason and the motive, neither of which, my dear Watson, I suspect you would be able to provide.'

There was a round of laughter before the little group fell silent, absorbed in their own thoughts.

'It is an intriguing thought, though ... I mean, what if St Anthony *did* push the old blighter? That would open up a whole new set of questions as to the why and wherefore, wouldn't it?' suggested Barrington.

'Perhaps it's just me,' said Rupert, 'but, if you catch Mrs Olivier at a certain angle, I've sometimes thought that there is a slight resemblance between...'

'Are we ready to go, then?' asked Collins St Anthony, suddenly appearing from behind the vehicle and cutting across Rupert.

'Yes, we are. We were waiting for you, actually,' said Stephen, who had started to find St Anthony's way of suddenly appearing as if from nowhere, both alarming and extremely off-putting.

'What were you going to say, Winfield?' asked Barrington, as he rose stiffly from where he had been sitting and turned to enter the vehicle. His shoulders and arm muscles had already started to pay the price for his quick-thinking bravery. 'A slight resemblance...' He left the question open, inviting Rupert to continue.

'Oh, I can't remember what it was I was going to say,' Rupert said evasively, looking at St Anthony as he spoke. 'It's gone I'm afraid.'

42

Iraq

Baghdad – Monday, 5th October 1931

Prince Abdul Salaam Abd al-Allah stood at the large window of his office in the complex of buildings which housed several of the government ministries of the British-mandated Kingdom of Iraq. He gazed out over the sprawling complex of structures that made up the growing, ancient capital of the new state. He smiled to himself at the thought that it was truly Baghdad and not Rome which should be honoured with the sobriquet the Eternal City. It was, after all, held by many to be the cradle of civilization. His self-satisfied gaze was suddenly arrested by a black speck high above in the pale blue, clear sky. A large bird, which he thought to be an eagle, was circling slowly in large ellipses, which carried it alternatively in and out of sight as it flew over the roof of the building – over his head, in fact. It was a good omen. Was it not the great Saladin himself who adopted the same bird as his own emblem in his struggle for supremacy against the invading infidel? He nodded slightly in agreement with his own thoughts. He was cousin to the king and saw himself assuming that very role in the very near future, once the British had left. For a moment he even envisaged a new national coat of arms, with the stylised image of Saladin's eagle of victory, wings outstretched, at its centre.

'Does Your Highness expect more finds of oil ... further away from Mosul?'

The prince, lost in his reverie, had almost forgotten that he had a visitor seated in the chair opposite his large ministerial desk.

'Your Highness must surely be circumspect with regard to the ownership of the oil, once the British have left us to ourselves...'

The prince turned to face his visitor who, either out of respect or simple curiosity, had left the sentence open ended, inviting the prince to finish it. He chose not to. Instead, he crossed back to his desk. It was obvious that there was not going to be a completion of the sentence, so the visitor continued speaking.

'Your Highness has, quite correctly and with considerable foresight, referred to the strength an independent Iraq will derive from such vast oil deposits. I must, with the greatest of respect, say that I am honoured, and at the same time a little mystified, as to why Your Highness has sent for me. I am, after all, not someone who has much knowledge of oil.'

There was a slight pause as the prince resumed his seat, unaware that he was being eyed with practised, concealed cunning by his visitor.

'I am greatly honoured, nonetheless,' concluded the visitor, showing the required obsequiousness expected towards one of such exalted station.

'My dear fellow,' replied the prince, unconsciously lapsing into the turn of phrase he had picked up during his days in England, 'we face considerable changes in the very near future. We must ensure that we are ready to meet and conquer any, shall we say, unforeseen stumbling blocks that might present themselves.'

'Does Your Highness anticipate trouble when the mandate ends?' asked the visitor, with a sudden steely abruptness, which, despite the veneer of politeness, alarmed the prince.

'Is it reasonable to expect that the British, simply because their mandate to interfere in our affairs is about to lapse, will haul down their flag, take their military bands with them and leave?' asked the visitor. 'They are untrustworthy. Surely they will try some ruse to keep their hands around the oil pumps?'

The prince sat and looked at his visitor. Rashid Ali al-Gaylami was forceful, charismatic, and undoubtedly had both Iraqi and his own interests at heart. What the prince was not at all sure about was the order in which this man had arranged these potentially conflicting interests. It had become quite clear to him that his visitor had his own personal agenda. 'You are possibly quite correct in that assumption,' replied the prince, as he took a cigarette from the gold box on his desk, before offering one to the other man, 'which is precisely why we need to ensure that *we* are in the position of strength when they leave. That is why I have asked you to come and see me. The time is approaching when we must act to ensure our sovereignty and independence. The oil is our greatest asset, but it could also be our greatest liability, if we are not prepared to defend our rights to it and fend off any future foreign aggression aimed towards it ... if you follow me.'

'Your Highness is as perceptive as your reputation gives you credit,' replied al-Gaylami.

The prince did not much like the obsequiousness in al-Gaylami's voice. It was not supported by the man's expression, which was totally impassive and devoid of either emotion or even the enthusiasm of political zeal. And yet the prince knew that this man was a powerhouse of political drive and was well known to the British for his activities promoting Iraqi nationalism. 'I have spoken to His Majesty about our future,' continued the prince, as he settled back into his ornately gilded chair, his smouldering cigarette clasped loosely between the fingers of his right hand. 'He is convinced of the necessity of creating a strong political front, ready to take over everything the minute the British are gone. Perhaps even before they officially do so...'

'Does His Majesty think that, possibly, we might not be ready to assume total control of our own affairs?' Rashid Ali al-Gaylami knew, as well as the prince, of the king's reputation for indecision. 'Does His Majesty have concerns about possible dissent from within?' continued the visitor, who had often wondered how the Palace had managed to hang on to power for as long as it had.

For a split second, the prince's eyes narrowed and tried to bore into this man's mind. Of course, he knew al-Gaylami to be politically active; the reports from his own clandestine agents, as well as official police reports had revealed that. And yet, as al-Gaylami sat erect in his chair, he seemed to be politely, cautiously inquisitive without being overly pushy. The prince suddenly wondered if it was, indeed, his visitor who was assessing *him*, rather than the other way around.

'His Majesty has no concerns for the internal stability of the kingdom,' added the prince. That, too, was a lie, but a lie which also contained an element of truth. *Cousin Faisal is not much concerned about anything,* the prince ruminated. *He doesn't seem to have progressed much beyond his exploits out in the desert against the Turks ... and that was years ago.*

'From the remarks Your Highness has made, however, I would venture to suggest that Your Highness does ... harbour some concerns,' proposed al-Gaylami quietly.

'It is a well-known fact that our country is made up of several different factions' replied the prince. 'There are bound to be differences of political opinion and we have to face that fact. We also have to be ready to act accordingly. It goes without saying that, despite our slight differences, we are all of one nation.'

'Within our borders there are also differences in the

interpretation of the words of the Prophet: *peace be unto him*,' replied al-Gaylami, for the first time allowing the faint hint of a smile to cross his lips.

'Indeed, that is so,' agreed the prince.

'Whilst the British are here, it is perhaps correct to state that we are all united as a single nation, with the avowed desire to get them out,' continued al-Gaylami, in a soothing tone, which belied the concealed menace of his words.

'I have sources which inform me of the British meddling in Persia, or Iran, as we are now supposed to call it. We must guard against similar events and situations in our own country, once they have finally gone,' the prince revealed.

'Once again Your Highness is well informed,' said al-Gaylami, hiding behind his ambiguous, obsequious smile. 'There is a saying in Tehran: *If there is something wrong, then the British will be the cause of it*.' He chuckled softly. 'It is hardly surprising. The British, who have never had a legal mandate over Persia, nevertheless take the lion's share of their oil revenues.'

The prince nodded in agreement, but beneath his calm exterior he was struggling to fathom the substance and depth of his visitor. What *was* this man's political allegiance? Or indeed, what were his ambitions? The interview seemed to have gone down an unexpected path, to the point where the prince had begun to wonder if summoning the man to the Ministry had been a mistake.

'But, naturally, as I have already said, Your Highness will know far more about matters concerning oil than I,' continued al-Gaylami, the smile now completely gone.

The remark rang hollow in the prince's ears. This man seemed to be well informed. *And I am the one with the official and unofficial information-gathering network*, the prince thought as he studied his visitor, *and not you, you upstart*!

'Our friends in the nationalist movement in India are presently in a very similar position to the Persians. Sadly, the Indians are not under a mandate the legal duration of which is about to expire.'

An alarm bell suddenly began to sound inside the prince's head. His visitor knew of the independence movement in India and obviously had contact with its leaders. So he did not confine his activities solely to Iraq; nor was he ignorant of the situation in Persia. He wondered again, this time with rising concern, as to the extent of this man's ambition: if it was similar to his own, he would be a potential threat rather than the ally the prince had hoped he would be.

'Are they expecting the British to leave India?' asked the prince.

'They hope for the day, but cannot as yet see it,' replied al-Gaylami, shrugging, 'but they have concerns that, when that day finally *does* come, they will have to deal with religious and possibly political dissent on a scale hitherto unimagined. Your Highness is wise to consult, with a view to ensuring that a similar situation is not allowed to arise here.'

In the prince's head the alarm bell could still be heard, as he continued to feel the unease rise within him. 'Are you suggesting that we could well have a civil war on our hands, once the common denominator of the people's anger and annoyance has departed?' he asked, stubbing out the remains of his cigarette in a large ashtray.

'I am sure Your Highness has informed His Majesty of the possibility of such an undesirable eventuality,' replied al-Gaylami impassively.

The prince waited for something further, but there was nothing. He suddenly felt that he was being drawn into a tight corner, which would leave him very little room for manoeuvre. Both of the men knew only too well that to lose power, or even to show weakness, was almost certain political suicide. Despite his visitor's quiet, subservient demeanour, the prince also knew instinctively that the man was dangerous. Despite his reputation for political rabble-rousing and nationalism, al-Gaylami was definitely someone who could not be trusted. It had become clear to the prince that the man harboured ambition certainly as great as, if not even greater than, his own. He was only too well aware that there was no room at the controls for two pilots, each bent upon following his own flight plan.

'Let me be frank with you,' said the prince, aware that the alarm bell was sounding louder than before, 'the security of the state must always be the paramount concern. It is of the utmost importance that all the strong factors within our political ... yes, and even our religious structures ... are of one accord in the national interest.'

'Under the guidance of His Majesty, I am sure that that will be the case, when the time comes,' said al-Gaylami, the smile hovering around his lips again, almost mockingly. 'It is essential that the nation has a strong figure to lead it.'

There was something about the way al-Gaylami voiced this last sentence. He did not know why, but the prince sensed that it was a veiled threat – a warning that he might not be the strong leadership figure that would be required. Did his visitor see himself filling this role?

'I believe that Your Highness has recently taken delivery of a new aircraft?' asked al-Gaylami, as he abruptly changed the subject. 'I trust Your Highness is satisfied with the machine?' He did not add that he knew of the further ten such machines the prince had just ordered. Information was a commodity which could be easily traded in Iraq.

For a moment, the prince was at a loss for words. He had been mentally outwitted and was still processing the implications behind what his visitor had said about the nation needing a strong figurehead.

'Yes ... I am most satisfied with the machine. It was flown out from England by the owners of the company; a brother and sister. They came in two of the craft...'

The interview continued for some twenty minutes. Despite

subtle probing and digging on his part, the prince was largely unsuccessful in his attempt to trap his visitor into unfurling his true political colours or ambition. In fact, the visitor gave away very little.

After al-Gaylami had been shown out of the office, the prince found himself feeling suspicious and disturbed. Had al-Gaylami, in the most subtle of ways, actually laid down some sort of gauntlet, even while the British were still in residence? The man was going to have to be watched – and watched carefully. If necessary, he would have to be removed.

The prince took another cigarette and lit it. Like his cousin, the king, he smoked far too many cigarettes. Getting up from his chair, he crossed once again to the window. There was a single remaining official function to perform later in the day and then he would have the opportunity to fly his new aircraft up into the solitude of the sky. He looked forward to that. He would be unquestionably in control, the absolute master. Up there, in the...

He stopped suddenly and stared up out of the window and into the sky above him. The eagle was no longer there. In its place circled a much smaller, blacker bird. Around and around it flew in diminishing ellipses, clumsily – narrowly avoiding the rooftop under which he stood. It had none of the elegance of the earlier majestic eagle. As the prince watched, it seemed to descend towards him, its large beak opening and closing rhythmically, in time with the ungainly flapping of its wings. He suddenly thought that the bird seemed to be laughing – laughing at him, Prince Abdul Salaam Abd al-Allah. Despite his Western education, he still harboured the deeply rooted superstitions of his desert background. Suddenly, they welled up inside him with as much energy as did the black gold, as it poured up the confines of the drilling pipes and burst free from the stricture of the ground that had held it prisoner for millennia. He took an involuntary step backwards, away from the window and the sight of the laughing crow. In the process, his hand clenched into a fist, breaking the cigarette in two, the lighted end cascading down his Savile Row suit and on to the floor.

This is a bad omen, he conjectured, a very bad omen...

43

Trans-Jordan

The King's Highway, near Petra – Tuesday, 6th October 1931

Uri pulled the little convoy of vehicles off the dusty highway and into a shallow wadi. His boys quickly unpacked and set up the red-striped canvas awning, which they slung between two of the vehicles. A horizontal pole, supported by two braced uprights, ran down the centre, giving the construction sufficient height for the tourists to stand under it. Collapsible chairs were produced and a fire lit. Afternoon tea was on its way.

'I hope you enjoyed your time at Shawbak Castle,' said Rupert, as he busied himself settling everyone down.

'It seemed to be quite a lot of effort getting there, for not much of any great interest when we did,' said Peter Olivier, as he dragged a chair nearer one of the open ends of the awning, where the first hint of an evening breeze suggested itself on the hot air. 'We'd seen the other castle, which was far more interesting and I'm still in some discomfort with my bruises.' He winced, almost on cue, as he sat down in the chair. 'There was also quite a lot of walking.'

'No doubt Barrington was in much the same boat,' said Stephen, who was standing at the opposite opening to that at which Olivier had placed his chair, 'wouldn't you say, old chap?' he continued, raising his eyebrows towards the hero of the previous Saturday.

'A little, yes,' replied Gordon Barrington quietly, 'but not so much as to put a damper on the day's activities. That would not have been very fair on the others. Besides which, there are several interesting features at the castle … the two churches within the walls, the baths, the rainwater pipes, not to mention the spring underneath the castle … and the three hundred and seventy-five steps leading down to it.'

Any subtleties contained in Barrington's response sailed high over Peter Olivier's head and floated away, out into the desert.

'A nice cup of tea is going to be welcome,' said Claudette, as she sat in the chair next to Jane Olivier. 'What do you say to that?' she asked, smiling broadly at the other woman.

'I'll be back in a bit,' said Collins St Anthony. He moved through the centre of the makeshift tent, passing close to where Jane Olivier was sitting. As he did so, she cringed visibly and moved her body away from him, all the time keeping her eyes on the sandy ground. As he walked on past her and out from under the awning, she seemed to fill out to her former self. Lawrence Hawkhurst raised his eyebrows to his sister, winked knowingly and nodded his head in the direction of St Anthony's receding back. She frowned back, as if to discourage him. Claudette also noticed the reaction of Jane Olivier, but she had no such scruples about observing the correctness of polite society.

'Are you all right?' she asked gently, placing her hand on the woman's arm.

'Oh!' responded Jane Olivier, startled by the contact. 'What … sorry, what did you say?' She tried to smile, but her face was lined with some burden, something that weighed very heavily upon her.

'Of course she is,' answered Peter Olivier, a little gruffly.

'It's probably the heat. She's been like this almost from the first day we started the tour.' Not looking in his wife's direction, he continued with his character assassination whilst surveying progress with the tea-making. 'She has a habit of being moody. She'll be quite all right in a moment. I have often suggested she sees someone at the Foundation about whatever it is that causes her moods, but she never takes my advice.' The delivery of this was without emotion, affection or concern in his voice.

Alexandra Hawkhurst shot him a glare of deep loathing and disgust that, had he seen it, could well have turned Olivier to stone.

'Of course, Peter is right,' Jane said in a brittle voice, retreating once again beneath her husband's dominating shadow. 'I really am most sorry if I cause you all any concern. You're all very kind. I'm sure that a good cup of tea will put things to rights.' She smiled at her husband, who ignored her. Then she turned the same forced smile on the rest of the party.

Claudette gave her a reassuring pat on the arm. 'Of course it will. It always does.'

This is a brutal landscape, as brutal as some people can be to their own kind. Morris Ginsberg had wandered out a short distance away from the vehicles and stood smoking a cigarette. He looked at the desert, trying to process the scene he had just witnessed between the Oliviers. Not liking what he saw – the lack of compassion and the subsequent injured emotions – he had preferred to leave the shade of the awning, in favour of a little solitude. The way Olivier treated his wife offended his sense of right and wrong. It upset his belief that everyone was entitled to a little respect and even to a little love in their lives. He had no time for either the overbearing and self-opinionated Mr Peter Olivier, or his precious Foundation. *All talk and very little action, except when someone in high authority is looking*, he thought, as the faint breeze played around his face and slowly teased the smoke from his cigarette. *In a world of their own ill-conceived righteousness they presume to tell everyone else what they see as wrong with them. Such an attitude would not...*

His contemplation was interrupted by the sight of Collins St Anthony, who came striding past and, without any acknowledgement, walked on the short distance back to the improvised tent.

There goes another one with a millstone of some description around his neck. Such people make a profession out of being miserable or angry... Morris flicked the butt of his cigarette on to the sand and ground it in with his shoe ... *Or, sometimes, both.*

Under the awning the mood had lightened and there was a general murmur of conversation. The tea had been brewed and, under Uri's guidance, Aaron and the boys had produced cakes and biscuits from one of the wicker hampers.

'I still find it hard to accept that the Crusaders would actually have chosen to live out here in these isolated castles ... in this heat,' said Alexandra Hawkhurst thoughtfully, 'and all for the sake of religion?' The upward inflection in her voice invited a response to her statement.

'There was a great deal at stake,' replied Gordon Barrington. 'In the rigid, codified world in which they lived there was no real room for individual, free thought. If you did not do what your feudal lord wanted, or what Holy Mother Church ordered, you usually came to a sticky end. They were extremely superstitious and the ultimate sanction of the Church was excommunication – no communion, no Heaven.'

'That just goes to show that not much has changed. The Church was just as intolerant then as it is now,' chipped in Lawrence Hawkhurst, smiling in Peter Olivier's direction.

'The question is whether the Crusades were about religion or temporal power and money,' said Rupert, attempting to diffuse the explosive potential of the last remark. He was becoming a little alarmed at the tension which Peter Olivier's presence on the tour seemed to generate at almost every opportunity.

'It is a matter of *faith*,' said Olivier, glaring at Lawrence. 'This is the Holy Land and *we* had every right to it.'

'I have read that the Christians *did* have the right to come here,' said Stephen. 'Islam allowed us in, provided that there was no evangelising or attempts at conversion. That sounds fair enough to me. It almost suggests that there was hardly the need for the Crusades in the first place...'

'There are those who ascribe some of the tensions in this area today back to the days of the Crusaders. They left a residue of deep-seated distrust and hatred on both sides,' added Barrington. 'It certainly is a consideration.'

'At least the Jews cannot be blamed,' said Morris quietly, as he stirred his tea.

'There was a lot of Arab knowledge, which was taken back to the West as a result of the Crusades,' continued Barrington, 'but the jury is still very definitely out as to whether the Crusades were a necessity of faith or simply a money-grabbing expansionist invasion. Whichever way you look at it, the outcome could hardly have been less satisfactory, apart from the knowledge we gained. It certainly was not a case of all's well that ended well, I'm afraid.'

'Very little in human endeavour seems to end well,' said Collins St Anthony, almost under his breath, from where he was sitting on the running board of one of the vehicles, almost directly opposite Jane Olivier.

Claudette put her cup back into its saucer. Out of the corner of her eye she noticed that Jane Olivier was visibly disturbed by something, but this time Claudette was more restrained and did not question the reason for this.

It was the mention of the word *well* – thrice in as many seconds – that had disturbed Jane Olivier. The image of that word suddenly flashed across her subconscious and sent her scurrying for a place of safety. In her mind's eye she saw, once again, the events amid the ruins of the Castle of Shawbak.

Earlier in the day they had been shown around the castle ruins by a young archaeologist from Amman, an affable young man, naturally dark-skinned and swarthy, who was leading a small team working within the walls. He was also enthusiastically talkative about his excavation.

'This castle is one of a chain part of ... by the Crusaders built,' he enthused, waving his arms wide to encompass the ruins, as he eagerly displayed his knowledge of the English language.

'Some of it still looks to be in good condition,' said Barrington, looking up at the towering bulk of the walls and keep.

'But of course,' replied the archaeologist, 'much of it was in the Mamluk period restored ... to fight against the enemies they are having. This is the way I am telling you this.'

Lawrence Hawkhurst, the corners of his mouth twitching in barely suppressed amusement, was about to launch forth with one of his witticisms. He was stopped by a frosty glare from his sister, who was only too familiar with her brother's sense of humour and of how embarrassing it could be at times.

'Here is much that we have still to excavate, but this costs too much of money,' their guide continued, as they strolled around the castle. 'Over here, being in the shade is a shallow well. It is using water from a large cistern under the floor. This cistern was in the Crusader period built, when the castle is also. There is a deep spring *underneath* the castle, which is giving water to the cistern.' He paused and turned to the group, a smile on his face. 'The water is very cool and sweet – this I am telling you to try some. Perhaps some persons are descending to all three hundred and seventy-five steps to the spring and are taste it.' He laughed encouragingly. 'And you can make a souvenir of the pleasant taste of the water.' They walked on a little further. 'And now we go to the church,' he continued, walking off ahead of them. 'The catacombs underneath are enough on their own to be seen. So come, please.'

Jane Olivier did not fancy the oppressive darkness of the catacombs and instead opted to wait for the rest of the group at the well. She had removed her large straw hat, which she had started to use as a fan, and was leaning against the stone wall that surrounded the well. Twisting around slightly, she stared idly down into its darkness.

'It's not very deep, is it?' The totally unexpected sound of a man's voice made her jump. 'In fact, it's almost as shallow as some people,' he continued, sitting on the wall of the well, just behind her.

She knew whose voice it was and froze as she awaited what would happen next.

'Isn't it truly amazing that humans can build a massive structure like this castle perched up here on top of this hill, live in it and feel safe, like some protecting womb, and then abandon it ... just like that?' he said as he clicked his fingers.

To her strained nerves, the click sounded like a gunshot, echoing off the sturdy walls. 'If necessity dictates that such a thing must be done, then it is the will of God that it must be so,' she answered, her voice quavering slightly, as she drew what strength she could from her faith.

'Do you not think that it is too convenient to thank the will of God for all the world's woes?' he continued, his voice raised to barely above a whisper. 'Wouldn't it be more realistic to say that *we* carry the responsibility for our actions, not some invisible divinity that, at best, can be only a vague concept? *We* are responsible, even if some think that such responsibility is guided by a higher force. In essence, that is what your husband says, through the offices of his Foundation. Is it not one of the main thrusts in his drive for a return to greater social responsibility within our fractured society?'

She had started to feel threatened by this man's conversation, although his voice held no menace. In fact, it had the gentle lilt of comfort and relaxed confidence. Not for the first time since the start of the tour she wondered why it was that she felt so uncomfortable in his company. And why had he not gone down to look at the catacombs with the rest of them? Why had he remained behind to speak to her?

'We have to take responsibility for our own actions,' he continued in the same soft, lilting way as he walked slowly around the well, gesturing up to the castle battlements as he did so. When he stood in front of her he stopped, facing her, his hands clasped loosely in front of him.

'Mr St Anthony, why are we having this conversation?' she asked, using a strength she had not realized she possessed, although her voice quavered slightly with nerves.

'Your husband was very responsible in his missionary work in Africa ... what was it now, just over twenty years ago? His responsibility was widely applauded, or so I read a short time ago...'

There was a pause, during which time Jane Olivier slowly started fanning herself again. She dared not look at the young man, not even for a split second. Instead, she stared stoically ahead of her, wondering how much longer her husband and the others would be. The situation had started to resemble the plot in one of those American detective thrillers she enjoyed reading – in secret, of course, as Peter would not approve.

'I became really interested and began to wonder if *you* could honestly acknowledge that you, too, had been a responsible person,' continued St Anthony.

Lost in the labyrinth of her memory, she didn't hear what he was saying.

'I was a quiet, almost depressed little boy, apparently,' he continued, looking straight at her, 'until I was three. Then I went to live with Mother and Father and I became a very happy child. They made me their son and I developed into a well-rounded young man. I am well educated, rich and a credit to my parents and the community.' He paused to pick up a pebble and toss it down the well shaft. 'Do you know how good it feels to have *responsible* parents?' he hissed. 'And then it all changed. Happiness and contentment plummeted to unexpected depths, just like that pebble down the well and all because of a chance remark made in the last few minutes of a long life.'

'I don't understand,' said Jane Olivier, half-turning to look at him, but all the while desperately hoping that her husband would appear from the church doorway that led down to the catacombs.

'Mother mumbled something about giving me a home as being the best thing she and Father had ever done. What do you think she meant by that?' he asked, but it was not a question which invited an answer. 'Collins is quite an unusual Christian name, wouldn't you agree?'

'I would like you to please leave me in peace; my husband will return shortly,' she said. 'I really do not see that we have anything to talk about.' For the first time, she found the courage to look the young man straight in the face. She had not taken a good look at him before. There was something about him that sparked considerable disquiet deep inside her.

'Oh, I think that we do. About the time before you became Mrs Olivier.'

She stiffened again and looked away from him, breaking her eye contact and giving him the advantage. 'What do you mean?' she replied, for the first time in years her voice holding the faintest suggestion of defensive anger.

'The time before you were even engaged to the rising star of Mr Peter Olivier, the doer of good works amongst the dispossessed and downcast; the upholder of strong morals and all that should be good and proper in society. It is amazing to think that he achieved his lofty, self-righteous purpose with the aid and support of a fallen woman. Miraculous I'd say, given the narrow-mindedness of society ... wouldn't you agree?'

'What on earth do you mean?' she snapped back in her own timorous way, as she felt her knees start to slacken. 'I have no idea what you are talking about.'

'Yes you do,' he shot back, 'and it is now time for you to take responsibility, Miss Collins.'

She swayed back against the wall of the well, reaching out with her free hand to steady herself. The mention of her maiden name came like a bolt from the blue. As Jane unscrambled the hints and insinuations that had been pouring out of this man's mouth, she realized that her feelings towards him were changing. The maelstrom of emotions that had been building up during the period since she had had the misfortune to come into contact with this young man was now flooding through her brain in a sequence of suspicion, loathing, anger and fear. Suddenly the confusion cleared as her most basic emotion erupted and was laid raw and exposed: maternal instinct. This was her son! But unable to respond as she would have liked, she fell back on the protection of respectability she had built around herself over the last two decades. To enforce this dreadful situation, this odious man moved even closer;

so close that the smell of his hair oil mixed with his sweat almost stifled her.

'Or should I say *Mother*? I've found you at last,' he whispered into her ear, with neither love nor affection in his sentiments.

'Don't be ridiculous,' she responded feebly, her words seeming to fall hopelessly down the well shaft.

'My parents ... my real mother and father, no thanks to *you*,' – he almost spat out the last word – 'were the most decent people you could hope to meet, Miss Collins. They educated me, gave me their name and left me very well provided for. I have my own business and we hold a Royal Warrant, you know. That is a sure sign of respectability.'

'You're making wild accusations,' she gasped, in an attempt to nullify the truth.

'Not really,' he retorted. 'I did some research at Somerset House ... and guess what I found? There it was beautifully inscribed in flowing script on my birth certificate: *Mother: Jane Collins. Father: unknown.* Father unknown ... God, but what a *scandal*! What must *your* father have thought? He must have been mortified. After all, he had his position as a highly regarded member of the congregation to consider. And then his pretty young daughter produces an embarrassment, which must be dispensed with. Not disposed of, thank goodness; Holy Mother Church wouldn't have liked that too much. No, just *removed* to the back of beyond ... out of sight ... removed to an orphanage, to be precise. How *responsible* your father was to protect the family honour like that! For this trip I decided not to use the name given to me by my parents; instead I devised a nomenclature to help *you* remember who I really am. I have my first name: *Collins* ... which was your name of course. Then there was the problem of what my assumed surname should be ... then I thought about St Anthony, the patron saint of lost and hopeless causes. That seemed ideal, as there was no reason why I should not take the name of the orphanage where I was abandoned. What an interesting name it is: Collins St Anthony.'

He paused, his eyebrows raised as if waiting for her to respond, but she knew that anything she might say would be pointless.

'And then there was this,' he continued, lifting his shirt out of his waistband to reveal a large birthmark across his stomach. 'It's all a bit like a penny-dreadful, isn't it, Miss Collins – *Mama.*'

The trembling that had started whilst her secret past was revealed now turned to severe quakes and she felt as if the yawning chasm of the wellhead was inviting her into oblivion and safety. She tried to speak, but the sounds refused to leave the refuge of her mouth. It was not meant to be like this: all the heartache and pain experienced twenty-three years ago came flooding back. Had she tried to imagine this moment of discovery, when she finally met her son? Yes, of course she had. In her dreams it had been a wonderful moment, full of love, tenderness and tears; the fulfilment of the most basic of human emotions with the strength of that biological bond that was unique and undeniable. This is what she had prayed for, not this hideous nightmare of hatred and loathing!

'Imagine how it feels to discover that your loving mother and father aren't who you thought them to be and that...' He tucked his shirt back into his trousers and turned his malevolent glare full on to Jane Olivier. '... And that your own mother didn't want you!'

'How much do you want?' she asked, suddenly angry.

'Please! Don't insult me ... *Mother*,' he replied, a menacing grin slashing across his mouth. 'I have more money than even *your* husband could waste on his stupid Foundation.'

'Then what do you want?'

'I want you to suffer. I want you to constantly look over

your shoulder to see if I'm there. I want you to live on your nerves, wondering if I'm going to suddenly appear and spill the beans, as it were. Imagine how you would like that ... I want you to go through what I've been through the last couple of years...'

She had fallen silent, the sunhat held limply in her hand by her side, her gaze fixed on the sandy ground in front of her.

'I'm going to wander off now. It was good that we had this conversation. Don't think of telling your husband. Anyway, he'd probably have you burned at the stake as a Jezebel.' St Anthony chuckled – a low sound full of menace and hatred. 'And I'm very happy that you are now going to live a life of unrelenting mental discomfort, as you spend it keeping the truth from your pompous husband. I can't imagine what he'd do if you let the cat out of the bag and caused his oh-so-respectable pillar of religious righteousness to collapse about him. But it would be appropriate though, don't you think? Rather like Samson in the temple, but from a different perspective, naturally.'

'I'll tell him that you're blackmailing me,' she gasped, her voice betraying her nervousness and desperation.

'*Am* I blackmailing you?' replied St Anthony calmly. 'I think not. I haven't asked you for anything ... Quite the contrary, actually. I am giving *you* something ... the gift of your *conscience*. It will be like a thorn in your side. No, think of it as your very own Crown of Thorns.'

Jane Olivier suddenly winced.

'I'm quite protected, you see. My late parents ... my *real* mother and father ... were highly respected members of society. It's that respectability that gives *me* peace of mind.' He chuckled again – the same, menacing sound. 'So ... I'll be off then ... until we have the opportunity of another little chat like this. Perhaps some time in the future? Who can tell? I'll make sure that the occasion is *responsibly* chosen, never fear. I might even offer your husband some of my money for his Foundation. So, in time, we *could* have another little talk ... at a Foundation meeting, perhaps ... Who knows?'

Just as Lot's wife had looked back and had been turned to a pillar of salt, Jane Olivier, too, had been forced to face the consequences of her past and had become rooted to the spot as she contemplated the significance of her current situation.

'We'd best move on,' said Rupert, as Uri's boys busied themselves packing away the awning and chairs. 'About another hour and a bit and we should catch our first glimpse of Wadi Musa and Petra. We'll have quite a descent, but the views are well worth the effort,' he continued, as he marshalled his flock into something resembling order.

'Pardon me asking,' Alexandra said softly to Jane Olivier, 'is everything quite all right? You look a little pale.'

'What ... oh, you are kind. Yes, I'm fine. Thank you. It's just a ladies' problem. You understand,' she replied, smiling wanly.

'Oh ... *that*,' replied Alexandra. 'It's a terrible inconvenience and quite a bind, isn't it?'

Jane Olivier smiled again and nodded her head in agreement. Alexandra Hawkhurst could not possibly have the faintest idea of just how much of a bind Miss Collins's unexpected 'problem' was.

44

Petra

Dusk, Tuesday, 6th October 1931

An hour and a half after the stop for tea on their way from Shawbak Castle down the King's Highway, the tour group arrived in Wadi Musa. The modern town was a poor substitute for the ancient grandeur of the lost rose-pink city beyond. In the gentle twilight of another slowly-cooling day, their equipment, supplies, tents and finally they themselves were loaded on to donkey-drawn carts and then, like some modern travesty of an ancient desert trade caravan, were moved through the Siq and into the large open area of flat ground outside the massive bulk of the ornate Treasury.

'Welcome to Petra,' called Uri, who had gone on ahead of them with the vanguard of their supplies and now stood at the foot of the triclinium steps. 'Please enter and enjoy some refreshment.' He gestured up the steps towards the spacious, cool interior.

Inside the cavernous building Aaron and the boys were busying themselves setting up trestle tables and folding chairs, ready to dispense a much needed sun-downer to the weary and dusty tourists.

'If you don't mind, I think I would like to lie down for a little while. I have found today's travel rather taxing, I'm afraid. Can I go to our tent now?' asked Jane Olivier, as she hesitated on the top step outside the triclinium.

'Even as we speak, it is being made ready for your comfort,' Uri said, flashing his white teeth in a broad smile. 'It should not be much longer. I will tell you when everything has been prepared. In the meantime, perhaps you would like to sit in the cool – over here?' He indicated the far left-hand corner of the wide verandah, which ran across the front of the ancient building. 'There is the suggestion of an evening breeze there, too,' he added, walking over and positioning a chair for her.

She smiled wanly and followed him.

Stephen watched her go and thought that she did so like a docile, well-behaved Labrador. He surprised himself with that analogy and realized how true it actually was. *There is something wrong with her*, he speculated, *and I'm not totally convinced it's not something of her mind, as much as something of her body. She's still quite well preserved, but she's carrying herself as if she were many years older. She suddenly seems to have withered.*

A little over an hour later, when the glasses had all been refilled and emptied, everyone went their separate ways to their respective tents either to rest, or to begin the evening ritual of preparing themselves for dinner. Even in the wildest outposts of civilization, the rules dictated by polite society still had to be observed in all things and at all times.

'Well, my dear chap, we're back,' said Stephen, as he offered Rupert a cigarette. They were quite alone, sitting on the top step outside the triclinium. Inside the vast, multicoloured space, Uri's boys were now busy laying the table for the evening meal. Off in the near distance, beyond the neat campsite, the enticing smell of something delicious had started to waft up from the kitchen tent and had already partially filled the air with the promise of what was to come.

'Yes, we're back, but this time we know what we are about,' replied Rupert, 'or at least we have a good idea …

which is more than we had the last time. What's our plan of attack?' he asked, turning to Stephen with a look of boyish enthusiasm on his face.

Stephen suddenly burst out laughing. He felt an uncontrollable, warm flood of affection for his friend. *This scroll business really is just another adventure to you, isn't it? Not much has really changed in that dear head of yours, has it?*

'What's so funny,' asked Rupert, a little taken aback by Stephen's unexpected outburst. 'Did I say something amusing?'

'Not at all, my dear chap,' replied Stephen, putting his hand on Rupert's forearm and squeezing it gently. 'I'm just very happy, that's all.'

'And that makes you laugh?'

'Of course ... why not?' continued Stephen, smiling.

'Well, that's all right then. So ... what's the plan?' repeated Rupert.

'I would suggest that we need to reconnoitre the area first. We've got the photograph to work from, but we need to get our bearings before we move in for the final assault. *If* there is anything there, another couple of days won't make any difference, considering it's supposed to have been there for a couple of thousand years.' He paused just long enough to blow out a perfectly formed smoke ring, which vibrated delicately, gyrating up and away from them. He had seen a detective do it in an American gangster film they had seen back in London. 'The question is what do we do with your tour group whilst we're out there searching? We don't want this lot tagging along, just in case there *is* something in all of this and we do find a scroll. Remember, the fewer people that know about any of this, the better.'

'And how are we going to just get rid of them?' Rupert asked, turning his head to look out over the campsite.

'I expect that Mr al Mohammed is still here with his archaeological expedition. From what he said when we were here last, they have enough work to keep them busy for years and that's just fiddling around with the bits they already know about, let alone the rest. He's a very obliging chap...'

Stephen's voice trailed off and, in the companionable silence that followed, each of them returned to their first visit to Petra, to the death of Professor Unsworth and to what a godsend it had been having al Mohammed to help them with the resolution of the problems that had arisen from that event. It had been al Mohammed who had, in large part, assisted them in avoiding what could well have been an extremely difficult situation. But they would not be visiting the professor's grave specifically – that had been decided shortly after they had returned to London. That was a time and an incident now firmly lodged in the past. For the two friends, Petra would always be synonymous with the professor and his death; for them the whole site represented his grave and would be revered accordingly.

'... Old al Mohammed's dead keen and passionately enthusiastic about his work. Perhaps he can take them off our hands whilst we go and investigate ... as honorary tour guide or some such thing,' Stephen continued, quickly drawing them back to the reality of the present. 'He doesn't have to know anything about the scroll.'

'It's worth a try,' Rupert agreed. 'It would certainly solve a problem, wouldn't it?'

'Which is more than can be said for the enduring problem of the old stump, I'm afraid,' muttered Stephen, rubbing his leg with his left hand as he moved slightly to adjust his sitting position. 'I'm afraid the Phoenix's old cane, here, is becoming a necessary accessory.' He raised the heavy black cane, with its ornate silver griffin-shaped handle. The bird's twin ruby-red eyes glinted for an instant as he did so. Then he caught a sudden movement out of the corner of his eye and half turned to see what it was.

'Excuse please, you wish for something?' The voice had

taken them completely by surprise. It had come from behind them, from the triclinium. 'What is it you desire?' It was Uri's younger brother, Aaron Ben Zeev. He had been busy supervising the laying of the tables and now stood a short distance behind Rupert and Stephen, easily within earshot.

'Er … no thank you, Aaron. I don't want anything,' Stephen stammered. He fished around for the right words, surprised by this unexpected intrusion into their conversation.

'Pardon me,' replied Aaron Ben Zeev. 'I saw you hold up your walking stick and I naturally assumed that you wished to have something.'

'No, I was just…' Stephen let his voice dissolve into silence. He saw no reason to offer any explanation. He was more concerned with the suspicion he suddenly felt rise within himself. Had this man made the simple mistake of misinterpreting a signal, or had he tried to disguise his own discovery?

'I hope that everything is going well, gentlemen,' continued Aaron, a smile on his face that bordered on the theatrical.

'Everything is going very well,' Stephen said, eyeing Aaron warily. 'Everything is up to the high standards we have come to expect from your brother and his team.' He used the phrase purposely, as he watched Aaron's face for any reaction to the remark. There was none – the younger man's smile remained as impassive as the carved rock that surrounded them.

'That is good,' Aaron replied, the hollowness of his smile barely concealed. 'Uri works hard and we all try to play our parts. Excuse, please,' he muttered, as he turned and walked back into the triclinium.

'Was he listening to us, do you think?' asked Rupert, as he watched him go.

'Yes,' Stephen replied, 'I'm sure he was. If I hadn't half-turned, he'd probably still be standing there. I wonder why?

What's he up to?'

'I wonder if...'

'Hang on,' whispered Stephen putting a warning hand on Rupert's arm, 'it would seem as if walls have ears here. Come on...' he continued, motioning Rupert to get up with him. They continued their conversation as they strolled around the campsite, away from any more eavesdroppers.

45

Petra

Shortly before dawn, Wednesday, 7th October 1931

The awesome sight of the ruined grandeur of the Nabatean capital or at least that part of the sprawling ruins that had been discovered and uncovered, rose sleepily from another night of cold slumber in the crisp desert air. The sun was rising, but had not yet clawed its fiery way up and over the surrounding mountains to bathe and then, as the day wore on, to bake the multicoloured rock in its heat.

Atop the High Place of Sacrifice two shadowy shapes stood in the pre-dawn gloom. They were waiting for the drab sandstone bulk of rock that spread out before them to be transformed into a curtain of fiery, blood-red orange, as the sun's rays licked hungrily down the rugged outlines of the cliffs.

'That could be the eagle stone,' said Rupert, in a voice a little more than a whisper, 'over there ... behind us.'

Stephen had retrieved the colour photo from its hiding place in his walking stick. Flattening it out, he replied thoughtfully, 'Quite possibly, my dear chap ... Not much longer now and we should know for sure. I must say that I can't really make out anything over there.' He pointed away across the valley that separated them from the sheer wall of cliffs rising up on the other side. 'There doesn't seem to be anything that looks even remotely the same as Harrison's photograph.'

'Well, we know from what he said that he *did* take it from up here and that it was at dawn,' said Rupert, thrusting his hands further into his pockets, against the cold of the pre-dawn.

'Why are you whispering?' asked Stephen, a little bemused, whilst speaking in his normal voice.

'Am I?' asked Rupert, surprised. 'I had no idea that I was. It's probably this place; it's supposed to be a place of mysterious sacredness and I suppose that some of the mystery has rubbed off on to me.'

Rupert's sensitive character was very much in tune with the beliefs surrounding this mountain. It was only four months before that they had last been on this mountain top and had discovered the mortal remains of Professor Unsworth. Rupert remembered the peacefulness of the scene and how the location seemed to be a natural place to meet one's death. That observation had been confirmed by the Reverend Fairweather as they had made their solemn way down the mountain as part of the cortege behind the body of the professor. He explained with great scholarly detail the significance of the site and how important it had been to Professor and Mrs Unsworth. Rupert also recalled how the Reverend had undergone a noticeable character change at the time of the professor's death: from that moment he appeared to no longer represent a faded symbol of religion, stuck in his ways and the rites of his faith. Suddenly he emerged as a force of intellectual thought and opinion, managing to present the contents of the Bible in a freethinking, refreshing and modern way. Without a doubt, The Holy Land and Petra Tour with its promised *Journey of Exploration through Two Thousand Years of Civilization* had certainly enlightened the Reverend Fairweather.

Sitting on top of the High Place of Sacrifice Rupert now also felt connected to this mountain and to the people who, over the past two thousand years, had climbed to its summit, as he and Stephen had today. But Stephen was the pragmatist and Rupert knew his friend would feel differently about the experience.

'Do you feel anything?' Rupert asked.

'Only the perishing cold!' came the reply. 'We didn't exactly bring the correct winter gear with us, did we? Not out here to the Middle East where it's never cold...'

Rupert smiled, as the response had been as expected. He and Stephen were completely different in so many ways and yet as a whole they complemented one another perfectly by each filling the void in the other's life. Together they were a solid unit and as such they had already faced various awkward situations and would, undoubtedly, face many more. Were they on the cusp of another adventure he wondered?

The two friends continued to watch and wait, during which time it grew steadily lighter as the sun, hidden behind the mountains at their backs, started to rise in its stately, unhurried progression. Stephen kept holding out the photograph in the direction of the cliffs, studying both it and the breathtaking vista in front of them.

'There is something I've been thinking about,' said Rupert suddenly. 'I was going to mention it when we were sitting on the triclinium steps, but got side-tracked by Aaron interrupting us.'

'And what might this profundity be, then?' replied Stephen, taking his gaze off the photograph and turning, smiling, to face Rupert.

'What I don't understand is why your uncle always seems to get us involved in things which are always so important to the national good. I mean, it's not as if we're anything to do with Military Intelligence or spying or anything like that, is it? That diamond business in Egypt was one thing, but, even so, everyone seemed to be in the right place at the right time, almost as if by accident. Perhaps that was a different thing... but this Scroll of Gershom business doesn't seem to be anything like that. If this scroll is *that* important, then why not send the properly trained people out after it? Why get us involved?' Rupert looked at his friend in the silence, as his voice echoed and faded amongst the ancient boulders.

Stephen seemed to be thinking, the smile still on his face. 'It's because that's the way things used to be done. It was a sort of ... gentleman's game, organized and played...' He paused, a wistful expression flickering momentarily across his face. '... By people like my uncle. On the one hand, they realize only too well that the world has changed way beyond what it was like when that *was* the way things were done; on the other hand, they still sometimes do things in the tried-and-tested way, because they know they worked previously.'

'But isn't that being just a bit out of touch with reality?' asked Rupert. 'If this scroll is so important, then surely there should be more thought given to recovering it ... before it falls into the wrong hands. That is, if it even exists in the first place.'

'You're probably quite right. It does smack of the idea of sending a gunboat to subdue the natives, I suppose.' Stephen chuckled. 'But, then again, I suppose it's one way of dealing with what could be a politically sensitive issue without drawing too much attention to what's going on ... just in case the whole thing *is* a wild-goose chase. Probably there is the need to be carefully cautious about the way these things are dealt with. I'm not sure though ... being only a humble medical doctor and not a politician.'

The two men stood in companionable silence waiting for the rising sun, each lost in similar, yet differing thoughts.

'You'll have to ask my uncle yourself, not that I think he'll pass on any more of his reasons for any of this than we already know...' said Stephen eventually, returning his gaze once again to the photograph.

'I say,' whispered Rupert, 'I need a pee. Have I got time?'

'You tell me, my dear chap,' replied Stephen, lowering the photograph and turning to his friend. 'You know your own bladder far more intimately than I.'

'I mean do I have time before the sun comes up?' answered Rupert.

'If you're quick, you should be fine,' answered Stephen, chuckling. 'I'd say we have a few minutes in hand before all is revealed. But I thought you were in awe of the mystery of this sacred place. And yet you're quite happy to pee on it?' muttered Stephen, amused by the seeming contradiction in Rupert's value judgement.

'It's either that or I embarrass myself. All things considered, I really don't think there is any option regarding the obvious choice to make,' he reasoned.

'Spoken with true rationality and clear logic,' answered Stephen. 'Off you trot then, but linger not, afore the disc is risen and be upon us, as Shakespeare might have said.' He returned to his study of the photograph as Rupert strode purposely away to the left side of the flat-topped mountain, where there were a couple of convenient outcrops of rock.

'Did you trip?' asked Stephen casually, as Rupert re-joined him a few minutes later. 'It sounded as if you'd dislodged a couple of stones. Sound carries well in this quiet, clean air.' He was still looking at the photograph, as at the very top of the cliffs the first, wafer-thin line of bright light, still only the faintest pink, had suddenly appeared.

'No,' replied Rupert, 'there *are* no stones over there. It's all very flat, even behind the outcrops.'

'Are you sure?' asked Stephen, looking up from the photograph for a second. 'I thought I heard something, over there, where you were ... engaged.'

'But I went over there,' said Rupert, pointing further to their left, 'not where you're pointing. You've got the wrong outcrop.'

'Oh...'said Stephen, turning to survey the whole of the scene on the mountain top, which lay spread before them. 'How curious, I was sure it came from over there. Perhaps it was an animal.'

'Must have been ... probably the local wildlife waking up and starting to look for breakfast. Just like that lot back at camp...'

The thin pink line at the top of the cliffs had started to widen and march down the cliff face, growing deeper and deeper in colour as it did so.

'We're off ... at last,' said Stephen, the unexplained sound of falling stones forgotten.

As they watched in silence, the curtain of light continued to slowly descend across the cliff face, changing colour all the while as it did so: first dark pink, then light red, then blood red and finally red-orange. It had reached a third of the way down when the combination of the colour of the stone with the millions of facets of mineral crystals it contained and the reflected colour of the climbing sun suddenly seemed to make the cliffs burst into flame, the iridescent glow resembling the embers of a well-established fire.

'My God,' gasped Stephen, 'look at that...'

'It's fantastic...' mumbled Rupert, who was as amazed by the spectacle as was his friend.

As the curtain continued to descend across the cliffs, the shape of what looked like a large bird suddenly appeared, wings outstretched, as if it had hovered and then landed on the cliff face, blotting out the flames where it did so to reveal the natural colour of the stone beneath.

'You were right, my dear chap,' said Stephen, taking a step forward and barely able to conceal the excitement in his voice. 'That *was* the eagle stone you pointed out.'

The shadow of the rock – the eagle-shape – seemed to flap its outstretched wings and float slowly down the cliffs, gradually distorting its shape as it did so.

'There!' shouted Rupert, suddenly stabbing his finger out across the valley towards a small patch of very dark grey, which appeared, as if by magic, at the end of the bird's beak.

'I see it,' said Stephen, pointing his finger to the same relative position on the photograph. 'I've got it marked.'

'So there *is* a ca—' Rupert stopped in mid-word. As the two men watched, the tiny blotch of the cave entrance seemed to vanish, as if eaten by the advancing beak of the giant bird. Suddenly, it was gone – just as silently and as quickly as it had first appeared.

'Almost unbelievable,' said Stephen. 'Here one second and gone the next, eh?' Then, taking a pencil from his pocket, he drew a circle on the photograph, marking the exact location of the cave mouth. 'Look, it's just above that ledge, which looks as if it's about forty-five degrees. Fantastic! Now the cave has disappeared completely.'

'But it's still there,' replied Rupert. 'It's just that now we can't see it any more. See how the light is changing. Everything looks so different.'

The bird-shaped silhouette they had witnessed a brief moment before had now distorted to the point of resembling nothing more than a large, irregular shadow, and the curtain of fire, which had consumed the cliff with its ferocity, had now almost reached the bottom of the cliffs, leaving the cliff face bleached out and drained.

'So far, so good, eh?' said Stephen. He quickly rolled the photograph into a tube before releasing the catch on the ornate silver handle of his walking stick and exposing the hollow central compartment. With practised skill he slipped the photograph back into its hiding place and clicked the handle back into position. 'There, that is safely hidden again. Suddenly, this whole affair takes on a new dimension and becomes rather more interesting, wouldn't you say?'

'Question is what next?' added Rupert, as they turned

and started to retrace their steps across the High Place of Sacrifice to the rock-cut steps, which led down to the valley floor below.

'What's next, my dear chap is to get into that cave and see what we can find,' answered Stephen. 'There must be a way of actually getting at it, either up from the valley floor or down from the top of the cliff; otherwise how did Gershom's lot hide the thing in the first place? And if there is no truth in any of this, despite the inscription on the marble tablet, then how come we've just seen the proof of what's written for ourselves? We need to think this one through and get the rest of the group out of our way for a while. We should go and see al Mohammed today and discreetly enquire if he would like to deliver a couple of lectures on his work here. That should give us a breather, eh?'

Stephen had become excited at the prospect of making progress with the hitherto fruitless search for the so-called Scroll of Gershom. Now, having seen the evidence of the truth of at least part of the story surrounding the scroll, he felt buoyed up by the sense of eventual success, even if he was, as yet, uncertain as to how that success was to be achieved. 'In the meantime, I could do with a nice hot cup of tea and some breakfast.'

For the first time in a very long while, as he strode off back towards camp, he paid no attention to the throb in the stump of his left leg. At that precise moment he had far more exciting things with which to occupy his mind.

46

Italy

The Ansaldo Shipyard, Genoa – Wednesday, 7th October 1931

'An auspicious day, would you not agree, *padrino?*' said Count Ciano. He had to raise his voice above the din of hundreds of excited people and the more melodious sounds of a navy band, drawn up on the quayside.

'Indeed, it is a good day for Italy,' replied Count Vittorio Contini-Aosta, treading the safe path of neutrality. 'Il Duce must be very proud to know that he has led us so gloriously to this day of celebration.' He pointed dutifully to the towering bulk of the heavy cruiser *Alberico da Barbiano*, the grey bulk of which towered above them like an eagle rising from its nest.

'But, forgive me! Of course, *padrino*, I know that it is you and your ministry that have planned and executed the new vision for our navy.' Realizing that he may have spoken without giving due credit where it was due, he tried to placate the count by adding. 'How stupid it is of me not to accurately assess the situation.'

Contini-Aosta smiled wanly and, with that peculiarly Italian gesture, shrugged his shoulders as if to dismiss any possible affront.

They were standing close to a large covered dais, which was draped in red, white and green bunting, and had been erected on the quay next to the new warship. Some of the minor dignitaries and Party officials had already taken their seats on the dais, well back from the more important rows of chairs at the front. Crowds of people lined the quay in a solid, packed phalanx, through the middle of which lay an open corridor lined on both sides by marines. It was down this walkway that Il Duce, accompanied by the king, would make his theatrical entrance. The full value of carefully organized, meticulously staged publicity and mass propaganda was never lost on Mussolini. It was a hot day, with only the slightest breath of a cooling breeze blowing in off the sea to disturb the flags. Of late, Contini-Aosta had found the uniform he wore uncomfortable. He was not clear as to whether the discomfort was merely physical or with the reason why he was wearing the uniform itself. He had also been doing much thinking: perhaps one thing led to the other – he was not at all sure.

He had also started to find these big military gatherings something of a strain. In fact, he now detested these carefully stage-managed Party events: the noise of the cheering crowd; the crowd itself, like so many lemmings; the endless saluting and the growing pompous arrogance of Il Duce himself. Whilst he could not show his irritation, he would have to continue to internalize these feelings; at least there was still room for private thought in Mussolini's Italy. He smiled to himself.

'You are amused by something?' asked Ciano, looking at his godfather.

'Oh ... yes. The band...' lied Contini-Aosta, careful not to reveal what it was that had made him smile. 'They are playing one of my favourites, the "Anvil Chorus"...'

'Ah, yes. *Il Trovatore.* Did I tell you that we saw an excellent production at La Scala, before we went out to Rio?'

'No ... no, you didn't,' replied Contini-Aosta, who much preferred Bellini to Verdi anyway.

'It was really quite excellent. There was...'

But Contini-Aosta had stopped listening; he was busy thinking instead. How appropriate, to hear the 'Anvil Chorus': just like Mussolini's words beating against all of our brains ... in the same way that the gypsy's hammers crash against their anvils in the opera. A smile of detached noncommittal had spread across his ageing face. In his mind he had gone back to the Villa Biranconi outside Rome – back to his beloved vineyard. The noise and bustle of the commissioning ceremony, even the massive bulk of the *Alberico da Barbiano* had disappeared, to be replaced by the quiet, tranquil refuge of his vines. He had had enough, he suddenly realized. He didn't want to be a part of all of this any more!

His attention suddenly returned to the noisy quayside. He turned and looked at his godson and wondered if Edda had ever passed on anything she had heard her husband – or, for that matter, himself – say. Her father had ears everywhere. *Is this what her* papà *and the Fascists have brought us to? Distrusting everyone ... even our own families?*

He was about to say something when the band struck up with 'La Giovannezza', the Party anthem, and a sudden roar erupted at the far end of the quay, at the beginning of the ceremonial corridor.

'They are coming,' said Ciano. 'Let us take up our positions to welcome them.'

The band was struggling against the roar of the crowd. The count wondered if the sudden outpouring of Party loyalty had been spontaneous or engineered by the Party officials. These days it was often difficult to tell. The noise steadily increased, as the crowd erupted into a chant: *Du-ce ... Du-ce ... Du-ce.*

What about the king...? Contini-Aosta questioned. Remember the king? He still counts for something!

It took several minutes for Mussolini and Victor Emmanuel III to make their unhurried, choreographed progress down the human corridor. The music changed and the band struck up with the Triumphal March from *Aida*. Those dignitaries deemed important enough and of sufficiently high rank, had all been marshalled at the foot of the small flight of steps that led up to the dais. They stood in a short line, ready to be introduced.

Even this ritual is absurd! Contini-Aosta thought. We know perfectly well who we all are. It is hardly necessary to be formally presented every single time there is a parade or function! And the endless bloody saluting...

He started to feel perspiration under his uniform and peaked cap. Was it the sun, or was it perhaps something deeper, something far more serious, that had caused him to sweat? The mood of the huge crowd remained buoyant, but the chanting had subsided. He felt his mouth become dry. Perhaps it was just the heat of the day. Then, without thinking, he returned the king's greeting with a military salute – not the approved Party one. The king seemed to be genuinely pleased. Perhaps he, too, was getting progressively more and more sick and tired of the Fascist approach to everything and was only too pleased to be reminded of earlier, perhaps less troubled times. A short conversation ensued between the two men, but Contini-Aosta remembered nothing of it. He found himself to be half on the quayside in Genoa and half in his vineyard at the Villa Biranconi. And the bloody music! Was it his imagination, or was the band playing *everything* forte-fortissimo all of a sudden?

'*Bravo*, Vittorio. Italy is proud of you. You and your Ministry have done well with your planning and today we commission yet another of our many fine, new warships.'

The king moved on and Contini-Aosta suddenly found that he was face to face with Mussolini. The count's arm shot out in the Fascist salute, almost as an involuntary action borne of many years' experience.

'Everything is under your direct leadership, Duce,' replied Contini-Aosta, once again using the automatic and politically correct Party response.

'Well, yes,' replied Mussolini immodestly, 'but you and your Ministry are delivering what it is that Italy needs, even if it is *I* who created the master plan. I would hate to lose you,' continued Mussolini. 'Our plans for the Empire have reached an important stage and I would go so far as to say that any change in our structure would be most unwelcome ... perhaps, even, detrimental to our united desire to create a new Roman Empire. In fact, it could not be tolerated. Italy is, after all, greater than any of us. Your work with the French will not be forgotten. Laval has requested an official visit to Rome next year. *Bravo*, Vittorio! Good work! In time to come, they will say that the empire was largely due to the efforts of people like you.'

After delivering the pronouncement, Il Duce moved on.

As he sat in his chair in the front row on the dais, Count Vittorio Contini-Aosta battled with his emotions. The paradise of his vineyard and the tranquillity of the Villa Biranconi suddenly seemed light years away from the noise and pompous bluster of the reality in the shipyard. As he sat and watched the commissioning of the new warship, something in the back of his mind started to disturb him. It was the way in which Mussolini had spoken to him. There was another feeling, too, from much deeper down. It was not a new feeling, but it was one which his memory recalled he had not experienced for many, many years, not since he had been a very young boy at his family's mountain retreat late one summer. He had become lost in the surrounding forests and had spent several uncomfortable hours in the late afternoon and early evening in the company of howling, hidden wolves.

The feeling was fear.

47

Petra

Early evening, Wednesday, 7th October 1931

It had been a tiring day in the sun-drenched ruins of the rose-pink city. The tour group had returned to camp, where they had first rested and then dressed for dinner, which had been served in the triclinium. They now sat, each with a cup of steaming Arab coffee in front of them.

'That was excellent, as usual, Aaron,' Alexandra Hawkhurst said, as she stirred a third spoonful of sugar into her strong coffee. 'Please pass my compliments on to your brother.'

'I am pleased you have said so,' Aaron Ben Zeev replied. 'Rest assured I will pass on your message.'

Lawrence Hawkhurst shot his sister a curious glance. Of late, Alexandra seemed to have been taking more than just a passing interest in the olive-skinned, swarthy young Jew. Her brother was certain that it had not just been his own overactive imagination. As he sipped his coffee, he decided that he would have to keep an eye on things. After all, wasn't that what she had always done with him? He would simply be repaying her thoughtfulness. He chuckled at the thought.

The evening meal had been prepared and served to the usual high standards and the tourists had done the meal justice, with the exception of Jane Olivier. Sitting next to her husband, she had just pecked at her food, like a sparrow.

During the meal Peter Olivier had become totally preoccupied with a discussion concerning the rights and wrongs of autocracy in a democratic society and, as a result, paid no attention to his wife at all. Lawrence Hawkhurst had gone out of his way to provoke him by trying to draw a non-too-discreet parallel between the Catholic Church and the draconian fist of Mussolini's Fascists in Italy.

'You don't seem to have much of an appetite this evening, Mrs Olivier,' enquired Collins St Anthony towards the end of the meal from his position at the end of the table.

He had waited until there was a lull in the conversation, so that his question would be heard by all the diners and would have maximum impact in its provocation.

'No ... not really,' she had mumbled in embarrassment without looking at him. She still had no idea of how she could best react to this man after the conversation they had had back at Shawbak Castle. Perhaps when the tour was over and this odious man had gone, things would be better. Then she remembered he had said that he would find her from time to time and she slid back into her pool of depression, from which there seemed to be no escape.

Before the coffee cups were cleared away, Rupert asked for everyone's attention.

'Ladies and gentlemen, I have some exciting news. Mr Hussein al Muhammad, the Trans-Jordan Assistant Director of Antiquities, who is presently on a large-scale dig here in Petra, has kindly agreed to be your guide for the next two days.'

There was a murmur of enthusiastic comment around the table. Not that the tourists knew it, but it had not taken much persuasion – al Mohammed was only too pleased to be able to pass on his passion about the site.

There followed another half-hour of general conversation, during which time Alexandra Hawkhurst and Claudette Catzmann chatted happily about shopping in Jerusalem,

Rupert was quizzed as to the credentials of al Mohammed, Lawrence Hawkhurst pressed home his advantage over Peter Olivier, and Jane Olivier sank lower and lower into her private well of depression. The others sat separately, largely saying nothing.

After the party had broken up for the night, Stephen and Rupert walked a short way up the Siq, away from the Treasury and the campsite, to enjoy the last cigarette of the day. More importantly, there had been the security aspect of not being overheard again, as they had been by Aaron Ben Zeev the previous evening. That was what he had been up to, despite the attempt he had made to cover it up. In a land where everything had its price – especially information – it paid to be cautious. Perhaps, even, overcautious.

'You know, my dear chap, for the first time since my uncle got us involved in this scroll affair, I am starting to feel very exposed and almost out on a limb. It was all very well and good to talk about this business in the comfort and safety of his office back in Whitehall, but the reality of our situation out here is as different as oil is from water.' There was a short silence, broken only by the sound of their crunching footfalls echoing off the walls of the Siq. 'Uri's brother being so inquisitive has unnerved me a trifle – question is, is he the only one? Are we going to get caught in the crossfire? Then what? We can hardly contact the nearest British Embassy from way out here and ask my uncle to send us help ... Things have moved on a lot since that business in Egypt...'

'Then why didn't you tell your uncle that you weren't interested in getting involved?' Rupert asked, as he flung the butt end of his cigarette into the empty stone gutter, which ran almost the entire length of the Siq and which had once carried water into the ancient city.

'Two reasons, my dear chap,' Stephen replied without hesitation. 'Firstly, you do not usually have the option of saying no to my dear uncle and, secondly ... well, to be frank, the whole idea of this *Scroll of Gershom...*' he overemphasised the words, '... with its politically dangerous message, seemed so preposterous that I didn't really believe it even existed – not until this morning, up there on the High Place of Sacrifice.'

'Well, at least al Mohammed will get the rest of them off our hands for the next couple of days,' Rupert said, as they turned in the darkness and began to retrace their steps. 'Is that going to give us enough time do you think?'

'It's going to *have* to be enough time,' Stephen replied, taking a long draw on his cigarette before exhaling the smoke into the night in a long plume. 'We can't expect al Mohammed to take them off our hands for any longer. As it is, it's very good of him to have them at all.'

They walked on for a short distance in silence.

'So ... if we *do* find the scroll, now that we seem to have found the cave or at least a cave that seems to match the description, what do we *do* with it?' Stephen questioned. 'Will it be fragile? What do you think it could be written on?'

'Most probably it will be velum ... or ... perhaps, even copper. Such examples are known to exist...' A whispered voice was heard floating down the Siq like a breeze, out of the darkness.

Rupert and Stephen stopped dead in their tracks, before turning together, as a pair of well-drilled soldiers, to face the direction from which the voice had come.

'Barrington?' Stephen whispered, as he recognized the voice.

'The same,' Gordon Barrington replied, barely audibly. 'You say that you might have located the repository of the scroll. I'd keep quiet about that, if I were you, certainly until we can be absolutely certain that there is no chance whatsoever of our being overheard.'

'What do you mean by *our*?' Stephen asked, still in little more than a whisper.

'We're all on the same side. Ask Professor Longhurst at the British Museum. We're looking for the same thing and we have the same reasons...' Barrington's face was suddenly framed in the glow of a match, as he lit a cigarette. It looked a lot more rugged and determined than it did in normal sunlight; the stark up-lighting from the match chiselled the features out of the darkness. 'I'm sure you were told about the missing bottom right-hand corner of the tablet and that Rabbi Mosheowitz was something less than helpful when he was summoned to Whitehall...' The match had gone out, but the end of the cigarette glowed red, as Barrington took a draw. '... And that the security of the oil in Iraq is of prime importance to our Imperial strategy, which would be compromised by a revolt in Palestine...' The voice was still little more than a faint whisper. '... Do I need to go on to establish my credentials?'

'Did someone send you?' Stephen demanded, but there was no reply.

'How did you know our business?' Rupert whispered. 'Have you been following us?'

'Good Lord, no...' Barrington whispered back, a chuckle in his voice. 'I didn't have to. You two were talking quite loudly enough and seemed to have forgotten that you were walking in a natural echo chamber. Think of the towering cliffs above you, on either side of the Siq. Everything you say in here is amplified. I heard everything quite clearly...' He chuckled again. 'We're going to have to tighten up security. Oh ... and one last point, Hopkins, *Cecil* asked me to give you his best regards.'

48

Petra

Early afternoon, Thursday, 8th October 1931

'This could be the way down,' called Gordon Barrington, pointing towards a narrowing cleft in the ground in front of them. 'What do you think?'

'It's possible,' replied Rupert, shading his eyes from the glare thrown out by rocks on the opposite side of the valley. 'That looks like the back of the High Place of Sacrifice over there, and this access seems to connect with that angled ledge down there, so we should be more or less in the right place. What do you think?' he asked, turning to Stephen.

'It could be,' he replied. He referred to the photograph in his hand, with the tell-tale pencil circle drawn on the cliff face.

'Shall we take a look, then?' continued Barrington, as he, too, turned to face Stephen, as if waiting for a decision. After fruitless attempts to climb up from the valley floor, they had finally climbed to the cliff top by a circuitous, steep path. They now looked down into the valley from a position to the right of the cave's location. They would have to make a diagonal descent towards the ledge that they were using as a landmark.

The three of them made their way carefully down the narrow cleft. As they descended, they became aware that the path, which had been barely discernible along the topmost ridge of the plateau, now began to take on the characteristics of a defined walkway. It did not look as if the rocks had been hewn to create it. Rather, it seemed to follow some sort of natural fault line.

'This definitely does seem to be a path of sorts,' called Barrington, who had taken up the lead position in the three-man file as it made its way carefully forward. 'Watch out when you reach this spot. The path is quite narrow and there is a sheer drop on the outside.' He paused and gingerly peered over the precipitous edge. It fell away towards the uneven valley floor, several hundred feet below them. 'It seems to open out a bit up ahead,' he added, moving back from the edge, 'and it descends a little more gently. I say, Hopkins, we're not going too quickly, are we?'

'No, not at all,' replied Stephen, 'it might look a bit of a struggle with this thing, but I'm used to it,' he said, waving the heavy black cane in the air.

They walked on for a few minutes, the stifling stillness of the afternoon disturbed only by the sound of boot on sand and gravel and by the occasional sustained scraping sound, as the incline and the sand underfoot combined to cause the occasional slippage of scree.

'It's just as well that the cliff face on this side is so irregular,' said Rupert, after he had slipped and stumbled, reaching out with his left hand to steady himself by grasping a small outcrop of rock. On his right was space and oblivion. 'At least there's something to grab hold of.'

'And so far it's a straightforward descent,' said Barrington, 'and we don't have to clamber over anything.'

'It's opening out into quite a flat area ... over there,' called out Stephen, after they had descended several more feet, 'and there's a narrow overhang, too. I think we should take a breather and have some water. It's unpleasantly hot up here, what with the heat radiating back at us from the rocks.'

They reached the broader area, which Stephen had

indicated, and paused to wipe their faces and to drink some water.

'Aah, that's better,' said Stephen, as he lowered his water canteen and wiped his mouth with the back of his hand. 'Pity there's no breeze down here,' he added, aware of the throb in his left leg.

'Too sheltered for that, I'd say,' said Barrington, as he, too, drank from his canteen. He also splashed a little water on to his handkerchief and wiped his face. In that heat, the cotton would be dry even before they continued on their way.

Rupert was standing behind the other two, leaning against the uneven surface of the cliff wall, looking straight ahead of him across the expanse of valley. 'Did you see that?' he exclaimed, standing up and taking half a step forward, towards Barrington.

'See what, my dear chap?' asked Stephen, as he took a second swig of water.

'I thought I saw a flash, or something. Just as Barrington was drinking...' Rupert looked at his companions in turn. 'Perhaps it came from you, Barrington. It must just have been the sun reflecting off your watch face ... when you tilted your arm to have your drink. That was probably what it was ... It was quite bright ... like a pinprick of light.'

'It could well have been something reflecting off the glass,' replied Barrington, turning to face Rupert as he spoke, 'except for the fact that we aren't actually standing in the sunshine. It's already far over the top of this mountain, so it couldn't ha—'

'There! I did see something!' exclaimed Rupert, taking another step which brought him level with Barrington. 'It wasn't your watch face at all; it was a reflection from the High Place of Sacrifice ... over the valley ... there.' He pointed past where Barrington's arm had held the water canteen to his mouth.

'No! Stop pointing,' hissed Barrington. 'Otherwise anybody up there watching will know that we suspect something.'

'I didn't see anything...' exclaimed Stephen, '... and do be careful not to get too close to the edge.'

'Well, neither of you *would* have done,' replied Rupert excitedly. 'You were both facing the wrong way just then. I was the only one facing out over in that direction. Look!'

The other two wheeled around and followed the direction in which Rupert was pointing. Barrington caught his arm and lowered it in time to see the last half-second of a glinting flash; Stephen, slower in his movements because of his leg, saw nothing but the rocky, parched mountain top shimmering in the afternoon heat.

'You could well be right,' said Barrington, shielding his eyes from the dancing glare and trying to see if anything moved. 'I thought that I caught the faint glimmer of something, too.'

'Perhaps it was just the rock crystals reflecting the sun,' offered Rupert, as he, too, strained to see if anything moved atop the High Place of Sacrifice.

'If that were the case, then surely the reflection would be constant, like a torch beam, as the sun traversed across the crystal?' asked Stephen.

'And yet, I'm sure I saw two glints, very close to each other ... two distinct flashes of light,' insisted Rupert, who had raised his hand to shield his eyes. '*Two* glints bouncing off *two* reflecting surfaces.'

'Such as you would find from the lenses on a pair of binoculars...?' asked Stephen.

'Just so,' replied Barrington thoughtfully. 'I learned that to reveal your existence through carelessness is very stupid and often lethal in a military context. Further to your hypothesis, Winfield, I'd say that the chances of two rock crystals being the same size, in perfect alignment with each other and thus capable of reflecting the same intensity of light must be practically non-existent...'

'So you think that we *are* being watched, but who would know we are here and who would have known to go up *there* to keep an eye on us,' Rupert asked, turning to look at the other two. 'If we're being followed ... even from that distance ... is anyone going to be able to see what we are trying to do?'

'If we saw their reflection, then it means that they definitely can see us, too,' said Stephen.

'And they would have seen you pointing at them, Winfield,' added Barrington, 'so that means that they'll stop watching us because they know that we've discovered them. Keep watching for another flash, but I would venture to wager that there won't be one: whoever it is knows that we've rumbled them. If we are being watched,' continued Barrington ominously, 'it means that someone else has an interest in what we're looking for...'

For the next couple of minutes, the three men stood on the broad, flattened area of the pathway, giving the impression that they were chatting and resting, but all the while vigilant for another flicker or glimmer. As predicted, there was none.

'Do you have any idea if there is another party interested in our little search?' asked Barrington, inviting either of the other two to respond and enlighten him.

'Not as far as we know,' said Stephen, casually looking out across the valley at the mountain again, 'but that could well have been a misconception. After all, we have only just found out that *you* are interested ... for all the right reasons. Depending on your point of view, it seems as if there is, indeed, a huge amount at stake in this business. If we have rivals in our search, then things have suddenly become a lot more serious.'

'And possibly a lot more dangerous?' queried Rupert.

'Then it's just a well I brought this,' said Barrington, who had turned his back to the High Place of Sacrifice and now held open one side of his cotton jacket to reveal a holstered Webley. 'From my Mesopotamia days,' he explained. 'She's getting on a bit now and I don't particularly like using her, but I will if I have to.'

'Good man,' said Stephen, grasping Barrington by the shoulder, 'I, too, have mine from the war. Regrettably, I did not have your foresight to bring it with me. It's down in the camp.'

'Let's push on,' said Barrington, letting his jacket return to its normal hanging. 'We need to try and give the impression that we have noticed nothing and were just pointing out the beauty spots, as it were.'

'Right,' said Stephen, 'let's go.'

As they walked further on along the path, it seemed to Rupert as if this Gordon Barrington, whilst deferring to Stephen, had almost taken command of the situation. He pondered on this as they trudged on, for it appeared to him that Barrington was suddenly displaying a very forceful and commanding nature. In the centre of the little column, Stephen was thinking along similar lines. This man had established his credentials through relaying a message from Stephen's uncle in Whitehall. Beyond that, neither he nor Rupert actually knew anything about Gordon Barrington, other than the belief that they could count on an extra pair of reliable hands, if the need arose. Given the incident of the unexplained flashes of light, and the man's immediate response to the situation, Stephen quickly revised the misgivings he had originally harboured about involving Barrington in this adventure. They could well find themselves in a situation where an extra weapon – even the short stiletto blade hidden in his walking stick – might come in handy.

'There it is!' Stephen called, pointing to the opening of

a cave in the cliff face ahead of them. 'It is easy to see from up here, but almost impossible to see from anywhere else. It doesn't look anything like it does in the photograph,' he said, as he paused and compared the image on the paper with the reality in front of him. 'It's hardly surprising that no one knew of its existence. You wouldn't know where to look. We only found it because of...'

'...the rocks which burn,' said Barrington, smiling.

'Indeed, the *rocks which burn*,' repeated Stephen, looking at Barrington with a quizzical expression. This man seemed to have been very well briefed on matters concerning the scroll and Stephen once again wondered what this man's background actually was. He also now realized that Barrington's story of having to take some of his accumulated leave from the British Museum was probably untrue, as any connection to that august establishment was almost certainly just a cover. However, his uncle had promised to look after him and it would appear that this man had been sent to keep that promise.

Stephen noted that the shadows were already well advanced up the sides of the Valley and served to highlight the fact that it had taken far longer than anticipated to find this cave. He was mindful that it really was a miracle that they had found the cave at all, considering they had only a dark smudge, seen against the cliff at sunrise the previous morning, as any kind of clue. The tangible proof that this dark smudge on the photograph had now turned out to be a cave was a stroke of luck.

'It looks as if the passageway narrows as it goes back into the mountain. Then it turns away to the right,' said Barrington, as he squatted at the cave mouth and peered inside. He was able to see a little further in, as his eyes grew accustomed to the near-inky gloom. 'There seems to have been a bit of a rock slide, too ... Hardly surprising in these parts, I suppose.'

'How bad a slide?' asked Stephen, looking over Barrington's shoulder. 'It doesn't look too serious, does it?'

'It just seems to have restricted the entrance and the passageway somewhat, but I think we could still get through,' advised Barrington. 'We'll just have to be careful to avoid any loose boulders or causing any further rockfalls.'

'Phew! It is hellish dark in there,' pointed out Stephen. 'I can't see much beyond the opening.' He turned to Rupert and smiled. 'Rather like some of your Egyptian temples and tombs, eh?'

'Well ... yes, I suppose so ... except that we know what we're doing with most of them by now,' replied Rupert, who had been keeping an eye on the High Place of Sacrifice, but had seen no more flashes. 'Perhaps if we came back early tomorrow morning, before the sun goes over the top of the mountain, the sun might shine into the cave and down the passage – like it does down the central passageway in the temple at Abu Simbel.'

'The passageway seems to turn to the right, just after you go through the opening, so I'm not sure that sunlight would be much help once we get inside...' said Barrington, '...other than to perhaps show us the way out. It is no good ... we're going to have to get some torches from somewhere. Lighters aren't going to be much good in there and I've not got that many matches left.'

'We've got a couple of torches back at camp,' offered Rupert. 'We *will* need to watch where we put our feet. It wouldn't do to go blundering around in the dark – just in case we tread on some priceless artefacts and damage them.'

'Or, to be more practical, in case one of us falls down an incline or other precipice we can't see,' muttered Stephen ominously; he wasn't sure if his friend was being serious or not. 'We have no idea of the internal state of these mountains or what damage millennia of earthquakes might have wrought. Do you remember the damage to the theatre down there?' he asked, gesturing away to where the impressive amphitheatre stood, its levels distorted in ancient times by some unexpected movement of the Earth.

A sense of disappointment had descended upon the party; they had got so close and now time was running out.

Stephen was slightly irritated with himself and with the others for not planning ahead: *why the hell didn't we bring the torches anyway?* Then to lighten the mood, he proposed, 'So tomorrow it is, gentlemen ... bright and early ... with our torches. I suggest that we place a pile of stones at the top of this pathway to mark our route down on the morrow.'

'That is the best plan, besides which, it will very soon be time for al Mohammed to return his charges to the comfort of the campsite and we should be there to welcome them home,' said Barrington. 'If we are on hand when they arrive it might go some way to allaying any suspicions as to what we've been up to today...'

They made their way back up the path, retracing their steps to the top of the plateau. During their ascent, Rupert kept glancing back at the High Place of Sacrifice, but did not see any further glints or flashes.

The three men, while fully engrossed with their discovery of the cave, had not seen the final, spluttering flashes on the opposite side of the valley.

49

Petra

Evening, Thursday, 8th October 1931

'Mr al Mohammed tells me that you had a very interesting day at his archaeological excavation,' said Rupert, addressing the table generally.

'It was a very *tiring* day, Mr Winfield,' said Claudette Catzmann, 'and hot, even under the canvas awning.' She had removed her shoes and under the discreet cover of the table was rubbing her feet against each other. 'But, despite the heat, it was interesting, hey Moshie?' She turned and looked lovingly at Morris Ginsberg. 'I don't really understand all of it, but to a *chanteuse* like me it was still interesting. To think that people have lived around here almost since the time of Moses...'

'Of course, it is highly improbable that Christ himself ever came anywhere near this place,' said Peter Olivier, peeling an orange he had taken from the large bowl of assorted fruits that were the evening's dessert. 'We would have to go further north to be able to see those locations he did visit. Still, al Mohammed is very knowledgeable and is a very polite fellow.'

The rest of the tour group had learned by this time not to provoke Olivier into a debate over anything religious. The prospect of a lengthy and often acrimonious confrontation, in defence of his rigid and often bigoted views, held no appeal to them. It certainly didn't appeal to Lawrence Hawkhurst whose Scaramouche-like character usually prompted him to entice those of a more rigid outlook into a sparring match, from which he usually emerged the smirking victor.

'Did you manage to complete all of your paperwork, Mr Winfield?' asked Alexandra Hawkhurst, as she reached across the table to retrieve a platter of dates.

'Most of it, thank you, Miss Hawkhurst,' lied Rupert, who had used the pretence of having to catch up with company paperwork as the excuse to absent himself from the day's expedition. 'There remains a small amount still to complete, which I will work on tomorrow.'

'And you, Hopkins,' asked Collins St Anthony, talking over the top of his coffee cup, 'where did you get to today? You missed some really exciting digging...'

Stephen looked at the young man uncertain as to whether he had meant his last remark to be what it seemed, or whether he was attempting to be facetious.

'I have trouble with an old war wound to my leg...' said Stephen, smiling at St Anthony in a most disarming way, '...and I find that a lot of walking or standing around sometimes makes it worse. Rest is the best remedy when that happens.'

'I also had a most interesting day...' Gordon Barrington leapt into the situation that had arisen through the suspicious questioning, and moved swiftly to diffuse it. '...I went and investigated a new tomb, which al Mohammed had told me was a very recent find...' Barrington had no idea whether it was or not. 'It's the tomb of a Roman centurion who was based here in Petra. A most interesting mixture of architectural styles and...' Barrington had never actually *seen* the structure itself, but he continued for some minutes, avoiding furnishing too much detail about the tomb, which, in truth, Hussein al Mohammed *had* mentioned in passing during a conversation they had had.

'Was there a big garrison here in Roman times?' asked Morris Ginsberg.

Barrington was not at all sure. 'There has always been a need to defend this part of the world,' he continued convincingly, 'because of its vital role as the key to the trade route to Palmyra.'

Morris nodded his understanding.

Barrington then continued, extolling the importance of the region to the Byzantine Empire, which, he reminded everyone, was his especial area of expertise at the British Museum. He prattled on to his audience, some of whom seemed genuinely interested in what he had to say, whilst others, after the heat and exhaustion of the day's activity, seemed too tired to interject.

Stephen smiled to himself at the thought of how they had all apparently perfected the art of lying – and lying rather convincingly.

'Al Mohammed said that he has plans for us to go much further than his excavation site in tomorrow's little jaunt,' said St Anthony, cutting into an apple without looking at anyone specifically. 'He plans to take us all up to the tomb called the Monastery. He says it is the best thing found so far and well worth the effort to go and have a look. Isn't that right, Mrs Olivier?' he added, suddenly turning and smiling at Olivier's wife.

Jane Olivier certainly did not appreciate this inclusion in the conversation. Instead, she saw it as a jibe and a dreadful reminder of the hopelessness of her situation. She kept fiddling with the spoon in her saucer. 'Yes...' she said in a voice which sounded far more tired than any of the others, '...yes ... he did.'

'If we have come all this way, then perhaps it is for the best that we make the effort and go and see these wonders of this ancient civilization,' said Morris Ginsberg. 'We are privileged to be able to do so. There are not many others who have...' He squeezed Claudette's hand gently as he spoke.

'Of course, you are right, *bubalah.*' She smiled back. 'But I'm not sure if my feet can take another day of all that walking and standing around, already. I can understand exactly how Mr Hopkins sometimes feels and *I* wasn't wounded in the war,' she continued, smiling her over-wide smile at Stephen. He reciprocated by raising his coffee cup to her and bowing his head slightly. 'Mr Winfield, do you think that I could possibly have the chance to spend tomorrow in the camp and just rest my feet? Would Mr al Mohammed be mortally offended if I didn't go and see this Monastery place of his?'

'I should imagine that he will fully understand your reasons for not visiting it,' replied Rupert charmingly, 'and I am sure that he would not like you to overtire yourself...'

For his part, Stephen was still trying to fathom out why these two had come on the tour in the first place. Ginsberg seemed a nice enough chap, capable of an interesting and even intellectual conversation, but his wife – as warm and chatty as she seemed to be – was definitely cast in a different mould and hadn't even brought appropriate walking boots with her; she was still tottering around in her high-heeled shoes..

'You must stay put and rest yourself, Claudie...' said Morris, taking her hand and kissing it gently, '...and I'll go and look for both of us.'

Rupert was touched by the gentleness and thoughtfulness of Morris's loving action. He smiled across at Stephen, who raised an eyebrow and smiled back in return.

'I might stay in camp tomorrow, too, if that's al—'

'Nonsense!' snapped Peter Olivier, without actually looking at his wife, '...Of course you can't stay in the camp when there are sights of historical importance to be seen and explored.'

'There might not be another chance to see these sights, Mrs Olivier,' coaxed St Anthony with a voice as smooth as treacle. She sat up suddenly and turned her head to stare at him. He smiled back at her – almost provoking her. For a moment she appeared to rise in her seat and by returning his gaze with eyes blazing, she seemed to be at the point of challenging him. But, as had happened previously, she lost her courage and stature before shrinking back into her own shadow.

Alexandra Hawkhurst had been watching this scene with interest and had picked up on the friction between the Oliviers and now the hostility between Jane Olivier and the odious St Anthony creature. Smiling across the table at the deflated Jane Olivier, she offered a compromise. 'If Mr al Mohammed thinks it is worth the effort to go and explore the Monastery, then I think it most probably is. He certainly showed us some very interesting artefacts today and I'm sure that he will allow us to progress at a comfortable pace tomorrow. It would be a real shame to miss the occasion and you may have the opportunity of taking some interesting photographs.' Over the last few days it had occurred to Alexandra that Jane Olivier seemed to have regressed in her general demeanour and attitude, until she resembled more often than not a young child after a parent had scolded it for some transgression. This was especially noticeable when she was in the company of either her husband or St Anthony.

Jane Olivier smiled wanly, but did not respond.

'Tomorrow should finally put an end to the scroll business,' whispered Stephen, as he, Rupert and Barrington strolled down the Siq back towards the campsite. They had agreed to go for a stroll after supper under the pretence of going for a final cigarette but, in reality, they needed to finalize their plans for the following day. They were whispering softly as the impending resolution to the question of the mysterious Scroll of Gershom added a certain frisson of nervous tension to their conversation.

'Well done, you two,' said Gordon Barrington, chuckling. 'Between the three of us we seem to have convinced them all that the operations of the tour are quite above board and are progressing smoothly, as intended. I have to admit that at one point I did think that we were going to have a tricky time trying to explain our absences, but I believe our stories have been accepted.'

'I hope it goes as smoothly tomorrow,' whispered Stephen seriously, 'because I'm not sure if we can pull the wool over their eyes for another day after that...'

'...And there's al Mohammed to consider. I'm not sure that even *his* indulgence would stretch to shepherding this lot around for a third day,' added Rupert. 'He's been very good about it, up to now...'

'...Not that he knows *why* you were suddenly so keen for him to share his passion and interest with your flock,' added Barrington, as he paused to grind out his cigarette in the dry sand.

Not for the first time, Stephen suddenly found himself wondering how someone from the rarefied, academic environment of the British Museum – where it was so easy to slip out of this world and lose yourself in another, much older one – was so capable and so able to take control, without giving the impression that he had done so. Barrington was quite unlike the men from Military Intelligence that Stephen had run up against during the war; they had seemed to be quite inept in comparison.

'There is one other thing,' whispered Barrington as they emerged from the Siq, the lighted campsite lying ahead of them. 'Young Hawkhurst is not as irresponsibly juvenile as his actions sometimes might lead you to think. He seems to have put two and two together and come up with suspicion as the answer. I've roped him in to help us tomorrow. Sorry

I didn't have a chance to ask you chaps first. It really was a case of channelling his enthusiasm to our cause, before his questioning gave the game away to the others.'

'Do you think it was him on top of the High Place of Sacrifice this afternoon, with the glinting binoculars?' asked Stephen.

'Unlikely,' replied Barrington, 'he was with the others and, besides, he would have asked us directly what we were doing up there, if it had been him. Tact and diplomacy are not his style ... but he might be useful in a scrum ... and Heaven only knows what, or who, we will come across tomorrow...'

'All hands to the pumps, if there's an emergency,' said Rupert lightly.

'You could put it that way,' replied Barrington, suddenly sounding very serious.

The conversation in the Siq that evening was not the only one to have a certain seriousness attached to it. In the dark shadows of the far reaches of the campsite, well away from the well-lit triclinium and where the camp's lights barely reached, two shapes were engaged in a heated conversation in Yiddish.

'It is your duty to do this,' hissed one, his voice barely audible. 'I need hardly remind you that you are greatly in our debt and that the debt now has to be repaid.'

'But why do you want an old scroll?' replied the other, older voice. 'What is so important about an old scroll? Can't you just ask to see it, if it is *that* important?'

'Are you being stupid on purpose?' snapped the first voice. 'Did you not understand the urgency of this matter when it was explained to you? Do you not realize that the fate of our entire nation might rest with this scroll?'

The older man bristled in the darkness – he was far from

being stupid and he disliked the arrogant tone of the younger man. 'I cannot see how an old scroll can be *that* important, even if it...'

'It is not your place to understand how important the scroll might be to us,' interrupted the younger man, his voice betraying his impatience and intolerance of the other's implied dissent. 'It is your job to do as I tell you and to repay your debt. It is as simple as that. Remember that we have eyes and ears *everywhere*. There is no escape from your obligation and there is no escape from *us*!'

'But what am I to tell my wife? How do I tell her about the Monastery, if I have not even seen it?' The tension of the conversation and of his position was now clearly manifested in the older man's voice. 'What am I to do if she asks questions?'

'That, my friend, is your concern and not mine. You have a few hours to think of something.' The younger man drew very close, almost touching the older man's cheek. 'Be ready tomorrow morning. We will leave after the others have gone. No one must see us. Here take this,' he continued, thrusting a hard, lumpy object wrapped in a soft cloth, into the older man's hand. 'I am told that you are good at using it...'

The still night air was suddenly tinged with the faintest whiff of something that brought unpleasant memories flooding back to the older man, who recognized it immediately – it was the smell of gun oil.

50

Petra

Mid-morning, Friday, 9th October 1931

Once the rest of the tour group had been escorted away from the campsite by Hussein al Mohammed, the coast was clear for the exploration group to set off as well. The four-man team was anxious to get to the cave as quickly as possible, as they had no idea how much time would be needed to search for the scroll once they gained access; they also knew that they had to be back in camp before the others returned from their trip to the Monastery. Accordingly, it had been a very fast and exhausting climb up the cliff, across the top and then down the marked pathway to the cave. It was at this point that Stephen, Rupert and Barrington, together with the newest member of their team, now stood sweating on the flat area directly in front of the cave mouth.

'Do you see, Hawkhurst, how well the entrance to the cave is hidden?' Stephen gasped, as he wiped his forehead with his handkerchief and replaced his hat. 'The mouth of the cave is at the bottom of a sort of passage in the cliffs, behind this outcrop of rock … No wonder it is almost invisible from down there … It remains secret until you are almost upon it.'

The mid-morning sun beat fiercely down on the cliffs and it was stiflingly hot, hemmed in as they were between the sheer rise of the cliff and the heart-stopping drop to the valley floor below.

'Let's get on with it, then,' said Barrington, as he switched on the electric torch Rupert had given him. 'Last chance to place any bets on whether this scroll business is real or not,' he said, smiling at the others. 'Any takers?'

There were none.

In the bright glare of the heat, the torch was totally ineffective. Barrington tapped it gently, to see whether it was working, and he was only convinced that it was when he shone it into the dark cave mouth and saw its feeble light hit a pile of rubble.

'Is your torch working?' he asked Stephen, as the two of them led the way into the cave.

'Ineffectually at the moment, but I'm sure things will improve once we get into the cave proper ... assuming that it does go back for any great distance,' Stephen added.

They had to pause for a moment, for their eyes to adjust to the near-pitch blackness of the passageway that lay before them. The two beams of light from the torches now assumed an importance far beyond the small, dual pools of light they cast on to the passage walls and floor. Without them, investigation of the cave would be out of the question. They picked their way gingerly along the passage, which suddenly narrowed considerably, leaving just sufficient room for them to continue in a single file.

'Watch where you're going,' advised Barrington, who was in front. 'It looks as if there might have been some sort of a cave-in here – the passageway is almost blocked off.'

'That's probably because of an earthquake,' suggested Stephen, once again aware that Barrington seemed to have taken the lead.

From the rear of the little procession and audible well above the noise of the footfalls on the passage floor there came the sound of shoe leather scraping across loose gravel.

'What was that?' asked Hawkhurst, turning back to look.

'It was only me,' said Rupert, who was bringing up the rear. 'I tried to walk over a boulder, but it rolled away. I nearly tripped, but I'm all right.'

'Careful where you walk... Keep close together – otherwise the light won't be any use to you, even if it does reflect off the walls a bit...' said Barrington, as he pushed further into the cave.

'Are you all right?' whispered Rupert, as he caught up with Stephen.

'It's a bit of a rum do, but it is nothing an old soldier can't cope with,' replied Stephen. 'If it gets any trickier, I might pass the torch to you. Trying to cope with the torch, the cane and a badly uneven floor might just prove too much. Better safe than sorry. I'll let you know...'

They had progressed well into the darker recesses of the cave. When the beam of light hit the walls of the passageway, it was as if the wall had been studded with sequins in places, where the facets of the mineral crystals reflected the unaccustomed light of the modern outside world.

'It's much clearer up here,' called Stephen thankfully, as they made their way further down the passageway, turning to their right as they did so. 'The walls are narrowing, but there don't seem to be any more rockfalls ... so far.'

The restricted width of the passage meant that, yet again, they had to keep in a single file.

'It's quite stuffy in here,' said Hawkhurst, as he felt his way along the wall, always focusing on the twin beams of light in front of him. 'Fusty, almost ... and it's getting hotter.'

'We don't seem to be going into the mountain much,' said Stephen over his shoulder. 'We're moving more in a direction parallel to the cliff face,' he continued. 'I would say that so far we're probably no more than twenty feet into the mountain.'

'It's opening out ... and it's turning again ... off to the left this time,' said Barrington, who had stopped to wipe his face with the long white scarf, which he had let dangle around his neck from under his lightweight cotton jacket.

'This could go on for miles,' said Stephen, shining his torch past Barrington and playing its beam on the rough walls. 'It was too much to hope that we would just enter the cave and see the scroll straight away.'

'Then again, perhaps not,' added Barrington, as he started walking again. 'This seems to be opening out even further, as we go around this bend...'

Their voices had become suddenly very loud, as the confined space of the passage suddenly gave way to a cavern-like void. Although the large, confined space acted as a kind of amplifier, the sound was clipped and dry lacking any reverberation or timbre.

'...And this is as far as we go,' continued Barrington, playing his torch over the curving walls, which marked the far end of the chamber.

'Nothing but piles of stones, sand and rough rocks,' said Rupert, as he brought up the rear of the procession and joined the other three in the chamber. He sounded disappointed, as the two beams of light flashed around the cavern like a pair of dancing glow worms. Perhaps he had been expecting the orderliness of the Egyptian tombs, but this was a different time and a different culture. 'No scroll ... or treasure ... nothing!'

'The first rule of archaeology...' reminded Barrington, as he moved forward into the cavern proper, '... is to leave no stone unturned, so let's take a closer look.'

The floor of the cavern was covered in sand and strewn haphazardly with boulders of various sizes. Here and there, outcrops of rock protruded into the cavern, some reaching from the floor to the ceiling, others ending at different heights short of the cavern roof. At the far end of the cavern the ceiling dropped considerably, causing the explorers to stoop to reach the furthest recesses.

'You two take the left side and we'll do the right,' said Barrington, clapping Hawkhurst on the shoulder. 'Remember, we are looking for anything that doesn't look like a boulder or a rock.'

'Surely, if the scroll was *that* important, then it would have been carried in some sort of a strong box or chest or something, wouldn't it?' asked Lawrence Hawkhurst, as he and Barrington moved forward, shining the torch light over the nooks and crannies of the cavern as they did so.

'It's subjective as to what a great treasure actually *is*,' said Rupert, who secretly felt a twinge of disappointment at not having discovered something along the lines of Howard Carter's Boy King, back in the Valley of the Kings. 'To us, it's usually gold or diamonds. To some it could be the wisdom of their civilization and to others it could be a steady and reliable supply of clean water. And if you're wandering around in the desert, as Moses and his tribe were supposed to have done, your concept of a great treasure would probably veer towards the latter, I should think.'

'Spoken like a true archaeologist,' said Barrington, laughing and turning to shine his torch beam on Rupert as he did so 'and who's to...' He broke off in mid-sentence. 'What's that over there?'

The action of turning to face Rupert had caused his beam of light to momentarily flash across a pile of stones in one of the niches at the bottom left of the cavern. He now turned the light back on to it.

'That's not a natural pile of stones. Look at it – it's like a cairn. Those stones have been carefully stacked around or over something. Perhaps it's an entrance to another chamber...'

Within seconds, all four of them had formed a tight semicircle around the area in question.

'Of course, we should be carefully notating all of this and photographing or sketching what we find, before anything gets moved' said Barrington.

'You cannot be serious,' replied Stephen in disbelief. 'In this instance I hardly think that would be appropriate. Don't take offence, old chap, but we didn't come up here on an archaeological dig; we are looking for something far more significant than...'

'Of course, you are quite correct, Hopkins,' said Barrington, 'but you must excuse my interest, and I am an archaeologist, after all.'

'I say, as there are four of us, why don't we make a chain and just pass the stones back over there,' suggested Hawkhurst. 'It'll get them out of the way and we can lay them out on the floor, so you'll still get an idea of what the original pile looked like, just in case it is an archaeological find and not the precious scroll. What do you think, Winfield?'

'Good idea, let's get cracking. How about if Stephen holds the torches, one in each direction and then the three of us can see what we are doing as we form the chain gang to disassemble the cairn and stack the rocks as Hawkhurst suggested,' Rupert said, his tendency to gabble slightly underlining his excitement.

Grateful for the thoughtfulness of Rupert's idea, Stephen propped his cane against his leg and held a torch in each hand as requested. Despite the terrain, he had found the going far easier than he had dared hope. Perhaps it was the excitement or the sense of danger, but for the first time in ages he had almost forgotten that he had a stump where the bottom of his left leg should be. Nevertheless he was glad of the chance to rest.

Hawkhurst squatted down next to the cairn and gingerly started to remove the top stone from where it had rested for millennia. It was heavy. He passed it to Rupert, who in turn passed it to Barrington, who laid it on the floor in the centre of the cavern. It was sweaty work in the airless, confined space and yet the growing excitement was such that it never occurred to them to remove their jackets. Within a few moments the air had also become clogged with fine sand, which had been disturbed when the cairn stones were moved.

'It might not look much like Carter's find, but I'm getting very excited nonetheless,' said Rupert, breathing heavily with the exertion of their efforts. 'And to think that this might have been put here at the same time as Tutankhamen was buried in the...'

'Shine the light over here more, Hopkins,' said Hawkhurst suddenly, as he removed a large stone from the decreasing pile and suddenly saw the dim outline of a shape that had not been formed by Nature.

'Look!' he exclaimed excitedly, 'that looks like the top of a jar of some sort.'

Within a second, they were grouped around the remains of the cairn. It had not taken that long to remove sufficient stones to reveal what looked like a small jar made from clay or terracotta.

'All this way for a jar of olive oil?' quipped Stephen. 'We saw jars just like that in Pompeii, but they were much larger...'

'I think you'll find it contains something more valuable that olive oil,' said Barrington, who was intently studying the neck and seal of the jar. 'The problem is how to find out what it is without breaking the jar...' He thought for a few seconds before continuing. 'It seems to have been sealed with wax ... beeswax possibly ... so it's probably remained airtight. That means that, if what's in there is organic, it'll probably start to degrade the moment we open it and let the air in.'

'We have no other way of knowing what we've found, do

we?' asked Hawkhurst. 'Unless you want to parade the thing back to camp and let everyone see it in the process, which, I'm led to believe, is *not* what you want...'

His words faded into the rocks, to be replaced by a silence that was broken only by the shallow breathing of the four men. In the confined space of the cavern, the air had begun to turn stale in the restricted atmosphere.

'We must open it and hang the consequences,' declared Stephen. 'We haven't come all this way to do otherwise. I'll do it and take the responsibility for any resulting unpleasantness...' Removing his penknife from his pocket, he opened the blade and reached out towards the jar.

'Very noble of you, but I think *I* should perform the honours. An archaeologist's privilege and all of that!' said Barrington, as he held out his hand and took the knife from Stephen. 'At least I only have to answer to Professor Longhurst back at the Museum,' he added, as he began to carefully dig into and remove the wax, which had hardened with the passage of time.

As he watched with the others, Stephen once again found himself wondering about this man. *Who else, apart from my dear uncle, will you really have to answer to, once we get back to London?*

A sense of excitement and expectation filled the cave. It felt as if all four explorers were holding their breath as the last vestiges of wax were removed and the dried stopper, which had once been a knot of tightly wound cloth, was prised loose of the neck of the jar.

'No sudden escape of the Pharaoh's curse, then...' said Hawkhurst, as the stopper was placed on the floor. '...Not like that Tutankhamen business in Egypt, I hope,' he added, but the other three were far too focused on the contents of the jar to answer him.

'This could be a scroll...' whispered Barrington, almost in disbelief, as he carefully removed a bulky, dark brown cylinder, 'but whether it's the one you were looking for remains to be seen...'

The cylinder, which was about twelve inches long, was wrapped in several layers of fabric strips, almost as if it had been encased in swaddling clothes. Most of the fabric looked to be still in a reasonable condition.

'Let's have the light over here,' said Barrington, as he held the scroll in his right hand and carefully unwound the outer layers of cloth, laying them out on the sandy floor next to the stones from the cairn.

'My God, but the good Professor Longhurst would have a fit if he could see what I'm doing,' he murmured. 'Still ... needs must...'

Suddenly, in the beams of light suffused with motes of dust belonging to previous ages, a thin scroll emerged from the thick, surrounding layers of cloth. Barrington held it reverently in both hands and like a priest performing an ancient rite on top of the High Place of Sacrifice, he offered it up for the other three to see.

'It's not very big for something that's supposed to be so important...' Lawrence Hawkhurst said with his usual glibness. In the stillness that followed, he immediately regretted such a ridiculous remark.

'We shouldn't proceed any further,' said Barrington, having decided on the possible enormity of their find. 'We should take this back to where it can be opened and conserved in the correct manner, before it is lost to us and all mankind. We can't do that here...'

'*Is* it the Scroll of Gershom, then?' whispered Stephen.

'Your guess is as good as mine,' replied Barrington, not taking his eyes off the scroll he held in his hands, 'but we're not going to know till we get this back to a conservation expert at a museum.'

'Back to *the* Museum,' corrected Stephen softly. 'It is out of the question that it is taken anywhere else.'

'Of course, you are quite right; it cannot be taken anywhere else.' Barrington put the scroll down on the fabric wrappings and quickly took off the white scarf he still had around his neck. 'We'll wrap it in this,' he said, smoothing out the scarf on the floor alongside the scroll. 'You must have thought I was completely mad, wearing this thing in this heat. Well, you'd have been wrong. It's only the very ends which are silk. The bit in the middle is oilcloth and there is a pocket stitched into it...' He prised open the double layer of oilcloth as he spoke and carefully inserted the scroll into it. '...Bloody uncomfortable to wear, I can tell you, but very practical when needed, eh?' He carefully wound the rest of the scarf around the central pocket of oilcloth until the scroll was hidden beneath several layers. 'It's not airtight, but it's better than nothing. The question is how do we get it back to London by the shortest route?' He stood up, putting the thin bundle containing the scroll into the inside pocket of his jacket.

'That's where we come in. Alex and I have one of our aircraft on the runway at the airfield in Gaza. We flew out two Avengers when we delivered one to our customer in Baghdad.' Hawkhurst was careful not to mention the name of their Iraqi client. 'If we can get the scroll to Gaza, then we can fly home with it. Much quicker than any other way...'

'What do you think, Hopkins?' asked Barrington.

'I think that could well be a good idea, but not one to be discussed in here. Let's make a move back to the camp,' he replied, starting to move through the cavern towards the passageway.

They retraced their steps, leaving the confines of the cavern and re-entered the narrow passageway.

'Do you think that it could really be a scroll written in the time of Moses?' asked Stephen, as they approached that part of the passageway where the rockfall made progress difficult.

'Only a very outside chance of that, I would say. Probably not from Moses' time,' replied Barrington, 'more likely from the time of the Roman occupation or possibly a couple of centuries before, I'd say. As far as we know, things didn't really get written down in Moses' time. This would have been written much later...'

The explorers, once again in single file, started to climb over the rockfall section before continuing along the constricted passageway towards the cave's entrance. Ahead of them appeared the dim glow of the bright sunshine outside.

'And what if it isn't this Scroll of Gershom?' asked Hawkhurst. 'Will it have any value, apart from its great age?'

'Everything in antiquity has a value,' replied Barrington, 'wouldn't you agree, Winfield?'

'To a greater or lesser degree,' replied Rupert, who, at the rear of the line, was starting to clamber over the larger of the boulders by supporting himself on the passage walls.

'Until the thing has been opened and read, it's anyone's guess,' continued Barrington, who had cleared the last pile of fallen stones and boulders and could see the opening of the cave ahead of him.

He was joined by Stephen and the two of them turned around to play their torches over the obstacles on the floor, making it easier for Hawkhurst and Rupert to see where they were going. Eventually all four had climbed over the rubble in the passageway and were approaching the cave entrance.

'We won't need these any more,' said Stephen, turning off his torch. 'We must try and adjust our eyes to the bright sunlight outside.'

'It a bit of an anti-climax, don't you think?' asked Rupert, holding Stephen by the shoulder. 'I mean after everything that's happened, we find a scroll and that's it ... We find a scroll and are still none the wiser.'

'That's the excitement of the profession though, Winfield,' replied Barrington, chuckling. 'You never know where any find will take you next, either back to the drawing board or on to goodness knows where in search of more. That's the surprise of archaeology...'

'And this is the surprise of Irgun!' snapped an accented voice from just outside the cave.

Two figures had suddenly appeared in the cave mouth. Standing against the intense glare of the sunshine outside, they appeared as two blurred, almost meaningless dark oblong blotches.

'Give me the scroll!' barked the shape in the front.

51

London

Whitehall – mid-morning, Friday, 9th October 1931

'This has just arrived, Sir.'

'Thank you, Collingwood,' said the Uncle taking the large envelope, the flap of which had been sealed with a large blob of red sealing wax. 'A cup of tea would be appreciated,' he continued, smiling fleetingly in his private secretary's direction before returning his attention to the envelope.

'Of course, Sir,' Collingwood replied as he turned to leave the room.

The envelope contained two sheets of paper, both of which were covered in lines of typing. The paper was not headed, nor were there any identifying marks. Across the top of the first sheet, in blue ink, were two lines of scrawled handwriting:

Our conversation refers.
Please advise where you think it best we go from here. M

The Uncle settled in his chair to read the report. As he did so, his mind went back to a telephone conversation he had had earlier in the day with Max Aitken, the 'Press Baron of Fleet Street' as he had become known.

'...Well, the wire service sent it through to us earlier this morning...' Max had said, '...You know that news is one of my pet loves, but I wondered if this little piece of intelligence ought to go through your hands first ... before we decide whether to print any of it or not. Remember, we both have the national interest at heart.' The soft Canadian burr had failed to hide the steely determination in the voice. 'The source is usually one hundred per cent reliable.'

'It's a dangerous part of the world at the best of times,' the Uncle had replied, 'so it could well be true. If it is...'

'I tell you what...' Max had cut in, abruptly, '... it's best not to say too much over the telephone. I'll have one of my people bring a typed version of the wire message around to you ... within the next two hours or so ... Okay?'

The Uncle began to read the first few lines of typing:

```
Rumours are circulating with increasing
regularity, which concern the present state
of affairs within the Iraqi political structure
surrounding the king. Our sources have
reported that there seems to be the beginning
of a power struggle in anticipation of the
British withdrawal after the end of the
mandate. This could well destabilise the
entire region and ferment Arab nationalism
in various guises further afield...
```

He paused in his reading, laid the typed transcript of Max's wire message down on the desk in front of him and leaned forward, supporting his chin in his hands. What he read was beginning to have a vaguely familiar, ominous ring to it.

```
It is widely rumoured that the Oil Minister,
Prince Abdul Salaam Abd al-Allah, cousin of
```

the king, has recently placed an order for several British aircraft of the latest modern design, ostensibly to facilitate movement and communication between the Iraqi oil fields...

Next to this, in the same blue ink as before, was written:

Could also be used for military purposes? Who is the manufacturer? HM Government clearance required??

The Uncle picked up a red pencil and drew a circle around the handwritten comment: *If a possible military context, then yes,* he wrote above it.

... But the motive could well be military use. Unrest seems to be growing in the southern part of the country, which could well have an influence on both Trans-Jordan and Iran, to the detriment of Britain's interests. Support seems to be split between Prince Abd al Allah and Rashid Ali al-Gaylami. The latter has recently emerged as a nationalist politician of some standing. Reports indicate an attempted alliance between the prince and al-Gaylami, but initial contacts between the two seem to have produced no results, leading to the present polarization...

The Uncle turned on to the second page of the typescript.

... this does not bode well for post-withdrawal Anglo-Iraqi relationships. It is thought that al-Gaylami, like the prince, favours closer ties with Italy. The role France would play in an independent Iraq is far from clear at this stage. If the extent of the new Iraqi oilfields proves to be as is presently thought, a power struggle between Great Britain, those European powers not allied to her, the independent Iraqi government and the present pro-British regime in Iran could well have devastating effects on the future well-being of the Empire and the sea route to India, via the Canal.

The Uncle sat back, his hands resting loosely on the arms of his chair. The multiple questions of oil for the fleet, Arab nationalism, security of the Suez Canal and the uncertainty of the durability of old, long-standing alliances had become something of a nightmare in recent years. Having read this latest revelation, he began to think that things in the new, post-conflict world were moving with a momentum that even his considerable authority and influence would ultimately prove almost powerless to influence, control or even stop. *Perhaps things are moving along too fast,* he contemplated as he stared across the large expanse of his well-appointed office. Suddenly, for the most fleeting of moments, he fancied that he felt the ghost of a previous time – of an age when the mere threat of a British gunboat appearing over the troubled horizon was usually sufficient to placate all but the most determined of would-be aggressors. He felt it float out of the very wood panelling and engulf him in the shroud of a past glory, which was no longer attainable. He shivered, involuntarily. *Am I being left too far behind? Are we all being left behind, as the century moves speedily on and grinds our former glory into the dust on the pages of history? Is our time drawing to a close?* He shivered a second time and then thought the unthinkable. *Are we fooling ourselves into thinking that we are immune to change and that the Empire is eternal? What the hell else can we do if we have no idea of what the 'new' way of diplomacy or world domination is?* He didn't know why he should have thought this. He could not remember ever having had a similar thought, or a similar doubt, before.

Rising from his chair, he crossed to the large framed map of the world which hung on the wall. He stood before it, staring at the red patches that indicated the possessions of the far-flung Empire. They covered the world in substantial areas of colour or, in the smaller territories, as if the map had been peppered with buckshot. As he stood staring, he felt as if a shroud had wrapped itself around him. Through a mirage of chill apprehension, he imagined he saw the red patches disappearing as the Empire slowly dissolved. To either side of the map were large portraits in oil paint. To the left, Field Marshal Burgess, the hero of Chandrapur and to the right, Admiral Fellingham, gallant defender with his small squadron of the embryonic colony of Hong Kong. Both seemed to be turning from their allotted poses to stare, horrified, at the Uncle. He shivered again. The room seemed to be even colder than before.

Nonsense, the Empire is eternal. He looked again at the two portraits and fancied that they had once again assumed their usual poses, secured under the thick coats of discoloured varnish. *We have to preserve the Empire, if we are to survive. What other choice do we have?*

There was a gentle knock on the heavy panelled door, which was then softly opened by Collingwood. He entered carrying a small tray.

'Your tea, Sir,' he said, as he placed the tray on the side of the large desk.

The Uncle suddenly felt the warmth return to his body. The shroud of cold, sombre gloom, which had consumed him a moment before, had vanished as quickly as it had appeared. On the map the red blotches still showed the Empire's possessions and the two heroes of an earlier age stared once again with impersonal, lifeless eyes, out into the large office.

'What was that?' asked the Uncle absently, as he turned to look at the other man.

'Your tea, Sir. Will there be anything else?'

'No ... not at present ... On second thoughts, Collingwood, there is. Wait a moment, would you?' He crossed to his desk and he sat down. Taking a small sheet of headed paper from his paper rack and unscrewing his pen, he wrote in his distinctive hand:

Max, Suggest silence until more becomes clear. We will instigate a check regarding the business with the aircraft. I concur regarding the question of national importance.
Yours.

He did not sign the note. He did not have to.

'See this goes off straight away, would you ... by hand for immediate delivery.' He placed the note in an envelope and sealed it. On the front he wrote simply *Lord Beaverbrook*.

After Collingwood had withdrawn with the envelope, the Uncle sat in his chair stirring his tea. He looked down at his hand and noticed that it was trembling slightly, almost imperceptibly. He tapped the teaspoon twice on the rim of the cup and then placed it in the saucer, where it made a sound akin to a tinny rifle shot. For a moment he sat and gazed blankly at the concentric circles which swirled about the surface of the warm brown liquid. A single stray tea leaf, spinning around like a Dervish, seemed to be in imminent danger of being sucked down into the vortex at the centre of the cup.

As could we all, he thought suddenly, *if we lose control of things.*

He had not given the question of the Scroll of Gershom much thought of late – not that he had forgotten it, but there had been no news of it and other matters had occupied his mind. He had not forgotten the physical awakening of nationalism amongst the Jews of the Diaspora and of Palestine in particular. Nor had he dismissed the threat of political upheaval that the discovery of such a scroll, with its blatant command from the Divine Authority to rise up and establish the Kingdom of the Children of Jehovah on Earth, would ignite.

As the tea leaf disappeared into the tight swirl, he glanced once again at the large world map. He had a momentary vision of the numerous pockets of red, like the single black tea leaf in his cup, being sucked down into the vortex of an insecure, changing world, in which the old certainties of control were becoming ever more unreliable. The thought frightened him. He felt a flickering pain of apprehension for the future.

This is ridiculous, he reasoned as he opened the top drawer of his desk and took out a round cardboard pill box. *You're overdoing things again. You're not as young as you used to be and the doctor told you to slow down a little.* He took a pill from the box and swallowed it. *If I don't take command, who else will? It is all well and good just telling a chap to slow down and take things easy...*

Had he known of the events that were currently unfolding on a narrow ledge outside an almost hidden cave on the other side of the world, his experience of the fleeting pain of apprehension could well have lasted for considerably longer.

52

Petra

Noon, Friday, 9th October 1931

'Give me the scroll!' barked the indistinct shape at the mouth of the cave, shouting above the sound of a revolver being cocked. 'I know you have it. Give it to me!'

From the darkness inside the cave, the two blurred forms at its mouth shimmered like beings from another world. They were both given an almost halo-like glow by the dazzlingly bright sunlight behind them. It was only as Gordon Barrington hesitated on the threshold of the cave, shielding his eyes from the unaccustomed glare, that the leading shape took a more recognizable form. It was not extending an arm in a gesture of welcome – it was holding a gun, which was pointed threateningly at the tightly packed group of four men in the cave passageway.

'Hello, Ben Zeev,' said Barrington. 'Does Uri know where you are?' The voice was calm and unsurprised.

Aaron Ben Zeev seemed to flinch for a moment at this question. 'You will do as I tell you!' he snapped back in reply. 'My brother does not tell *me* what to do. It would be better for him if he would listen to *me*. I am getting tired of asking – give me the scroll!' The arm holding the gun moved a little higher.

Stephen, Rupert and Hawkhurst squashed into the opening of the cave behind Barrington, their eyes having to adjust to the light before being able to focus on the menacing figure in front of them.

'I don't know what you're on about, old chap.' Barrington answered calmly. 'What scroll?' He went to take a step forwards as he spoke, but stopped in his tracks as the revolver was pointed directly at him.

'Do not come any nearer!' snarled Aaron Ben Zeev. 'Do not make the fatal mistake of thinking that Uri's *nice little brother* cannot use a gun and is afraid to shoot. Do not try my patience any longer.'

'Did Irgun teach you to shoot?' Barrington enquired. 'Was that at the university? Or perhaps it was in the countryside outside Haifa. And what must your family think? Are they proud to have a member of Irgun in their home?' Despite his calm exterior and level voice, Barrington was desperately thinking of the next move. His brain was racing faster than the propeller on one of Hawkhurst's aircraft.

'So you *were* listening to us the other night ... in the triclinium,' said Stephen, as he edged his way further out of the cave, until he was standing almost shoulder to shoulder with Barrington. They were shielding Rupert and Hawkhurst, who stood close behind them, looking over their shoulders.

'Not just the other night, I would suspect,' said Barrington.

'You are right. You were overheard at that time and also on several occasions. It was not difficult to hear what you said, no more than it was for others to hear you in the Petra Hotel in Jerusalem,' Aaron Ben Zeev added, a smirk pulling his lips into a twisted smile. 'You bloody British think that you have all the answers and that the rest of the world owes you some kind of eternal debt of gratitude for ... for what? For enslaving the people of the world, even the People of Israel ... in their own land?'

His voice was alternating between an ominous whisper and a high-pitched shout, as he stabbed his left hand in an accusing gesture of defiant hatred at Barrington and the other three explorers who were now all tightly grouped together in the small opening of the cave.

'And now you think the natives are simply going to let you carry on like that?' His voice had risen in intensity and the flare in his eyes demonstrated an ignited passion burning with as much intensity as the sun itself. Despite the obvious emotion displayed in the defence of his cause and the animated finger stabbing of his left hand, the gun remained rock-steady with its aim held directly at Barrington.

'Now look here, I don't know what you're talking...'

'That is enough! Stand still. Do not move any nearer ... any of you, or I *will* shoot!'

'But what's stopping you, then?' asked Lawrence Hawkhurst, speaking over Stephen's shoulder. 'If you think we have this scroll of yours, what's stopping you?'

'It is easier to explain four broken bodies at the foot of a steep cliff, than it is to explain four dead bodies that have bullet holes in them,' snarled Ben Zeev. 'And it is easier to take the scroll here, than it would be to have to climb all the way down there,' he continued, flicking his chin towards the edge of the pathway and the horrendous drop to the valley floor.

Barrington had only seconds to assess their predicament and to decide on a course of action. He had tried to take a couple of steps out of the mouth of the cave to allow Rupert and Hawkhurst more room to manoeuvre, but he knew that none of them could move anywhere to the left of the cave, as the natural formation of the rock doubled back on itself forming a kind of blind alley. Realizing that there was no escape in that direction – only the towering sheer face of the rising cliff – he had tried to move to the right, where the path led back up to the top of the mountain and where the precarious pathway leading up from the cave widened slightly. That idea had not worked either. All he had managed to achieve was to gain one or two more inches of space for the two behind.

'Block them!' shouted Aaron Ben Zeev, suddenly flinging out his left arm to indicate the open patch of pathway that Barrington had tried to reach, 'and shoot them if they try anything stupid!'

Up to this point, everything had happened so quickly that the four explorers, hemmed in at the mouth of the cave, had not had a chance to take much notice of the second blurred shape, which had been largely hidden behind the other, more forceful form of Aaron Ben Zeev. Now, in response to the barked command, the second man moved slightly to his left – almost reluctantly – to block off any escape to the beginning of the path back up to the mountain top. He was also armed, but, unlike Ben Zeev, he did not hold his revolver with unnervingly constant accuracy, ready to drop any dissenter in his tracks. It was held low and seemed to oscillate slightly, from potential target to potential target, as if unsure of what to do next.

'Hello, Morris, fancy seeing you up here,' said Stephen flippantly. 'How's Claudette this morning?' There was more than just a hint of sarcasm in his voice.

'As you know, Hopkins, she is resting, as she told you at breakfast. Why do you...'

'Shut up!' ordered Ben Zeev, making an irritated gesture with his left arm. 'Do not talk to them!'

'What's she going to say about this, then?' added Rupert, following Stephen's opening lead and taking a shuffling step out of the cave mouth. 'And you a decorated war hero, too!'

'Have they got you involved in this as well?' added Hawkhurst, as he, too, finally managed to just clear the mouth of the cave. 'Are you part of their ... what did you call it?' he asked Ben Zeev, a quizzical smile on his face in defiance of the imminent danger. '... *Igloo*?'

'No...' blurted out Morris, the revolver quivering and then lowering even more towards the ground.

Stephen knew that they had to tread carefully – as a gunshot at that angle would still inflict a nasty leg wound if fired.

'...I am not part of Irgun,' Morris continued. 'They tricked us and we owe them for the mon—'

'Enough of this old woman's drivel...' interrupted Ben Zeev in Yiddish, taking a sideways step and moving closer to Morris, but never taking his eyes off the four men. '...You are a fool and an old woman. I was wrong to even listen to them when they told me you would help me.'

'But they are my people ... there *is* no war,' replied Morris, the revolver sinking even lower towards the ground, as his shoulders visibly drooped, 'and there was no talk of shooting people ... *my* people ... in cold blood.'

'You are a Jew and *we* are your people,' hissed Ben Zeev out of the corner of his mouth, never once taking his gaze off the four men in front of him. The hatred in his voice now seemed to be directed in equal measures towards Morris and the other four men on the ledge. 'Search that one ... now!'

Morris made as if to take a step towards Barrington and then stopped. The gun slumped to his side, as his arm hung limply. 'He says I have to search you,' he said in English, 'but I am not sure if I want to get mixed up any further in all of this...' He looked straight into Barrington's face, flicked his gaze to Stephen and then back to Barrington again. 'I had no idea that...'

As he spoke, Morris Ginsberg had done as he had originally been told to do and had moved to block the escape route up the narrow pathway away from the cave. Unwittingly, he had also moved closer to where Aaron Ben Zeev stood. Realizing that his ally had now become almost as much of a liability as the four men in front of him – men whom he considered to be his mortal enemies – Ben Zeev suddenly brought his left fist up in a swinging arc from waist level and struck Morris across his face with a blow of considerable force – a force generated by both anger and resentment. The blow took Morris completely by surprise, knocking him off balance and spinning him around in a tight semicircle. He tottered backwards, propelled by the accurate energy of the attack and spiralled down to the ground. As he collapsed, his body fell length-wise, like a pack of falling playing cards, so that his head finally smacked against the rough surface of the cliff face. He seemed to have been knocked senseless and lay on the sandy ground, sprawled like a felled tree trunk blocking the way to freedom.

Ben Zeev's blow had caused Morris's arm, which had held the gun lamely by his side, to involuntarily fly upwards as his body spun around and tottered backwards. The sudden movement had caused a reflex action in the muscles of his hand and arm and he had squeezed the trigger before the pistol had left his hand. A single shot rang out, bouncing and echoing around the valley walls and beyond, before the revolver arched out over the edge of the narrow path and sailed gracefully through the air, before commencing its final plunge to the distant valley floor below.

Lawrence Hawkhurst let out a sharp cry of pain and collapsed to his knees, his left hand clasped to his right shoulder. He crumpled to the floor, gasping. At the same instant, Barrington launched himself at Ben Zeev. He did so with such velocity that he covered the few feet that separated them in a second, taking Aaron completely by surprise and preventing him from using his gun, which was knocked from his hand. The two men shot backwards, staggering along the ledge in a tangle of limbs and flapping clothing until they caught the corner of the protruding rock formation that hid the entrance to the cave. Then, they seemed to rebound off the rough surface and into the small open space directly in front of the entrance to the cave proper. It resembled a grotesque dance routine, but one devoid of music. As they staggered across the sandy ground grappling with each other, they tripped over the recumbent form of Morris and came crashing to the ground, almost on top of him.

They wrestled with each other, first Ben Zeev and then Barrington appearing to have the upper hand. They squirmed and wriggled in the soft sand like a pair of salamanders, all the while drawing nearer and nearer to the innocuous border of oblivion. Almost on the precipitous edge of the pathway, Barrington's jacket flew open, the action of their fight having caused it to ride up his torso. The ends of the white scarf had worked free of his pocket and were flapping around like a pigeon trying to escape from its cage. The two men were both still struggling on the ground in a tangle of limbs. Ben Zeev suddenly noticed the flapping scarf and grasped it, pulling it completely out of Barrington's pocket.

'You do have it,' he wheezed, almost inaudibly, between short gasps of hot breath, 'and now it is mine!' He started to laugh, raising himself up slightly on his elbow, one hand holding the scarf and its contents, the other hand trying to fend off Barrington's aggressive attack.

The look of triumph on his face suddenly froze into a petrified smirk, his mouth still half open. Almost in the centre of his forehead an angry, uneven circle of ruptured skin suddenly appeared, the edges of the circle torn and jagged where the skin had been rasped open, allowing the surface blood to ooze out. As the large, jagged stone flew off his forehead and bounced once, twice, in the sand of the pathway, Aaron Ben Zeev seemed to raise himself even higher on his elbow until he reached the point where he overbalanced and rolled backwards, propelled by the force of the impact of the stone against flesh and bone.

From where Barrington was lying on the ground, he felt the release of the pressure of the other man on his own chest and witnessed the startled look of truncated victory on Ben Zeev's face, as it rose up into the air above him, like some grotesque fairground balloon.

'He's going to fall over!' shouted Rupert, his hand and fingernails scratched from the rough stone, which, in sheer desperation, he had prised free from the cliff face and flung at Ben Zeev. 'Quick ... hold him ... he still has the scroll!'

He lunged across the few feet to where Ben Zeev was balancing dangerously between the reality of the pathway and the unknown of the eternity below. As he did so, Barrington slithered around on the ground, like an agile cobra, and lunged at Ben Zeev's raised arm. To the other witnesses to this spectacle, everything seemed to play out in slow motion and had the sense of being surreal. But *this* action was real – very real.

As Barrington slithered around, Rupert tripped over him and fell head first to the ground, landing almost on top of him. As he fell he lunged out for something – anything – to break his fall. His fingers closed around the wrist of Aaron Ben Zeev, whose balance on the side of safety now seemed to be as hopeless as was the angry, bleeding eruption on his forehead. As he fell backwards over the crumbling edge of the precipice, he slowly dragged Rupert with him – closer and closer to the point of no return. There was no sound from Ben Zeev, only the startled look in his eyes and the blood from his forehead, which had started to cover the lower part of his face. From his talon-like hand streamed the flapping ends of the white silk scarf with its ancient cargo.

Rupert let out a muffled cry as he realized what was happening. Barrington had also assessed the urgency of the situation: the two men were about to slip over the edge of the cliff. Instinctively, he reached up and caught Rupert's right leg with both of his hands.

'I've got you!' he yelled, as he twisted himself around, desperately fighting to hold on to Rupert's leg, but his hands were slipping down the trousers, towards Rupert's ankle. 'Hopkins! Help! He's slipping...!'

Ever since the single shot had been discharged and Hawkhurst had collapsed to the sandy ground, Stephen had been attempting to stem the flow of blood from the injured man's shoulder. Stephen cursed himself for leaving his medical bag back at the campsite again. Before they had set off earlier that morning, he had rationalized the need for taking it, but had decided against it as he knew he would have to use his heavy cane in one hand and would need his other hand to support himself against the rocks on the climb down the cliff. He had, however, slipped a couple of gauze bandages and a small bottle of iodine into his pocket, thinking that they might come in useful to treat an unexpected graze or fall inside the cave. Even so, not having his bag was a decision which he now bitterly regretted. Hawkhurst was coughing and wheezing erratically. The frothing blood stain on the front of his shirt, just under the right clavicle, was matched by another, similar one at the back, where the tear in his shirt and jacket showed the exit path the bullet had taken.

'You're lucky, old chap,' Stephen said, as he quickly inspected the wound, ignoring as best he could the drama on the ledge behind them. 'It's towards the top of your lung. I'm going to have to bandage it ... This won't hurt,' he lied, as he poured some of the iodine on to a patch of gauze. He had propped up Hawkhurst against the wall of the cave passageway, out of the sun, and had made him as comfortable as he could. Now, in response to Barrington's call for help, he abandoned his patient and turned back to the edge of the pathway.

'My God ... Rupert!' yelled Stephen, as the realization of the impending disaster hit him.

'Take hold of his other leg ... quickly! I ... I can't hold him on my own,' screamed Barrington, as the knot of writhing bodies slid over the sand towards the yawning drop.

'I've got him! It's all right!' shouted Stephen, grabbing hold of the lower part of Rupert's other leg, which was flailing the air.

Between Barrington's low angle and Stephen's higher one, Rupert was quite safely held on the path side of the precipice. The same could not be said for Aaron Ben Zeev, whose semi-conscious form hung head down over the edge.

'I'm not sure I can hold him!' shouted Rupert, his hands claw-like and white with the immense effort of trying to hold on to the inert, dangling body. 'He's slipping ... and he still has the scroll.'

'Bugger the scroll!' yelled Stephen, only now taking in the awful scope of Rupert's position and the implied loss he, himself, would suffer if rescue were not successful. 'Let him go!' he barked, with renewed vigour and sense of purpose. 'We've got *you* and that's what counts!'

Morris Ginsberg moved his head slightly and moaned softly, but the first signs of his impending return to consciousness went unheeded by the others.

Barrington moved his right hand up Rupert's body, under the jacket and felt for the leather belt he wore in his trousers. He found it, wrapped his fingers around it and, with a superhuman strength born of sheer desperation, pulled backwards with all of his might. At the same time, Stephen held even tighter to Rupert's leg, oblivious to the dull, aching pain that had registered the angry protestation of the stump of his left leg. Rupert was hauled back from the edge of the walkway with such unexpected force that his grip on Ben Zeev gave way. Rupert, Stephen and Barrington all cascaded back on to each other, forming an undignified, winded heap on the ground.

Peripheral sounds from Morris Ginsberg as he tried, yet

again, to cross the threshold back into consciousness and from Lawrence Hawkhurst crying out in pain, went unheeded as the other three men on the ledge caught their breath after surviving the life-threatening fracas.

'Are you all right?' asked Stephen, as he clawed over the tangle of limbs to take Rupert in his arms.

'Yes ... of course ... I ... it's gone,' he replied, as his mind cleared and returned him to the scene on the pathway of a few moments before. 'The scroll ... it's gone...'

'To hell with the bloody scroll...' said Stephen, his voice a mixture of anger at the all too recent close proximity of sudden death and of grateful acceptance that the danger had now passed. He smiled as he looked into Rupert's sweaty, sand-streaked face. 'You do look a mess,' he said, laughing with relief.

'It's still with us,' said Barrington excitedly. He had extricated himself from the tangle of bodies to peer over the edge of the drop. He lay prone across the path, scrutinizing something below in the abyss. 'Down there ... only a couple of feet. It's caught up in the branches of a bush! Who'd have thought that *anything* would grow up here, never mind about something growing out of a cliff? Look!'

The white scarf hung lazily, cradled in the gnarled and twisted twigs of a small bush, which had seeded itself in a crevice in the cliff face. The swollen bulge in the middle of the bush, where the folds of the scarf lay thickest, told them that it still enfolded the mysterious scroll.

'It's not yet a totally lost cause,' said Barrington with a note of jubilation in his voice. 'If you two hold me by the legs, I might just be able to reach it.'

'I'm a little taller than you are,' said Rupert, 'and I am of a slighter build, so I'll be the one who does the dangling. Besides which, I've had *some* recent experience at being stretched and having my legs pulled.'

Although the danger of the previous few moments had

passed and they all fully realized that the next, necessary step of recovery was probably going to be just as dangerous, a lighter mood seemed to have suddenly descended on them.

They set about the task of retrieval, as they had discussed, and it was barely ten minutes before the scarf, the scroll and Rupert were all safely back on the level, if uneven, ground of the pathway. The scarf had become hopelessly entangled in the twig-like branches of the little bush, which had only been persuaded to abandon its precarious foothold with a hefty pull from above. This had dislodged its tenuous root system from the small fissure that had grudgingly given it sanctuary. Once safely on the narrow pathway, the scarf had been removed from the spindly branches, and the bush unceremoniously flung out into space to cascade out and down into the valley – the third casualty of the day.

By now, the sun had risen past the top of the mountain and the cliff face, though still radiating the accumulated heat of the morning, was at least in shadow. Barrington and Rupert sat resting, their backs against the cliff, wiping the sweat of their exertions from their grimy, sand-streaked faces. They took long draughts from the water bottles that were slung across their shoulders over their jackets; the thick webbing straps from which they were suspended had miraculously survived all the pulling and shoving of the recent engagement. The scroll was once again safely ensconced in Barrington's jacket pocket. Stephen automatically returned to his role as a doctor and turned first to Hawkhurst, whose breathing had eased somewhat, and then to Morris Ginsberg, who had finally regained full consciousness.

'It's just a bang on your head,' said Stephen, as he squatted down next to him. 'Your jaw might ache for a bit and there will be some bruising, but you should be right as rain in no time. I'll give you a couple of aspirin when we get back to the campsite.' He had done what he could with what little he had.

'Thank you,' said Morris, 'thank you for taking the time to trouble with me.' He looked sheepish and embarrassed and could not look Stephen in the face.

'Have some water,' Stephen advised, holding out his flask. 'You don't want to add dehydration to the bang on the head. How would you explain *that* to Mrs Ginsberg?'

'You are very kind, Doctor,' said Morris. softly. 'I thank you again for bothering with me. Particularly after...'

'After ... what...?' Stephen asked.

'After what ... back there...' stammered Ginsberg, motioning towards the mouth of the cave, '...the scroll business ... and young Hawkhurst, I mean.'

'You did not intend to shoot anyone. You made that much perfectly plain,' replied Stephen, 'the gun discharged as you were spinning around from Ben Zeev's blow. So, if anyone is responsible, it is Ben Zeev and he is now answering to a far higher court than anything we have. I am sure that Hawkhurst will be all right. There should not be too much internal damage as there are clean entry and exit wounds, which I've cleaned as best I can.' He turned to look back towards the cave mouth as he spoke. 'We just need to get him down from here as soon as possible and off to a hospital. He needs drugs and possibly a drain in his lung, at least until it heals.'

'And the business with Irgun...' muttered Morris, looking Stephen straight in the face for the first time. 'What about Claudie? I don't care about myself, Doctor; they can have me ... but what about my Claudie?'

'I'd say that you redeemed yourself,' said Barrington from across the pathway. 'If you had carried out Ben Zeev orders, things could have ended up very differently. But you didn't, thank God; you stuck to your own high principles, for which we are extremely grateful.'

'But now I am a condemned man as far as *they* are

concerned,' Morris remonstrated, looking down at the ground. 'My poor Claudie.'

'What is this Irgun anyway?' asked Rupert.

'It's a resistance group, vowing to establish a Jewish homeland in what you call Palestine,' said Morris. 'That was why they wanted this scroll. It is something to do with an instruction from above to set up this homeland. I was not told everything. They offered us a new beginning ... a new life...' He fell silent for a few moments and then looked determinedly into the faces of each of them in turn. 'But they never said anything about shooting my own kind in cold blood. In the war ... that was different ... that was the enemy...'

'No one else need know anything about what happened up here this morning,' said Stephen, as he got to his feet.

'*They* will know,' said Morris. 'They no longer have Ben Zeev; neither do they have the scroll. But they do have me and they will come looking for answers,' he added, ominously.

'You said that they offered you a new life ... a new beginning,' said Stephen. 'I know someone who might be able to arrange that for you, in a place far away from here, where you'll be safe ... from *them*.' Morris Ginsberg looked up at him enquiringly. But there was no further explanation as Stephen was turning his attention back to his other patient. 'First, we must get Hawkhurst down from this place,' he continued. 'Any ideas? He won't be able to walk.'

'Hawkhurst's quite slender, so what about a sort of piggyback lift to get him up the cliff?' offered Barrington, 'and where the path is too narrow, perhaps someone else can support him from behind and keep the two of us steady. It might not do him much good for a bit, but it's better than leaving him here for the next four hours whilst we go for a stretcher ... if there is one in the camp.'

'I can help with him,' said Morris Ginsberg. 'I will take my turn to carry him.'

'In that case, when we get on to the flat surface at the top of the cliff, the two of you can take each end of my cane and Hawkhurst can sit on it. Winfield here can support him from behind. I think he should be kept upright as much as possible.'

'And we can revert to a piggyback where the path narrows,' added Barrington. 'At least we can get Hawkhurst down...'

'...Which, as you said, is better than leaving him here,' repeated Stephen, as all four of them, including Morris Ginsberg, prepared for the ascent.

'What are we going to tell the others?' asked Rupert, unexpectedly.

'The bare minimum to make it convincing,' replied Barrington. 'Ben Zeev came up here with water for us; to avoid us getting dehydrated and all of that... very thoughtful, etc. Poor soul missed his footing on the sandy, narrow path and fell over. After all, was it not he, himself, who said something to the effect that it was easy to explain a broken body at the foot of a cliff? Well, he's got his chance now, except that it is we who will be doing the explaining.' There was no trace of amusement or humour in his voice.

'And young Laurence Hawkhurst?' asked Morris, concern showing on his face.

'... He was knocked over when Ben Zeev fell off the cliff, fell against the rocks and broke his arm,' replied Stephen. 'I'll put the right one in a sling and that should hide the wound underneath.' He smiled at Hawkhurst and then continued. 'But we have plenty of time to finalize things once we get out of this place. Barrington, I'll try to give you a hand to get Hawkhurst up ... We just have to go as carefully as we can with him.'

53

Rome

Sala del Mappamondo, Palazzo Venezia – Friday, 16th October 1931

The over-large, opulent room with its marble-clad walls and floor and the single large desk in the far corner, seemed to grow strangely still and more than just a little cold. Even allowing for the first faint hint of approaching autumn weather, which twisted wisp-like around the dazzlingly white columns of the nearby Vittorio Emanuele monument, the room seemed cold.

```
... and this should in no way detract from his
service to the Party or the brilliant record
of service to the Fatherland in the recent
war. There must, however, be a source of concern
from the security point of view. The count has
access to so much information which is of a
highly confidential and potentially inter-
nationally explosive nature. Given the count's
years and possible complications arising from
speculation as to his mental health, it is the
opinion of OVRA that Il Duce be respectfully
informed of this present state of affairs.
```

Seated behind the desk, hunched in his chair like a predator about to spring upon its prey, Mussolini glared at the sheet of paper he had been silently reading. In the ominous silence that filled the room, he scanned the sheet for a second time, his eyes drawn to a single sentence, which he read again: ... *a source of concern from the security point of view.* That phrase stuck in his mind.

'Tell me honestly Arturo, this *concern*, how seriously do you view it?' he asked.

Arturo Bocchini, Chief of the OVRA, sat impassively on the other side of the desk. He had not relaxed into the welcoming softness of the ornate padded chair, but sat ramrod straight on the edge of it. He was one of the very few visitors Il Duce received regularly who was accorded the honour of being invited to sit during the audience.

'It is of sufficient concern, from the point of view of state security, to be brought to your attention, Duce,' replied Bocchini coldly. 'The count's behaviour has hinted at becoming...' He paused whilst fishing for the most appropriate word, '... shall we say *erratic* of late...'

Mussolini put the sheet of paper down on the desk and glared at his chief of secret police. 'Give me a concrete example of this *erratic* behaviour,' he said softly. 'I expect you to know about these things.'

'There were reports of a discussion the count had recently with French Prime Minister Laval, during his visit to Paris...'

'Last month?' cut in Mussolini. 'That went well, did it not?'

'Yes, in the sense that the French seem to be warming considerably to the idea of ceding us part of their African possession of Somalia. There are even vague suggestions that they might, in the future, support us in our goal of expanding the Empire...'

'So where is the evidence of his erratic behaviour in all of that?' repeated Mussolini, his jaw thrust out. He had no time for mere speculation. He also knew that Bocchini was not one to act without proof.

'The count took it upon himself to mention that we would also need a substantial supply of oil and that we had almost secured the same through negotiations with foreign powers.' The evidence was delivered in the man's usual, clinically cold manner. He had been charged with upholding state security and nothing and no one was going to get in the way of his discharging this duty. Bocchini held no grudge against the count, but if the man was becoming a security risk...

'He said that? Are you certain?'

'I am,' replied Bocchini. 'Luckily there were very few journalists present and our translators managed to phrase his remarks in such a way as to present them as the fact that we would welcome the opportunity to *purchase* oil from any friendly country. Not quite what the count had said...'

Mussolini's face clouded over with the threat of an imminent downpour.

'As you well know, Duce, although your plans for the new empire are well advanced, we are not yet ready to implement them. Nor are our negotiations concerning the procurement of crude oil with the Iraqis, the French or any other foreign power intended to be public knowledge.'

Once again, the room fell into a cold silence. Bocchini continued speaking. He held no notes, nor did he refer to any documents. He did not need to – he had the information in his head.

'There is also a report of uncharacteristic behaviour at a recent parade in Bologna, where the count seemed to be distracted to the point of boredom. There was also his inconsistent behaviour at a recent commissioning ceremony at the Ansaldo shipyard. There were those present who thought that the count seemed to be in a trance or a daze for some of the time.' Bocchini paused for a second, before continuing, 'This latter behaviour was attested to by an implacable source...'

'Count Ciano,' said Mussolini, coldly. He had heard of Contini-Aosta's odd behaviour during the ceremony via his son-in-law and daughter.

'The same, but we have no record of any recent illness, either mental or physical, which could possibly excuse such behaviour,' concluded Bocchini. He sat impassively, waiting for a response.

Eventually, Mussolini rose slowly to his feet. Bocchini did the same, but was motioned to remain seated with an impatient wave of Il Duce's hand. Mussolini walked slowly across the polished marble floor, with its intricate patterns of coloured inlay, the heels of his highly-polished cavalry boots resounding like rounds of artillery fire in the high confines of the cavernous room. When he reached the window he stopped, flung his arms behind his back and spoke to Bocchini again, without turning his head. 'I have worked hard to give Italy peace and quiet ... work and calm.' There was a lengthy pause. Bocchini knew from past experience that it was unwise to say anything in the pauses during which Il Duce was thinking or reflecting. 'I give these things to the people with either love if possible or with force if necessary, for the better good of the Party and the Fatherland.' There was a second, even longer pause. 'What is *your* advice concerning this matter?' he asked abruptly.

'It is my opinion that the Count Contini-Aosta be watched with the utmost scrutiny to prevent any future serious lapse of state security. His loyalty to the Fatherland is beyond reproach, but his loyalty to the Party and to the cause of the new empire has to be regarded as a separate issue. There is the question of the count possibly developing anti-Fascist opinions, either intentionally so, or through slips of the tongue caused by the march of his years.'

Outside, across the busy street, the glittering white monument perched atop its mound like the spectacular centrepiece of a huge wedding cake, had already started to cast long shadows over the Eternal City; shadows which could be as long as those which would inevitably fall across the Count Contini-Aosta.

'And then?' asked Mussolini.

'Then we will have to match the means to the end...' replied Bocchini in the same clinically cold voice he had maintained throughout the audience, '...when circumstances dictate.'

54

England

Extract from the early edition of *The Times* newspaper – Friday, 30th October 1931

Fears are being expressed for the safety of the well-known aviatrix Miss Alexandra Hawkhurst, who, together with her brother, Mr Lawrence Hawkhurst, is joint owner of Hawkhurst Aviation Limited of Suffolk.

Miss Hawkhurst took off from Gaza in Palestine, on the Monday before last, at the controls of one of the new Hawkhurst Avenger aircraft, the design and speed of which have aroused much interest in both the aviation industry and at the Air Ministry. It is understood that Miss Hawkhurst's brother is convalescing in a Jerusalem hospital, following an unfortunate accident whilst on a recent holiday to the Holy Land, during which he broke an arm.

Miss Hawkhurst was attempting to return home following a land route, via Athens, Zagreb, Zurich and Paris. The last reported sighting of her aircraft was as it ascended from Orly Aerodrome, outside Paris. The weather was poor and predictions were that it would probably deteriorate alarmingly over the following few hours. She was expected to have landed at Croydon Aerodrome during Saturday, 23rd instant.

The last reported sighting of her aircraft, in almost

zero visibility and appalling weather, was by the crew of a Dutch trawler in the southern part of the North Sea. This important information has only recently come to hand, as the vessel was obliged to ride out the atrocious weather at sea. If this sighting was, indeed, that of Miss Hawkhurst's aircraft, it would indicate that she had flown many miles off course and was heading in completely the wrong direction. This would have taken her further north-north-east, out over the North Sea. The information we have is that the fuel capacity of a Hawkhurst Avenger is more than adequate for the flight from Paris to Croydon, but would probably not allow for a lengthy, circuitous diversion out over the North Sea. Flying in such poor weather would increase the aircraft's fuel consumption considerably. In turn, this would reduce the flying time available to the pilot.

As Miss Hawkhurst is now almost a whole week overdue, HM Coastguard has been requested to commence a search at sea for possible signs of wreckage or other signs of the unknown location of the aircraft. It is understood that the Royal Navy will also commence a sea search of the area, as part of their regular patrol duties.

Hawkhurst Aviation Limited was not available for comment.

EPILOGUE

Donnington Castle, Bedfordshire – Saturday, 7th November 1931

The first frigid claws of the approaching winter had already grasped the bare branches of the trees that encircled the vast expanse of lake. Wraith-like tendrils of dawn mist had ridden over the flat mirror of the water's surface, like mysterious seahorses at play, but the eventual emergence of the feeble sun had banished them to whence they had come. The crispness in the air brought the massive grandeur of Donnington Castle into sharp focus as it stood brooding, keeping watch over the hundreds of acres of surrounding countryside as it had done for nearly eight hundred years. The outward signs of it having been a defensive structure had long since been transformed to accommodate more peaceful times, so that now it resembled more a miniature version of Versailles than a crenulated bastion.

Like the country of which it was a part, Donnington Castle displayed the ravages of unforgiving time and of its gradual decline from what had once been a position of opulent grandeur and power. Indeed, there had been a time when the house – for that was how the Hopkins-Donnington-Boughton family regarded it – had been mentioned in the same admiring breath as that other statement of position and power occupied by the Marlboroughs in Oxfordshire.

Now, although still massive in extent and grand in concept, the castle suffered from an almost constant need for ongoing repair and preservation. Even the extensive gardens, which surrounded the castle and its huge artificial lake and which had been designed by Capability Brown, were showing the ravages of the Great War. The army of gardeners, who had laboured so diligently to preserve the artificial neatness and order fashion imposed upon Nature, had seen it as their duty to march off to join another army. Out of the original thirty-two, only fourteen had returned and of those five had been so badly wounded and maimed that Stephen's uncle had seen it as his moral obligation to allow them to retire on a generous pension, as the reward for their burning patriotism. The way things were going, it was difficult to see how things would ever revert to what they had been, before those fatal shots had been fired in far-off Sarajevo.

Despite the circumstance of modern times, Donnington Castle was still the family retreat. It was a place to which regular returns could still be made; a place of peaceful tranquillity and calm, almost completely at odds with the reality of the so-called Brave New World outside.

The previous afternoon, Stephen and Rupert had caught the 1.35 p.m. train from London.

'You are certain about this?' Rupert had asked, once they had settled themselves into the upholstered plush of their first-class compartment.

'Good Lord, yes,' Stephen had replied, a faint smile pulling at his mouth, 'my dear uncle might not always be possessed with the most up-to-date thinking on many things, as I've said before, but I'm quite certain about this.'

This referred to his uncle's open invitation to visit him at the castle. Recently, his uncle's insistence that Stephen spend more time at the family home had grown: ... *and why not bring young Winfield down with you when you come.* It was more of a command than a question. His uncle had met Rupert on several occasions, either at the opera, the club or at some other function to which Stephen had been invited *with partner*. He had taken an almost instant liking to the fresh-faced young man. Even if his nephew had not yet married, it had pleased him to see that he had found himself a regular male friend. So many long-standing friendships had been savagely destroyed in the war. The flippant nature of modern society suggested to him that the forging of enduring friendships might be something easier remembered than either achieved or maintained.

As the train gradually gathered momentum and sped past the restrictive outskirts of the sprawling, tired old Mother of Empire, both of them relaxed more into their seats. It was as if they had crossed some unseen barrier, releasing them from the strictures and confines of the formalised, almost artificial London society in which they were sometimes obliged to move. It was as if they were not only heading up the line to Donnington Castle but, at the same time, moving back in time to an age where people were far more deferential, where the actions of the few were far less scrutinized and far less questioned by the many.

'Are you absolutely certain that you're happy about me joining the family at the castle?' Rupert asked cautiously, without turning away from the window. The question was more of an aside than a direct enquiry; he knew the delicate tightrope they were obliged to tread in the public view and things could hardly be more public that a large family gathering.

Both of them were only too well aware of the prejudice a union such as theirs provoked in the often bigoted minds of those who simply did not understand. When those minds occupied a position far higher up the social ladder than the average, and if some transgression became open knowledge, that prejudice could not only be far more focused, but also more virulently dangerous as well. Rupert was uncertain about his reception at the castle: being on the family's home ground and being entertained at the Uncle's London club were two totally different things. He tried not to let his apprehension show on his face, but simply continued looking out of the window.

'Perhaps it's up to us to move things on a bit ... into modern times and all of that,' said Stephen, who had started to fill his pipe. 'Bright lights shouldn't *always* be kept hidden under a bushel now, should they? As far as I'm concerned, lights don't shine any brighter than you do, old chap.'

Since the business in Petra and the struggle over the scroll, his stump had increasingly bothered him. It had worsened once they had returned to England with the damp, oppressive autumn weather. Smoking a pipe seemed to help numb the ache a little. As the days shortened and headed towards the inevitability of the approaching bleak winter, so the discomfort in what was left of his upper left leg grew. He kept this to himself – Rupert had often thought that the grimaces and groans were as a result of their passion for each other, but Stephen had kept the reality to himself. He had also kept quiet about the appointment he had made to visit Harley Street. Long ago he had acknowledged how lucky he was to have found a life's companion like Rupert, but the realization that there could be unexpected complications ahead and that the possibility existed – at least in his own mind – that Rupert could well soon be saddled with a near-cripple for the rest of his life bothered him greatly. He had resolved not to give in to any possible future incapacity. He had also, of late, come to understand the true meaning of what was *really* meant by putting on a brave face. As proof of that, the heavy black cane, a little scratched and worse for the recent wear, was propped up against the wall of the carriage, at his side. The ornate silver handle still held its two blood-red ruby eyes, which, in support of Stephen's resolve, flashed their defiance at Fate.

'We are what we are,' he continued, smiling, 'and the rest of them are going to have to come to terms with it. You and I will simply be ourselves and relish every single second of what we have together.'

In the empty compartment, Rupert leaned forward and patted his friend's knee.

'And I'm more than happy with that,' he said softly.

When the train arrived at Donnington-under-Meadow the two travellers were met by Rivers, the Uncle's butler of over forty years, before being driven to the castle in time for dinner. Upon being shown to their quarters, the two friends discovered that their rooms were joined by a connecting door and were able to settle in quickly and still had sufficient time to bathe and dress for dinner before joining the rest of the family in the burgundy sitting room for a pre-dinner drink. Dinner itself was the usual formal affair. Around the table sat several of the Uncle's other house guests for the weekend, including a retired field marshal and his wife, both of who talked incessantly, and the local vicar and his wife, neither of whom seemed to have much of interest to contribute to the conversation. Both Stephen and Rupert fitted into the company very easily, listening politely and making the appropriate responses as the opportunity presented itself.

It was nearly eleven o'clock before the party broke up and each had gone to their respective rooms for the night. Now, with the chimes from the clock atop the distant stable block marking half-past midnight, Rupert knocked softly on the connecting door and entered Stephen's room. He crossed to the armchair, which stood in front of the fireplace and removed his robe, throwing it over the back of the chair. As he turned to face Stephen, his naked frame was encased in the glow from the fire, which burned brightly in the hearth, safely restrained behind its fire screen.

'Just like being back at home in Westminster,' said Stephen, admiring what he saw with genuine affection. 'Same as the scene at number fourteen, Wellington Mansions. Except that this room is a lot bigger,' he added, smiling. 'In fact, *everything* looks bigger...'

Rupert looked reproachfully at his friend. In his left hand he held a folded newspaper. 'That's as may be,' he said tantalisingly, 'but first take a look at this.' He crossed the floor and snuggled in beside Stephen. 'I read this whilst taking my bath. The society pages are a mine of information.'

'Or a mine of purest poison,' chuckled Stephen, 'depending on your point of view.'

Rupert smoothed out the copy of that morning's *The Times*, which they had brought with them on the train, but which had gone largely unread during the journey. On the society pages there were several wedding photos. Rupert pointed to one of them.

'Well, I never!' said Stephen. 'So our friend Harrison actually wooed and won the delicious Miss Madeira Barnfield after all.' He laughed out loud. 'And I'd say the aggressive Mrs Hester Barnfield was none too pleased about it,' he said, pointing to the glaringly miserable figure in the furthest corner of the photograph.

'I would say that the mother of the bride was lucky to have been included in the picture at all,' added Rupert with a chuckle. 'Isn't it amazing what financial independence and a headstrong nature can do for you?' He opened out the paper, turned back a couple of pages and then pointed to the bottom right-hand corner of the page. 'Our friend Mrs Unsworth,' announced Rupert.

'So it is,' replied Stephen, moving the paper nearer to the bedside light and reading the article which accompanied the photograph. 'She's set up a scholarship in the professor's name. What a marvellous way of perpetuating his memory.'

For a moment neither of them spoke and the room was filled with the staccato crackling of the burning fire.

'Do you think we'll be like them in thirty years' time?' asked Rupert, holding his friend tightly with both arms and crumpling the paper between them.

'My dear fellow, if we are a quarter as happy then as we are now, we'll still be as rich as Croesus. Wouldn't you say?'

Rupert squeezed even harder.

'But I'm as rich as Croesus now,' whispered Stephen softly, as he kissed his friend. 'And now ... before a little sport, let us rid ourselves of the unnecessary,' he continued, folding the crumpled pages and moving to throw the newspaper to the floor.

'Wait a moment,' said Rupert, catching his friend's hand in mid-air before smoothing out the pages on Stephen's chest. 'Turn back to the society pages. I've saved the best thing till last.'

'Correction, my dear fellow,' said Stephen, 'what you're about to show me, as interesting as it will no doubt be, cannot possibly be *the best thing*. That very definitely *will* come last!'

His smiling face was very close to Rupert's and was almost entangled in the spread pages of newsprint, which Rupert now held in his hands.

He gave Stephen a gentle nudge with his elbow and smiled back. 'Thank you for that,' he whispered, 'but first, you simply have to take a look at this...'

'Good God,' exclaimed Stephen, looking at the photo and reading the caption, 'it's old Olivier ... *minus* Mrs Olivier.'

It was a photo of the opening of a new branch of the Catholic Foundation for Family Values in Society, at which the Cardinal Archbishop of Westminster had officiated.

There was also a sentence to the effect that Mrs Olivier, who always accompanied her husband on such important events, was indisposed due to her having to take complete rest for a recent nervous condition.

'She was more than a little highly-strung at the best of times,' muttered Stephen, 'so perhaps Mr has finally succeeded in sending her over the brink ... poor woman.'

'She certainly had changed somewhat by the end of the trip, hadn't she?' said Rupert, 'and weren't those two the complete *opposite* of the Unsworths?'

'As different as chalk is from cheese,' replied Stephen, reaching the end of the article. 'Which makes me feel even more strongly that we are very lucky ... you and I. Not to be like them...'

'To be like we are with what we have,' added Rupert, with deep-seated affection in his voice, 'and not to be like poor Mrs Olivier. She *did* seem to be as jumpy as a Mexican jumping bean most of the time. Perhaps she was bothered by something that came up...'

'Speaking of which...'

The morning dawned crisp and cold. After a leisurely breakfast, the rest of the day passed off pleasantly enough. Stephen took Rupert to look around the parish church, where most of his ancestors were buried and which boasted the remains of two late medieval wall paintings. On the way back to the castle, they stopped off at the local public house in the village of Boughton and enjoyed a ploughman's lunch, a pint of the local ale and a conversation with the landlord. On their return to the castle they were met by Rivers who had instructions for them to attend the Uncle later that afternoon.

'...That is correct, Sir...' said Rivers, his voice echoing around the marbled grandeur of the entrance vestibule as he took their coats, '... in the private study at precisely four o'clock, when tea will be served.'

At the appointed time Stephen and Rupert entered the Uncle's private study. This was a grand, wood-panelled room with a high ceiling consistent with its classical cube proportions. Two large sash windows, heavily draped, gazed out across the sloping order of the gardens, towards the lake. Two of the walls were lined from floor to ceiling with leather-covered books of various sizes, their spines ornately tooled in gold. The room resembled more a room in a grand London club, rather than a study in a private house. Already the sunlight was fading outside, but the room was comfortable and quite warm; it invited private conversation. The three men sat in leather armchairs around the fire.

'... It's a bit of a do, in fact...' continued the Uncle. He broke off his dialogue when a knock on the door heralded the arrival of tea. He waited while the two housemaids, supervised by Rivers, pushed in a generously filled tea trolley and positioned it close to the fire. Tea was poured and distributed in the time-honoured fashion.

'Thank you, Rivers,' said the Uncle. 'A splendid effort, as usual.'

The butler made no reply, but simply bowed slightly as he ushered the housemaids out of the room before closing the door quietly behind him.

'... Everyone's looking, but there is still no sign of her...' There was a slight pause, as he stirred the tan-coloured liquid in his cup, '... or of the scroll.'

'Hawkhurst is making a complete recovery and should be back with us before Christmas,' said Stephen. 'He took the news about his sister very badly, I'm afraid. They were very close to each other. Wouldn't you agree?' he asked, turning to Rupert.

'Indeed. In fact, I'd be very surprised if Hawkhurst doesn't blame himself for what happened to his sister,' Rupert replied. 'I mean to say, if he hadn't had the misfortune to get in the way of that bullet, then both of them would probably have been at the controls of their Avenger aircraft ... and they would have been together.'

'Of course, there is the very real possibility that the scroll is at the bottom of the North Sea by now and beyond anyone's reach, which could be a good thing apart from the sad loss of Miss Hawkhurst, naturally,' continued the Uncle.

'Or could it have fallen into other hands somewhere between Paris and ... well, anywhere, I suppose?' added Stephen, putting his cup down and resting his hands on the heavy black walking stick.

'That, of course, is the other undesirable possibility,' said the Uncle, his brow clouding over as he spoke, 'but there have been no reports of any aircraft crashes on the Continent. At least, none that we know of...'

'Or of any unexpected landings at foreign aerodromes?' questioned Stephen.

The Uncle raised his eyebrows in a gesture of uncertainty. 'This whole scroll business could yet spring out of nowhere, like an angry tiger, and bite us on the backside.'

Rupert was about to laugh at the Uncle's remark, but was just in time to realize that it was not intended to be in the least bit funny. He stopped himself in the nick of time. There was a lull in the conversation, during which the room filled with the sharp crackling of the logs on the fire. The three men entertained their own thoughts on the matter of the scroll and the ramifications of its possible reappearance.

'How did you chaps manage with the body of that Irgun chap in Petra?' asked the Uncle suddenly. He helped himself to another sandwich from the tea trolley.

'Aaron Ben Zeev?' replied Stephen.

'Despite the threat of loaded firearms,' continued Rupert,

'we were fortunate in as much as he fell off the cliff, rather than having to be *shot* off it. Naturally, Uri Ben Zeev was extremely upset by his brother's death, but he seemed to accept the explanation that it *was* an accident with some considerable stoicism. That's actually a characteristic of the Jewish race; an acceptance of Fate, as it were. We told him that his brother had thoughtfully come after us with some water bottles ... You know the sort of thing, looking after the climatically unaware and ill-prepared English. We told him that his brother must have missed his footing on the path. It was, after all, very narrow in many places.'

'No one knew anything about what happened up there on the cliff face, apart from those who were actually present,' added Stephen, 'so no one was any the wiser. It was quite easy for us to present a unified explanation, which was convincing and which went largely unchallenged. That held true for Hawkhurst and his bullet wound. He's made of stern stuff and kept quiet when we reached the campsite. We said he had fallen against the rocks and had broken his arm.'

'And our chaps in Jerusalem sorted out everything else,' added the Uncle, lighting a cigar, 'and they'll see to it that Hawkhurst gets home safely. He might well have to be invited to sign the Official Secrets Act when he does. We don't want any of this getting out. The Middle East is as dangerous as ever and the scroll, now presumed lost for good, is just one small part of the problems we have in Palestine...'

'Excuse me asking, Sir,' said Stephen, 'but did you manage to sort something out for Ginsberg and his wife?'

'After all, if it hadn't been for him, we might well have ended up dead ourselves, Sir,' added Rupert, looking uncharacteristically serious.

'Our people have sent them out of harm's way...' replied the Uncle. 'We have packed them both off to Cape Town.

There's a sizeable Jewish community down there and they'll blend in as a pair of new immigrants. They have new identities to go with their new life ... in gratitude for services rendered. Obviously, it's in their own interest to keep their previous lives a closely guarded secret. And it goes without saying that the service you have both rendered is also acknowledged.'

Stephen took a breath and was about to ask his uncle why it was that, in the dangerous world of the modern age, he seemed to persist in involving the likes of himself and Rupert in such dangerous affairs: they were, after all, rank amateurs. The world had moved on considerably and the sight of a gunboat flying the White Ensign had most definitely lost all of its former power of political persuasion. The age of the *Boys' Own* stereotypical hero was also very definitely a thing of the past. Stephen was stopped in his tracks, even before the words had formed themselves on his lips.

'And, of course, we must not forget young Barrington,' continued the Uncle, 'a very clever chap.'

'Was he really who he said he was, Sir?' asked Rupert. Despite being a little in awe of Stephen's uncle, Rupert was nevertheless very comfortable in his presence. 'He certainly knew his onions regarding the archaeology side of things, but he also seemed to be competent in a great many other areas as well...'

The Uncle smiled and said nothing for a few seconds, as if he was thinking carefully before speaking. 'Let us just say that he has training in things other than archaeology. There are moves afoot to develop our secret service, which means that we will need very able and highly competent people, if the plans are to reach fruition. I'll leave the rest up to your own imaginations.'

It was obvious from the Uncle's expression that that was all he was prepared to say on the subject of Gordon Barrington.

'Was anything ever resolved concerning that French oil exploration team we bumped into in Trans-Jordan, Sir?' asked Stephen, suddenly remembering their adventure in the desert.

'Nothing,' said the Uncle simply. 'Naturally the French denied everything, as expected. It all had to be handled very delicately in carefully couched diplomatic language. We usually find that the more vehement the protestations of innocence, the higher the level of guilt involved, despite the protests to the contrary.' He laughed heartily. 'It really is a stupid game when you think about it: posturing, politeness and hypocrisy in equal measures.' He did not tell them that the latest intelligence reports hinted very strongly at some sort of a close alliance between Paris and Rome, in the latter's ongoing search for reliable supplies of crude oil with which to feed their seemingly uncontrollable desire for territorial expansion.

The three men chatted on amicably for a further forty minutes, before the Uncle announced that he had matters to attend to before the party was due to assemble for their evening drinks and dinner. After his nephew and Rupert had left, he crossed the thick pile of the Axminster carpet and sat in the padded leather armchair behind the large mahogany desk, which was an almost exact replica of the one in Whitehall. Only the familiar, comforting surroundings of the rest of the room told him that he was as removed from the Heart of Empire as it was possible for him to be.

He opened the desk's central drawer and took out a buff folder, which was tied closed with red tape. He took out the top sheet of paper, adjusted his spectacles and once again read the lines of type:

> ...the prospect of a palace coup d'etat against the machinations of His Royal Highness Prince Abdul Salaam Abd al-Allah is now thought of as a certainty.

THE GERSHOM SCROLL

It is assumed that such a move will be aimed to coincide with British withdrawal, following the expiry of our mandate early next year. It is assumed that, under His Majesty the King, the new political power in Iraq will be headed by Rashid al-Gaylami, a nationalist politician who is known to us and whose activities have increased markedly in recent months. Any form of political alliance between HRH and al-Gaylami, once thought to be a possibility, now seems out of the question. HM Government is well advised to reconsider the future of British oil interests in Iraq, as al-Gaylami is known to have sympathies with Rome and, to a lesser extent, Berlin. Iraq's close proximity to Persia and our oil supplies in that country should also be borne in mind, as should the possibility of any future destabilisation of Iraq subsequently producing a similar, knock-on effect in Iran.

The Uncle continued to hold the sheet of paper in his hand, as he turned and looked out of the window opposite his desk. The view that met his gaze was a million light years away from the international problems he had just absorbed and which now filled his brain. It was almost as if life at the castle – with its carefully arranged, but constantly predictable routine, its gardens and its lake – was a fiction and that the reality of the modern world, where everything was changing and nothing seemed to be either predictable or constant – at least not in the way it had been in his younger days before the war – was reflected through what he had just read.

The old ways were changing, the old securities a thing of the past. These days, events seemed to be moving at a dizzying rate. What had once been straightforward and clear-cut now seemed highly obtuse and far from clear. Old enemies now seemed to be forging new alliances and old allies seemed to be drifting further and further apart. And then there were the Americans. From the safety of their isolationist homeland across the Atlantic, they seemed to be having more and more to say for themselves on international matters. There had even been instances recently where they had ventured thinly disguised and unwelcome comments regarding certain aspects of Imperial policy within the Empire. To those who comprised the Old Guard at Whitehall, these unwelcome comments from the one power with the strongest claim to a mutual heritage had been the last straw.

O, brave new world that has such people in't! He leaned forward suddenly, supporting himself on the desk. Why had he been reminded of Miranda's positive declaration of joy to Prospero, her father? This tempestuous twentieth century was no reason for joy; it was moving on far too rapidly – almost too rapidly to allow space for men like the Uncle to be carried along with it.

Despite the excellent tea, the affable company and the cosy comfort of his study, the Uncle once again felt the gnawing emptiness of doubt in his stomach. He had started to feel this emptiness more and more over recent months. His doctor had given him some pills, but they didn't seem to make that much of a difference. They had done little to counter the feeling of near hopelessness – the feeling that events were spinning around him and that he now found himself increasingly unable to manipulate or affect them as he had done in the old days. He returned his gaze to the now crumpled sheet of paper in his hands. Absently, he laid it down on the buff folder and removed his spectacles. Crossing his arms across his chest, he stared down at the paper and his spectacles. He sat there for some time, but he did not really register them. His mind was occupied with far more serious matters.

As he sat in his chair, gazing down blankly at the desktop

in front of him, he allowed himself to face the stark realization that, perhaps, he was out of phase with the times, like some once-omnipotent, but now marginalized, character in a Shakespeare play. He sighed.

Was it time for him to move on?